ETHAN CROSS

manipulat... isure & ...e."

"The surprises are fast and furious
and will leave you breathless to read more."
Lisa Gardner, #1 *New York Times* bestselling author of *Find Her*

"A fast paced, all too real thriller with
a villain right out of James Patterson and *Criminal Minds*."
Andrew Gross, #1 *New York Times* bestselling author of *Reckless*

"*Silence of the Lambs* meets *The Bourne Identity*."
Brian S. Wheeler, author of *Mr. Hancock's Signature*

"An intense novel that will have you locking your
windows and doors, installing a safe room and taking
Ambien so you can sleep through the night after finishing."
Jeremy Robinson, author of *Pulse and Instinct*

"A superbly crafted thriller skillfully delving into
the twisted mind of a psychopath and the tormented soul
of the man destined to bring him down."
D.B. Henson, bestselling author of *Deed to Death*

"A taut, violent and relentless nightmare."
A.J. Hartley, bestselling author of *What Time Devours*

"A great mix of gruesome murders,
a psychotic killer, revenge and great writing."
Crimesquad

By Ethan Cross

THE ACKERMAN THRILLERS

I Am the Night
I Am Fear
I Am Pain
I Am Wrath
I Am Hate
I Am Vengeance

I
AM
HATE

ETHAN CROSS

HEAD
of ZEUS

An Aries Book

I Am Hate
was previously published as
Only the Strong

First published as *Only the Strong* in the United States in 2018 by
The Story Plant, The Aronica-Miller Publishing Project, LLC

This edition first published in the United Kingdom by Head of Zeus in 2021
An Aries book

9 7 5 3 1 2 4 6 8

A CIP catalogue record for this book is available
from the British Library.

ISBN (PBO): 9781838931025
ISBN (E): 9781838931018

Printed and bound by CPI Group (UK) Ltd, Croydon, CR0 4YY

MIX
Paper from
responsible sources
FSC
www.fsc.org   FSC® C020471

Aries
c/o Head of Zeus Ltd
5–8 Hardwick Street
London EC1R 4RG
WWW.HEADOFZEUS.COM

To my best buddy, Gizmo, for literally being
by my side when all of these books were written.
May you rest in peace, my friend...

1

Francis Ackerman Jr. had lost track of the number of lives he had taken and the level of destruction he had wrought. He barely remembered much of those dark years. They were merely a blur of blood and pain. If a man truly reaped what he sowed, Ackerman knew the kind of harvest he deserved. Still, he couldn't make himself worry about consequences or fear judgment. He had stared into the darkness on numerous occasions and imagined the smell of brimstone and the sound of weeping and gnashing of teeth. But he couldn't harness the proper emotional and physical response. Fear remained as elusive to him as sight to a man whose eyes had been carved from his head.

Ackerman hadn't been born blind to fear and addicted to pain. His own father had subjected him to every form of torture imaginable and forced him to experience traumatic events from the lives of the most notorious killers in the world. When that wasn't enough, his father surgically ravaged the portions of his brain which controlled the response to fear and the fight or flight instincts.

Despite those inherent setbacks, Ackerman was proud of what he'd accomplished so far. He had found his way back to his younger brother and, through Marcus, had gained a family. Since then, he had saved several lives and, by his count, aided in the capture of eight serial murderers. And the biggest catch yet—a man they knew only as Demon who ran a network of sadistic killers for hire—was scheduled for transfer from Foxbury Prison to ADX Florence, one of the most secure correctional facilities in the world.

Ackerman should have been in a better mood. But he couldn't allow himself joy or pride over the capture, since he hadn't directly beaten the Demon. Part of him knew that while they both still breathed, their struggle would never be over.

He watched his brother from the rear of a briefing room with speckled floors and white block walls that stank of cigarettes and gun oil. Special Agent Marcus Williams—Ackerman's younger brother—wore a black suit and a dark-gray dress shirt, no tie, his brother having vowed to never wear one again. Marcus outlined the details of the transfer to the team of law enforcement and correctional officers arranged in a grid of folding chairs crowded into the room's center. Ackerman wasn't allowed to directly participate in the transfer, since his status was merely that of a "consultant." But his skills would be put to use soon enough. What coach left the star player on the bench for long? And if killing were a sport, then Ackerman was certainly the Michael Jordan of murder.

His brother's plan was simple, but had merit. Three teams would leave the staging area at staggered intervals. Each convoy would consist of a forward scout in an unmarked sedan, two patrol cruisers, the armored prisoner transport, two trail cars, and a helicopter on overwatch. In addition, they would have state police diverting traffic to insure that their route was clear of innocent bystanders and potential threats. Each armored transport would be loaded with a hooded man. Not even the guards would know which convoy held the real prisoner.

Marcus would ride shotgun with a state trooper behind the real prisoner, while the others from their team occupied the trail cars of the decoys. Ackerman and Special Agent Maggie Carlisle would be in the overwatch chopper for Marcus's group—him as a special consultant and her as his keeper. Ackerman had grown quite fond of Maggie and considered her family, though his brother had yet to pop the question to his longtime girlfriend and officially make her Ackerman's little sister.

Marcus finished the briefing and motioned for Ackerman and Maggie to join him at the side of the room opposite the exiting officers. Marcus said, "I want you two to be scouting ahead for possible ambush points. We'll send the forward car up to check out any spots that could pose a threat."

Ackerman said, "I still don't think we should be sending him in any of those transports."

"Drop it, Frank. It was hard enough getting all of this approved once. We're not going to do multiple waves. But don't worry. That transport isn't stopping for anything."

Ackerman shrugged. "You're the boss, little brother."

"Don't call me that. At least not in public."

"That hurts my feelings."

"Considering you enjoy pain, you're welcome."

Ackerman smiled. "When do I get to say goodbye?"

"Are you sure that's a good idea?"

"The only ideas I have are good ones."

Maggie rolled her eyes. "Let's just get on with it. I wouldn't mind spitting in that prick's face before he's hauled off."

Ackerman said, "Majority rules."

Marcus shook his head. "This is not a democracy. That being said, I think the three of us could possibly get him to give something away. Some clue to his identity or where we can find his friends. Keep that in mind when we talk to him."

Ackerman's heart rate increased and his anticipation grew at the thought of once again coming face to face with the Demon. The feeling reminded him of the girl who took his virginity, or at least what he felt was his true virginity—all his other encounters being of a forced and violent nature. She had been a Mayan girl he had picked up along the road to Cancun, and she had served as Bonnie to his Clyde. For a time anyway. He now trembled with the same kind of adrenaline he had felt when she had dropped her flower dress from her shoulders.

Marcus led them down a concrete-and-block corridor into a room that smelled exactly as it should: like six men with shotguns in full tactical gear baking in the Arizona heat. Demon was strapped to an industrial dolly in the center of the six men. As they approached, Marcus ordered one of the guards to remove the hood, straps, and bite-stopping mask covering the prisoner's face.

Demon rolled his head from side to side and opened his mouth to stretch out the muscles of his jaw. He had long black and gray hair that hung down over his face. The tissue over his left eye had been melted, and he had no eyebrows. Knife wounds and slashes intersected most of the rest of his face, but the most prominent of the disfigurements was his Glasgow smile—a wound achieved by cutting the corners of the mouth and then torturing the victim. When the victim screamed or moved, the flesh of his face would tear.

Demon's Glasgow smile stretched nearly from jawbone

4

to jawbone. But it wasn't straight across or turned up like a smile. It looked more as though a giant axe had cleaved the bottom of his head off at a slight angle.

When Demon spoke, his voice flowed out in a mellifluous Scottish brogue. "This is not even close to the level of comfort I'm accustomed to when traveling. I'm definitely going to leave you a bad Yelp review."

Marcus's lips curled back in disgust. "I'll call up the captain and have him send in your wine, jackass."

"You've seen me take life before, Agent Williams, but that was for business. You've never experienced the beauty of what I do for pleasure. I like to lead my subjects through a representation of each level of hell."

Marcus stepped close and whispered, "It's good you're into that kind of thing. Because that's where we're sending you. Hell."

"Are you referring to the prison or a plan to send me to the grave?"

"Pick one."

Demon shook his head, black strands of hair whipping back and forth over his face like inky tentacles. "You've probably heard 'Seek and ye shall find' in regard to the Kingdom of Heaven and God, but that applies in the opposite direction as well. For every thesis, there is an antithesis. If you pursue the devil, he'll find you ... and everyone you love."

Marcus was about to respond, but Ackerman had sat back long enough. It was time to establish dominance. He punched Demon in the center of his face, snapping the dark-haired man's head back against the metal of the dolly. Demon laughed and spit blood on the floor.

Ackerman said, "Whoever my brother calls family is my family as well. And I dare any man to try and take what's mine."

"I offered you a way out before, but I'll give you one more chance. Your team can let me go and forget all about me. Or, if you choose to oppose me, I will burn your family alive and shake their dust from my feet as a testimony against them."

Ackerman grinned. "If I was capable of fear, I would be worried."

Demon's gaze traveled from Maggie to Marcus. "This is one of life's binary choices, boys and girls. There's only one path or the other, no in between. It's like choosing whether to believe or not believe or have children or not. Your only options here are to let me go now or face the consequences."

Maggie said, "I've heard enough."

"Then a cloud appeared and covered them," Demon said, "and a voice came from the cloud: 'This is my vessel of wrath, whom I hate. Fear him.'"

Ackerman tilted his head at their prisoner. "I've heard that the Almighty doesn't look kindly upon those who pervert the Gospel."

Demon whispered, "I'm not even sure I believe in all that. But I do know this, my boy. I'm going to give you a tour of hell, and when you ask me for the bread of mercy, I'll give you razor blades instead."

Ackerman chuckled. "Sounds like a party."

2

Special Agent Marcus Williams—a team leader in the Department of Justice's black ops program known as The Shepherd Organization—strapped on his Level-4 tactical gear. The armor had been designed to withstand rounds even from a high-powered rifle. He cycled his M4A1 assault rifle to make sure it was locked and loaded, clean and lubricated. He had a terrible feeling that he would be needing the weapon and the body armor in the next few hours. He had hunted several serial murderers—including, at one time, his own infamous brother, Francis Ackerman Jr.—but Marcus had never encountered anyone quite like the man they knew only as Demon.

Marcus had apprehended Demon just beyond the borders of Foxbury Prison as the madman aided in the escape of the leader of one of the world's most dangerous gangs. He had learned from Demon's former apprentice, the now-deceased Judas Killer, that the Scottish-born man with the scarred face had actually recruited and organized a network of the most depraved members of society and given them direction and purpose. He had banded this interconnected web of psychopaths and malcontents into a money-making machine, which allowed Demon's influence to grow in both power and reach.

It was the kind of case the SO had been created to handle, the sort of work Marcus had been born for.

Ackerman had told him that a man with Demon's resources wouldn't remain in custody for long, but that only led Marcus to take a more personal role in Demon's transport and incarceration. He had succeeded in the apprehension of a killer whose criminal influence spread out like a fibrous cancer across the dark underbelly of society, and Marcus had no intention of letting such a prize slip from his grasp.

He waited in the long dark tunnel leading from Demon's holding area to an armored transport that would carry the criminal mastermind to the supermax prison known as ADX Florence—a modern dungeon surrounded by a barren wasteland which housed everyone from the world's most dangerous terrorists, including Al-Qaeda operatives and Unabomber Theodore Kaczynski, to several organized crime figures. One of those inmates had a very personal connection to Marcus and Ackerman—their own father, the mass murderer known as Thomas White.

His real name was Francis Ackerman Sr., but the SO had kept that information under wraps, allowing the name of Thomas White, the killer's last-used alias, to become his permanent name. Even Marcus had grown accustomed to thinking of his biological father as Thomas White. It made it easier to distance himself from the madman who had used Marcus and his son, Dylan, as test subjects, just as he had done with his brother many years prior.

Marcus had no plans to visit his biological father upon dropping off his current prisoner. He hadn't spoken to Thomas White since his apprehension, after the madman tried to blow up a group of school children in Kansas City, which only came after his torturing Marcus in a dark hole for months on end. If God answered his many prayers, Marcus would never have to look in the eyes of his biological father again. His brother felt differently, even though Ackerman had endured even more torture at the hands of their sperm donor. Ackerman had gone so far as to request visitations with their father, and the Director had reluctantly indulged his brother's forays into the dark mind of Thomas White.

He wondered if his brother's control and willpower had now surpassed his own. He couldn't stand to be in the presence of the man who had brought him into this world. He had even fantasized many times about his father's violent death and didn't know how Ackerman could look the bastard in the eyes. But he supposed that his brother's total lack of fear helped when facing their own personal monster.

As the guards marched Demon down the long dark corridor of concrete and rebar, Marcus white-knuckled his weapon and resisted the urge to end the mastermind's life. Part of him wished he had killed Demon when he had the chance in the tunnels beneath Foxbury.

"Take off the headgear. I want to say goodbye," Marcus said to the guards.

With the hood and protective mask removed, Demon smiled and puckered his lips as if for a kiss. Grabbing the killer by the throat, Marcus said, "If you try anything, I'm going to put a bullet in you. The biggest part of me hopes that you'll attempt to escape, because nothing would bring me more peace than to have you lying on a slab in some morgue."

Demon, quoting Nietzsche through rancid breath, said, "Whoever fights monsters should see to it that in the process he does not become a monster. And if you gaze long enough into an abyss, the abyss will gaze back into you."

Marcus looked to the lead guard and said, "Get him out of my sight."

The officers loaded Demon into an armored prison transport, and Marcus took his position inside the rear patrol car. He had tried to plan for the worst and consider all possibilities, but some dark intuition told him it wouldn't be enough.

The caravan rolled out from the holding facility in Arizona early that morning, expecting to arrive at the secure facility at ADX Florence around 11:30 that night. Marcus had actually informed the prison of a much later arrival, but the early departure was another attempt at sabotaging any potential rescue attempts. Demon had the resources necessary to stage a dramatic escape, and unfortunately, any countermeasures he could dream up could be outthought by the opposition. He just hoped he had planned one move ahead of the unseen adversary.

The first eleven and a half hours of their journey proceeded without incident.

Marcus could barely keep his eyes open most of the drive. The Colorado scenery whipping past the window was probably beautiful during the day, but now the view was nothing but vague silhouettes and the occasional flash of an animal's eyes illuminated by the periphery of the convoy's headlights. He nodded off for a moment, always surprised at how much easier it was to fall asleep when he was trying to stay awake. But he sprang to attention as the cruiser bumped its way over a dead animal, some small carcass that flashed out of sight before he could really look. His hand rested on his pistol. He tried to relax while keeping his eyelids from dropping like castle gates.

The state trooper behind the wheel of the cruiser—possessing about as much personality as an earthworm—was little help. The short but muscular man had barely spoken a sentence since they left. Marcus disliked people who were comfortable in their own silence. The quiet moments left more time to think. More time for questions with answers he didn't really want to know.

The cruiser's radio crackled to life and a voice said, "Command, this is Overwatch 2. You've got a car parked along your route about twenty miles ahead."

Before Marcus could give the order, the scout came back with, "10-4. This is Forward 2. Proceeding to intercept."

The next few moments dragged on as Marcus waited for the scout to reach the site of the potential ambush. He held his breath in anticipation. Finally, the senior officer in the scout car reported, "Appears to be a genuine breakdown. Male and a female are outside the vehicle flagging me over."

Marcus grabbed the radio receiver and said, "Go in hot! Take them down and ask questions once they're secured."

"They seem scared to death. If it's a real breakdown, they've been out here for quite some time with no traffic flowing past. They—"

"That's an order. Take them down hard and fast. Apologize later, once the scene is secured."

"Roger, Command."

A moment passed, and Marcus said, "Overwatch, do you have eyes on?"

"Affirmative. The suspects have been subdued."

After another pause, one of the cops in the scout car said,

"Command, we've got a nine-month-old baby in the back seat. Should we arrest her as well? I don't think my cuffs will fit."

Marcus gritted his teeth and took a deep breath before responding, "No need for cuffs. But you may want to have the dog sniff the kid's car seat for explosives. Don't forget for a second the kind of people we're dealing with. The type who would slaughter that whole family and wear their blood like war paint if it furthered their cause. Don't let your guard down for a second."

"Roger, Command."

Marcus added, "And the rest of you, remember … I don't care if your grandmother or your baby sister is in the middle of that road. We stop for nothing."

3

Corin Campbell now saw the skull face everywhere she went. At first, she thought it was a prank, some kids hacking Facebook accounts and messing with people. But now, she had seen the face in real life.

At least, she thought she had. Or maybe her eggs really were scrambled, as her sister had been proclaiming for years. Corin wasn't sure anymore. If all she knew of reality was to be believed, then some nightmare from a slasher film had come to life and now stalked her every movement. The fear was almost crippling, and Corin was not the type to scare easily.

She had first noticed the skull face appearing in the background of some of her Facebook and Instagram selfies, mostly group shots walking down the street or standing outside a restaurant. In the most recent photo, the figure had been standing right outside her window.

She was almost positive the skull face hadn't been there before, when she had first posted the pics. The appearance of the nightmare figure could have been the simple result of a hacked account, just some teenager with a MacBook Pro and a rudimentary knowledge of Photoshop.

Still, she couldn't say that with certainty. She had checked for evidence of photo doctoring and received the response from a local computer repair shop that the photos "appeared to be doctored, but results were inconclusive."

She still hadn't figured out what the hell that meant. It was a politician's response, one that said a whole lot and absolutely nothing in the same breath.

Then, yesterday, she had glimpsed the skull face in a passing car and again on the shadowed visage of a man standing in a doorway across the street. But that had to be a product of her imagination. Lack of sleep from studying had teamed up with a sick social-media prank, assaulting her subconscious to the point of delirium.

After all, she hadn't been the only one affected. A Google search revealed that the hacking had affected several woman throughout the northwestern United States. The case had grown to full-blown urban legend status. *Skullface*, as someone on the Internet had named the man in the skull mask, had joined the ranks of other digital-era folklore like Slender Man and the Shadow People.

Her searches had turned up claims that other hacking victims had gone missing, but she dismissed them as false news, like those fake celebrity death articles that kept popping up all over social media. Still, part of Corin kept thinking that if Skullface was real, then his message was obvious: *he was watching, and he was coming for her.*

The skull mask, in what she hoped were doctored pics, had been fashioned from some sort of blood-stained metal. But the bone structure of the skull couldn't have been that of a man. More like a demon or an extinct predatory creature, like a T-Rex. Or some hybrid of both. The metal fangs were less like teeth and more long, jagged shards of torn metal, broken and misshapen and curled up slightly into a sadistic smile.

If it was real, then it was obviously some sort of hideous

mask. Halloween costumes didn't scare her. But guys who wore them while stalking her most certainly did.

She considered taking the whole thing to the police, but with no proof other than a few inconclusively doctored photos, the cops would be more of a hindrance than a help. She could take care of herself. She had done so her whole life. And if this nut-job in the mask thought she would be an easy target, then he was in for a surprise.

Exiting the building after her last class at San Francisco University, Corin pictured Skullface around every corner as she made the long, dark journey up the concrete parking structure to her car. The images were fresh in her mind's eye as she heard footsteps slapping concrete.

Someone was following her. Should she turn around? Face her pursuer? Attack? Make a run for the car? Scream?

Trying to move casually, Corin slipped her hand into the pocket of her jacket and gripped the handle of a spring-assisted knife. She could pull the weapon and release the blade swiftly with a mere twist of her thumb.

Timing the approach of the footsteps, she played out each movement in her mind.

Duck, twist, pull the blade, kick.

The footsteps had increased in rhythm. The sounds growing closer.

"Hey!" he yelled.

He was rushing her blitzkrieg-style. He had underestimated her, which wasn't surprising. Even her fiancé called her "Mouse," and sometimes she truly hated him for it. Corin was petite, with bronze skin and dark hair inherited from her Brazilian mother, but being five foot four hardly meant she was defenseless.

Although, she supposed that was the image she had chosen to portray. Just a normal girl. Just like any other college student. Only Corin and her sister, Samantha, knew the truth.

Again, the man shouted, "Hey!" just as the footsteps reached her.

Not waiting for the rest of the sentence, Corin spun on her attacker, pulled her blade, and kicked out at groin level. Her foot collided with the man's crotch, doubling him over in pain and dropping him to his knees. She stepped forward, jamming the knife against his throat as he wheezed in agony.

Corin fought to calm her breathing as she stared down at her pursuer's face.

His name was Michael.

She recognized him from the accounting class she had just completed. Her phone lay on the ground beside Michael's feet, where he had apparently just dropped it.

She felt like a complete idiot. The poor guy was simply trying to return her property, and she had gone all Jason Bourne on him.

"I'm so sorry," she said, closing the knife against her thigh and slipping it back into her pocket.

"Phone," Michael wheezed as she helped him to his feet.

"I saw that. Thanks. But hey, a girl can't be too careful these days, right?"

"I think I'm going to throw up."

She winced. "Yeah. How are your nuts? They didn't, like, go back up in there or anything, did they?"

4

About an hour into their journey, the helicopter passed over an affluent suburb. Looking at the expensive dwellings, which were barely used—most sitting empty during the day and half the night—Ackerman pondered: If the Creator were to look down upon the poverty-stricken lands of the third world and what some called "civilized" society, would Elohim judge prosperity in the same way that humankind did? Or would the world be seen in reverse?

Over his radio headset, Maggie's muffled voice said, "Anything interesting in those files I gave you?"

Ackerman had wondered how long it would be before Maggie asked him about his review of the files regarding her brother's abduction at the hands of a serial offender known as the Taker. He had wanted to wait until Demon was safely stowed away before broaching a subject that could become a distraction.

"I'll tell you later."

"Tell me what later?" She leaned forward and grabbed his arm, meeting his gaze. "Did you find something?"

"Perhaps, but I know how easily distracted you normals can become and—"

She squeezed his arm, her nostrils flaring and her eyes going wild.

With a roll of his own eyes, Ackerman said, "If you insist. How silly of me to think that the current assignment takes precedence over a twenty-year-old cold case, but regardless, as I was reviewing some of the police reports I discovered that your father consistently said things like '*They* took my son' and 'Why aren't you out finding *them*?' He always referred to the abductors in the plural."

"My father's not a reliable witness. He was probably too out of it to have seen anything."

"Yes, it seems the local police felt the same. They focused so heavily on him as a suspect that it tainted their entire view of the case. And, of course, we know for certain that your father was not the culprit, don't we, little sister?"

"What's your point?"

"Their view of your father's story subconsciously biased their questioning of the neighbors. One of the investigators was kind enough to record his interviews on cassette. Do you know how hard it is to locate a Walkman these days?"

She grabbed his arm again, this time digging in with her nails. The pain shot sweet tendrils of ecstasy through his body. He pulled his arm away and said, "I will kindly ask you to refrain from showing me your appreciation. I feel it's strangely inappropriate given the nature of our common-law sibling relationship."

Maggie sat back, gritted her teeth, and closed her eyes. Her lips mouthed the numbers from one to ten as stray strands of her blonde hair blew across her face. He assumed he must have somehow inadvertently angered her. The encounter warranted further study during a quiet moment.

Finally, she said, "Will you please just tell me?"

"See. Was that so hard? You lived at the end of a dead-end street just off a county highway, with well-traveled roads to the north and south. People probably turned onto your road accidentally and wheeled back around all the time. The abduction occurred on a Saturday, and all but one of your neighbors were home. It was a nice day. Chances are some of them could have been outside and seen the vehicle."

"Okay, great. Get on with it!"

Ackerman whispered, "If you'd shut your mouth long enough to listen to what I'm saying, perhaps you could use your brain to make the same deductions I have. Alternatively, you could allow me to finish explaining this nonsense. Maybe even soon enough to get back to the task at hand before we miss the whole escape. We're supposed to be on *Overwatch* not *Overlook*."

"Fine. I'm sorry. Please go on," she said, eyes closed.

Ackerman doubted her sincerity but soldiered on nonetheless. "The investigators asked your neighbors if they'd seen anything 'suspicious' or 'out of the ordinary.' They didn't ask if they had seen any cars drive past at the time of the abduction, which could have corroborated your father's story."

He finally saw the wheels turning in Maggie's eyes. She sat back and turned her eyes to the convoy. He did the same, happy to retrain his focus on things of more pressing significance.

5

From above, ADX Florence looked like a Martian colony viewed through a telescope. The buildings seemed to hunker low to the ground, as if hiding from the unhindered attacks of the wind. Ackerman watched out the chopper's side window as the convoy pulled through the facility's front gates and wound its way to the concrete bunker that would be Demon's new home. The vehicles came to a stop in waves like the curling humps of a caterpillar. The officers in the lead cars fanned out to cover the transport. Marcus had told them all several times that they were not to let their guard down until they were driving home. The armored vehicle came to a stop in front of a set of large metal doors in the side of one of the squat structures. The trailing cars flowed in behind it, and with armed prison guards opening the doors through which Demon would be wheeled inside, the officers stacked up and opened the rear of the armored transport.

Even from hundreds of feet in the air, Ackerman could tell something was wrong.

The tiny forms of men stood absolutely still for a few seconds and then turned their attention outward. Another small dot ran over to the transport. Ackerman guessed that to be his brother.

Thinking of his younger brother, Ackerman caught himself rubbing at the base of his skull. The powers that be had deemed him too much of a risk to let loose on the world without a leash, and so they had surgically fastened a satellite-controlled chip onto the base of his spine, loaded with a small charge adequate to blow a hole in his spinal column. They explained that the chip couldn't be removed by anyone but their doctors without also removing his ability to walk, and if he tried to block the signal, the chip would detonate after a certain amount of time.

He hadn't liked the idea of the chip, but he also wasn't afraid of a challenge. And he still wasn't completely convinced that they had even inserted a tracking chip, or that they had the power to remotely terminate his life.

After a moment, Marcus's voice came over the radio, crackling inside Ackerman's headset like an angry blowfly. Marcus said, "It's empty. Demon's gone. He just disappeared from a moving vehicle."

Turning to the pilot, Ackerman said, "Get me on the ground."

"We don't have clearance for that."

"It's better to ask for forgiveness than permission. Now, put this thing on the ground, or I'll toss you out and do it myself. And I'm not just saying that to sound tough. I will literally throw you out and land the chopper myself."

The pilot's brow furrowed. "Do you even have a pilot's license?"

"I have five thousand hours."

From the rear of the cabin, Maggie said, "Just do as he says. Now. Or I'll let my colleague here be all that he can be."

6

The Gladiator most enjoyed watching the women in the days right before he took them. He regarded this period as the *haunting* of the victim because he was always there in the background, watching and waiting, like a hungry poltergeist. It was all about the anticipation, that pregnant joy before the main event. In many ways, he approached martial arts in the same way he did hunting. He *reacted* to an opponent if necessary, but, whenever possible, he would set a trap and wait.

Although she wasn't his normal type of prey, Corin Campbell was his adversary on this evening. Typically, his victims were more physically imposing than the petite college student. Still, he had no moral objection to harming a weaker creature. He didn't believe in morality. As Nietzsche had said, "Fear is the mother of morality," and the Gladiator had yet to find an opponent worthy of his fear.

Corin wouldn't put up much of a fight, unlike his preferred victims, but she was very special for other reasons, which was why she had been chosen.

Now, standing in the closet of her spare bedroom, wearing the skull mask—which he considered his true face—the Gladiator's excitement grew.

He wondered if Corin could taste the anticipation as well. He had been following her for the past few days and giving her glimpses of Skullface, an Internet-born nomenclature which he didn't particularly care for. He wanted her to feel him coming closer, a mythical urban legend haunting her every step.

The Gladiator had worked hard to nurture that legend, at least within a one-hundred-mile radius of San Francisco.

He had begun by hacking the Facebook accounts of several women throughout his hunting zone. He would then doctor their photos, adding the face of death somewhere in the background. But photos weren't enough to build a legend and infect the subconscious minds of a populace. It had made him a trending topic among young women between the ages of twenty and twenty-five, but it was just a silly prank. At least, that's what they told themselves. The kind of thing that was as inevitable as getting the flu in the digital age: a simple hacked account.

Things became a little more real for the ladies when the digital lines of communication sparked with strange tales of hacking victims going missing, simply vanishing into thin air as if the boogeyman had carried them off to his dark realm. And, in truth, that wasn't far from what had actually happened to those other missing women—the same thing that was about to happen to Corin Campbell.

7

Marcus closed his eyes against the onslaught of dust and chips of gravel kicked up by the chopper's rotor wash. Tiny splinters of rock stung his skin like a pissed-off hive of hornets. He was always a little surprised at the strength of those blades, even from a good distance away.

His brother and Maggie dropped from the chopper's cab, hunched against the power of the rotors, and hustled toward him. Ackerman yelled, "Show me the transport."

"We've been over it. He's gone. Don't worry about where he was. I need to know where he's at right now or where he's headed."

"If he isn't in that transport, then he's beyond your reach."

"Then why do you need to see the truck?" Marcus yelled over the thumping of the blades.

"Because he could still be in there," Ackerman said as he reached the transport and looked inside. He added, "Has anyone actually stepped up inside?"

"Of course we have. I had guys crawling all over this thing. He's not hiding in there, but we'll tear it apart to be sure."

"Have you verified the identities of the guards who were driving?"

"Yes, before they left with the prisoner and then double-checked here. This is definitely their vehicle. It hasn't been switched out or anything like that. It's secure."

One of the officers ran up and asked Marcus, "Sir, we're moving the transport inside. Should we have the drivers go ahead and take it in there?"

"No, have someone else drive it. And keep those two in custody and under guard until we figure this thing out."

Maggie cursed under her breath and asked, "What about the camera in the back? Weren't the guards checking on him during the drive?"

"According to the camera, he's still in there," Marcus said. "The video feed has been compromised. Not sure how yet."

Cocking his head to the side like a curious puppy, Ackerman stared into the empty vehicle. The rear of the transport was all gray metal, with the world's most uncomfortable benches along each side. But there was no way out except for the rear doors. Not so much as a window. Considering that Marcus and the officers with him hadn't noticed the rear doors opening up and their prisoner jumping to the ladder of an awaiting helicopter, how did he escape, leaving nothing behind but his empty shackles?

Marcus felt the weight of guilt pressing down. He had dozed off a few times during the drive. Maybe he had missed the whole escape as it took place right in front of him. He balled his fists until his nails penetrated the skin of his palms.

Abruptly, Ackerman started laughing. A small giggle grew and swelled into a coughing belly laugh. It took a moment for him to stop and collect himself. Finally, he said, "It's a locked-room mystery. That. Is. Awesome."

Doing all he could to keep from choking his brother, Marcus slammed the rear door of the transport four times in quick succession, each impact shaking the armored vehicle with four clangs of metal on metal.

"Nothing about this is funny!" Marcus screamed.

"You seem to be taking this rather personally."

"We may never know how much innocent blood is on that bastard's hands. Putting him away could be the one good thing that you and I are meant to do, the whole reason we exist."

Ackerman shook his head. "Hardly. Merely one episode in a grand saga."

"Just tell me where he is. Come on, Frank. You're the escape artist. Where should we be looking?"

Ackerman seemed to consider this for a long moment and then replied, "I have no idea."

Marcus leaned in close and, through clenched teeth, whispered, "You're always looking for a chance to show off. Here's a golden opportunity."

"Don't try and play on my vanity, little brother. It's bad form. And it doesn't really matter at this point. I'm afraid our Scottish friend is long gone."

"If you have any idea how he did this, I need you to tell me now. Please. Besides, you want to know how just as much as I do."

Ackerman rolled his eyes. "Touché. If you insist, we'll need to start by going for a little ride."

8

Corin could tell something was wrong. Her home had an energy. An aura. It was as if she could sense a disturbance in some type of force. She never understood why some people laughed in her face when she shared such feelings. A friend had once explained that it was in reference to some popular film, but Corin had never been interested in stories or games.

All she cared about was increasing her quality of life and furthering her own knowledge. At least, those were the only two things she could allow herself to care about right now.

Her fiancé, Blake, had been boring her to tears lately, and she didn't fully understand why. But that was an issue to contemplate at a later date. All her brain power had been used up for today.

She slowed the Subaru in front of their jointly owned condo and whipped into their single reserved parking space, which Blake had insisted she use. He was always making nice little gestures like that. It made him hard to hate. And she didn't really want to hate him. She simply wondered if Blake, soon-to-be doctor, was truly the man with whom she wanted to spend the rest of her life. Her doubt about him was hard to quantify. Blake looked great on paper. But there was something missing. Some spark that had either burned out or was never there to begin with.

Thoughts of Blake and their eventual nuptials filled her attention for the rest of the walk inside and up the stairs to her condo. It was a two-bedroom unit, but all the dimensions had been shrunken down. It made her feel claustrophobic, as if it was one step above a cardboard box.

She pulled out her knife and released the spring-assisted blade before placing her key in the lock and going inside. She shut the front door behind her without turning on the lights. Then she stood in the threshold, waiting, the knife up in a fighter's stance.

She listened for sounds of an intruder, but the constant murmurs of the city around her made it hard to distinguish between the yuppies cackling at the bar around the corner and the slow, deliberate steps of a stalker.

Thirty seconds passed.

Forty-five.

She flipped on the lights.

One good thing about living in a shoebox was that you could look from left to right and pretty much see the whole place. It made searching for an intruder easy. She scanned both bedrooms, checked the tiny kitchen and eating area. All clear.

But should she take it a step farther?

A voice that sounded an awful lot like her sister Samantha whispered, *Don't be an idiot. You're just being paranoid over some stupid prank and a fake article. The whole thing was probably a trick to drive in ad revenue for a fake website. The same trick that all of those faux celebrity death articles capitalize on.*

But still, Corin didn't move.

Should she check the closets?

Samantha's voice in her head replied, *And then what? Under the kitchen table?*

She wished Blake was there. He would have gladly checked the house for her. And, if the man in the skull mask was waiting in the shadows, Blake would die first, giving her a chance to escape.

Waiting a few breaths longer, she stuck the folding knife into her pocket. Refusing to give in to irrational fears, she threw her keys and purse onto the counter.

But, again, a small voice against the back of her neck told her to, *Check the closets.*

The skull face popped into her mind.

Pulling out her phone, she tried to check her Twitter account as if everything was normal.

Part of her subconscious whispered, *Just get it over with. Like pulling off a band-aid.*

"Ughhhh! Fine," she said aloud.

Pulling out the knife and extending the cutting edge, she marched into her bedroom and ripped open the closet door, ready to plunge the blade into Skullface's chest.

Nothing jumped out at her.

She probed the depths but found no signs of life. Feeling like a frightened child, she moved to the closet in the spare bedroom.

She tore open the door quickly, just as she had with her own closet, the knife leading the way, ready to bury itself into any terror that may lurk in the shadows.

But this time, as she pulled open the bi-fold door, a dark form erupted toward her. She didn't even have time to scream before it was on top of her.

9

Ackerman sat with his eyes closed, his feet shackled to his hands, and both shackled to a metal bar running across the bench seat of the armored transport. He could feel Marcus's impatient gaze on him from the opposite bench, but he didn't share his brother's sense of urgency. Demon was long gone; he could feel it. There was no reason to rush.

Besides, he didn't believe in rushing. Every moment should be savored, whether that moment be one of pain, pleasure, or both. Discovering how Demon escaped wasn't something that could be rushed; it would simply take how long it was going to take.

"You better not be wasting my time here, Frank."

"If I were in Demon's situation, I would be listening and studying. But I've always been a solo act. My escape would depend upon unearthing an inherent flaw or weakness in the current system. On the other end of the spectrum, Demon has nearly endless resources and a whole agency of murderers at his disposal. I assumed he would go big and bloody. It wouldn't take all that much firepower to take down the convoy."

"But they didn't know which convoy actually held the prisoner."

"Information like that is hard to keep hold of. Doesn't really matter anyway. He didn't attack. He chose to disappear right under our noses. As if he were truly a creature of immense power whom we could never contain. It's beautiful psychological warfare."

"Focus, please. If you had Demon's resources, how would you do it?"

"I'd cheat. Kind of like stacking a deck of cards. I would arrange the playing field in such a way to ensure my victory."

"You're saying the truck has been sabotaged in some way? We're interrogating the drivers now, but they say it's the same truck they drive every day. They claim to know it like the backs of their hands."

"Demon's associates probably altered the actual vehicle while it sat on the lot."

"The transports are under twenty-four-hour surveillance in a secure area. Nobody is going to roll up with a cutting torch and start going to town on the thing."

"Perhaps they copied the vehicles and switched them at some point. It would require a moderate degree of analysis, but it could definitely be done. All the details wouldn't have to be exact. You'd just need to find a few of the vehicle's major character flaws, and the ape brains of the two officers would fill in the rest."

"Okay, let's assume for now that they were able to switch or alter the vehicles, which would be another lead to follow."

Ackerman said, "That avenue of investigation will be a dead end. A waste of our time and resources."

Marcus cocked his head to the side, cracking his neck. It was a small tick, indicative of anger and fight mode, an idiosyncrasy that Ackerman had witnessed his brother display on numerous occasions. Marcus said, "Assuming the van is altered in some way for it to allow his escape, what would the alterations be?"

"I think you could be better at this game than me, dear brother. Just close your eyes and listen. What does that beautiful mind of yours see? Break down each element. Find what's wrong. What doesn't make sense? What's broken?"

Marcus didn't close his eyes, but Ackerman could see the wheels turning. His brother's brain was falling down a rabbit hole, analyzing every small sound inside the moving transport. After a moment, Marcus reached out, grabbed the bar securing Ackerman's shackles, and began to twist and push. After a little work, it broke free from its supports. This allowed Marcus to slide the bar down a couple of inches, which in turn gave Ackerman unrestricted movement inside the cabin.

Ackerman laughed. "Nice work, little brother."

"That only gets him away from the bench. He would still need something to pick the locks on the cuffs that he left behind. But you were right, Frank, I did notice a few odd rattles and scrapes. And a few details that don't belong. Like this bolt."

Reaching down, Marcus squeezed the head of an inconspicuous bolt on the floor and pulled it free. He didn't need to twist it because it wasn't actually a bolt. It was a key.

Marcus handed it to Ackerman. "Well, I guess that confirms the transport was altered somehow. But how did he get out of the back without us noticing?"

Ackerman used the hidden key to unlock the shackles on his wrists and ankles. Then he said, "Switch benches a moment." Marcus moved over to the metal seat on the opposite side of the transport's rear cabin. Ackerman got down on his hands and knees and started pressing against the bottom of the van.

Marcus said, "We've been over all of that. There are no secret escape hatches."

"But you didn't check while the vehicle was in motion. I have a feeling that the mechanism was designed to withstand close inspection."

Marcus leaned back with a nod and a narrowing of his eyes. "And a close inspection would never be done while the transport was in motion."

Running his hand across the metal and feeling for a release of some kind, Ackerman looked back fondly on his days inside so many cages. He hated being confined like an animal, but even though he hated cages, he found great pleasure in escaping from them.

Toward the end of the bench closest to the main cabin, Ackerman pushed and was rewarded with the click of a lock being released. He pressed up on the bench, and it moved easily, having been hinged to the sidewall. The hidden hatch opened into the vehicle's wheel well and undercarriage.

Ackerman studied the craftsmanship of the concealed release mechanisms a moment and then closed the bench, shutting out the sounds of the road. He sat down and said, "Well, there you have it."

Marcus shook his head. "Okay, now he has access to the undercarriage. But he still can't go anywhere while the convoy is moving and two other vehicles are right behind him."

"It was dark. We were all tired. He merely waited for a switchback turn while we were in the mountains. When the transport slowed to round the sharp curve, he rolled to freedom."

Marcus banged on metal leading into the front cab of the transport, telling Maggie to drive them back. "Nice work. We'll find every spot along our path that held switchback curves and focus the manhunt there."

Ackerman sighed. "I told you that searching for him like that is pointless. What you seem to be missing is that Demon had no contact with his associates and yet all of this went down, and he knew that it would. He knew exactly how his minions would orchestrate the release. Probably because it's a plan of his own design. Now, do you honestly think a man with his resources wouldn't have a car waiting? Or a helicopter? Keep in mind that we're dealing with a killer as talented myself, who has nearly unlimited resources. Imagine the kind of things I would have done with his power and finances during my dark years. He's already five steps ahead of us. Most likely, he's already slipped the nets and traveled far beyond your reach."

"I'm not giving up!" Marcus yelled. "If he's five steps ahead of us, then let's start gaining ground. How do we catch him?"

"Our deceased friend, Judas, left his diaries and a path for us to follow. Why did he do that?"

"Because he wanted to use us as an instrument of revenge against his mentor. And yes, he clearly states that Demon's files are in the possession of another killer he mentions, but those leads have stalled out. We don't know where to find this *Gladiator* he talks about in the journals."

"We're overlooking something in what he's left behind for us. Judas's big production isn't over yet. Don't forget that Dmitry Zolotov grew up in the theater. We may not even have reached the end of act one."

Marcus ran a hand through his brown hair. "We've been over those journals a thousand times. And we can't trust Judas anyway. His whole game was about betrayal and proving superiority and never allowing yourself to trust others."

"But that's the point. He's not playing against us. He's playing us against Demon. He wants us to win. Avenging the murder of one's soulmate is a pretty damn personal vendetta." Ackerman was referring to the betrayal which set all of this in motion—Demon's murder of Judas's soon-to-be wife.

"That may be, but I'm not letting Demon just walk away from this. I'm not giving up yet. We're going to run him down. Trace back whoever helped him and how. He's only a few hours ahead of us."

Ackerman sighed. "I want to go on record as having told you that all that is a waste of time. We need to play Judas's game. Our path to the Demon's network of killers and his files is through the Gladiator."

"Then find me the Gladiator. Until then I'm going to chase that Scottish bastard to the ends of the earth."

Ackerman smiled. "As always, brother, your stubborn, mindless determination is simultaneously endearing and yet as annoying as stepping in excrement."

10

The Gladiator listened as Corin stomped around the house. He heard her check the first closet and approach the second.

Then his trap sprung.

She screamed in terror. Then she grunted some unintelligible curse words.

He smiled beneath the skull mask.

At the last minute, he had decided that leaving a decoy to frighten her in the closet would cause her to lower her guard, which extended the experience and allowed her to be more easily overtaken.

With this in mind, the Gladiator had crept from the closet in the spare bedroom, found Corin's ironing board, and propped it up in such a way that it would fall out onto the next person who opened the door.

He had known she would check the closets. She had followed the same routine on the previous two evenings. He was inside her mind now, her personal boogeyman. Every noise she heard became his footsteps. She could feel him coming for her.

After laying his trap, he had moved to the bathroom, pulled back the curtain, and stepped into the shower. He stood there in the dark now, waiting for Corin to follow the rest of her nightly routine and take a shower before going to bed.

He listened as she opened drawers and gathered a change

of clothes. She entered the bathroom and reached inside the curtain.

He stood at the opposite end of the shower stall, trying not to make a sound, trying not to even breathe. He watched as she rotated the faucet's handle, tested the water temperature, and pulled the shower release. Water, cold at first, struck his boots and jeans, but still he didn't make a sound.

11

Ackerman had just dropped from the back of the modified prison transport when a man in a black suit pushed past him and intercepted Marcus, jamming a handheld radio toward his brother's face. Breathing hard, the man in the suit said, "There's been a development."

Grabbing for the radio, Marcus said, "Special Agent Williams on the line. Someone give me a sitrep."

A deep voice crackled through. "Agent, this is Warden Polly. I need you and your team at the west gate immediately."

"Why? What's happened?"

"Someone just pulled up and asked to speak with you by name."

Marcus caught Ackerman's eye and shrugged, seeming to ask for input. Ackerman responded by snatching the radio from his brother's hand and saying, "Was this person on foot or in a vehicle?"

"They pulled up in a black stretch limo."

Ackerman's heart began to race. It had been a long time since anything had truly surprised him. Even when he saw the back of the empty transport, part of him had expected as much. But this seemed to be uncharted territory, and for Ackerman, greater uncertainty and danger led to greater amusement.

But, in this case, he felt differently somehow. He felt a

strange *tingling* sensation that shook him to his core, and he had no idea what to make of it.

He said, "Tell the driver to get us over there immediately. I would hate to keep our guest waiting."

"Who's in the limo?"

Ackerman crawled back into the armored transport and replied, "Let's go find out."

Two minutes later, the transport skidded to a halt in front of ADX Florence's western security checkpoint. Marcus had radioed the rest of the team, including the police officers who aided in the botched prison transfer, to meet them at the gate. Most of those officers had already arrived, positioned their vehicles as cover, and drawn their weapons—good soldiers ready to fend off an assault. Ackerman could almost taste the gun oil and testosterone.

Marcus keyed his procured radio and said, "Open the gate and let them in."

The large metal gate slid back into a wall of reinforced concrete and a long black limousine pulled inside, the barrier slamming tightly shut behind the luxury vehicle and its occupants.

The driver stepped out first, all guns coming to bear on the man, who was dressed in a formal chauffeur's uniform. He hesitated a step at the sight of the officers, but apparently having strict instructions, the driver walked back to the limo's rear door. He pulled it open and unrolled a short velvet carpet.

Ackerman wondered who would step out. Could it be Demon? Perhaps some representative of his? Someone from the government?

With the fanfare complete, a well-built and well-dressed man stepped into the frigid Colorado air. The limo's passenger wore a black tailored suit over a black dress shirt and silk tie. It was the middle of the night, but the man wore dark designer sunglasses. A styled mane of gray and black hair had been swept back from the passenger's face, allowing a clear view of the man's many scars, which were only partially concealed beneath a salt-and-pepper goatee.

Demon said, "Sorry I'm late, but you boys know how I like to make an entrance."

12

Marcus had refused to speak to Demon until the killer was in a holding cell with his Italian suit replaced by the standard white-and-gray sweatsuits worn by the inmates at ADX Florence. For good measure, Marcus also had them add a straightjacket and manacles. Now he stood on the observation side of the glass, staring in at a man who had pulled a dramatic David Copperfield-style escape, only to turn himself in a short time later.

"What the hell is his game, Frank? This is why you're here. Get inside his head."

From behind him, Ackerman said, "That's a frightening—yet intriguing—proposition. Can you imagine the night-marish landscape which occupies his subconscious?"

Marcus looked to Maggie for support, but she merely shrugged. "Sometimes I feel like I have to translate everything for you. Why would he turn himself in? He beat us in a big way. He clearly had the resources in place to slip our nets. He was a free man, and now he thumbs his nose at us like he's untouchable."

"Perhaps because he is. Or, at least, he perceives himself to be."

"I just can't wrap my head around it. This is where we keep terrorists. Al Qaeda couldn't break someone out of this place."

Ackerman said, "Yes, it doesn't bode well for those working here the day he decides to make his exit."

"He's not going anywhere."

"Remember, when dancing with the Demon, we must consider what someone like me would do with unlimited financial and political resources."

"At the first sign of trouble, they would lock the place down and call in reinforcements. This is a fortress. And politically, the Director assured me we've kept Demon's incarceration under wraps for now. Only Deputy AG Fagan knows about it. No one over his head. So even if he had political allies, they—"

Ackerman rolled his eyes. "I'm sure he made a few phone calls after he escaped and was picked up in the limousine with his tailored suit at the ready. If I had his means and proclivities, in order to escape, I would kill every person working here at the same time."

"And how the hell would you accomplish that?"

"Would you like me to make a list?" Ackerman asked.

"Actually, yeah. Make a list. Then we'll use it to make sure *he* can't pull off any of *your* plans."

With a wink, he said, "Good thinking, little brother. You'd be well served to put my genius to use."

Marcus fought the urge to punch the glass partition separating them from Demon as he watched the smug son of a bitch just sitting there like the cat who ate the canary. He said, "The question remains: Why did he turn himself in? If he wanted to play a game with us, it would have been a hell of a lot easier on the *other* side of the bars. He could have sent us coded messages or something."

"I'm perfectly aware of all he could have done. He's

obviously playing with us. But to what end? I can't say I have the slightest idea what he's up to, but I think it's time we went in there and asked him."

A moment later, Marcus and Ackerman occupied two chairs on the other side of the glass. Demon sat in front of them, straightjacketed and seemingly helpless, but the madman's eyes were as gleeful and wild as ever. The Scottish killer looked as if he was in complete control and loving every moment of it.

Marcus wanted to pound Demon's face into ground chuck, see if that wiped the smug grin away. Instead of striking, he said, "Did you have a good time?"

In his thick Scottish brogue, Demon replied, "I certainly enjoyed myself. You?"

"We figured out how you did it. It was no magic trick. We're going to work our way back to whoever modified that transport."

Demon shrugged. "You are detectives of a sort. I would expect no less, and you certainly have a lot of investigating to do. You see, I want to help you. I want to sing for you like a good little jailbird."

"We're not cutting any kind of deal."

"I'm not asking you to."

"Then what do you want?"

"As you're well aware, my former apprentice betrayed me. He couldn't have pulled all of that off without help. And there was only one person in the world who Judas may have considered to be a reasonable facsimile of a friend. His name is Gladiator. I want you to kill him for me."

Marcus cracked his neck. "We don't work for you, and we don't *kill* for anyone."

"That's not what I hear about your Shepherd Organization and its checkered past. I hear you're a regular pack of dragon slayers. Taking on Gladiator will be right up your alley. We can argue about semantics later."

Marcus popped his knuckles and was thankful that, for once, Ackerman was keeping his mouth shut. "Fine. Tell us about the Gladiator. Where do we find him?"

Demon laughed. "I'm not going to serve him up for you like a roast pig. Make no mistake, gentlemen, you're here to work for me while I take a little vacation. I'm not here to do your job for you. One clue, that's all you get. You work on that one, and maybe, if you get stuck, I'll throw you boys a bone."

"So what's our clue?"

"Two words … *Mister … King*."

Marcus reached up and squeezed the bridge of his nose. "Is that Martin Luther or Stephen?"

Demon chuckled and rattled his chains. "This would technically be a second clue, but it's neither of those fine fellows. I don't know exactly where Gladiator hangs his hat. That's why I need some good trackers. But the first step on your path to finding Gladiator is through *Mr. King*."

"And where do we find him?" Marcus asked, but Demon didn't respond. The madman simply closed his eyes and refused to say another word.

13

Marcus paced a hole in the floor of the prison conference room. The place had a strange odor, like that of a zoo. Finally, the door opened and Maggie entered with a laptop procured from the warden's office. It was the only computer they could find that was allowed Internet access. Maggie typed a few keys and then sat the laptop down on the imitation wood laminate of the conference table.

Through the laptop speakers, the team's technical director said, "You are a go for Stan. What do you need, boss?"

Marcus leaned over into view of the MacBook's webcam and said, "I need to know everything you can find about 'Mr. King.' Maybe it's the name that some news anchor gave the Gladiator or ... who knows? We can't say anything for sure. How long will it take for you to do a full search?"

Marcus watched Stan's eyes fluttering back and forth as the tech genius did his thing. The tick-tick of Stan's fingers flying over his keyboard reverberated out of the laptop's speakers.

Within a couple of seconds, Stan replied, "Already done, boss man. That's why you pay me the big bucks. I found two interesting entries for the search string of Mr. King— of course, filtering by a lot of other parameters to remove any obvious false positives. The first possibility is a crime lord in San Francisco who has taken gangland brutality to a whole new level. We're talking reclusive millionaire living in a fortress on a hill kind of thing. The second—"

Marcus interrupted. "Is this first Mr. King believed to be responsible for the wave of flayings and decapitations in San Francisco? I heard about that on the news."

The case had piqued Marcus's interest one night as he lay awake and listened to a news broadcast in the neighboring room of a hotel with extremely thin walls. The brutal nature of the murders and the presentation of the bodies had made an impression. Using his eidetic memory, he tried to recall the details of the broadcast and his feelings at the time …

The newscaster had taken a moment to warn about the content of the next segment and then said, "Two boys in Golden Gate Park discovered another victim today in a series of gruesome killings, which investigators believe to be gang related. The two boys had planned to throw away the remnants of their lunches in one of the park's trash receptacles. Instead, they found a mutilated corpse."

A skinned torso had been all that remained of each of several victims dumped inside a garbage can, just like the one the two boys had discovered. The perpetrator or perpetrators in the series of murders would often leave the garbage can with the lid open in the middle of a spot buzzing with civilians—places like playgrounds, parks, shopping centers, and school buildings.

A female investigator's voice had taken over the sound of the muffled broadcast, and Marcus recalled her saying, "We believe the victims were left in specific locations to send messages to rival criminal organizations. We have no indication that this is the work of a single serial murderer, but we …"

He remembered thinking that it was the kind of message routinely carried out in places like Juarez, but this was one of the first incarnations of such organized brutality to pop up in the United States. Still, it wasn't his type of case, and so he hadn't dug any further.

Stan replied, "Yep, that's the one. The investigators think it's all gang warfare. King's group has its hands in most of northern California's illegal businesses—everything from drugs and guns to human trafficking. King and his crews hit San Francisco like a storm of blood and bullets a few years ago. They took power quickly and ruthlessly, following the examples of the cartels. King has a reputation for brutality and for publicly executing anyone who gets in his way. The second possibility I found on my search is an alleged serial killer who they just captured in Oklahoma City."

Maggie said, "That sounds promising. Tell us more about him."

"Harvey King is the guy's name. He's charged with the torture and murder of twelve prostitutes."

Ackerman shook his head. "That doesn't sound right to me. I get the sense, based on the name of his alter ego, that our Gladiator wants worthy opponents to battle."

"Sorry, I forgot to mention that they were *male* prostitutes," Stan said.

"Ah, I stand corrected, Computer Man. Perhaps Harvey King could be Gladiator's true identity."

Maggie said, "I found that little exchange to be pretty offensive and sexist."

Ackerman cocked an eyebrow. "Apologies, little sister. I was merely considering the fitness levels of the average male and female prostitute, not judging superiority of the genders as a whole. I think it's safe to assume who would come out on top if we dropped groups of male and female prostitutes into a large pit together and had them fight to the death."

She merely scowled back in response.

Marcus said, "What about the name Gladiator? Any connection to either the gang leader or serial killer on that."

After a brief pause, Stan said, "Sorry, boss. No connection with the term Gladiator or anything directly related to fighting or arenas or anything like that in either case."

Rubbing his eyelids, which felt as if they were made of sandpaper, Marcus said, "Of course not. It couldn't be that easy. It never is." Turning to Maggie, he asked, "Where's Andrew? I'd like to get his opinion on this."

Still scowling, she said, "He's updating the Director on everything that's happened. Not that you care about my opinion, but I think it's pretty clear that we head to Oklahoma City and pay a visit to the serial killer they have in custody. This turf war case isn't our kind of thing."

Ackerman said, "Our expertise is not a valid consideration. The question is whether or not it's Demon's 'kind of thing.' Ultimately, little brother, it's your call. Personally, I've always wanted to visit San Francisco."

14

Two weeks later...

Saturday

FBI Special Agent Jerrell Fuller woke in a state of panic. He didn't know what had happened, where he was, or how he had arrived there. All he knew was that he couldn't see. The world had become an impenetrable darkness, and it took him a moment to find his bearings and get his breathing under control. He reached out into the darkness but felt nothing. He sat there on the cold concrete floor for a moment while he waited for his eyes to adjust, but after the moment passed, he realized that not a single ray of light penetrated this prison.

He was naked—except for a pair of lightweight sweat pants. They weren't his own. He had been wearing a suit, last he could remember, at one of Oban's gatherings.

Jerrell searched his memory for any clues, but his mind was a fog. He felt sluggish. Had he been drugged?

Or was it something worse? Had he been killed somehow? Was this hell?

He hesitated to search out the boundaries of the room, for fear that it would have no end. Just darkness eternal, stretching as far as human eyes could never see.

Jerrell shook his head and slapped his own face. What

was he thinking? The drugs must have still been affecting him. He was an FBI agent, undercover in a brutal syndicate built on blood and fear and lorded over by the infamous Mr. King. This being some hitman's basement was a more likely scenario than darkness eternal.

Still, a memory floated up from the back of his mind. A former foster parent, a kind, elderly lady, who maybe enjoyed showing off her "Afro-American" foster child a bit too much to her group of white friends. But he had been in homes that were much worse. The memory was of her reciting a Bible verse. "In that place there will be weeping and gnashing of teeth."

Searching for his last tangible memory, a vision of something terrifying floated up from the ether of his hazy recollection. The face of a monster, something that must have sprung forth from a nightmare rather than reality. The image in his mind was that of a metal skull, only the metal looked as though it had been melted and elongated, giving the impression that it was the skull of some kind of demon, rather than that of what had once been human. The image of the thing's teeth assaulted his dizzy faculties. The fangs had been long, jagged shards, broken and misshapen and curled up into what was almost a sadistic smile.

Pushing the memory aside and telling himself it had merely been a twisted dream, he concentrated on repairing his memory. But whatever drug he had been given was still clouding his thoughts, and the last several days seemed a jumbled blur of feelings and images.

Jerrell felt around on the floor, which seemed to be swaying back and forth as if he was on a boat. In the blackness, he didn't know which way was up or down.

All directions seemed to become one spinning vortex of darkness and memory.

He took a deep and calming breath, telling himself he was an undercover FBI agent. He had been trained for this. He had once been forced to take LSD to keep from blowing his cover. If he could fight his way through that strange trip, he could fight his way through a dizzying darkness.

Hands searching and straining, he felt something. A small deviation in the smoothness of the cold concrete. The floor dipped downward toward a small impression, and his fingers felt the metal cover of what seemed to be a small floor drain. He knew what it was for. He had seen rooms where men were tortured and bled out into drains just like this one.

Jerrell was only twenty-nine years old. The thought that he wouldn't live to see thirty had never occurred to him, despite the dangers inherent in his line of work. He was a good agent. He didn't take unnecessary risks, and he never tried to push himself deeper than was necessary. It was all about finesse and gaining trust. It took time and patience. And he had done everything right. There was no reason they should have suspected him. Unless there was a leak in the Bureau. He couldn't imagine one of his fellow agents ratting him out for money, but it had happened before. He had seen firsthand the power of greed and how easily the promise of riches could corrupt a righteous person's soul.

And in this day and age, his betrayer needn't be an actual person. Mr. King had the resources to crack FBI encryption and infiltrate the Bureau's databases. Whether by greed or technology, the fact remained that his cover must have been compromised.

He tried to remember their security protocols. How long would it be before his handlers came looking for him? Dropping out of contact for a few days wasn't uncommon during such a deep-cover assignment, and so he figured he would be long dead before help arrived. His survival depended solely on his own initiative.

But what could he do to help himself in an environment that spun like an amusement park ride and was so pitch black he couldn't see his own hands a foot in front of his face?

One small step at a time, he told himself. Explore the environment, discover your boundaries. He felt his way along the concrete until he reached an outer wall of concrete blocks. He followed that around to gauge the dimensions of the room, which was about twelve by twelve. Then he explored every inch of the walls themselves. In one wall, he found a four-foot-by-four-foot square of glass inset in the blocks. He pounded his fists and shoulder against the barrier as hard as he could, but in his confused state, he had no idea whether his blows held enough power to break a car window, let alone what he suspected to be reinforced glass or even bulletproof polycarbonate.

As he slowly regained his faculties, a disturbing thought bobbed to the surface. He had heard the rumors about the Gladiator, who acted as Mr. King's hatchet man. He had heard the horror stories of the Gladiator eliminating the crime lord's enemies over days of torture and physical abuse and ultimately skinning them alive after defeating them in a sort of bloody combat reminiscent of what slaves endured in the Roman Coliseum.

Was that to be his fate? Was he at the mercy of the Gladiator?

Special Agent Jerrell Fuller didn't have to wait long to find out. As he was exploring his small prison cell and searching for cracks in the defenses, light bombarded the room. Through squinting eyelids, he recognized that the source of the illumination came from beyond the glass partition. After a few seconds, his eyes adjusted, but what he saw caused him to stumble and fall backward away from the glass.

It was the face of the monster from his nightmares, the shining skull of an otherworldly beast.

His foggy brain recognized in that moment that he hadn't felt a door to the room, and he wondered how the nightmare figure had placed him inside the claustrophobic concrete prison. Had he been dropped through the ceiling? Had the door been walled up after he had been deposited on the concrete floor?

A disembodied voice, which was deep and electronically distorted, said, "Hello, *Agent* Fuller. That's right. We know that you are a traitor, a *Judas* in our midst, and Mr. King pays me a substantial amount of money to deal with such unwelcome interlopers. His payments serve to finance my own pursuits, and your blood, if you are worthy, will further the same purpose."

"I don't know what the hell you're talking about!" Jerrell screamed. "I was running one of Mr. King's distribution centers. I didn't do anything wrong. I would never steal from Mr. King. I would never betray him. Tell him that. I'm a loyal soldier. I'm thankful for all the opportunities he's given me, and I would never betray that trust."

"We're way beyond all that, Agent Fuller. Your mask has been removed. Your true identity and your insidious machinations have been exposed. Now is not the time to plead for your life or further taint yourself with more lies. Now is the time to prove yourself. To prove that you are worthy of survival. Worthy of being a member of a species which rules this planet in both mind and body. You will be tested, and if found worthy, you will face me in the Diamond Room."

One of the blocks near the floor fell inward, revealing a small panel of light. A paper plate containing a bloody steak, a baked potato, and a bottle of water dropped through the opening before it clamped shut.

Jerrell rushed forward on shaking legs, trying to catch the panel before it closed, but he only succeeded in kicking his meal onto the concrete.

The Gladiator said, "Eat. You'll need your strength for the trials ahead."

Then Special Agent Jerrell Fuller's world plunged back into darkness eternal.

15

Special Agent Marcus Williams lay atop the motel room sheets with his eyes closed. His alarm would be going off soon. His girlfriend and fellow SO agent, Maggie Carlisle, slept peacefully beside him, but that kind of serene slumber had always eluded Marcus.

He had fought insomnia for years, unable to turn down the volume on his brain long enough to sleep. Attempting to thwart the condition, which he hated to admit had affected his job performance, Marcus had tried music and reading, but neither seemed to work. If he listened to music, he would simply analyze the different instruments and tones for hours on end. If he read, he would simply finish the book. The only technique that seemed to work for him was something that the Shepherd Organization's counselor, Emily Morgan, had suggested: a sensory deprivation chamber known as an isolation tank.

The unit, which resided back at their base of operations in Rose Hill, VA, looked like an old iron lung. The chamber was a lightless, soundproof monstrosity filled with Epsom salts and water heated to skin temperature. It created a natural buoyancy where he achieved a sense of weightlessness coupled with total isolation from the typical waves of overwhelming input.

Now, lying in this motel-room bed, he heard the noise of cars outside, analyzed the sizes of their engines as well as the possible makes and models based upon the unique growls and hums. He could hear the neon lights of the motel sign buzzing like a thousand wasps in his brain. He analyzed Maggie's breathing to see if he could determine the nature of her dreams. Someone had a television running in an adjoining room. He couldn't make out the details of the broadcast, but he guessed that it was a news program, a conjecture founded upon the beats and pauses of the muffled words and sounds pumping from the TV speakers.

He had given up on sleep hours ago, and instead, he replayed the events of Demon's escape, scrutinizing his every move and decision to determine if a flaw in his own thinking had led to the almost-disaster.

Even though Demon was now locked away in one of the world's most secure prisons, Marcus felt they had failed in every way and were only playing out whatever demented scheme the madman had concocted.

The Shepherd team had already spent two weeks analyzing, searching, and investigating in Oklahoma City, but just as Ackerman predicted, they had reaped nothing but a series of dead ends and wild-goose chases. Everyone was beginning to feel that they were barking up the wrong tree, even Maggie. The more they dug into the serial killer in custody in Oklahoma City, the more Marcus was certain he had made the wrong call, a decision that may have killed their chances of catching the Gladiator.

Not wanting to dissect the case and his failure any further, his thoughts turned to other questions: Was he a good father? Should he have allowed his brother out of a cage?

But it wasn't long before the case crept back to the

forefront. Unanswered questions were like thorns in his brain, and this case was all questions and no answers. He fought the urge to scream in frustration. He yearned for sleep, wondering why it had been so hard to keep his heavy lids from falling during the drive from Arizona. Why couldn't he do the same now?

Checking the time, he turned off the alarm ten minutes before it sounded and got up. He showered and threw on a black T-shirt and jeans. Several days of stubble poked out from the skin on his face, but he didn't have the energy to shave and told himself it made him look tough, instead of merely lazy.

The Director had called the night before and told him to be at the diner across the street at 5:00 a.m. for a meeting. The team had been working long hours, with every pursuit proving fruitless. They were all exhausted, but he hoped the old man had somewhere for their investigation into the Gladiator to begin. Making a command decision, he hadn't informed the rest of the team about the early-morning rendezvous, figuring they could use the extra rest after the disappointments of the past two weeks. In truth, he was envious of their tranquil slumber, something which seemed so alien to him.

He would have been better off working through the nights rather than lying there *trying* to pass out. But Maggie always wanted him to lie with her until she fell asleep. There were some nights when he would simply listen to her breathe in and out until she guided him down into dreams. But even those nights were filled with nightmares so vivid that he sometimes forgot whether his surroundings were real or imaginary. He had once caught himself dreaming about a case and then thinking the next day that the dream had actually happened.

The diner across the street reminded Marcus of Mel's Drive-in, which had been featured in the film *American Graffiti*. The 50s and 60s atmosphere alleviated some of the tension in his chest, reminding him of the simple pleasures of greasy food, ice cream, and another of his loves: classic cars. He spotted the Director and joined him at a booth in the corner.

Noticing that two drinks already rested on the table, Marcus asked, "Who's your guest?"

The Director didn't look up from the menu. "Val wants to speak with you. He's in the restroom."

He hadn't been expecting to see Special Agent Valdas Derus of the FBI's Behavioral Analysis Unit again so soon. Val had been a member of the director's former team at the SO, and then later, during the Judas debacle at Foxbury Prison, Val had run interference with the media for them. Marcus looked over the menu and tried not to worry about the FBI agent's sudden appearance.

As Val approached, Marcus analyzed the agent, as he almost involuntarily did with everyone. Val was Lithuanian by birth, but only a very slight accent remained to betray his country of origin. A very handsome man with flowing black hair and only a hint of gray, Val's age was impossible to ascertain from his features, and the Director had explained that Val was a notorious flirt and always in search of wife number three.

Valdas moved his coffee to the same side as the Director's and slid into the booth. In stark contrast to his virile former teammate, the Director had been on a noticeable decline for months. Marcus guessed that some disease ravaged the old man's body even now, but personal information wasn't something the Director shared with his underlings. His superior's behavior shouldn't have surprised him, considering the Director was a man who insisted on being called by title alone. He had only learned the Director's real first name because of Ackerman's hacking of the SO's personnel files. Marcus wondered what other secrets his brother had learned while poking around in the digital shadows.

Val said, "Good to see you, kid. Although I wish it was under better circumstances."

The waitress arrived and took their orders. Marcus opted for coffee and the Elvis Scramble—three scrambled eggs loaded with chorizo, green chili peppers, and Monterey Jack cheese.

When the waitress was gone, Marcus said, "You should know as well as anyone, Val, that we don't have better circumstances than these at the SO. Just blood and death."

"That's depressing. I don't remember it that way during my tenure."

"Why are you here?"

The Director said, "Marcus, show some respect."

"Sorry. Why are you here, sir?"

Valdas chuckled. "He reminds me of you, Philip." The comment earned an eye-roll from the Director, but Val continued, "The bureau needs your team's help, Marcus. We had an undercover agent recently go missing in San Francisco."

At the mention of the city they should have been in during the past two weeks, Marcus's stomach flipped as if he had just boarded a rollercoaster. Before he had even heard the details, he could sense that this missing agent wouldn't have been missing if it wasn't for Marcus choosing the wrong Mr. King.

Cursing under his breath, the anger rising, he said, "And let me guess, this relates back to our other Mr. King possibility. How recently did your agent go missing?"

"He failed to check in two days ago. And yes, our agent, Jerrell Fuller, was attempting to infiltrate a crime syndicate led by a man known only as Mr. King."

Marcus withstood the urge to break something. "What can we do to help?"

"We believe most of the mutilations to be gang related, but the corpses' appendages and skin were removed, and so the police have been unable to identify all of the bodies."

"Dental records?"

"What's left of the head is usually just a completely shattered skull and a mound of flesh. There are no teeth to identify."

Marcus thought about that, imagining a skull splitting. How much force would that require? From somewhere deep in his brain, the face of a scientist saying "a skull fracture requires five hundred kilograms of force. A man would have to weigh five hundred kilograms to fracture a skull by stepping on it." He made the conversion in his head. That would equal about eleven hundred pounds. Another memory from a visit to Ripley's Believe It or Not told Marcus that the heaviest person in medical history was Jon Brower Minnoch.

Marcus didn't specifically memorize those minor details, but his memory was like a series of detailed mental snapshots that he could refer to later. In his mind, he traveled back to that memory and conjured an image of the small metal plaque containing the information. From the plaque, Marcus learned that Minnoch weighed nine hundred and seventy-five pounds.

The laws of physics told him that it was nearly impossible for a human to exert enough force to crack a human skull. Break the jaw, cause internal damage to the brain, sure. But to actually crack the skull …

He said, "What did he use to smash the heads?"

"The examiners think it was a sledge hammer."

Marcus didn't need to remember any figures. He knew a sledge would get it done. He'd seen it before, back in his days with the NYPD.

Valdas continued, "The case is getting a lot of political heat. No one wants the public to believe that America is susceptible to the kind of violence seen south of the border. But there's something we haven't shared with the press."

"Don't keep me in suspense."

"The autopsies show that the male victims were always severely beaten prior to their deaths. These people fought for their lives."

"Why is that unusual? They could have been tortured for information or tried to escape."

Val shrugged. "Possibly. But we have been able to identify a few of the bodies who we can't tie back to anything illegal or gang related. A marine was identified by some shrapnel wounds and a boxing champion by some pins in his shoulder. We can't find any reason those men would be targeted by King."

Marcus shrugged, but his mind was starting to make the

connections. "Could have been in the wrong place at the wrong time."

Val added, "Except there's one more thing. Before Agent Fuller went missing, he recorded a conversation between an unknown party and King's righthand man, Oban Nassar, during which Nassar refers to 'The Gladiator.'"

Pulling out a cell phone, Val played an audio file for Marcus. He had to hold it up to his ear to hear the one-sided conversation and the exotic accent of Oban Nassar.

... Hello. Yes, sir ... I understand ... That is very unsettling news ... Decisive action is certainly required, sir. He's already seen too much. He must be dealt with quickly, in order to mitigate the damage ... With all due respect, sir, I don't believe this is a job that would require the services of the Gladiator ... I wouldn't argue that, sir, but you know how I feel about the prices that the Gladiator and his handler have been charging for their services ... Do you think it's wise to send this man to the Diamond Room? ... Of course, sir ... I understand. Consider it done ...

Marcus's body went rigid as his mind wove the various threads of the investigation into an intricate pattern. "So we know Demon's organization is built on turning serial murderers with a special talent into killers for hire. And now, you think that King has the Gladiator on his payroll and these dismemberments are being carried out by the Gladiator on Mr. King's behalf."

The Director said, "My guess is that Demon offers a package where he ensures that the killings can't be traced back to the client because the killer involved does his thing on more than just the people who could be tied to the group paying for the murders."

Marcus nodded in agreement. "A smoke screen to insulate the client if the killer is ever apprehended. But in this case, we can work it in reverse. We know the client and can use him to lead us to the killer. Exactly like Demon planned for us to do."

Val said, "Our agent disappeared shortly after that recording was sent. We have to assume that Agent Fuller is the man who Oban Nassar mentions as 'knowing too much' and requiring 'decisive action.' If we're right, then we have very little time to get our man back alive."

"You think the Gladiator plays with them? Forces them to fight? That would explain how he earned the nickname. And that also explains the boxer and the marine. He's choosing worthy opponents," Marcus said. "But from what I've seen on the news there were also a couple of female bodies found skinned. That doesn't seem very sporting for someone who considers himself some kind of ultimate warrior."

Val took a sip of coffee and replied, "Judging from the female torsos, they were actually rather petite women. Not well muscled. So it's not as if they were MMA stars. And we haven't found a way to positively identify the female victims to see if they could be tied back to King."

The Director chimed in, "But we have a theory. I asked Stan to reach out to some of his contacts in the digital underworld to see if any of them had ever heard of the 'Diamond Room.' There is apparently some site out on the Dark Web known as the Diamond Room."

Marcus knew the basics of the Dark Web. It was a term used to refer to websites found on Darknets, overlay networks which use the public Internet but require specific software, configurations, or authorizations to access.

The waitress returned with their food, placing a plate filled with grease and protein in front of him. Marcus said a quick silent prayer for the meal and the victims of such carnage before digging into his Elvis-inspired breakfast. With a mouth full of eggs, he said, "So what's on this site, the Diamond Room?"

"Stan can't access it, and neither can his friends. The rumor is that it's a place where you can watch people fight and die on a live video feed."

Val's breakfast was a bowl of fruit and vanilla yogurt. He mixed the two together and said, "I inquired with our cybercrimes unit, and they told me that the Bureau has been trying to get a glimpse of the footage or access to the site for a couple of years now."

"Sounds like our friend, Gladiator, is streaming his killings to the web," Marcus said, shoveling the eggs into his mouth and trying to remember the last time he had eaten.

The Director said, "Stan's friend has apparently seen one still image from the Diamond Room. He said that the Gladiator wears a metal mask in the shape of a deformed skull. That led us to—"

A small cough grew to a full, body-shaking hack, and the Director held his napkin up to his face. Marcus thought that he saw blood when his boss wadded it up in his fist. Even after he had brought the cough under control, the Director couldn't catch his breath.

Coming to his old friend's rescue, Valdas said, "The skull mask connection led us to a recent urban legend in the San Francisco area that they're calling *Skullface*."

Marcus rolled his eyes. "An urban legend?"

"Someone hacked into a bunch of woman's social media

accounts and doctored their photos, adding a man in a skull mask somewhere in the background of every photo. Really freaked a lot of people out, but harmless, right? Until some of the hacking victims went missing. The SFPD has a task force trying to track down the missing girls and this Skullface hacker."

"And you're thinking that the Gladiator and Skullface are actually the same guy?"

The Director, eyes still watery and his voice like brittle leaves, said, "Yes. We'd like you to work with the local task force and see if their investigation has uncovered anything useful."

Marcus replied, "But we also need to focus on King and his organization. And we're going to have to hit hard. We'll need to color outside the lines and get to information faster than the Bureau can through strictly legal means."

Val sucked in his lips as if he wanted to hold back his next words.

Marcus asked, "What aren't you telling me?"

The Director slid a manila folder across the table and said, "We don't have the time to work a plea deal or anything like that in order to get a reference or quick access to King, or at least someone high up in his organization. Without a reputation or connection, we can't get anywhere close to King. But we think you may be able to convince an old friend of yours to do us a favor."

Marcus didn't have to open the file. He saw a name on the folder's tab that told him all he needed to know: *Caruso, Edward*.

He dropped his fork, ran a hand through his hair, and leaned back in the booth. "You're kidding me, right?"

The Director said, "You have history, and you know damn well that he'll help you. If you swallow a bit of pride. Kiss his ass a little. Tell him what he wants to hear. It's just words, kid."

Marcus started to object, but the Director added, "And that's not all. Once you earn Caruso's help, we plan on sending Ackerman in undercover with you."

"Absolutely not. He's not ready."

Val said, "He did a hell of a job during the Foxbury incident. Saved a lot of lives."

"It's out of the question. He shouldn't be put in a position like that. Listen, I really think he wants to help, to make amends for all he's done. But he's not afraid of anything, including the consequences of his actions, and he simply doesn't understand how to behave. He needs a filter, someone to guide him."

"You'll be there with him. But let's face it, Marcus, they'll smell cop all over you. Ackerman will help establish your ... credibility."

"It's out of the question. I can go in undercover alone. I grew up in Brooklyn and knew a lot of guys from the families, and I've never been much of a cop."

The Director said, "Let's take this thing one step at a time. You just worry about Eddie Caruso, and we'll go from there."

Marcus hadn't talked to Eddie since leaving the NYPD, and their last conversation had not been a pleasant one. "I think you've misjudged my relationship with Eddie."

The Director laughed. "I know more about you than you do yourself, and I'm confident you can persuade him to help."

Val added, "We don't have time to get anyone to turn. Agent Fuller is probably being tortured as we speak. This guy used to be your best friend, and now he's a capo working for Tommy Juliano. He's our best shot at getting close enough to King's organization to learn something useful."

"I haven't been back to the city in years."

"Then it's time for a stroll down memory lane," the Director said. "Also, you don't really have much choice in the matter. Val and I and Deputy AG Fagan are all in agreement that this is the best use of our resources to find the Gladiator as quickly as possible and recover the missing agent. The Bureau is loaning us two of their Gulfstream jets to fly you and Maggie up to New York. Emily and your brother will head to San Francisco in the other jet to prepare for the meeting with the task force. But I'm afraid I'm going to need to steal Andrew for a bit."

"This just keeps getting better and better. You're taking my most dependable team member, and I'm ranking him above me on that, and you want to leave our rookie agent alone with my brother."

The Director said, "First of all, I think your brother may be in love with Emily, in his own twisted way."

"He killed her husband and destroyed her life."

"Exactly. Combine that with her many psychology degrees, and it makes her the perfect candidate to keep Ackerman in line. Plus, we always have the implied threat of our failsafe option."

"You just better hope that my brother doesn't figure out the truth of what you implanted in his spine. What if I say no? To all of it. What if I say that I can't knowingly carry out orders which I feel could put the lives of my team and myself in danger?"

"Could you give Marcus and me a moment, Val?"

Without a word of protest, Special Agent Valdas Derus dropped his napkin on the table and headed to the restroom.

"Listen up, kid," the Director said. "I've put up with your bullshit this long because you're very good at what you do, but I'm getting way too old and way too damn tired to coddle you anymore. You do as you're told or you can go back to being the pariah you were when I found you, and the DOJ will hand your brother over to the CIA to do whatever they want with him. I had guessed that they wanted to put him to work for them, but maybe they really just want him so they can cut open his brain and find out what makes him tick, find out exactly why he's the man with no fear. I suspect it would be pretty useful for them to be able to recreate such qualities in their own assets. So in response to your 'what if' question, you either follow orders or you're out on the street and Ackerman goes back to being a science experiment."

"Frank isn't ready for this."

"Your brother is the meanest, toughest son of a bitch I know. He can handle himself undercover."

Marcus leaned across the table and looked deep into the old man's eyes. "First of all, don't ever talk about our mother like that. Next time, I'll feel compelled to defend her honor. Second, for the record, this isn't going to end well. You remember I said that. And third, to be clear, I'm not worried about Frank's safety. I'm worried about everyone else."

16

Dr. Derrick Gladstone didn't believe in God—whether it be the Judeo-Christian God, Allah, or any of the minor deities imagined to rule over the forces of nature. He believed all religion to be superstition and nonsense. His religion was science, and looking at life from a purely scientific standpoint, he could find nothing to suggest he should deny himself any pleasure or follow any kind of moral code. After all, we are here, and then we are nothing—what more is there than to pursue one's own goals and fantasies? If it benefited him to be kind, then he would do so. If murder or rape or robbery was for his own benefit or the benefit of science and his place in history, then he had no problem with those acts either.

He knew that people couldn't simply run around lawless, killing and stealing from whomever they wished. But if you were smart enough not to get caught, then what reason was there not to commit the crime? The answer, Derrick supposed, was *fear*. The only reason not to act on your own self-interests was for fear of a deity, fear of consequences, or fear of your own ignorance. The first because you may face an inescapable punishment upon your death. The second because you could possibly face criminal repercussions for your actions. And the third because you fear that you are ignorant in your belief that the first two don't exist and shouldn't be feared at all.

What did he have to fear from an imaginary deity or from the law of the land when he was a *golden god* himself?

Derrick found it astonishing the things a man could accomplish when he abandoned the laws of gods and men and became his own master.

He dropped the patient's file he had been reading atop his desk, rubbed his eyes, and stretched out his arms. A whole stack of neglected paperwork sat beside the discarded folder. With everything going on in his life right now, he found it impossible to concentrate on work. But the privilege of owning an extremely successful company allowed Derrick a lot of freedom with his time. Still, there were some tasks—and some special patients—which required his personal attention and couldn't be entrusted to one of his many underlings.

Grabbing the push bar of his wheelchair, Derrick spun himself over to the side wall of his office where a small table of all glass held a crystal carafe in the shape of a skull. Fine cognac filled the skull. Four snifters and a few photographs of himself rested beside the liquor.

One picture showed him in a black wetsuit at a beach in Brazil holding his Mayhem Driver surfboard, which he had preferred because of it's ability to navigate dead sections and link waves together. He missed his time in the ocean.

Thanks to good genes, a strict diet, and an intense dedication to his own fitness, Derrick had always possessed a body which rippled with muscle and held no excess fat. Even while bound to a wheelchair, he refused to allow his muscles to wither and had continued a rigorous workout regimen.

Derrick supposed he would have been the perfect mate. He provided everything any partner could have possibly wanted. If it hadn't been for his injury ...

His impressive physique coupled with a square jaw, perfectly symmetrical features, flawless bronze skin, perfectly coifed head of sandy blond hair, and pale-blue eyes had always made it exceedingly easy for Derrick to attract the opposite sex. But even before the accident, he had little use for the fairer sex, beyond their necessity in procreation. His last long-term relationship had been his high-school girlfriend, and even then he had only put up with her because she was the head cheerleader and the most popular girl in school, and her adoration and the envy of his classmates served to augment his stature as star football player, valedictorian, and all-around alpha male. It was a place of honor that he had achieved through meticulous planning and hard work. Still, beyond the social aspects and satisfying his active teenage libido, she soon became a liability rather than an asset. In college, he found there were more than enough females ready to satisfy his physical needs without the emotional investment required by a mate.

Derrick picked up another of the photographs. This one showed a younger version of himself on one knee in full football pads. The younger Gladstone leaned over on his helmet and showed that million-dollar smile. Memories of his time on the gridiron filled him with a strange warmth. In another life, he could have played in the NFL, possibly both sides of the ball, offensively as a running back and defensively as a linebacker.

They had called him Derrick "The Gladiator" Gladstone.

The phone on his desk chirped, and his secretary said, "Dr. Gladstone, I have your brother on line two."

Derrick growled in disgust as he wheeled himself back to his desk. "Thank you, Susan, but I'm quite busy. Did he say why he's calling?"

"Dennis said that he's planning a visit and wanted to work out the details with you."

Gritting his teeth, he tried to remain calm. He counted to five and took a few deep breaths. "Thank you, Susan, I'll take the call."

His fraternal twin brother had always been Derrick's opposite. Dennis had struggled with grades and his weight and had shied away from sports and popularity. Where Derrick had fought with every fiber of his being to be extraordinary in every pursuit, his brother was more than satisfied with mediocrity.

"Hello, Dennis, to what to do I owe the pleasure of a call from my little brother?"

"You're older than me by like ten minutes."

"And I always will be."

His brother laughed and said, "Same old Derrick. Listen, we're going to be coming up to San Francisco next week and would love to spend some time with you and Mom."

Dennis always was a momma's boy. "Now's a really bad time for that."

"We both know you can make time whenever you want. That's the perks of being a big-shot doctor, and Mom isn't getting any younger. In her condition, there's no way she'd survive another stroke."

"She's fine. She'll be alive and well for Thanksgiving and Christmas. You can see her then."

"I've already made all the arrangements, and I've booked a hotel for Helen and me and the kids. The youngsters would love to spend a little time with their uncle. They adore you."

Of course they do, Derrick thought. *They probably wish I was their father instead of you.*

"Yes, I love them too, but as I said, now's not a good time. I have a lot going on with the business, and—"

"That's fine. If we only get to see you in the evenings or for dinner, we'll make do. But we're still coming up to see Mom. And…I was thinking maybe she could come stay with us for a while."

"That's out of the question. She's settled in here. Her doctors and caregivers are here."

"Yeah, but Helen's at home and could take care of her, and in your condition, we thought it might help to—"

"My condition?"

"You know what I mean. You're a busy guy and—"

"I said no."

Silence hung over the lines, and Derrick pictured his brother as a little boy bleeding from the nose and mouth. Derrick recalled himself pummeling Dennis's face, driving his fist up and down as if it was powered by strong hydraulics. Their mother had stood over them, a glass of Everclear and apple juice sloshing in her glass as she forced them to fight for her own amusement. "Only the strong survive in this armpit of a world, boys. You have to fight for everything you have."

Despite the fact that Derrick was always the victor in their mother's encouraged brawls, it was always Dennis who would receive her attention afterward as she stroked his dark hair and called him her "poor baby."

Over the phone line, Dennis finally said, "Well, we can discuss it more next week. Send Mom my love."

Derrick hung up without a word of goodbye, his anger swelling at his brother's insistence on a visit. This couldn't have come at a worse time. His plans were almost ready. Soon, he would have the necessary funds to solidify his legacy, and before that could happen, many preparations needed to be made. He couldn't accomplish anything with his sniveling little brother staring over his shoulder, still vying for the old witch's affections.

Closing his eyes and picturing his fist slamming into his brother's face, Derrick laughed and shook his head. He wouldn't let his brother stand in his way.

One of Derrick's many strengths was his ability to adapt and overcome any circumstance. After all, the ability to adapt to one's environment was crucial to being selected by nature as the instrument of advancement for one's species. And Derrick Gladstone intended to carve his name into the evolution of mankind.

17

Baxter Kincaid stepped from his front door onto Haight and Ashbury, the long stretch of concrete where Jimi Hendrix and Janis Joplin and other icons of the hippie movement had lived and spread their unique philosophy. Baxter didn't consider himself to be a hippie and was a disciple of no man. Still, he respected the efforts of the hippie founding fathers and mothers. The messages of peace and love were ones that he strongly identified with, but he also realized that it was not Hendrix and Jerry Garcia who had originally spread such a message.

The sun shined brightly, and the weather was beautiful. As he stepped out onto the sidewalk, having descended from an apartment where Hendrix himself had once resided, he spread his arms and thanked God for such a wonderful day.

Then he stuck a joint in his mouth and flipped open his Zippo lighter. The ace of spades adorned its face over an inscription declaring the greatest commandment: "Love the Lord your God with all your heart, your mind, and all your strength, and love others as yourself."

He inhaled deeply and took the sweet herb into his lungs. As he did so, he said a silent prayer, honoring the Father, Son, and the Holy Spirit.

Then Baxter headed down the street to Amoeba Music. He was in search of a Beck album on vinyl, but his ulterior motive was to spend a bit of time flirting with the goth chic whom he knew to be on duty that morning. Jenny Vasillo was the most attractive woman he had ever encountered. Perhaps not the most beautiful, but she possessed an inner strength which filled Baxter with a sense of excitement and warmth every time he entered her orbit.

As he walked, he stuck a small Bluetooth headset into his ear and brought up a recording app on his phone. His neighbor Kevin, a young techie whom Baxter suspected to be a paranoid schizophrenic, had convinced him to start a website and blog for his private investigation agency. Baxter had considered the idea a waste of time. If he needed clients, the universe would provide them; he was not concerned about searching them out. But Kevin had been adamant and promised to handle everything for free, and so Baxter had let the kid have his fun. A few times a week, he would record something and send it on to Kevin to correct and post on the website. The blog had actually earned a bit of a following, although Baxter wasn't sure why. He mostly just rambled about whatever popped into his head at the time.

Starting the recording and thinking of a time in the not-so-distant past when people thought you were crazy when you walked down the street talking to yourself, he said in his slow, south Texas drawl, "Baxter's Log, star date … whatever the hell date it is … There's darkness in us all—I've seen that time and again—but I don't believe in evil. Evil is an illusion. It doesn't truly exist. That may seem like a strange thing to say, especially from someone like me who often pays the bills exploring the darker side of the human soul. You may ask: How can he say that evil doesn't exist when we can see so much of it in the world? You don't have to look very far or think very hard to conjure up some fine examples. I'll give you an easy one. Adolf Hitler. The unspeakable acts of barbarism and cruelty committed by the leader of the Nazis and his regime are pretty universally considered evil. Pol Pot, Ted Bundy, Richard Nixon, the list goes on. So how can I possibly say that evil doesn't exist?"

Baxter paused to fist bump one of his neighbors who owned a vintage clothing store.

He continued, "To answer that question—Is evil real or merely an illusion?—we must ask another. What is darkness? Can you touch darkness? Does it have shape and form and substance? No, darkness is merely the *absence* of light. So what is evil? Evil is merely the *absence* of good. And we as human beings cannot be one hundred percent good or one hundred percent evil. We all have the capacity for both. Most would agree that only a loving God or a hate-filled Satan would be able to achieve the pinnacle of that spectrum. I would argue, however, that even the Devil isn't one hundred percent evil. After all, he started his career as an angel and was created by the same Universe that breathed life into every one of us. It's just that old red is as far away from the 'light' as one can travel. I can almost guarantee you that Lucifer doesn't see himself as the bad guy. I suspect he feels somehow justified in his torment of mankind and disobedience toward his creator. And the same can be said about our friend Adolph. He thought he was saving humanity from itself through racial and ethnic cleansing. Evil isn't something we are; it's something we do."

He paused to consider that, taking a long drag from the joint. "So how do we determine whether our actions are good or evil? I think it's simple. Do your deeds sow the seeds of love and peace or hatred and discord? Unlike evil, hatred is very real. It's not merely the absence of love. Hatred is the conscious decision to choose destruction over creation, despair over repair, judgment and condemnation over joy and harmony. So remember, brothers and sisters out there on this digital web of interconnected thoughts and information, step into the light and let your love shine bright."

He laughed as a car drove by right after he ended the recording blaring out a Beatles song, which proclaimed that love is all we need. It was as if the Universe was giving him a big thumbs up. He continued to chuckle as he puffed the last of his joint and stamped it out in a small, sand-filled ashtray and trashcan beside the entrance to Amoeba Music.

As he stepped into the store, security checked his fanny pack, which contained an eighth of herb and a small metal pipe. The security guard knew him and had no problem with the weed, for which Baxter possessed a medical card allowing him to legally consume marijuana—which wouldn't matter in a few months when California officially legalized recreational use. The guard was merely verifying that he held no weapons, which was something Baxter rejected on principle, but he allowed the big man to follow his routine. The kid didn't know that Baxter had once been a homicide detective and, after leaving the SFPD, had vowed to never pick up a gun again.

As he approached the counter, Jennifer Vasillo's pale cheeks flushed with red. Her skin was the color of alabaster, and her hair was an artificial match for a raven's feather. A round nose ring pierced her left nostril, and tattoos of unicorns and roses adorned her forearms.

Baxter tilted his trilby hat and said, "I bid good morning to you, fair Jennifer." He gave her his best smile, showing off the dimples in his cheeks. Chicks always dug his dimples.

Jenny V rolled her eyes and said, "As always, Mr. Kincaid, you're full of something that starts with an 'S.'"

"When are you going to let me take you out on the town?"

"'Out on the town'? Seriously, who says that? How old are you? And I'll think about allowing you to 'date' me when you get a real job."

"That's harsh. I do pretty well as a private investigator. And I'm captain of my own ship. Master of my own destiny."

"I'm sure you're great at being a 'dick' for sale. So great that Faraz, that greasy pimp, was in here looking for you this morning."

"What did he want? And why did he come here?"

"Said he needed to hire you, and he didn't have your number or address. I figured he would be your ideal client."

"I do most of my work for lawyers and the cops."

"Okay, then I guess the pimp is actually far more respectable than your typical clients."

"You cut me deep, fair Jennifer. Did he leave a message?"

"Just to stop by his place."

Baxter Kincaid unbuttoned his white Hawaiian shirt adorned with pale red flowers and struck a pose like an underwear model, showing off his muscled abdomen. He said, "Do you think maybe he was wanting to recruit me as a male prostitute?"

"No shirt, no service."

Baxter buttoned up and said, "Has my vinyl arrived?"

"Do I look like your secretary?"

"Yes, you do actually. And I have a crush on my secretary."

She rolled her eyes and said, "That sounds creepy, not sexy. And if I'm your secretary, then it's not flirting, it's sexual harassment. Go check the rows, Romeo," Jenny V said, returning to the magazine she had been reading.

Baxter headed toward the aisles of records and vintage concert posters, noticing the sign over a hallway which read, "Medical Marijuana Screenings." This was where he had received his own medical card. He smiled, thinking how lucky he was to live in the fabulous city of San Francisco. And not just because of the counterculture. Baxter had even loved *The City* during his days as a homeless kid on her streets.

Working his way to the proper row, he found the vinyl album he had used as an excuse to come in, checked out, and headed over to the pimp's house. Curiosity drove him more than anything else. Baxter had befriended most of the malcontents who resided on Haight and Ash and in the other sketchy neighborhoods of the city, like the Tenderloin district where he'd cut his own teeth.

Baxter had been originally raised in San Antonio, Texas, but his family moved a month after his thirteenth birthday. He would never forget the days of soup kitchens and homeless shelters as a young teen. He knew these were his people, and the city would always be his home. It was the only place where people understood the pain of growing up hungry and destitute and why letting your freak flag fly was nothing to be ashamed of.

The pimp's apartment was a couple alleyways off Haight and Ash. Most of Faraz's business was done in hotel rooms, but he maintained a small bordello within his apartment building, which doubled as a home for the girls who couldn't afford a place of their own. Baxter had clandestinely removed most of the truly noxious influences in the neighborhood through his SFPD connections, and more radical means, but Faraz wasn't all bad. He didn't necessarily agree with the man's profession, but at least Faraz respected his ladies and gave them opportunities to rise above working on their backs. Many of his girls had earned their GEDs and moved on to more respectable lines of work. Faraz had actually grown more successful because of the opportunities he afforded his girls.

Baxter would not typically answer a summons from a man like Faraz. He paid the bills by working for high-priced lawyers and using his network of informants to help his old colleagues in the SFPD, but Faraz had earned his respect enough to warrant at least a consultation.

The face of the apartment building was covered in flaking white paint, and the apartments had been built with bay windows and high ceilings. At one time, the building had probably been an expensive hive for the city's elite hippies. Now, it was Faraz's personal domain and a high-priced brothel catering to the many businessmen visiting the city in search of the free love found back in the 60s, and finding that this brand of loving was hardly free.

The building smelled vaguely of urine, herb, and cigarettes, but so did most of the back alleys here. A brooding hulk of a man stood guard just inside the front entrance. As Baxter crossed the threshold, the hulk stepped in front of him and said, "Do you have an appointment?"

"No, but Faraz left a message that he wanted to see me."

The big, bald-headed white guy wore gold aviator

sunglasses, and the lower half of his face protruded out like the countenance of a chimpanzee or monkey. The Monkey Man said, "Mr. Faraz is busy and not receiving visitors."

Baxter raised an eyebrow. "Busy sampling his own wares?"

Monkey Man didn't understand. Instead, the guard said, "You need to leave. Come back later."

"I was summoned, big man. And I'm not a dog that merely comes when you call. If he doesn't see me right now, then he can take his case to the National Society of Pimps and Assholes and see how that shakes out for him."

Monkey Man shoved Baxter away and said, "The boss is busy. Bounce."

"Are you positive you don't want to at least ask him? Just in case his business with me is more important than getting his knob polished?"

"I said get to stepping, prick!"

Baxter pulled a cell phone from his pocket and held it up to take a picture. Clearly frustrated and wanting to get back to staring mindlessly at nothing, Monkey Man said, "What are you doing?"

"I just wanted to get a picture of you. I'm going to send it to the Discovery Channel. They'll pay big money for a shot of Bigfoot in his natural habitat."

The punch from Monkey Man was fast for a big man, but still much too slow for Baxter to allow it to connect.

He deplored violence, but some people refused to listen without a slap to the face. He ducked beneath the big man's right hook and punched him squarely in his nut sack. When the Neanderthal bent forward in pain, Baxter threw his elbow up into the man's jaw, mostly using his legs to supply the force of the blow. The move connected with a crunch, aviator sunglasses flying from his elongated head as the big man fell back unconscious.

A memory of his father swam to the surface of Baxter's consciousness. "Don't ever start the fight, Bax," his father had said, "but make damn sure you finish it."

He snatched up the primate's Aviators and slipped them over his ears. They were the version with brown-tinted lenses, just like Baxter preferred. His pair had been broken by a pissed-off lawyer almost a week prior. The brown lenses gave the world a warm, sepia-toned quality. It made him feel as if every moment was a fond memory captured by some department store photographer.

Reaching into his fanny pack, he loaded a bowl as he ascended the stairs to Faraz's "penthouse." Striking his Zippo and lighting the herb, he reached the second floor. The walls were old plaster but had been re-painted recently. The place was clean and smelled of jasmine. The six small apartments on this floor belonged to Faraz's girls. The third floor had once been the same conglomeration of tiny one-bedrooms, but the self-aggrandizing Faraz had knocked down all the walls and converted the third floor into his private domain and business office where he ruled over his harem like a medieval lord.

Baxter supposed a lot of men would envy such power, but he knew it to be a hollow existence. Love could theoretically be cheap, but it was never free.

By the time he reached the third floor, Baxter had started to sweat. Temperatures in the city were usually only in the high sixties and low seventies this time of year, but today was an anomaly with the heat index pushing eighty-five degrees. Like most buildings and homes in the Bay area, Faraz's bordello wasn't equipped with air-conditioning.

Baxter removed his straw trilby—the kind worn on the beach, resembling the fedora of the old-time gangsters only smaller in diameter—and ran a hand through his damp mop of curly blonde hair. Despite his south Texas roots, he wasn't accustomed to this kind of heat.

He took a long puff of the sweet leaf as he reached the third floor and blew it out into the open space. He could still see where the walls of the apartments had once been, but Faraz's home looked relatively clean and hospitable despite a mishmash of old plaster and new drywall. The whole floor was one big open space. The air here smelled like sweat and vanilla-scented incense.

Faraz lay atop a bed in one corner of the penthouse, oblivious to Baxter's approach. The detective had a strange talent for approaching people without making a sound, perhaps something inherited from distant Native American ancestors. The Iranian pimp's buttocks were exposed and moving up and down as he pressed himself into a girl who, to Baxter's eyes, looked to be about fourteen. He assumed she was probably older. Faraz was actually a pretty stand-up guy, as far as pimps were concerned, but Baxter would check her out to be sure. If she was underage, then he knew a few people who didn't take kindly to pedophiles of any kind. With a phone call, Faraz would be dead or wishing he was.

"Am I interrupting?" Baxter said.

Faraz rolled off the girl in a tumbling mass of flailing limbs and snatched a 9mm Beretta pistol from the nightstand beside his bed. The Iranian huffed and puffed, his face red with exertion.

Baxter didn't even flinch. He said, "I heard you were looking for me."

The pimp muttered something in a language that was unintelligible to Kincaid as he laid the pistol back on the nightstand. In English, Faraz said, "How did you get up here?"

"Your pet monkey was taking a nap. How old is that girl?"

Faraz shook his head. "Don't worry, Kincaid. She's nineteen. I checked her ID. Even I have a code of conduct."

"I'll be checking into that. So is this her interview for employment?"

"I have to make sure all of the girls under my employ are top notch. You're not a cop anymore, remember."

"I'm well aware. And I understand that brand management is important. As long as she knows what she's getting into and makes a fair wage for her troubles, she can make her own choices. Now, why are you wanting to see me?"

Around his naked waist, Faraz wrapped a robe which sported a three foot dragon beside Bruce Lee's face and said, "One of my best girls, Sammy, she has a sister in college who's gone missing."

"How long has the girl been unaccounted for?"

"Nearly two weeks."

"That's a mighty frigid trail, partner. What about the cops?"

"They didn't do much more than file a report."

"I doubt that."

Baxter considered his options. He didn't really need the money, and he didn't want to earn a reputation for working for the dregs of society like Faraz. But he also had a soft spot for the downtrodden and the underdogs, which had earned him the nickname of the "People's Pig" through his pro-bono work catering to all those who normal society would prefer didn't exist.

He said, "I'll need to speak with Sammy directly, and if this is some attempt to trick me into tracking down one of your wayward harem, then I'll come back here and circumcise that turtlehead between your legs with a rusty spoon. You dig, brah?"

18

Ackerman moved his chess piece across the board, unable to hide a small smile. His elation didn't stem from the fact that he intended to win the game. Not that he was typically of a mindset to let anyone defeat him. But, in this case, he couldn't help but allow the boy to take him. Dylan— Marcus's son and his nephew—wasn't even double digits yet and here he was trying to emulate the famous chess game known as Kasparov's Immortal in which the Russian grandmaster defeated Topalov in forty-four moves. Ackerman couldn't resist playing the role of Topalov as the boy astounded him with his ingenuity. Either Dylan had inherited Marcus's amazing memory or Ackerman's genius. Perhaps a bit of both. The thought filled him with a strange warmth—what great and terrible things could be achieved by someone who was an amalgamation of he and his brother. Dylan fascinated him. The boy seemed more and more like a tiny version of himself by the day.

Dylan said, "Checkmate."

Ackerman beamed with pride. "So it is."

"Want to play again?"

"Maybe after a bit, young Kasparov. Let's chat for a while."

The hotel room was much like countless others Ackerman had played in over the years. Off-white walls and no overhead lighting, which he suspected was to hide the dust and grime. Low quality prints of beaches and sunsets adorned the disgustingly tropical walls. Ackerman felt like Jimmy Buffet had puked all over the entire motor inn.

Emily Morgan sat in a chair beside Dylan, reading a paperback novel. She looked up with suspicion as Ackerman mentioned having a "chat."

Her impeccable intuition served her well. He suspected that she wouldn't be entirely pleased with the nature of the following conversation.

Ackerman said, "How do you feel about spending time with other kids your age?"

Dylan didn't make eye contact, and Ackerman had noticed that he seldom did. "They tend not to understand me."

Tend not ... Dylan spoke with a formality and polished adultness that was unusual for a boy his age.

"You say they don't understand you. But do *you* understand *them*?"

"Not really. It seems like I always say the wrong thing."

Emily Morgan, his babysitter and Dylan's self-appointed protector, said, "What are you doing?"

Ackerman ignored her. "Dylan, would you prefer to play alone with your Legos or play baseball with other kids?"

"I like playing chess with you."

"But what about boys your own age?"

"Not really. I prefer to play alone."

Emily stood and took Dylan by the hand. She shot Ackerman a scathing glance and said, "Let's go see if your dad is back yet, buddy."

Dylan scowled but followed her from the room. A

moment later, Emily returned, slamming the door behind her. "What exactly was that all about?"

He didn't look up at her. He busied himself breaking down the chess set and putting it away. She walked closer and said, "I could have you thrown back in the darkest hole they can find. Is that what you want?"

Ackerman met her gaze and shook his head. "I have a better question. When do you plan to share Dylan's diagnosis with my brother?"

19

The area they were using for the briefing was called a corporate center. It was basically just one of the normal hotel rooms with everything stripped out of it and replaced with a conference table and some flat-screen monitors. Having taken custody of the room as their informal staging area while in Oklahoma, Marcus had wasted little time making the space his own. Almost every wall was covered with printouts and pictures, but he had left the conference table.

Marcus waited for everyone to take their seats before starting the briefing. He said, "I met with the Director and Valdas this morning." He went on to explain about the organized-crime connection, the mutilated bodies, Mr. King, the undercover agent, and the urban legend.

Andrew asked, "What about the bodies?"

Marcus gestured to the packet of information. Just seeing the physical file folder made him angry. He had been in the process of moving all of the SO's files over to digital. Unfortunately, Ackerman always insisted on reviewing paper records.

"There's the file on the bodies. You tell me, Dr. Garrison."

Andrew, a former medical examiner in Boston, opened the file and scanned the documents. After a moment, he commented, "All the limbs were removed postmortem. Cause of death is hard to determine in the reduced state, but the ME notes bruising, broken bones, and internal bleeding all over the cores of the male victims. Which happened while they were still alive. Like they were beaten to death."

Studying the photos with a curious fascination, Ackerman added, "The person doing the skinning has an experienced hand or some formal training."

"Doctor? Medical student?" Marcus asked.

"Possibly. At least a taxidermist or seasoned hunter," Ackerman said. Then he walked over to an easel and a giant pad of presentation and meeting paper. Marcus also hated the old-school paper and markers method. He had a high-tech organic LED touch screen mounted to one wall, but his favorite digital display board had hardly been used since his brother had started working cases with them.

At the board, Ackerman continued, "Let's look at everything we know so far. Let's dissect this thing, just crack the breast bone, separate the ribcage, and reach up to the heart of it ..."

Ackerman wrote "Gladiator" across the top of one page. Then he wrote down each thought as he spoke it.

"He works for Demon. How did that happen? Where is he from? What is his...*hunger*?"

Marcus added, "Contracted to King to murder and leave bodies in public places."

Leaning back with her feet on the conference table, Maggie said, "What about the two bodies that they've identified but can't connect to King?"

"Probably just part of one's smokescreen and one's hunger," Marcus replied. "It leads the trail of evidence away from King, and those two bodies that were identified—the marine and the boxer—they were worthy opponents."

Ackerman smiled. "Right, they were two victims whom

the Gladiator chose himself. So he's definitely wanting a challenge, looking for a worthy adversary."

"Then let's not keep him waiting," Marcus said in a voice that was half growl.

Stepping up to the easel, marker in hand, Ackerman said, "Let's look at the methods of execution." As he spoke, he wrote a note about each point. "He removes their hands and feet and skin. Possible trophies. Or it could simply be to obscure their identities. If it's the latter, then those acts are just part of the job. They serve a purpose. They don't fulfill any of his *personal* desires. So what parts of these crimes do fulfill his desires. We need to isolate what's part of the job and what's part of the killer."

Marcus said, "The beatings are his thing. He's picking worthy opponents and then pummeling them to death, probably arena style."

"But what about the women?" Ackerman mused.

Marcus said, "What really stands out to me is the faces and the skulls being crushed. If they're already dead, or at least very close to it when he finishes with the hammer, that act has to have personal significance. If he's already planning to remove the skin and appendages, he could simply cut the head off with the rest. He doesn't *need* to destroy their faces like that. He *wants* to do it."

Andrew added, "Like maybe he hates his own face. Maybe he has a deformity."

They all stared at the boards without speaking for a few moments. Checking his watch and remembering they had flights to catch, Marcus smiled over at Emily Morgan, the newest addition to the team. He said, "Agent Morgan, or should I say Dr. Morgan?"

"Agent is fine," she said with a bow of her head.

"You're going to have to step up, Agent Morgan, since Andrew is going to be off on urgent shadow government bullshit."

Andrew chuckled. "You sound upset. Are you going to miss me? Don't worry, little buddy. As long as you don't drink anything at least two hours before bed and then—"

"Okay."

"—you go potty right before you go sleepy night, then you should be fine."

"Thanks for that," Marcus said with a small smile.

A little chuckle interrupted every few words as Maggie said, "Being his partner is liking raising a baby goat, isn't it, Drew?"

Andrew said, "I think he's more like a baby rhinoceros."

Ackerman said, "You are aware that bedwetting is an early warning sign for serial murderers. Do you experience night-time bathroom malfunctions, brother? Or is it night terrors?"

Everyone fell silent.

Marcus said, "I'm fine. He was just kidding. Sometimes I can't tell if you're joking or being serious."

"I'm always serious. And bedwetting is also very serious to someone who suffers from it. I never had to worry about the delicacies of childhood development like that, since I never had a bed or possessions as a child."

"Thank you, Frank. Anyway," Marcus said, raising his coffee cup, "I just wanted to take a moment to officially welcome you to the field team, Agent Morgan. But I also wanted to let you know that we're going to need you more than ever while Andrew is off dissecting aliens at Area 51, or wherever the Director's super-secret mission takes him."

"Area 51 would be my dream job," Andrew said. "If that's what he has me doing, I'm staying there. I'd abandon you guys in less than a second to study alien biology."

Marcus said, "Would you stop interrupting me. As I was saying, welcome to the team, Emily, and while Maggie and I are back east, you'll be in charge of feeding *Kong* over there." He gestured toward Ackerman, who feigned offense. "So good luck and God's speed."

20

Baxter Kincaid stepped into the hall and closed the door to his apartment, a space once rented by Jimi Hendrix himself. When he turned away from his door, he came face to face with a man in dark sunglasses and a gray hoodie pulled down over his face. Baxter jerked back from shock and leaned a hand on the doorframe. The man didn't move at all, except for the occasional muscle twitch. Once he'd regained his composure, Baxter said, "Good morning, Kevin."

"I need your latest blog post."

"Now, Kevarino, we've talked about this. When someone says 'good morning,' you say …"

"It's two in the afternoon."

"I was referring to my personal morning," Baxter said in his South Texas drawl. "Some refer to morning in regard to the rising and setting of the sun. I think morning is more a state of mind."

Kevin's shoulders and neck twitched, sending ripples across the fabric of his hoodie. The kid smelled as if he hadn't bathed in a couple of weeks. "I consider whether it's morning or not by the time of day."

"You need to open your mind a bit, Kevster. What do you say to this? You and I can get together later, take our shirts off, and play some bongos."

Kevin said nothing.

Baxter lightly punched him on the shoulder and said, "I'm

just messing with you, buddy. Don't burn out a microchip. I'm glad I caught you. I was wondering if you found out anything about Corin Campbell for me."

"Wait here," Kevin said and then unlocked the three deadbolts on his own apartment door, cracked open the door, and slipped inside, the door shutting behind him. Kevin had been Baxter's neighbor for many moons now, and he still had yet to catch a glimpse of the youngster's domicile.

A moment later, Kevin returned with a manila folder, which he handed to Baxter. "Corin Campbell, inside and out."

"Excellent, my man. Put yourself down for a raise."

"You don't pay me."

"I know. That's what makes it a funny comment."

Kevin said, "I need to ask you something."

"What's on your mind, big guy?"

"You know a lot of lawyers and stuff. So I thought you could ask one of them. I was wondering about the legal precedent for how close a drone can get to a person's residence before you are considered to have violated their air space. And also, if it's actually illegal for the police to shoot down your drone. I was thinking that, since they're classified as aircraft by the FAA, it could be considered an act of terrorism on the part of the cop."

Baxter thought about that a moment and finally said, "I think it's around fifty-eight feet. It has to do with some precedent set by airplanes taking off and coming too close to some old man's farm. And you're actually correct that, to the letter of the law, said officer's actions could be construed to be shooting down an aircraft, since drones and passenger jets are classified the same under FAA guidelines. But in reality, Kevaramadingadong, no judge in his right mind would prosecute that case."

"So I need a judge who's *not* in his right mind?"

"That's one way to go."

"Thanks, Mr. Kincaid. Send me that file for the blog post as soon as you can. I mean, you know, at you're earliest convenience."

Baxter tapped his temple, tipped his trilby, and said, "It's on my list, Mr. Unabomber."

Kevin's gaze shot around the hallway, and he whispered, "Don't say things like that. There could be surveillance."

With an uncontainable little chuckle, Baxter said, "I do say a lot of interesting shiznit, don't I? Hey, whoever's listening, I would love a copy of the recordings or transcripts, 'cause I speak so much awesomeness that it's impossible to write it all down." He couldn't contain his laughter any longer, cracking himself up as he spouted the last line.

Kevin didn't say a word. He simply stood there, his head cocked slightly, his face barely visible beneath the shadows of the hood. He really did look like the Unabomber, only lacking a bit of facial hair. Like a cross between the sketches of Unabomber and Timothy McVeigh. The whole thing made Baxter laugh even harder. The longer Kevin remained frozen, the more it made Baxter laugh. Until he was hunched over, fighting for breath, holding himself up with one hand on Kevin's shoulder.

After a moment, he was able to regain his composure. Kevin still hadn't moved. Baxter slapped the young man on the shoulder and said, "Good times, Kevmeister. Good times."

21

Derrick Gladstone wheeled out onto San Francisco Hospital's third floor and expertly guided his utilitarian but functional wheelchair over to the nurse's station. He had requisitioned the chair's creation for his specific needs. The first of which was to make the chair as visually unobtrusive as possible. He had heard the term "murdered out" in reference to a car being painted all black, the chrome powdercoated, and the windows tinted. He liked to think of his chair as also being "murdered out." It was a flat black that reflected no light and blended with nearly any environment.

His second condition regarding the chair was that it appear modern and elegant. He wasn't about to push himself around in the same wheelchair that someone of a lower station could also afford.

As he approached the nurse on duty, LuAnn smiled and said, "Dr. Gladstone, good to see you. I didn't know that one of these babies was yours."

He returned the smile and made some small talk, although he had no affinity for the fifty-year-old obstetrics nurse. She was a single mother and poor. She smelled of cigarettes and halitosis. He hated that the children would have to smell her as she swaddled them.

Derrick rotated his chair toward the viewing window, which was thankfully handicap accessible. LuAnn walked up beside him and asked, "Which one is yours?"

"The Jefferson child. A boy. I don't know the name yet."

She pointed at the glass. "He's the third one back." Peaking over the edge of the window, Derrick observed the newborn squirming in the hospital bassinet. The baby was healthy and strong, wide awake and alert.

LuAnn said, "Would you like to hold him, Doctor?"

"I would love to," Derrick replied as he wheeled over to the door for the nursery. He knew the drill here well. He had visited numerous children at this hospital. Every child born under his care deserved at least a visit.

LuAnn retrieved the baby and laid him in Derrick's arms. The child blinked up at him, and Derrick rubbed the child's tiny hand with his own. No matter how many times he had done this very thing, he was always a little surprised and overwhelmed at how tiny and fragile human beings were when they entered the world. Many animals could walk from the moment of their birth, but homo sapien offspring were little more than balls of flesh, utterly helpless and dependent. Somehow, human-kind had topped the food chain despite that inherent setback.

Referring to the chart, LuAnn said, "And, by the way, his name is Leonardo."

Derrick winced and whispered to the child, "Sorry, kid. You were probably named after the ninja turtle, not the painter or actor. But I'm afraid what they name you is out of my control."

"What did you say, Doctor?"

"I was just speaking with little Leo," he said with a large grin.

She laughed. "I think it's great that you care so much

about your patients. It's a shame you don't have children of your own. You would have been a great dad."

Derrick maintained his smile, but his mind turned to the scalpel in the pocket of his white lab coat. He imagined himself standing up from the chair and jamming the scalpel into one of the cigarette-stained nurse's eyeballs. He pictured the shock on her face when he rose from the chair and the confusion when she noticed the scalpel in his hand. The blood spurted from her wounds as he sliced her neck and face to pieces. It rained a red mist over the top of the squalling and squirming children.

Pulling him back to reality, LuAnn said, "I'm assuming you want a picture with your new patient, as usual?"

"I never miss a visit or a photo op, LuAnn."

He handed over his phone and posed with the baby. She snapped a few photos for him and then asked, "Do you want me to put him back for you?"

He wanted to scream at her that he was much stronger and more capable than she was, but instead, he held the fake smile and said, "I'd like a few minutes with him, if that's okay."

"Of course. I need to take him back to his parents soon, but you can wait with him until then."

"Thanks, LuAnn. You're the best."

She winked at him and said, "Anything for you, Dr. Gladstone. I wish we had more like you here. That young couple was truly blessed to find you as a doctor."

He shrugged in deference. "Thank you. That's very nice of you to say."

When she was gone, he stared into the boy's eyes. The child already showed thin strands of blonde hair, very close to his own color. But the newborn's build reminded Derrick more of his youngest brother, Simon.

He thought of the first time he had laid eyes on Simon in a hospital nursery much like the one he was sitting in now. The twins, Derrick and Dennis, had been five years old when his mother had told them that she was pregnant. It had been at the kitchen table in their old two-story colonial. His father, learning of the surprise pregnancy at the same time as his two sons, had been quiet at first.

"Say something," his mother had said. "I just told you we're going to be having another child."

Finally, his father had smiled and said, "We're adding a new lion to the pride, boys. And you're going to have to teach him all that I've taught you."

Derrick had taken those words to heart and had considered that duty as he first saw his baby brother. There had been something off about Simon even then. When a five-year-old Derrick Gladstone looked into his newborn brother's eyes, he instantly noticed the boy's strength. Simon's body was strong and muscular compared to other newborns, but the thing that had struck Derrick was that Simon never cried. His brother had been born tough, and Derrick had loved the boy from the beginning, feeling a kinship with Simon that he had never experienced with his own fraternal twin, Dennis.

His mind turned then to the day when, out of kindness, he and Dennis decided to murder Simon. Looking back, Derrick wished they had killed their mother instead. His little brother didn't deserve to be erased from existence, but the same couldn't be said for the woman who wanted the boy gone. Still, there was little Derrick could do about that now, other than make the old witch pay for her sins, which he was already doing.

Leaning in close to little Leonardo's face, he kissed the boy's forehead and said, "Your parents certainly were blessed to have met me."

22

Marcus fought the urge to roll his eyes when Emily Morgan, the SO's resident counselor, asked for a few minutes alone with him. The others were preparing to leave, and so Marcus and Emily pulled out a couple of chairs from the conference room table and sat down facing one another.

"So what's up, Doc? How do you feel my brother is assimilating, or whatever you want to call it?"

"I believe Mr. Ackerman is learning and growing by leaps and bounds. But I wanted a moment to talk about you."

"I'm an open book. Ask away."

"What if you don't like the question?"

"That sounds like a loaded response. Did the Director order you to talk to me about Eddie Caruso?"

"He strongly suggested I discuss your old friend with you before you board the jet. But, as always, my primary concern is your health and well-being as a member of this team and someone whom I consider a friend. You helped me through my husband's death more than anyone else, Marcus. You are my number one concern. And from the way the Director described it, this Eddie Caruso is not someone of whom you think highly."

"I'm sure that's not quite the way the Director tactfully phrased it."

"He's a colorful man. But we're not here to talk about

him either. How do you feel about going back to see your old friend Mr. Caruso?"

"I appreciate the concern, Doc, but it's nothing to worry about. Eddie and I were best friends when we were practically babies. We had a falling out, and we ceased being friends, spent some time as adversaries, and ended up just trying to pretend the other person didn't exist."

"Does that situation sound healthy to you?"

"You always tell me not to live in the past. Not to overanalyze all my decisions and question whether I could've made different choices. It is what it is. I haven't thought about Eddie Caruso in years. It's not anything that still bothers me."

"I think that may have been the most you've ever spoken during one of our counseling sessions. So I would say that it obviously is bothering you."

"Bullshit! I've talked a lot more than that at least a few different times. You realize that when we go out there in the field I'm your boss, right?"

"Yes, but there's one area of management where I'm the boss. And that is when it comes to the well-being of this team."

"No worries. I'm all good."

Emily raised her eyebrows.

"Okay, we were close. We had a falling out. After that he teased me a lot, really made life hard on me. And I can't fault him for that. We were kids. That kind of thing happens. But the deal with Eddie is that after my parents were murdered he didn't lighten up on me. In fact, he started in harder. Made my life a living hell. It was so bad that I took a year off from school. Which everybody thought was completely understandable, considering that my parents had just died. No one really questioned it. But the real reason I needed to get away was because of Eddie Caruso."

"But you eventually came back to the same school?"

"Yeah, after taking some time away and looking at the situation objectively, I remembered that I could beat the living hell out of Eddie Caruso. So, first day back, I cornered him, and under threat of violence and humiliation, I offered him a truce. Kind of a North and South Korea type of deal. The kind of agreement where we don't want to work out our differences and so we're just going to pretend that the other party doesn't exist."

"Again, very healthy. But I totally understand, and you're right about one thing: we should learn from the past, but we should never worry over it. However, your unresolved history with this man could quite easily become a problem when you go to see him."

"It's not a big deal, Doc. Water under the bridge."

"After your parents died, what was the worst thing that Eddie did to you?"

"He said that my mother was a whore. He called my dad a dirty cop. The same dad who had just fought and died for me. He told me that they were probably relieved when death came, because at least they didn't have to put up with me anymore."

"I'm sorry you had to go through that, but as you said, it was a long time ago. I'm sure both you and Mr. Caruso are very different people now."

"I can't help thinking that anybody who would say that kind of thing to another kid whose parents had just died ... I don't know, that just seems like an issue with a person's heart and soul. A darkness that's never going to change."

"Perhaps, but one of the limitations of this mortal existence is that we can never truly see into another person's heart and soul. We spend so much time trying to chart a roadmap of what's in everyone else's heart, but we forget that the most important thing is what's in our own. We can't worry about what's in the hearts of others because our own soul is the only one over which we have any control."

"And how does that help me with Eddie?"

"You need to examine your own heart. We should forgive others in the same way we hope others forgive us. If you go in with a humble spirit and a forgiving heart, then you'll be fine. But here's a question: What if, as you suspect, Eddie still possesses a spiteful personality? What if he responds negatively? Will you give in to your anger?"

"Just because people make me angry, doesn't mean I have an *anger* problem. It seems more that I have a *people* problem."

"Last week, I was told you had an incident with a local sheriff."

Marcus gritted his teeth and growled deep in his throat. "We needed this Podunk sheriff to serve a warrant on one of the security guards who was supposed to be protecting the truck that Demon's cronies altered. The guard turned out to be dirty. He had taken a bribe to look the other way and erase the security footage."

"I don't believe the guard's culpability was the issue. This sheriff claimed that you defecated in his breakfast. He threatened to file a formal complaint with the Department of Justice."

Marcus laughed at the memory and Emily's description of it. "That's only partially correct."

"How do you partially defecate in someone's breakfast?"

"This local sheriff, I find out, is running for re-election, and he's in there at some greasy-spoon diner jibber-jabbering and won't go with us to serve the warrant until he's finished his breakfast. We tell his office that this is a time-sensitive investigation. They respond that we'll just have to wait. So we wait. For forty-five minutes. Finally, I go in and find this sheriff laughing it up with a bunch of old banker types. They're just sitting there, cackling like a bunch of old hens and sipping their coffee."

"How does that connect your excrement to his breakfast?"

"I'm getting there. So I walk up and introduce myself. I ask if he's the sheriff. Anyway, long story short, he gave me attitude, and I pissed in his coffee cup."

"You urinated in a fellow officer's coffee cup in the middle of a crowded restaurant?"

"No, I took the cup into the bathroom. Then I urinated in it and brought it back out to him."

"Do you feel that was an appropriate and proportionate reaction to his behavior?"

"To be honest, Doc, considering some of the other things I thought about doing to him, I think pissing in his coffee was a pretty measured response on my part. I actually think it displays some real personal growth."

23

It was the biggest house Marcus had ever seen.

And probably the most famous place he'd ever been, if you didn't count the lady in the bay or other New York City landmarks that had become commonplace to someone born and raised in the city. This was even in a whole other state: New Jersey. Other than a few camping trips with his dad, he had never been anywhere that didn't begin with "The New York ..." His dad, NYPD Detective John Williams, always said, "Why go on vacation? This is the greatest city in the history of the world. If you can't find it here, it doesn't exist."

But Marcus Williams, now seeing his teenage years within reach, had a sense that his world was finally starting to grow beyond the old neighborhood of brick and concrete.

It was a far cry from what stood before him now. The sprawling green of the manicured grounds and the massive white-and-black mansion seemed to be composed of colors he had never seen before. Or maybe they were only more vibrant than he had ever seen.

He still couldn't believe he was here, and he even had the permission of his parents. He hadn't necessarily lied to them, merely withheld information. He had waited for a busy moment to ask if he could go to a birthday party with Eddie from school, knowing they wouldn't question him. They were just glad that he was getting out of the house and away from his action figures and the "damn Nintendo."

Of course, Marcus didn't volunteer which Eddie from school he was going with, even though he knew his father didn't want him hanging around Eddie Caruso or ever spending the night at the boy's house. His father had told him that Eddie's father was a criminal and "not a very nice man." But Marcus didn't care about that. Eddie's father was never around anyhow, and he wanted to be Eddie's friend, not his father's.

Marcus didn't know the kid whose birthday he was about to celebrate. Eddie had told him that the party was at the home of an associate of his father's—someone named Tommy Juliano. The birthday boy, Nicky Juliano, was turning two years old. Eddie had said that the party was just as much for Nicky's brother Junior, who was graduating from eighth grade, so there would be lots of kids of different ages there. Maybe even some older girls.

Eddie, who had never been without a girlfriend since kindergarten, was always talking "about" girls, when he wasn't talking "to" them. Marcus wasn't completely oblivious to the opposite sex. He noticed them. They sometimes noticed him. But that was about as far as the interaction ever went, and when it did go farther, he usually said or did the wrong thing and scared them away.

The mansion had its own parking lot, and the whole lot was filled with the shine of the newest model cars. Eddie's mother parked the big Cadillac, which was also brand new. Eddie had bragged incessantly about his father just bringing it home from the dealership.

The inside of the mansion was as clean and sparkling as the exterior. Junior Juliano met them at the door. He and Eddie exchanged an elaborate handshake full of fist bumps and finger wiggling. Eddie was much younger than the eighth-grade graduate, but the older kids always seemed to like Eddie. Everyone seemed to like Eddie.

"This is my boy, Marcus. He's part of my crew, but his dad bleeds blue, so watch what you say around him."

Marcus, having no idea what it meant to bleed blue, punched his friend in the arm, which earned a little chuckle from Eddie and the response, "It just means that your dad's a cop, asswipe. Don't spaz out on me."

"Why does it matter if my dad's a cop?"

"It doesn't. Just don't mention it to anyone."

Sometimes he hated being a cop's kid. The others treated him like he was a junior officer, and he felt obliged to live up to everyone's expectations. At least, he had, before he became part of Eddie Caruso's "crew"—which was really nothing more than a scared and insecure group of kids mobbing together for survival.

In the years before he had become Eddie's best friend, on the same playground he now ruled, Marcus had felt as if he died more days than he survived. He hated school. It was a constant barrage of overwhelming input. All those social interactions. All those people to analyze and quantify. When he became Eddie's friend, people started liking him even if he said or did the wrong thing. None of the other kids screwed around with Eddie and his "crew."

Junior Juliano laughed and said, "We have almost an hour before the kids from my class are supposed to get here, and my little brother, Bratman, has already dug into the cake and opened his presents, so … You two little scumbags want to see something cool?"

24

Corin Campbell was a gorgeous young woman. Her sister, Faraz's girl, had paled in comparison when she had handed Baxter the photo of Corin. He wondered at the time if drugs had caused the contrast between the two siblings. If the roles had been reversed and Corin were handing him a picture of Samantha, Baxter wondered, would Sammy have been the beautiful sibling?

He didn't think so. He had a feeling that Corin had always been the golden child. Prettier. Smarter. Catching the eye of all her sister's potential boyfriends ... Jealousy was always a good motive, but not one he planned to pursue.

He knew within seconds after meeting Corin's sister that Sammy Campbell wasn't involved and didn't know where her sister had gone. He knew that not only because of the answers to his questions, but from watching Sammy answer them. She simply didn't have the capacity to harm her sister and lie about it. She barely had the capacity to form complete sentences, let alone link those sentences into complete thoughts.

Unfortunately, that also meant she didn't possess any information that could help him find Corin. All she really had for him was an old photo and the knowledge that her sister had disappeared.

But Samantha had introduced him via phone call to the first of the usual suspects.

Corin's boyfriend, Blake, had suggested a coffee shop to meet. Baxter had insisted on meeting at the couple's condo located in the city's trendsetting Dogpatch neighborhood. He claimed he wanted to get a better feel for Corin, but that was only one reason. An old detective's rule of thumb was to find the person the victim was sleeping with, and you've found your killer. But Baxter didn't know if the boyfriend was the one she had been sleeping with or if Corin even was a victim.

When he opened the door to the condo, Blake reminded Baxter of a former Nickelodeon teen heartthrob, about five years past his prime. Handsome but haggard. When Baxter looked into the kid's eyes, he saw something else. The hollowness of loss and grief.

The handsome medical student ushered him into the small apartment. The space was cramped but elegantly decorated with modern art furnishings. Everything had a certain enforced symmetry.

Baxter concluded that Corin had been the one who decorated the condo.

The other element that stuck out was the smell of old garbage. The dishes overflowed the sink. Takeout bags and empty junk-food boxes littered the counters and table tops.

Baxter concluded that Blake had been the one who destroyed the condo.

Obviously, Corin had been in charge of cleaning, and judging by the preciseness of her decorating, he suspected she'd be pissed to see what Blake had done with the place.

The kid said, "So you're a private investigator?"

Baxter smiled warmly. "Something like that. But, if I may say so, that is quite a suit. Didn't know medical students wore that sort of thing."

Blake had brown hair, slightly receding into a stylishly spiked widow's peak. He wore a suit more expensive than Baxter's fees would be for this whole case, and he smelled like cigar smoke and gin and tonics.

Blake said, "Don't let it fool you. The suit was a gift from my father. I had lunch with him today at the club. He insists I look the part."

"And what part is that?"

"Son of a high-priced lawyer."

Baxter nodded and made notes in a pocket-sized, leather-bound notebook.

He wrote: *FIL=lawyer. Enemies? Revenge? Ransom?*

He said, "Has he been helping in your search for Corin?"

"Why do you ask?"

"No particulars. Just figuring that high priced meant money and resources and access to the police chief and a whole swarm of private investigators."

Blake's gaze fell to the table covered in burger wrappers and Chinese takeout boxes. And beneath those, flyers displaying Corin's face and a 1-800 number.

Baxter didn't shy from the obvious. "So let me guess, man. Your dad didn't want you to become a doctor, and he felt threatened by your relationship with Corin."

Blake's lip curled in disgust. "My father simply doesn't care. At all."

"Sounds like a difficult sort of dude."

"As long as I don't ask for money and don't make him look bad, he could care less."

"My dad was just the guy who drove our house around when I was a kid. So I feel you on that, brother."

Blake shrugged it off. "I honestly don't think my father

could have gotten anything more done than what's being done already."

"The cops have been helpful?"

"Yeah, they've been fine. Not that I would know any different. I'm not an investigator."

"No leads?"

"Nothing they've shared with me. We've put up thousands of flyers. I've been on TV twice, offering a reward. My father did offer to pay that."

"Yeah, that's probably tax-deductible, and good publicity. Nothing came in on the wires?"

"No. The only thing the cops found was that her Facebook account had been hacked and some photos altered. Apparently, it's a kind of Internet prank going around right now. Adding some skull face in the background of people's pictures to freak them out."

Baxter made a note of that. "Do you have any of those pictures?"

Pulling out his cell phone, Blake swiped around and then showed the device to Baxter. It took him a moment to find the skull face, a twisted game of *Where's Waldo*. He stared at the face a moment, feeling a vague familiarity with it. As if he'd seen it before.

"Can you send me those pictures, please. Number's on the card I gave you. Another thought. I'm just putting this down to see if you pick it up, brother. Are you absolutely sure she didn't make it home that night?"

Blake shrugged. "I can't say anything for certain. But nothing was out of place, and the police couldn't find any signs of forced entry. Plus, her car would have been here if she was abducted from the condo."

"Unless the person who took her also took her car. But that's only if someone else is involved."

"What does that mean?"

"It wouldn't be the first time that a person put on one face to the world and hid their true self. Maybe she just split."

"Why would she ever—"

"I don't mean to imply anything or twist you up, man. But the questions have to be asked and answered and contemplated. In a case like this, with a missing person, you have to establish a lot of questions that have simple yes or no answers. The first is: Did she leave or was she taken?"

Anger filled Blake's eyes. "She wouldn't have run. She was happy. She loved her life, and she loved me. The only reason she would be gone is that someone took her."

Baxter had studied Blake's eyes and facial expressions throughout the whole exchange. He was an avid student of kinesics, the study of body language and facial expressions, and from every indication his trained eye could identify, the young man was being truthful.

"Okay, the next questions I would ask are: If she was taken, did she know the person or was it a stranger? A single perpetrator or a group? That sort of thing."

"You think Corin is dead?"

Baxter measured his response. "The odds aren't in her favor. But I'm a bit like an old bloodhound. Once I'm onto a scent, I don't let up. Dead or not, I intend to find out what happened to her."

"How can I help?"

"Enemies?"

"None."

"Guys who may have taken a perverse interest? Even if she thought they were just friends."

"Nothing like that. She didn't even have many girlfriends."

"Where was she seen last? Or where was she supposed to be last?"

Blake seemed to consider his answer carefully, not as if he was hiding anything but as if he wanted to ensure that his answers were precise. "She would have come home after her last class."

Baxter considered this. The car was an obvious point of abduction. She could have also parked in the wrong spot and been accosted by someone out to rob and mutilate her, but Baxter's gut told him this was premeditated. "Where did she usually park for class?"

"In the parking garage, but it has security. The footage shows her getting in and leaving the lot. She must have stopped somewhere between here and there."

"If you had to guess what happened to her—and be honest—what do you think?"

The young medical student looked toward the oak floor. "I hate to even speak it aloud, but Corin was tough and smart. She knew how to defend herself. She wouldn't have been taken by some crackhead, and she wouldn't have abandoned me and her life. The only thing that I can think is that she was kidnapped. But we haven't received any ransom demands ..."

The implications hung in the air like flies buzzing over a fresh corpse. Baxter asked, "Nothing else that seemed strange? Nothing she was worried about? Any changes in behavior? Listen, brother, don't hold anything back. Finding her may depend on the most insignificant of details."

"Just the skull-face thing in her pictures. But the cops said that particular hack has affected thousands of people. If there was anything else, I would have told the cops and would tell you now. It's like she vanished into thin air."

25

Corin Campbell tried to mentally project herself to a happy place. A meadow or a park or playing in the snow with Sammy on some early childhood vacation. Anywhere other than this cold, concrete chamber. She had completely lost perspective on how long she'd been here. Several weeks at least, but she supposed it could have been any amount of time. She could have been in this hell for days or weeks or only a matter of hours, and she wouldn't have known the difference. Everything was relative. Pain could make seconds seem like hours, and pleasure could make days seem like a matter of a few moments.

She couldn't say that her time here had been marked by nothing but pain. There was also the fear. Which she found to be even more soul-crushing than the pain. Corin had been in a constant state of fear and despair from the moment she had seen the man in the skull mask. Even when her tormentor wasn't with her, she could feel his presence in the air pressing down on her, pushing inside her.

The only way she was able to mark time was by his visits to her lonely corner of hell.

She wondered if Blake would still want her after all this. Not because of the physical aspects; she didn't doubt his understanding. But her mind was shattered in a way now that made her doubt she could even look at him the same. The world would never be bright and safe to her again.

She would never be the petite brunette in love with life, the girl Blake had fallen for. Although, she supposed that the woman he had fallen for wasn't truly the *real* her either.

Corin rolled over on her bare, sweat-stained mattress. Her legs shook with spasms of pain at the slight movement. That was another reason she doubted that she actually was in hell. She reasoned the genuine Satan would not feel the need to break the shins of his captives in order to ensure they couldn't escape. That act itself inspired hope in a strange way. If her tormentor felt the need to cripple her, perhaps that meant help was within reach.

The thought had faded after the first days spent searching for weaknesses in her cell, pulling herself along the concrete floor, trying to find a way to escape or a weapon of any kind. She found neither. There was nothing her five-foot-four broken body could do against a man of his size and strength.

No way out and no way to resist.

He owned her. She was his property to use as he saw fit.

People would be looking for her, but she doubted they would make it in time to save anything of the college student and girl she had once been. That woman, that sister and lover and friend, seemed like a person she had dreamed up in another life. The tears, a mattress on the floor, and the rape of her mind, body, and soul seemed to be her whole existence now.

And she wasn't the only resident of this hell.

She had heard doors opening. The muffled whimpering of other women as the devil chose to visit them. Trying to communicate, she had pressed her face to the door and yelled for someone to answer her. But the only reply had been the man in the skull mask shocking her with a cattle prod. The other girls, if she hadn't simply imagined them, had apparently learned not to speak up.

Still, a small part of her former self had clung to life. A room inside her heart where she refused to succumb, where the girl with the genius-level IQ still listened and waited for a way to turn the tables on the devil himself.

Corin clenched her fists and thought of Blake and her sister. She thought of that other girl in that other life, the one who now hid somewhere deep inside her mind, struggling to stay alive and sane. She refused to let that girl die.

Long ago, she had heard of the concept of memory palaces, a technique which some used to retain vast amounts of information through internal visualization. Corin had constructed a memory palace of her own—not for the purposes of preserving memories, but for the purposes of preserving the girl who refused to die.

Separating herself from the cold darkness and the helplessness of her situation allowed her to, in essence, become two people. One who lay naked on a filthy mattress in an empty concrete cell, and one who lived in a bungalow the color of driftwood with steps leading to the beach. She tried to make that place her reality, stealing the details of the bungalow from a memory of the last family trip before her mother's untimely death.

The strong woman inside her mind now stood at the railing of the vacation house's deck, looking down at the beach, detached from the horrors of reality, ever thinking, ever plotting.

She wouldn't die here. Instead, she would kill the devil himself.

She tried to maintain her cognitive distance and suppress fear and revulsion as she heard a key turn in her cell's metal door. Imagining herself still in a place of sun and sand, she made mental notes of the number of seconds before the door closed again. His footfalls seemed to be louder than before. Normally, he entered her room naked, except for the skull mask, but now she heard the slap of leather on concrete. She dared not open her eyes or look at him, for fear of her mental barriers crumbling, allowing the despair of her reality to shatter what was left of her fragile defenses.

Corin had been naked since the moment she awoke, as if she was merely a piece of cattle or a sex toy built solely for his sick gratification. But now, something had changed. Instead of violating her, the devil threw a blanket over her bruised and shivering body and said, "Your blood tests came back. Congratulations, you're going to be a mother."

The barriers she had worked so hard to erect crumbled at those words.

At first, she didn't comprehend the implications. She heard the devil's footfalls retreating from the room as the full meaning of those words pierced her heart. *Pregnant?* She heard the door close as the man who called himself the Gladiator raped her again with this knowledge and left her to drown in her own hopelessness.

Corin Campbell wanted to scream. She wanted to cry. Instead, she pushed down both urges and made up her mind that, at this point, survival had become a secondary concern. Her primary goal was now to murder the devil himself, even if it cost her own life.

Although, she supposed it wasn't only her life she needed to consider now, but the life of her alleged child. She pulled the blanket close to her body, curled into a ball, and wept, dreaming of bungalows on the beach.

26

Francis Ackerman's family had never owned pets, even before his mother escaped with his brother in her womb. Father didn't understand the concept of bringing animals into a home. Why take on the excess baggage of another living thing? At least human children could be put to some use.

Still, Ackerman had befriended the rare insect or arachnid that wandered into his concrete cell, and he could understand the appeal of pet ownership. The eight-legged predators fascinated him, but they didn't make for good friends. They were too much like him, and he wanted to form a friendship with a being whose personality would provide balance to his own. He and the spiders had spent most of their time in each other's company devising ways to kill and eat one another, which hadn't seemed to be a good basis for a lasting kinship.

His favorite childhood playmate had been a pill bug. Although, he had later learned the little gray bug—which earned its name by rolling into a ball when threatened— wasn't a bug at all, but, rather, a crustacean, more closely related to shrimp, crabs, and lobsters. He supposed that the tiny creature had actually been his only toy as well as a companion. The best of both worlds, a bug and a ball.

He was reminded of pets because Emily Morgan now approached with a small black-and-white canine tugging at a retractable leash. Emily wore a gray pantsuit with a purple shirt. Her dark hair was cut short. The sun lit upon subtle, dark-red highlights that she had recently added. A small smile unconsciously formed on his lips as he imagined running his hands along her porcelain skin.

She and the small vermin on the leash approached across the black asphalt parking lot of the Golden Gate bridge info center. The wind licked at the shortened strands of black and red, making it easier to picture what it would be like to run his fingers through her hair.

Then the little dog thing spoiled the moment by jumping on his leg and looking up at him with a closed mouth and a tilted head. He scowled at the little beast, fighting the urge to dropkick.

Emily said, "I think he likes you. I've never seen anyone have that reaction before. Not initially, at least."

"I thought a counselor would build up my self-esteem, not tear me down."

"Under normal circumstances, that may be true. But in your case, your self-esteem *needs* to be dialed down. How do you like the dog?"

"I don't work with animals. Too unreliable and unpredictable."

Emily chuckled. "You think this little Shih Tzu puppy is here to help track down serial killers?"

"I assume he's to be used as some kind of cover or distraction. A trojan horse, perhaps? How many pounds of explosives do you think it would be able to carry?"

She shook her head as if she was trying to wake from a dream. "We're not blowing up the dog. He's just here to be your friend. He's for you. I think it would help you to have another living thing under your care."

"Take it back. And if you insist on pursuing this 'living thing' therapy technique, then buy me a nice fern."

"Fern's don't make good friends. They aren't very intelligent."

"That's a rather stereotypical and offensive way of thinking. Every fern is different. There may be a strain that is quite personable."

She held out the leash with a rigidly extended arm.

"I'm not taking that."

"He's yours now. Take him."

"I will do no such thing."

"Don't be a baby. Take him on a walk and get to know one another."

Ackerman ignored her and the vermin. Trying to change the subject, he said, "I've been thinking about the Gladiator. If the pattern of the victims being competent opponents continues, then he would need to be quite a skilled fighter. Local mixed martial arts training facilities would be a good place to start. But I've heard over the years that there is a thriving underground fighting scene in San Francisco. I would suggest we visit the gyms, and while there, we gather intelligence on the underground."

The dog hadn't moved. It had only cocked its head to the other side. It was looking up at him as if it smelled he wasn't human. He shook the vermin from his leg.

Emily jammed the leash in his chest. His skin briefly electrified at her touch. These were the moments during which a reformed Ackerman had the greatest difficulty controlling his hunger.

Over his shoulder, his father's voice said, *She's yours. Take her.*

Ackerman had no fear. He didn't worry that she would reject him. During the dark years, he lived by simply taking what he wanted. And *who* he wanted. His had been a world of endless possibilities and zero restrictions. And he had once planned to take what he wanted until someone worthy could kill him and take it all back.

In those days, he would have seen no reason not to give in to his desire at that very moment.

But from analysis of past experiences, he understood that the rest of the family may frown upon such actions. In the dark years, he had no greater purpose beyond the joy of the moment. Now, he felt something greater than himself guiding his path. And he had a sense that the *something greater* would also frown upon choices like rape and murder.

And although Ackerman couldn't find a way to *fear* any deity, he had great respect for the Creator and his plans. In accordance with the grand scheme, he wished to find his own unique purpose, the reason he had felt so much pain and tasted so much death.

Emily said, "The gym idea sounds good. I'll call Andrew and run it past him. Now, your dog needs to go potty. Take him over to the grass."

"If I take that thing, it will be only for the purposes of killing and eating it. How did you even capture one of those so quickly after our flight landing?" The info center for the Golden Gate bridge had been their first stop after the FBI's Gulfstream hit the ground in San Francisco.

She frowned and eyed him angrily over the top of her sunglasses. "Capture? Do you think Shih Tzus are running wild in the hills around San Francisco?"

"I was thinking more like a group of inbred strays banding together in the sewer systems."

With a roll of her eyes, she said, "I called ahead and had this arranged. Shih Tzus are wonderful animals. My grandparents had three of them. They don't even shed."

"I was unaware that any canines shed their skin."

"Their hair. Never mind. This is non-negotiable. A direct order."

Ackerman growled and looked down at the furry, flat-faced vermin. The dog tilted its black-and-white head to the other side, its ears perking up. The creature seemed to be looking at him with some type of expectant energy. "What does it want? It's eying me strangely."

"I think *he* wants you to pet him."

"I already find it annoying and repulsive."

"He'll grow on you."

"Why is it so small and ugly? Is it deformed?"

When Ackerman looked back at Emily, he found her hiding a small smile. It looked nice on her, an expression she didn't often share with him. She said, "He's a Shih Tzu. This is what they look like. And he's still young, but this is about as big as he gets."

"If you insist on this madness, I think a larger dog would be more suited to my needs. Perhaps a Doberman?"

"This isn't about *your* needs. You're not supposed to train it to attack. You just need to take care of *his* needs and show him love."

Ackerman picked up the animal and held it out like a baby with a soiled diaper. He wanted to protest further, but he knew how strong willed and unyielding Emily could be. He said, "This is absurd. What do I call it?"

"I figured you could name him."

"How about *Annoying Bag of Useless Flesh*?"

"I think you'd get tired of saying that name all the time."

"I'll call him *Douchebag* for short."

"Be serious. You might as well get used to him. He's going to be with you for the next decade or so."

"I doubt that. I'm sure animals like this die of natural causes all the time. Or run out into traffic, fall off a bridge, leap out a five-story window. These things happen. I'm sure the numbers would support the possibilities."

"None of those things better ever happen to this dog, or I will make sure you share his fate."

He reluctantly took the leash and asked, "What now?"

"Take him for a walk over in that grassy area. He needs to go potty."

"Please don't refer to his defecation as going 'potty.'"

She pulled out a clear cellophane glove from her purse and replied, "Fine. When he *defecates*, pick it up with this."

"If I take that bag from you right now, I will slip it over this creature's head and suffocate it to death. I do not want to be responsible for this thing's droppings and maintenance. I consider this cruel and unusual punishment, and I have too much self-respect to allow such a waste of my time and energies to stand."

"Fine. But you will no longer be able to see Dylan."

"That's ridiculous!"

"If you can't show me that you're capable of caring about the needs of another living being over your own needs, then you don't deserve to be in Dylan's life."

"My brother—"

"Is on my side about this."

Ackerman gritted his teeth, closed his eyes, and counted to ten. He imagined jamming the mutt into a microwave and serving the ground remains to Emily as paté.

Then he opened his eyes, took the plastic glove, and dragged the small vermin toward a grassy knoll along the edge of the parking lot.

27

Stefan Granger finished his reps with the two-hundred-pound dumbbells and tossed them to the mat. One entire wall of his apartment was a giant mirror, like they have in the nice gyms. But Stefan didn't work his body to show off or have a bunch of people staring at him. He kept fit because that was the right thing to do. The right way to live, the only way, was to be the strongest and the smartest.

This was the third apartment he had rented in the city. The other two had become a problem because he had neighbors beneath and to the side of him. His new place was over the top of a garage. A nice young couple had rented it to him. It was originally built to be a nurse's quarters for an old couple that had lived there, but after they passed away and a younger family moved in, they didn't know what to do with the nurse's quarters. So they decided to make some extra rental income.

Granger had become quite close with the young couple. The wife was pregnant. Due any day now. He had dinner with them at least once a week and had already volunteered to paint the baby's room for them.

The situation suited him perfectly. It was a mansion compared to his dad's place at the cemetery. He was able to work out whenever he wanted. He could make as much noise as he wanted. And it was perfect camouflage for a man in his profession.

He stretched and stood up and then went down into the splits, stretching out his legs and arms.

Falling into a state of meditation, he heard the cell phone ringing. But he didn't answer. He tried to tell himself it was only a telemarketer or scammer. The only people who ever called him were telemarketers and a select few who actually had the number. But thinking of those who did have the number, he couldn't concentrate. Knowing that anyone who did possess the number would only use it for an important reason.

He rolled to his feet, ending the movement in a powerful haymaker to his punching bag. Then he stepped over to the kitchen and picked up his phone. As he had feared, it was one of the important calls.

Granger started to hit redial while reaching over to turn off the stereo—which was pumping out AC/DC's greatest hits—but then he realized that simply calling that same number would do no good. That number had already been erased. The protocol for the client was to wait fifteen minutes and call back.

He checked the time of the call. Fourteen minutes to go. He considered getting in some more reps before the call but then decided against it. He didn't want to sound out of breath when Mr. Demon called back.

28

The building looked nothing like the old gym in which Rocky had trained, the kind of place that reeked of testosterone and poor grooming habits. Ackerman had actually viewed part of the film in a theater at one of those retro film festivals. When the fire started to spread, the cinema enthusiasts had forced their way to the exits like pigs fighting over a morsel of food. Ackerman had sat in the center of the theater as the fire raged around him, eating popcorn and becoming genuinely interested in the film. He hadn't feared the fire, but it was still a force to be respected, and so he had missed the last third of the movie. Ackerman assumed that Rocky must have proven victorious and become the champion, considering the Italian Stallion became the protagonist of a franchise spawning seven sequels.

The gym he and Emily were now entering had walls lined with mirrors. One section in the back was filled with exercise bikes and elliptical machines. The floors were a cedar hardwood, and the walls were gray brick. The air smelled vaguely of sweat, but the odor was nearly camouflaged by the strong scent of vanilla and cinnamon. The place reminded Ackerman more of an upscale coffee shop than a setting where warriors were born. He wondered if the waters here were served with slices of cucumber.

Looking around at the pristine equipment and the trailer-park champions staring at themselves in the mirror,

Ackerman felt acutely disappointed. Where was the grit and fire of the Mickeys, and the underdog hunger of the Rocky Balboas? It seemed to have been replaced with a bunch of wannabe tough guys slash pretty boys who cared more about how swollen they looked in their selfies than the fire of competition and the drive to be a champion. Ackerman could plainly see that none of these men possessed the eye of the tiger.

The atmosphere and clientele made him feel sick to his stomach.

His disappointment turned to anger, and he suddenly felt an overwhelming urge to hurt these men. Which was difficult to do without touching them. Still, Ackerman didn't believe in impossibility.

Emily asked the young woman at the reception desk where they could find Leland Unser. She directed them to a thick-necked black man dancing around the main sparring ring. Large padded gloves covered Unser's hands. He bobbed and weaved as he yelled instructions at some kid punching the pads.

To Ackerman's trained eye, he could tell that Unser was one of the only true fighters in the place. And even the tough-looking trainer seemed about twenty years past his prime.

Approaching the sparring ring, Emily called out, "Mr. Unser, can we have a word, please?"

Unser screamed at the trainee, "You're still dropping your elbow! You do that tonight and that monster will put you on your ass."

Emily said again, "Mr. Unser, we just need a few minutes of your—"

In a gravelly baritone, Unser said, "As you can see, little girl, I'm busy. The kid here has a big fight tonight, and we have a lot of mental work to do before then. You'll just have to come back another time."

Ackerman climbed to the side of the ring and ducked under the ropes. He wore a black, long-sleeve shirt made of a skin-hugging, dry-fit material. He had selected the shirt for the purpose of displaying the thick cords of muscle stretched across his body. Not out of vanity, but as a type of psychological warfare.

The trainee had stopped throwing punches and stood beside his master, breathing hard. Leland Unser was a short, muscular black man with tattoos crawling up his neck, horn-rimmed glasses, and a perfectly shaved head. The muscles in Unser's jaw and neck were rigid and his nostrils flared.

Ackerman walked toward Unser and said, "Do I look like the kind of person who comes back later?"

Unser snorted in derision. "What are you supposed to be? Whatever it is, I'm not impressed, pretty boy. I get a lot of guys like you coming in here thinking they're big stuff, but any one of these other guys would eat you alive. They're real fighters. And you ain't got what it takes. Save us both some time and energy and get the hell out of my gym."

Ackerman laughed. "You're adorable, and I didn't know this was a training gym. I thought perhaps it was some sort of dance studio."

"You're about to have a very bad day. Now, last chance. Take your girl and your cocky attitude and get the hell off my property."

Emily had followed him into the ring and said,

"Mr. Unser, I think you have the wrong idea. We really just need a few moments of your time."

Ackerman said, "We've been asking around about the city's underground fighting scene. I hear there's a lot of money getting thrown around. Our sources told us you were the guy to see about getting an invitation."

"You heard wrong. I have no idea what you're even talking about. I'm a legitimate fight promoter. I don't associate with anything illegal."

Ackerman shrugged. "I know, I know. 'The first rule of Fight Club is that you don't talk about Fight Club,' but you're going to have to make an exception. All I need is a time and a location, and I'll handle the rest. No introductions or invitations necessary."

Other thickly muscled selfie-takers gathered around the perimeter of the sparring ring, obviously ready to jump in and defend Unser against the apparent interloper. Unser said, "I don't have anything to say. Now go."

Ackerman looked toward Emily, who had backed to the corner of the ring. She gestured to the door. She was angry about his handling of the situation and wanted to cut their losses. But she knew him better than that. Ackerman never backed down from a fight.

He smiled. "I know you don't know me. I'm merely some guy who walked in here off the street. You wouldn't risk exposing your less than legal income sources to a stranger. I completely understand. So why don't we do this ... I'll prove myself and help your fighter prepare at the same time. A little sparring match. No offensive moves on my part. See this gorgeous face. If he's able to land even a single punch or kick to this face, then I'll leave your baby-oil factory and never return. You can even tie my hands behind my back."

Unser's eyes narrowed, and his gaze locked with Ackerman's. "Why are you asking about underground fighting anyway? What kind of game you playing here?"

Emily said, "We could make it worth your while, Mr. Unser."

Ackerman cocked his head to the side but maintained the focus of his unblinking gaze on the washed-up brawler staring him down. He let the smile build onto his face like a slow tide sliding over the sand. He allowed the madness, the bloodlust, the darkness to swell up in him. He could almost taste the moment when Unser saw the insanity in his eyes.

Ackerman had always found that you can win a battle before it begins by merely asserting your dominance. After all, the whole point of the battle was to prove one's superiority over the opponent. If he could make his opponent fear that he or she had already lost, then his victory was assured.

One of the quickest ways to accomplish this was with a simple look. The gaze of something primal and wild that dwelled in him would reach into the other person's soul, triggering what he imagined to be some sort of biochemical reaction that informed his adversary that it's life was in clear and present danger. The instinctive part of his victim's body would then send out all kinds of signals, neurons firing, adrenaline pumping, all manner of subconscious warnings, all screaming to the soon-to-be victim that he or she was in the presence of an alpha predator.

He said, "You wouldn't much like the games I play, Mr. Unser."

As he spoke, Ackerman could almost taste the cold chill as it fell like rain down the trainer's spine. The words didn't matter, it was the way they were spoken. Like a hungry wolf growling at its prey.

Unser shivered and asked, "You look like a guy who's done time in the Ding Wing."

With all too intimate understanding, Ackerman knew that Unser referred to the psychiatric wing of a prison. Using another common prison term, he replied, "I'm actually out on jackrabbit parole right now."

Unser looked from his trainee to Ackerman and then back again, as if he were a chess master considering the sacrifice of one of his pawns. "All defense and no offense," Unser said. "And all he has to do is land one punch, and you'll let me get back to work?"

"That's right."

"And we can tie your arms behind your back?"

Ackerman bowed his head in acceptance of the terms.

"Somebody grab a jump rope and get up here. Tie this fool up."

The man Unser had been training—a Latin gentlemen with a head shaved into a mohawk—had kept his mouth shut during the entire exchange, deferring to his superior. But now the young fighter seemed hesitant. "Are you sure about this, Mr. Unser? He can't defend himself."

Unser squeezed the fighter's shoulder and, through clenched teeth, said, "I want you to knock this crazy bastard's head off with one swing. Can I count on you to do that, or should I have one of these other guys in the octagon tonight instead of you?"

The fighter shrugged his shoulders, looked at Ackerman,

and said, "Sorry, player, but you 'bout to get knocked out."

It would have been simple enough for Ackerman to slip free of the rope, but he had no intention of doing so. The objective here was not to demonstrate his skills of escape, but to establish his dominance to every other alpha male in the room.

The young fighter rushed forward, preparing to deliver the knockout blow but still half expecting Ackerman to kick or dodge the attack. The kid's fear made him hesitate.

Unfortunately for the hungry young fighter, Ackerman had catalogued every flaw in the kid's technique as he had watched him train earlier. The kid always shifted his weight and raised his left arm before throwing his right, and when throwing a left, his right shoulder tensed up.

Since the fighter's unconscious muscle movements choreographed his every attack, Ackerman was easily able to dodge a long series of punches. With every unconnected blow, the fighter's frustration grew. With anger and embarrassment clouding his judgment, the young Latino's technique became even sloppier.

Ackerman intentionally backed himself into the corner and then read the twitches of the boy's muscles like a shaman seeing the future in smoke and fire. When the kid was about to throw a huge right cross, Ackerman ducked under the blow and spun away from his opponent.

The fighter's momentum carried him forward, off balance, his fist striking the corner post of the ring. But then confusion turned to anger, and the kid rushed him with the intention of taking him to the ground.

Up to this point, the young fighter had been relying on his fists, but this wasn't boxing. It was mixed martial arts, and kicking and grappling were all on the table.

As the boy rushed forward, Ackerman waited until the last moment and then dropped low and spun, sticking his foot into the boy's path. Already out of control, the impetuous young fighter ran right into the trap, lost his balance, and ended up with his face planted into the mat.

Ackerman couldn't help but laugh out loud. He looked out at Emily, hoping to see some admiration and respect in her eyes. But her face was emotionless except for a few tight lines of concentration and concern. She reminded Ackerman of a zoologist watching a lion devour his evening meal.

Amid the chuckles and jeers of onlookers, the young fighter slapped the mat. It seemed the entire gym had taken time away from flexing in front of the mirrors to watch the show.

Pushing himself to his feet, the kid took a second to collect himself and control his breathing.

Ackerman said, "There's still time to forfeit."

Changing tactics, the kid feigned a right cross and then kicked Ackerman in the thigh with his right leg. Landing a blow for the first time, the kid seemed rejuvenated. He followed with a flurry of kicks, both low and high. The low kicks Ackerman caught with his thigh, enjoying the jolts of pain. When the kick came high, he deflected the blow with his shoulders.

Much like his punches, every one of the young fighter's kicks had a nearly imperceptible giveaway, allowing Ackerman to easily deflect the blows.

The fighter's right leg shot toward Ackerman's face

with the speed and strength of a knockout. But before launching his attack, the kid had shifted his weight and pulled his right foot back two inches. Knowing exactly where the kick was headed, Ackerman offered a kick of his own. This was designed to intercept the incoming blow at the ball of the fighter's ankle. Crying out in pain, the kid stumbled backward.

Ackerman tilted his head and said, "'The clever combatant imposes his will on the enemy, but does not allow the enemy's will to be imposed on him.'"

Breathing hard, the fighter said, "Did you memorize that from a fortune cookie?"

Ackerman grinned. "Close. It comes from an ancient Chinese military treatise dating from the fifth century BC. Sun Tzu, *The Art of War*."

The kid squared up again, but Ackerman had grown bored with the display. It was time to put an end to the sparring match. The next kick from the impetuous young man was an all-in type of move that seemed to work better in movies than in real life. It was a knockout move, a full round-house kick aimed at Ackerman's head. The kid didn't even try to feign another attack or hide his intentions, as if he were daring Ackerman to stop this blow from connecting.

As soon as the boy's muscles betrayed his intentions, Ackerman turned to the side the kick would be coming from and launched a hard straight forward kick of his own. No spin. No fancy technique. Merely a jackhammer blow aimed directly inside the fighter's calf.

The blow connected with a crunch, spinning the boy around and dropping him to the mat. The young man rolled in pain.

When he saw the blood on the mat, when he smelled its sweetness, he heard his father's voice: *Kill them all and the pain will stop. You are the night, Francis. No fear of death. No purpose in life but to cause pain and kill.*

Ackerman clenched his fists until the nails broke the flesh of his palms. He concentrated on the pain, centering himself. Using the pain as a compass to guide him to serenity.

Unser, his rage returning, said, "That was an offensive move. You cheated!"

Ackerman replied by slipping free from the rope and dropping it to the mat. Then he removed his shirt, exposing the roadmap of pain and suffering that covered his body. There wasn't an inch of his torso and arms that wasn't covered in scar tissue. Burns covered huge portions. Multiple bullet holes. Countless knife slashes. His back even showed the marks of a scourging, similar to what Jesus Christ experienced before his crucifixion. Father had tried to be historically accurate and fashioned his whip from several leather thongs with sheep bones and sharp metal balls grouped at intervals along the ends of each thong. Ackerman vividly remembered the whip embedding itself into his back and ripping out whole sections of flesh as the flagellum was pulled free.

Many of the onlookers gasped at the exposed scars, but Ackerman's eyes didn't move from Unser's. He said, "As you can see, many have attempted to kill me over the years. Care to venture a guess at how many succeeded? Now, I know you're a tough bunch and you probably think you could overwhelm me by your shear numerical advantage. But let me remind you that this time my hands won't be tied behind my back, and I won't be playing nice."

Unser ran his eyes over Ackerman's scars a moment and then pulled out a business card from a wallet in his back pocket, whispering, "Somebody give me a damn pen." One of the onlookers tossed him one, and Unser wrote on the back of the business card. Then he said, "There are a few different underground circuits in the city. I put the times and addresses of the two best on the card. Now get out."

Unser looked to Emily and added, "The places you're headed, baby doll, I once saw a guy get punched so hard that his eye flew out. His opponent picked it up and ate it. The crowd cheered him on."

Ackerman chuckled. "You know eyeballs have a very rich and buttery consistency. They sort of melt in your mouth. But there's this hard sphere in the center. It's best to just spit that part out."

Unser's face curled up in disgust. He held out the card and said, "Please leave."

Taking the business card, Ackerman stared at the two addresses and debated about whether to press his luck. "The real reason I'm in town, Mr. Unser, is because I've come to bet on the next fight in the Diamond Room. Do you have any connections there?"

Upon hearing the words "Diamond Room," Unser's demeanor instantly changed, his eyes darting around from his men to the newcomers. "Who are you? Who sent you?"

"I'm just a man with provocative proclivities and money to burn."

Ackerman saw two trainees creeping up behind Emily, but he also recognized that Unser possessed information vital to their case. He had often found that the easiest way to extract information was to simply allow your target to tell you themselves.

The two goons grabbed Emily from behind, searching her pockets and placing the edge of a knife to her throat. Ackerman felt a strange, protective rage fill him. He wanted to rip out the two men's tracheas for laying their probing hands on his partner.

In his mind, Father said, *Kill them all.*

Lip curled in a snarl, Unser said, "I think maybe it's time we start asking the questions. And if I don't like your answers, then I'm going to kill you both and have your bodies burned down to nothing but ashes."

Ackerman's gaze remained locked on Unser. It took every ounce of his hard-earned self-control to keep from listening to Father's instructions. He wanted their blood, their pain, their fear.

One of the two trainees pawing at Emily said, "She's packing, and she's got a government badge! Department of Justice."

Unser's eyes narrowed in suspicion. To Ackerman, the barrel-chested trainer said, "You don't seem like a fed."

"I'm a special consultant."

"Why didn't you two just tell me you were cops?"

Ackerman was tired of playing with these men. "Here's what's going to happen. Your men will remove their hands from my colleague, or I will detach their hands from their bodies. Then you will tell me all you know about the Diamond Room."

Unser was silent, transfixed by Ackerman's cold stare. With a nod to his men, Unser said, "Everybody get back to work. These two are leaving." The two trainees released

Emily, returning her weapon and ID. His glasses were becoming fogged up from his erratic breathing, and so Unser removed the horned-rims and wiped them on his shirt. Then he removed another business card from his pocket, wrote an address on the back, and said, "All I can tell you is that if you're wanting to find the Diamond Room, this is a good place to start."

29

Get them before they get you.

That had been one of her mother's favorites. She used to impart that wisdom to her daughters regularly. At least, she did before that day when she hung herself in the bathroom.

Corin Campbell could still see her mother's feet spasming and searching for a foothold. The kicks slowly died down as her mother's face turned purple and her eyes rolled back in her head. Corin had been four years old, but she still remembered the event in vivid detail. She supposed it wasn't the kind of thing a person easily forgot.

She had tried to kill her mother's memory many times, but her current ordeal had exposed how alive and well that pain truly was, how closely it lay below the surface. Although, even her worst memories of her previous life were preferable to this hell.

The door creaked open, which was strange. She normally heard his heavy footfalls echoing off the concrete walls long before he opened the door. This time, she heard nothing.

Light blinded her. She held up an arm as her eyes adjusted. Instead of the man in the skull mask, a young woman about her age or a little older emerged angelically from the light. The angel laid a tray in front of her. It held a bowl of water, some wash cloths, and a pile of white silk, which looked to be some sort of house dress.

As her vision cleared, Corin saw that the Angel had dark skin and curly black hair pulled up into a utilitarian bun. She wore a white dress and a pair of fuzzy brown house slippers. When the figure from the light spoke, she didn't sound at all like an angel.

Her voice was hoarse and dry, as if she had been screaming or crying or perhaps hadn't spoken aloud in a long time.

The woman standing over her said, "Wash up. Change your clothes." Then the angelic figure turned to leave.

Corin said, "Wait. Are you … Who are you?"

The woman's gaze fell to the floor. "Just get cleaned up, and then we'll talk."

Watching her leave, Corin wasn't sure how to react. She stared at the bowl of water and the clothes. When the woman left the cell, she neglected to shut the door. Corin twitched with anticipation. She waited a couple of seconds and then crawled over to the opening. She was growing accustomed to the pain of her broken shins.

Corin peaked around the corner of the door. It opened into a concrete service corridor. Conduits and pipes ran along the ceiling. A single bare bulb lit the barren space that smelled of mold and rot. The dark-skinned woman in the white dress was ten feet down the concrete corridor, smoking a cigarette.

Her dress shimmered in the sparse light. The woman shook her head and said, "Get yo ass cleaned up. I'll bring down a wheel chair when you're ready. You don't want to hurt the baby crawling around on the damn floor."

30

Marcus seethed when he saw that his old *friend*, Eddie Caruso, had sent a limo to pick them up, but refusing the ride would have drawn more attention than accepting it. He had noticed the curiosity in Maggie's eyes when she learned that he had an old friend now involved in organized crime. An interrogation would be coming soon. She had a way of rooting out all of his insecurities and secrets and calling him out on them, and he definitely didn't want Maggie digging into his relationship with Eddie Caruso.

As they descended the escalators and saw the limo driver holding a sign for "Emma Williams," he realized how difficult it was going to be to protect his secrets on this one. He closed his eyes and cringed as he motioned to the driver, hoping Maggie hadn't seen the sign.

"Who's Emma Williams?"

He rolled his eyes. "It's a really bad joke."

"What does it mean? Is she an old girlfriend or something?"

"Nothing like that. It's my initials. M.A. Marcus A. Williams. M.A. Williams. Only pronounce it 'em-ah.' It's pretty childish, but in Eddie's defense, we were like ten when he came up with that."

"This was your *friend* who would call you by a girl's name?"

"It's the kind of thing guys do."

She gave him a guys-are-stupid look but said nothing. He shook hands with the driver, a white man with a round face and the beginnings of a neck beard. The man's suit was well tailored, neat, and unwrinkled. He analyzed the driver's appearance, cataloging the visual data for further reference.

He said, "We just need to grab our duffles," and received a smile and a nod from the driver. Unfortunately, they had been forced to check their bags because of the weapons carried in each, but it was worth the extra time. He didn't plan to visit Eddie Caruso unarmed.

After they had retrieved their bags, the driver led them through the airport and outside to a long, black stretch limousine. As Maggie slipped inside, she said, "This Eddie must have been some friend. He sent a car for you and thirty of your closest friends. Did you travel with an entourage back in the day?"

Marcus didn't reply. He just fell into the seat beside her. She was already playing with buttons and digging through the liquor cabinets like a kid with a new toy. He wondered if she'd ever ridden in a limo before. She certainly hadn't done so in the time he'd known her, and she'd never mentioned being a bridesmaid or attending prom or any other instance where limo rides were common. Being a solitary person himself, he had never noticed before, but in that moment, he realized he'd never heard Maggie mention any of her old friends. There were a few women they'd met on cases with whom Maggie kept in contact—such as Lisa Spinelli, the lead tech person from Foxbury Prison, and Eleanor Schofield, the former wife of a serial killer the *Chicago Tribune* had dubbed the Anarchist—but she'd never talked about anyone from her life before joining the SO.

He felt a little hurt that she didn't trust him with that part of herself, but then he felt a pang of guilt for always doing the same to her.

As she poured a glass of champagne and flipped buttons that changed the pattern of the lighting in the vehicle's interior, she said, "Tell me about Eddie."

Marcus felt like a swimmer who saw the shark fin heading his way but could do nothing to escape. Maggie was moving in for the kill. "What do you want to know?"

She downed the champagne from her glass, pulled out a bottle of twenty-year-old scotch, and poured herself two fingers. "You've never mentioned him."

"He was my best friend in junior high. What was I supposed to say?"

Maggie shrugged. "Guess I just have some tough memories from the last time someone from your past popped back into your life," she said—referring to Dylan's mother, Claire Cassidy, who had revealed that Marcus had a son.

He hoped Eddie wouldn't be divulging any such life-changing revelations. "I can make you a one-hundred-percent promise that Eddie did not have my baby."

She downed the scotch and said, "That's hilarious. Who moved away? You or him? Which one of you moved away after junior high?"

"Neither. Why do you ask?"

"It seems strange to me that this guy was your best friend in junior high, and then your friendship was just over. If neither of you moved away, then why didn't you remain friends?"

Marcus considered his words carefully. His Brooklyn accent bubbled to the surface as he fought to stay calm.

"Life happens. We drifted apart. His dad was a made man. Mine was an officer of the law. It was only a matter of time before the ways of the world stood in the way of friendship."

Refilling her scotch, she asked, "Did something happen?"

"I'd rather not talk about this. Can we just drop it?"

"Fine."

"There was some strange emphasis on that 'fine.'"

"I just wonder what secrets you're keeping from me this time."

He shook his head and growled deep in his throat. "There's nothing to tell."

"Fine."

"It's not like you don't have your fair share of secrets, darling."

Maggie took a long swig from her second glass of scotch. "Well, aren't we a pair."

31

Every bedroom was a suite with its own sitting area and bathroom. And each bathroom had some crazy deal that shot water back up at you. It was like nothing Marcus had ever seen before. But that wasn't the cool thing Junior wanted to show them.

"You see the strip of color here in the marble," Junior said, referring to a two inch line of emerald green which traced the walls. "If it's green, that means you're in an area of the house open to the public. If it's red, then that means it's restricted access."

"That's so cool," Eddie said.

"It's just something my Grandpa Angelo came up with. This was originally his house, before my pop inherited it."

Marcus said, "Your grandpa must've been some guy. I can't imagine how much money it would take to build a house like this. What did your grandpa do for his job?"

Eddie quickly said, "Don't worry about him, Junior. He don't know nothing."

"What did I say?" Marcus asked.

Junior stepped up into Marcus's face. The eighth-grader towered over him like Goliath to David. The older boy seemed to be challenging him for some reason, but Marcus couldn't understand why. Still, he had learned early on that you never run from a fight and you never back down from a bully.

He imagined that he was a stone gargoyle, the kind that stood watch on some of the older buildings. Nothing could hurt stone. And stone was neutral and unchanging. Marcus simply stared back at the older boy and stood his ground.

Junior finally said, "My Grandpa Angelo was one of the greatest men who ever lived. He built this town. He was in the family business, little boy blue."

"Oh, I understand," Marcus said, even though he really had no idea what that meant.

Eddie acted differently around Junior. It was as if they had fallen into a strange hierarchy where Marcus answered to Eddie, and Eddie answered to Junior. He didn't know who Junior answered to, but he was sure there was a bigger fish above him.

"I need to know that you are cool, little boy blue," Junior said. "Because I'm about to take you babies deep into the red zone."

Eddie seemed to be bubbling at the prospect, but Marcus was fine playing in the green area. Stepping forward, Eddie said, "He's cool. Take a chill pill."

"If he sees something and squeals," Junior said, "then it's my ass. Which means it's your ass. And your pop's."

Eddie hesitated, apparently considering the consequences for the first time. After a few seconds of thought, he turned to Marcus and said, "I was thinking about that birthday cake. It's going to be gone soon, and I really want a piece of that. Marcus, you fly down there and grab us three pieces, so we don't miss out. Better yet, grab four, so you can have two for your trouble."

Junior seemed relieved, as if Marcus was a burden he was glad to be rid of.

Marcus wanted to scream. His supposedly best friend had just stabbed him in the back. He wanted to explode. He wanted to flip over all the furniture in the hallway and ram his fist through the walls. He felt the anger rising up, the red creeping over his eyes, but outwardly he kept pretending that he was a stone gargoyle.

He said, "Sure thing." Then he headed back down the hall toward the stairs.

Over his shoulder, he heard Eddie say, "I told you it was cool. That fat freak does whatever I say."

32

Francis Ackerman checked the address a second time and then growled like a wolf about to strike. "I don't understand this."

From the driver's seat of the rented white Impala, Emily Morgan looked at the entrance of Oakbrook Cemetery and said, "I take it this is Unser telling us to drop dead."

Ackerman cracked his knuckles over and over. "My honor demands retribution to be swift and bloody."

"Don't be silly. You don't have any honor."

"Words hurt, and now is not the time to provoke me. This just doesn't make sense. Feels like we're missing something. Maybe he's directing us to one of the current residents of the cemetery?"

She shrugged. "It's a big cemetery, and it's raining. Do you really want to walk the rows, looking at headstones for clues?"

"We wouldn't even know what to look for. Why can't people be more precise with their language? His instructions were so vague."

"I think we may have to accept that he was sending us a message to get lost. He may have sent us here just to waste our time."

Ackerman looked back on the encounter with Leland Unser inside the sparring ring. He said, "Unser would never have knowingly defied me."

"Really? He seemed pretty defiant to me."

"But I gave him the look."

"What look?"

"The one that tells him if he challenges me then I'll butcher him, his family, friends, his pets, and then everyone in his phone's contact list."

Emily said, "That's a pretty powerful look. Do you think something may have been lost in translation?"

"No."

"Okay, so you gave him 'the look' of murdering his whole family tree, but at any point did you ever intend to carry through with that implied threat? If he crossed you, did you intend to kill everyone in his phonebook?"

"I suppose not, at least not right now, but maybe someday. We're too busy at the moment for such distractions."

"And the old Ackerman? What would he have done?"

"Are you saying that I'm going soft? Am I losing my edge?"

"Don't make a big deal out of it. You're just becoming less of a monster and more of a human being."

He stared at the rows of gravestones beyond the wrought-iron fence. "But what if the monster is what we need? I was born to be a predator, and every moment of pain from then on has sharpened me to a razor's edge. I can't allow that edge to grow dull."

"Life has phases, Frank. To everything there is a season. Maybe it's time to put the knife down."

"That's ridiculous. It sounds like you want to put me out to pasture. Killing, fighting, hunting. It's all I've ever known."

"Then maybe it's time to learn something new."

33

With Blake's reluctant permission, Baxter had searched the whole condo for any clues or insights. In the bathroom, he found a high dosage of anti-depression medications in Corin's name, but little else. She was clearly the dominant personality, but Baxter had the sense that she established her dominance passively, possibly through manipulation. The drawers in the bedroom were each labeled with his or her initials, and there was a small chalkboard on the bedroom wall beside the light switch. At the top, it said, "Blake's List." It then contained a chalk run-down of all their activities over the next few days and a task list for Blake on each. The dates were nearly two weeks past.

The only room left to check was the spare bedroom. He wandered through it with a trained eye. The devil was always in the details, and the details often went overlooked.

Finding nothing, he moved to the closet. As he parted the bi-fold doors, a dark shape shot toward him. He deflected the attack with a forearm and muttered a curse under his breath.

Looking down at the object that had fallen on him, he said, "You always keep your ironing board in the closet of the spare bedroom?"

"No, that is strange. Corin has a spot for it in the hall closet. She likes to iron while I watch TV."

"She doesn't watch with you?"

"Corin prefers books. If she picks out what we watch, it's usually a boring documentary."

Baxter asked, "So did you or the police move the ironing board into here?"

Blake shook his head. "I don't use it, and the cops didn't move anything. Corin must have stuck it in there."

"Seems rather peculiar, the way it fell out at us like that."

"I guess. She was probably in a hurry."

"When does she usually do her ironing?"

"Like I said, while we watch TV."

"But does she ever use the ironing board in the morning before school, or does she press your Italian suit before you head to the club."

"No, I have it dry cleaned and pressed. And Corin always has everything ready and laid out for the next day. She seldom irons anything in the morning."

"So when was the last time she used it?"

Blake paused to consider that. "Probably the night before she went missing."

"Probably?"

Another pause. "Definitely. I watched the 49ers game, and she ironed a couple of outfits and then worked on homework."

"And what did she do with the board afterward?"

"I can't say for sure, but I think I remember her putting it away in the hall closet. Where are you going with this?"

Baxter shrugged. "Could be nothing, but it makes me wonder if the site of Corin's abduction was actually here in the condo."

"You mean that the person who took her moved the ironing board? Why would anyone do that?"

"I don't know, but the real question to ask is: Does her being abducted from here change things?" He checked the time and said, "I have another appointment, but I'll be back in touch soon. Probably later this evening. You be around?"

Tears forming in his eyes, Blake replied, "Anything you need. If there's even a chance it could lead to Corin, I'll do it. Whatever it is. I just need her back."

34

Stefan Granger parked the Buick a block down from Haight and Ashbury. It was a nice day. Low 70s. Granger still wore jeans and a hoodie. The weather in San Francisco was always perfect for identity concealment. The sky had gone dark but a steady stream of people still flowed down the streets once walked by some of the most iconic musicians and activists in history.

Granger had placed an antiviral mask over his face before leaving his apartment. He didn't even want to be recognized while driving. From the visor, he grabbed his low-light glasses. They weren't quite as effective as night vision, but they hid his eyes, and the large green goggles associated with night-vision technology could be a bit conspicuous. Still, in his profession, even the slightest edge over an opponent could make all the difference.

The white antiviral mask he had chosen was a cross between one designed to collect dust, like a painter would wear, and one designed to protect from infection, like those worn by surgeons. It was the perfect tool for concealing his face. When the average person saw a man in a hoodie and a ski mask walking down the street, they immediately became suspicious. Fake beards and prosthetic noses and the like could be employed as camouflage, but the easiest option by far was to pretend he was merely another germaphobic or germ-infected citizen. People generally steered clear, and he could even wear such a mask while indoors.

His gloves were the most popular brand, purchased from a chain store, and paid for in cash. While not as innocuous as the mask, the gloves were still not enough to make anyone suspicious.

But the one tool he had yet to choose for this job was his weapon. Granger had an arsenal in the trunk of the old Buick, but he didn't want someone to see him staring into a trunk full of guns, and so he took a moment to consider the options.

There was his trustee Walther PPK, threaded for a top-of-the-line suppressor. It was chambered for the 380 auto, a small caliber which, combined with subsonic ammunition, could be virtually silent. Then there was his father's old shotgun, which he had sawed off and retrofitted into a weapon of mass destruction. It had originally been an over-under hunting gun, and he enjoyed the frequent reloads that the two shot capacity required. It made the game fairer for his opponent. Like a handicap in golf.

But neither of those seemed to check the boxes for this evening's contract. He wanted this to look gang related. So he decided on the Mac 10—a fully automatic machine pistol with a long magazine filled with hollow-point 9-mm rounds. It was brutal, effective, and easily concealable. And unlike those used in drive-by shootings, his Mac 10 had been customized and upgraded for reliability and accuracy.

His hooded sweatshirt was two sizes too large, which left ample room to conceal the machine pistol.

The last thing Stefan Granger did before exiting the vehicle was to stick in his wireless earbuds and direct his phone to play AC/DC's "Back in Black." He'd started the practice of listening to music while killing a few months back, in an effort to heighten his other senses and to give another handicap to his prey.

After retrieving the Mac 10 from the trunk of the Buick, he walked toward the target's apartment building, which had been converted to an inner city bordello. As he moved, he kept his head down and made eye contact with no one. He cleared his mind and visualized what was to come.

When Stefan Granger was a boy, his favorite games had been the *Mortal Kombat* series. He still remembered the first time he had visited a friend's house, one who could actually afford a Sega Genesis. It was there that he saw a digital cartoon character tear out the spinal column of another cartoon character. He was instantly hooked. Not because of the violence, although that didn't hurt; but for him, it was the thrill and strategy of the gameplay. He found it to be much like real life. In the game, when a character performed a certain move against you, one needed to be able to counter and return the attack. This was done by pressing a certain combination of buttons. And Granger had become an expert at responding to his opponents' attacks with the perfect combination.

He smiled beneath the antiviral mask, thinking of the day that his father brought him home his very own Sega Genesis. It was a little used and abused, but his dad had picked it up at a yard sale with extra controllers and over twenty games, including some bloody fighting games like *Mortal Kombat* and *Eternal Champions*.

Still musing over childhood memories, he reached the

front stoop of Faraz Tarkani's whorehouse. A large, bald white man in a black T-shirt stood beside the entrance, smoking a cigarette. The apelike sentry was laughing and joking with another man, a big black fellow wearing a sleeveless shirt and a stocking cap. Granger couldn't hear what they were conversing about because of the earbuds, but he read their lips and ascertained that the discussion centered upon the anatomy of a new employee.

He tapped a button on his earbuds to pause the sounds of classic rock. Then he said to the two thugs, "I'll make a deal with the two of you. The first one of you to tell me where I can find Samantha Campbell gets to live."

The overly muscled ape man flicked away his cigarette and said, "Get lost, freak."

Stefan Granger smiled, but then he realized they couldn't see him beneath the mask. Rolling his shoulders and warming his muscles up to pump on all cylinders, he tapped the earbud and the tiny speakers began to pump with AC/DC's "Shoot to Thrill."

The bouncer seemed to register that something was wrong, some primordial alarm system dating back to the early days of man. Granger had the gun out and was squeezing the trigger before the sentry knew what had happened. He aimed low, the bullets shredding the ape man's legs and dropping him to the concrete.

As the bald bouncer shrieked in pain, Granger turned his machine pistol on the man in the stocking cap. The large black gentleman was smarter than his comrade. He raised his hands and said, "Sammy's upstairs with the boss. She's showing him her appreciation."

"Appreciation for what?"

"I don't know, man. Something to do with her sister who went missing."

The first man flailed about on his hands and knees, leaving a trail of blood on the pavement as he tried to crawl toward his fallen weapon. Granger raised the Mac 10 and squeezed off another line of projectiles. This time, he aimed for the man's large, bald head. It reminded Granger of a giant egg, and it cracked just like one.

The other man kept his arms raised and trembled with fear. Granger took aim and said, "Thank you," before ending the informant's life. On his earbuds, Brian Johnson sang about pulling the trigger.

After performing a tactical reload, Granger headed for the top floor. He wasn't here to kill the girls or their clients, but he also had a rule about witnesses: *never leave any*. The mask and glasses were camouflage against video surveillance, but he didn't trust them or take chances. He mowed down three of the girls and two of the clients before he reached the pimp's penthouse suite.

Granger approached the top of the stairs cautiously, knowing what would await him on the other side. While on the floor below, he had heard the footfalls of at least two other gunmen. They would be waiting somewhere in that hallway.

He reached the top of the stairs and placed his back against the wall, keeping himself concealed from the point of view of the hallway. Then he grabbed one of his empty magazines and tossed it back down the stairs. It thudded and clanked. He listened and waited.

Back in his video game days, Granger had faced numerous opponents who found success through button mashing, essentially just going crazy and getting lucky. But in every instance, he had found that button mashing was no match for proper technique and strategy. Even then, he knew that the most patient of two opponents always had the upper hand.

Just as he expected, he saw the barrel of the man's Glock pistol before he saw the man himself.

Granger grabbed the guard by the wrist, jerked him forward, and unleashed his weapon into the man's abdomen. His victim screamed in pain and discharged his own weapon. Granger slapped the Glock pistol away and spun the dying guard around to use as a human shield.

With his arm around the first guard's neck, holding him up like a rag doll, Granger rushed into the hallway. The other sentry had his gun raised and ready, but Granger was concealed behind the man's partner. His Mac 10 roared and spit hot shell casings toward the ceiling. The controlled burst caught the second guard in the chest, driving him back and painting the walls with red.

His human shield had yet to die like a good boy and was even trying to wriggle free of his grasp. In his ears, AC/DC still thumped along with his heartbeat. Granger wasted no time in turning the gun on his human body armor and squeezing the trigger against the man's temple.

An empty forty-five round magazine fell to the floor, and Granger slammed a fresh mag in place. Then he jacked back the slide and headed toward Faraz's penthouse.

Over the earbuds, "Shoot to Thrill" ended, and "What Do You Do for Money Honey" began.

35

The dark-skinned woman in the house slippers pushed Corin up to a concrete landing as she unlocked a door with two deadbolts. Corin asked again, "Where are we?"

Without responding, the woman propped open the door and returned to the wheelchair's handles.

Corin felt a strange sense of vertigo as they crossed the threshold. They moved from what was bare and utilitarian to something finished with expensive flare. The carpet was dark red, like old blood stains. The hallway looked as if it could have been inside an overpriced hotel, if not for the unkempt and deteriorating look of it all. Corin's mind flashed back to a scene from some movie, creepy twin girls standing at the end of a similar hallway.

Doors marked with large consecutive numbers lined each side of the endlessly long hallway. She had no way of knowing whether the doors opened into more concrete service corridors or lavish guest suites. Trying to get a feel for the layout made the whole place seem surreal and menacing, as if each door opened into someone else's personal hell.

Finally reaching the end of the hall, the woman in the slippers unlocked a set of double doors. The contents of the room beyond also caused Corin's head to spin. Her mind fought to find solid ground, any anchor to orient herself with respect to where in the land of the living she could be.

The woman pushed her into a massive ballroom lined

with lacquered cedar planks. She guessed the space to be a hundred feet long and fifty feet wide with cathedral ceilings reaching to at least twenty-five feet at their pinnacle. The far wall was mostly glass, containing rows of custom windows formed into a pyramid. Beyond the wall of windows, Corin saw the sandy shore of a small lake or pond, surrounded by the dense green of a forest.

She guessed by the type of trees that she was still somewhere in northern California. That was good. She knew the area. And she wasn't in hell. At least, she didn't imagine they had trees in hell.

Eight beds had been arranged into neat rows in the center of the ballroom. But they weren't simple cots or mattresses on the floor. They were like something found in the bedchambers of a princess. Each intricately carved four-poster bed was wrapped in a translucent white curtain, giving the impression of individual tents. Beside each bed stood metal clothes racks, several different white garments hanging from the rods.

The woman in the slippers rolled her past the beds, toward the wall of windows, where a circle of leather couches formed a sitting area around a bearskin rug. Two other women in the same white dresses lounged on the couches, both reading old hardcover books. One girl had Asian features, and the other was a petite blonde with short hair. The Asian girl looked to be a few months pregnant.

Corin didn't allow herself to think about the alleged baby growing inside her own stomach.

Over her shoulder, the woman said, "This is Sherry and Tia. And I'm Sonnequa. This is Corin, girls. The Master's newest addition."

When Corin spoke, the words exploded out breathlessly and forcefully, as though she was spitting daggers at each woman. "What the hell is going on here? Why are you all just sitting around? We need to escape? Who are you? How long have you been here? Does anyone know—"

The slap across her face silenced all her questions. Her hand reflexively went to her cheek where the warm sting still resonated over her skin. Sonnequa's hand hung in the air, trembling.

Corin didn't say a word. She had always found that the best defense mechanism was to keep your mouth shut and play dead.

Sonnequa's voice shook as she whispered, "We're not allowed to converse with each other when the Master isn't present."

"What? I don't—"

"Tia," Sonnequa said, "show Corin what happens when we don't obey the rules."

The Asian girl sat up, leaned closer to Corin, and opened her mouth. It took a few seconds for Corin to realize what she was seeing, what was missing from the picture.

When she understood, Corin started to shake uncontrollably. She wanted to run, but her legs were broken. She wanted to vomit, but she had nothing in her stomach. She wanted to cry, but dared not make a sound.

Tia, the pregnant Asian girl, was missing her tongue.

36

Marcus wasn't at all surprised by the name of Eddie's nightclub. It was just the kind of thing his former friend would come up with: both self-aggrandizing and egomaniacal. He and Maggie pulled up to The Great Caruso at ten after nine, but already the party was in full swing. All manner of Italian sport and German luxury automobiles lined the mansion's massive parking lot.

As they reached a security gate, a muscular man in a black tuxedo and white gloves stood at attention. The guard approached the driver, said a few words, and then, approaching their descending side window, said, "Identification, please?" Marcus recognized the bulge of a pistol beneath the guard's jacket.

Maggie held up her DOJ credentials. The guard smiled back and said, "Mr. Caruso welcomes you to the party." The attendant bowed cordially, and the security gate parted.

The whole place made Marcus want to puke.

The guy had acted off a script and had clearly been trained to allow entry to the "party" in a very specific manner. Marcus wondered if his former friend had choreographed the employees personally on how they should speak and behave. Eddie always was a control freak, down to every last detail.

The element that disturbed Marcus most was the syntax the attendant had been instructed to use. It wasn't "I welcome you" or "We welcome you." It was, "*Mr. Caruso* welcomes you to the party." As if Eddie had downgraded the guard from human being to robotic slave, as if the kid wasn't even allowed to have his own identity. He was merely an extension of "The Great Caruso."

The guard followed the limo through the gate and then up to the mansion's *porte cochère*. He opened the door for them and said, "Mr. Caruso awaits you in the grand ballroom."

As he stepped out, Marcus said, "Buddy, Mr. Caruso is a douchebag, and your life will turn out a lot better if you quit this job and get yourself a respectable one. Maybe apply at Burger King."

The guard looked dumbfounded, as if he were searching for a scripted response to such a statement.

Marcus didn't wait for the canned retort. He started up the marble stairs toward a pair of French doors—twelve feet tall, white with gold accents. The entrance made Marcus feel as if he was walking up to the pearly gates.

Inside was a grand foyer with a coat check and several small sitting areas around a giant rotunda. Men and women sat in some old leather chairs surrounding the periphery of the foyer. Some laughing, some kissing, others smoking cigars or fluted cigarettes.

The doors to the "Grand Ballroom" were just as large as the entry doors, but these were made of a dark mahogany. Two more men in tuxedos stood on each side, ready to allow entry farther into Eddie's little kingdom.

It wasn't until the doors parted that Marcus finally realized that Eddie's club was a themed hangout. The entire show had been designed to make people feel as if they were in *The Great Gatsby*, or at least some cellular generation equivalent. Most of the women wore lace flapper dresses. They spun on the dance floor, their many-colored sequins glittering like a sea of rubies, emeralds, diamonds, and sapphires. The men wore tuxedos and stylish formal suits. The outfits, the decorations, the atmosphere screamed 1920s New York, but the music was some kind of bastardized amalgam of techno, hip-hop, jazz, and blues.

The pulsing beat hurt Marcus's chest, and the lights made his world throb. But it seemed successful in pushing the wannabe gangsters and flappers to grind closer and lower.

A sprawling staircase climbed each side of the long, rectangular ballroom. Eddie Caruso was descending the closest staircase with the swagger of a film icon. And, Marcus had to admit, Eddie looked the part. He wore a simple black tuxedo and a bow tie. His hair was slicked back and looked to be professionally styled. He even had the boyish good looks, but the suave persona crumbled a bit when Eddie opened his mouth.

His voice was soft with a thick Brooklyn accent, but it was also low and scratchy like an old man who couldn't catch his breath. During their sixth-grade year, Eddie's house had burned to the ground. Eddie and his younger sister had been trapped in the fire, and Eddie came away with scarred lungs and scorched vocal cords. Marcus recalled that Eddie didn't really mind his new voice. In fact, Eddie had used it to his own advantage, letting it add to his tough-guy reputation.

Eddie spread his arms and, in his sandpaper voice, said, "What do you think of the place?"

Marcus glanced around at the extravagance and excess for a few seconds and then said, "It reminds me of a low-budget musical at a community rec center. Do people have to pay to get in here?"

Eddie smiled and said, "So you're still an epic prick. That's good to know."

"And you're still a flaming narcissist. In my experience, when someone keeps telling you about how 'great' they are, that usually means the opposite is true."

"It's a themed club, jackass, and it makes money like we have the printing press in the basement. Whole thing was my idea. I noticed that a lot of rich kids and suburbanites were having these Gatsby-themed parties. It started as a tax write-off, but apparently there was something to it, and The Great Caruso was born. But it's all for show."

"If it's just a show, then why not make it legitimately 'Gatsby' themed and hire someone to play Gatsby instead of inserting yourself into the role."

"Then we'd have to pay for the rights. As it stands, our theme is just the 1920s, and using my real name adds to the mystique."

"Or you just like to stroke your own ego."

Eddie smiled. "I have people lined up to stroke it for me, Old Sport."

Maggie intervened, saying, "Mr. Caruso, thank you so much for agreeing to meet with us. Your place here really is something. Isn't that right, Marcus?"

"Sure, it's beautiful, Eddie, and not creepy at all. Just like if Robert Redford had a baby with Lady Gaga."

Eddie laughed, but his eyes showed his annoyance. "Don't hold back, Marcus. Tell me what you really think."

Maggie said, "Do you have somewhere private that we can talk, Mr. Caruso?"

"Of course, come on up to my office. And beautiful women call me Eddie. And you, Marcus, I'd prefer you call me Mr. Caruso."

37

The past…

Once Eddie and Junior were out of sight, Marcus took off in a full sprint down the massive, marble-floored hallways. He flew down the stairs, rounded the corner, and followed the sounds of voices. The party was out back on the patio. The kids' parents had gone all out on the festivities, with bounce houses, ball pits, and magic shows. The place reminded Marcus of Coney Island. More than once, he considered just staying down there and stuffing his face with cake. But whatever it was Eddie and Junior didn't want him to see was too good to miss.

He rushed over to the cake table, secured three pieces, and made his way to the kitchen. He explained to one of the caterers about the cake, and she was glad to help. She took the three pieces and said she would wrap them up and leave them on the counter. With a rushed thank you, he hurried back to the stairs, the second floor, and back to the hallway where his supposed friend had betrayed him and called him a fat freak.

Marcus stopped, breathing hard and heart pounding. He sucked in a few gasps and forced his lungs to calm. He listened. The sounds of the party, the air-conditioning, waiters in the kitchen, children giggling and playing in the backyard, the hum of fluorescent lighting, the rush of water flowing through pipes, and there, somewhere beneath it all, the muffled voices of Junior and Eddie.

Marcus followed the sound down the hall and to the point where green became red, public versus restricted, safe versus dangerous. He hesitated at the boundary, knowing that he should turn around. As he stepped across the threshold into the red area, he could've sworn that the air grew colder and the light dimmer.

He followed the sound of their voices, needing to know the very thing they didn't want him to. The murmurs originated from a bedroom on his left, but Marcus waited in the hallway and listened. He knew Eddie would just tell him to get lost again.

Marcus arrived just in time to hear the phrase: "secret passageways." Junior continued, "My Grandpa Angelo was a real nut job."

"I thought you said he was the greatest man to ever live?"

"No, he was looney toons. I just told little boy blue that to shut him up. During Grandpa A's younger years they called him the Butcher; during his older years, they called him the Mad King. He built this place in his older years. My pop had all the entrances to the secret passageways boarded up. But I re-opened this one, so I can sneak around the house."

Eddie said, "That is so awesome."

Marcus peeked around the corner and saw Junior opening a secret passageway by twisting a piece of trim and pulling it off the wall. Then he pushed against a portion of the wall, which clicked open to reveal the hidden entrance.

As he grabbed a flashlight from a nearby bookshelf, Junior said, "Come on. Let's do some exploring. But once we get in there, you stick right by me."

"Why? What's in there?"

"Don't be a baby. Nothing's in there. It's just that some of the passageways have been sealed off, others are dead ends. It's easy to get lost. I thought I was gonna have to spend the night in there one time. Before I got the hang of it. So stick with me, okay?"

"Like glue," Eddie whispered.

Marcus, although concealed outside the doorway, could still picture Eddie's face. That moment where his stiff bravado cracked and the scared little boy beneath shined through. Marcus had seen that look on Eddie's face several times before. It had once been an endearing quality, and somehow, knowing that it was all a cover made it easier to put up with Eddie's egomania.

He waited for the other boys to leave the room and then gave them a moment to travel down the secret passageway before working up enough nerve to pursue.

Repeating Junior's procedure, Marcus followed the other boys into the bowels of the Mad King's castle.

38

Stefan Granger didn't ascend the last set of stairs up to the small-time pimp's own version of the Oval Office. Instead, he kicked into one of the rooms on the southern wall and headed toward a fire escape, which he had already scoped out earlier. Most buildings had changed over to inner stairwells rather than external fire escapes, but there were always a few preservation holdouts and those too poor to update.

Granger followed the metal stairs up to the penthouse, but he made sure to stay out of sight. With a quick glance through the window, he saw the pimp dressed in nothing but a pink bathrobe. Faraz held a scantily clad woman out in front of him, his arm tight around her neck, her eyes bulging. His other hand held a gold 9-mm Beretta.

He assumed the woman to be Samantha Campbell. She was needed alive. Granger took aim with the Mac 10, but there wasn't enough separation between Faraz and Sammy. Even though he was accustomed to the weapon and could control the bursts, his instrument of choice for this assignment simply wasn't designed for pinpoint accuracy.

The antiviral mask hindered his ability to spit, and so he growled instead. He knew a variety of different attacks, both physical and mental, but he didn't have time for subterfuge. The police were already en route. Still, he saw no other open moves with his current resources.

Quickly analyzing the situation, Granger stepped behind

the bricks beside the window. Then he reached down and knocked. As he had expected, the pimp whirled toward him and opened fire. The window shattered, but Granger was relatively protected behind the wall from a 9 mm. There was a slight chance of a bullet ricocheting off the metal framework of the fire escape. But random instances such as that were also why Stefan Granger had all his clothes lined with a carbon nanotube composite—a revolutionary new material that was pliable under normal conditions but hardened like steel with any impact.

After Faraz finished his tantrum, Granger leaned forward and said, "I'm just here to talk."

"You seem to let your machine gun do the talking!"

"It was your guys who drew on me. I just needed a word. And they must've taken one look at me and decided to shoot first and ask questions later."

"You lie!" Faraz yelled.

"Think about it. I could've killed you just now. I had the drop on you. I could've taken you down, but I didn't. Instead, I knocked on the window to get your attention. I'm only here to talk. Now, can I come out without you trying to shoot me."

"You go ahead and come in real slow, but if I don't like any twitch, I take you down."

"Fair enough," Granger said as he climbed inside, the Mac 10 still in his hand but his arms raised up in surrender and the weapon's barrel pointed at the ceiling.

Which was, in reality, an attack position.

With a flick of his wrist, he could direct his fire back to the pimp, but most people without a law enforcement or military background didn't recognize such a threat.

Faraz said, "So talk. And part of what you want to talk about better give me good reason not to kill you."

Sammy wailed and cried as Faraz loosened his grip enough to allow her to breathe. With the woman now facing him, Granger could see that she wore a crotch-less Wonder Woman costume. He said, "It's okay, Ms. Campbell, I'm not going to let anything happen to you."

Her response was only more blubbering, but she did look up and make eye contact. In that moment, he saw confusion, and he realized his mistake.

The room was only lit by candle, but with the low-light glasses, Granger could plainly see that this woman was not Samantha Campbell.

With a roll of his eyes, he bent his wrist to reacquire his target and squeezed the trigger. The result was one dead entrepreneur and one dead employee on the floor. He had wasted precious seconds assuming this woman to be his target. They possessed the same blonde hair and same artificially enhanced forms. Still, he cursed himself. His father had always preached against assumptions.

His gaze swept the room, and he listened for any sounds. But the police were close, and the sirens made it impossible to listen for an individual's breathing. He didn't have time to play hide and seek, and so he stitched a line of bullets high into the walls all around the room.

Then he listened for the whimper.

When hunting, fear was often the most effective method to draw out one's prey.

He aimed the machine pistol at the source of the small cry.

"Come out now, or I open fire," he said, bluffing.

Samantha Campbell stepped into the light. She had been cowering on the opposite side of her employer's bed. Sammy, as her sister had always called her, was naked in all the spots she should have been clothed, while black leather covered all the patches of skin that could have acceptably been exposed.

Through a zippered opening, she said, "Please don't kill me. I didn't see anything."

"Remove the leather from your face."

She pulled off the zipper-clad mask.

With positive visual confirmation on his target, Granger lowered his weapon and said, "Don't worry, Ms. Campbell. I'm here to take you to see your sister."

The young woman's surprise exceeded her fear, and she asked, "You know my sister? Are you the one who took her?"

"Don't worry. Everything is going to be just fine." His eyes searched the room for her regular clothing, but not seeing anything else, he reached down and pulled the pink bathrobe from the dead man's shoulders. He held it out to Sammy. "Put this on."

"It's covered in blood," she said, tears streaming down her face.

Granger examined the garment and saw the spots where bullets had pierced the fabric and then penetrated the pimp's flesh. Blood had rushed from the wounds and stained the robe. He said, "It just makes it look like pretty red flowers. Put on the robe, or I'll give you a few blossoms of your own."

Once Sammy had on the robe, he rushed her down the fire escape and away from the building, heading toward the Buick. He was unarmed now, having discarded the Mac 10 in Faraz's penthouse. It was a street gun, no serial numbers. Perfect for a job like this. He half-carried the terrified woman as she stumbled and dragged her feet. Luckily, his own strength was more than adequate for the task.

When they reached the Buick, he turned to Samantha Campbell, and in his mind, he overlaid an internal diagram of a woman's brain and spinal column onto the side of her face. Then he struck her in the temple with a blow designed make her head rotate, twisting the spine and disrupting function between the upper brainstem and the higher brain, causing unconsciousness. Once she was out, Stefan Granger popped the trunk and deposited Sammy inside. Then he slid in behind the wheel and headed for the compound, his assignment complete.

39

Corin Campbell would have normally backed away in horror at the sight of Tia's mutilation. The young Asian woman, who didn't look to be over eighteen, had only a mangled nub where her tongue should have been. Corin wanted to run as fast as her deceptively strong little legs could carry her.

Unfortunately, Corin was behind enemy lines with two broken legs, and she could do little more than look away and tremble.

Sonnequa said, "This is your world now, baby girl. You'd best get used to it."

"Get used to it?"

"This is your life now. I'll explain the rest of the rules. Only ask questions if it's pertaining to that specific rule. Nod if you understand."

Corin nodded.

"Good." Sonnequa pushed Corin's wheelchair over to the massive window. "Nice view, isn't it? You can have a decent life here, Corin. A quiet life, perhaps. But not an uncomfortable one. As you can see by the view."

"And that is a view of where?"

"Northern California, and that's as much as you need to know about that right now. The first rule, as you heard, is no communication of any kind unless the Master is present or you are acting under his orders."

"Where is the Master? Is he here all the time?"

"He joins us for dinner most evenings. The time varies depending on his schedule. It's always a five-course meal. Prepared by us, of course, but the Master often brings in takeout to give us a break from even those duties."

"So he's not here right now?"

"Sometimes he is. And sometimes he isn't. Doesn't really matter. Rules stay the same."

"But if he's not here, then how does he know—"

"There are sophisticated surveillance and audio detection systems installed throughout the compound. If you speak to one of the other ladies or attempt to communicate, he will know. Someone is always watching. Trust me on that. Tia thought she was being smart too. She didn't plan to get caught."

"If that's the outside world, right there, and he's not even here, then what's to stop us from getting away. We could smash that window and run. All of us."

"That brings us to rule number two. We have wonderful facilities here. A stocked kitchen abundant with healthy snacks. A swimming pool. Sauna. Gym. Jacuzzi. Lots of books to read. A television with an endless supply of movies. And very little work to do. This place provides us with a life of luxury."

"As what?" Corin asked. "Sex slaves for some psychotic pervert?"

"If I were you, I would keep thoughts like that to myself. The Master will probably cut you some slack since you're new. But I would never count on mercy here, baby girl. Not from anyone."

Sonnequa dug into a pocket of her dress and handed a

stack of pictures to Corin. Staring at the first photo, Corin felt the urge to vomit, but there was nothing in her stomach to heave out. She looked away from the photos and asked, "What is this?"

"Keep looking at the photos. Rule number two: don't ever leave the protection of the Compound."

"Or what? The Master will butcher you?"

"The Master didn't inflict those wounds. That's what happened when the hellhounds—a trained pack of Rottweilers—got hold of a girl who decided to break rule number two. The hellhounds protect the compound from intruders, but they're also trained to tear us to pieces if we venture outside. You can explore, if you wish. Just don't try to open a locked door, cause a problem, or step outside these walls. Keep looking through the pics."

"I don't need to see any more."

"That wasn't a request." Sonnequa snatched the photos from Corin's grasp and stuck them up in front of her face. "You look at these, baby girl. I've been here the longest. I've seen what happens when you defy the Master, and breaking the rules has swift and serious consequences."

Sonnequa kept sticking photo after photo in front of Corin's face. "You look at them! These were my sisters. That's what we are here. A family. You can have a good life here. You just need to be a good wife."

"A good wife?"

"He has bought you as his bride with his strength and blood."

Corin felt as if she'd stepped into an alternate dimension. "I'm no one's property, and I'm no one's wife. Good or otherwise."

"Rule number three is a catch-all. Do anything to incur the wrath of the Master, and the sentence is death. He has no mercy for those who defy him."

"This is insane. I'd rather die than live on my knees."

Sonnequa slapped her hard across the left cheek and then leaned down into her face. "You best wake up, baby girl. There are much worse things he can do to you than kill you. And when one of us breaks a rule, we all suffer. Things aren't as dark as they seem now. When you see the Master tonight at dinner, I suggest you show him respect and reverence. You can have a good life here."

40

Special Agent Maggie Carlisle guessed that Eddie's office had once been the mansion's library. Two-story bookshelves encircled the room, with a ladder on rollers providing access to the top volumes. Like the rest of the club, it was something from an old movie. The enormous room held a sitting area with brown leather couches and a desk that looked as if it belonged in the Oval Office. Individual display cases filled with antique weapons from various eras, each with a small plaque, lined a path to the desk. On the way in, Maggie noticed that one contained a tommy gun that supposedly belonged to John Dillinger. She wondered if the collection had been designed to add to "The Great Caruso's" mystique.

Eddie took his position behind the massive desk and directed them to a pair of leather chairs facing him. As Maggie sat, she noticed the chairs were shorter than normal, as if the legs had been altered to ensure that everyone looked up toward the desk.

She glanced over at Marcus. His nostrils were flared and his lip curled as though they had just stepped into a garbage dump. She had lectured him about playing nice on the drive from the airport, but he often seemed incapable of filtering himself.

"So, to what do I owe the pleasure?" Eddie asked.

Maggie said, "We're here to ask for your help, Mr. Caruso.

We work for the DOJ as part of a task force tracking serial murderers."

"Yes, I'm aware. I had my people check into both of you. It seems that your group's activities are veiled in secrecy. To be honest, I was surprised that Marcus was still in law enforcement, after being drummed out of the NYPD."

Marcus said, "My resumé isn't really any of your concern."

"Considering that you're sitting in my office, in my club, I think it is my concern. I don't like to associate with unsavory types, and the word on the street is that you've gunned down more bad guys than you've caught. Sounds like you're nothing but a glorified trigger man."

Leaning forward, Marcus said, "You heard wrong. I don't need a gun. I could come across this desk and rip your lungs out with my bare hands."

"Anytime. Anywhere."

Marcus smiled. "How about right here and right now?"

Knocking three times on the desk to get the attention of the two little boys, Maggie said, "Okay, I think both of you need to relax. You can go in the bathroom and measure later, but first, let's have an adult conversation."

The two men stared at each other for a few seconds, but then Marcus said, "We're not here to dig up old bones. It was all a long time ago."

"You still think you're better than me, don't you?"

"Yes, I do. But it's kind of a moot point. Homeless winos have more class than you do. It makes this whole 'Great Caruso' shtick even funnier." Marcus stood and added, "Come on, Maggie. I knew this was a waste of—"

She snapped, "Sit your ass down. I didn't come all this way to watch you throw a tantrum."

Marcus looked as if he'd been slapped.

Turning to Eddie, she said, "You want to prove you're better than him. Here's your chance. Forget about the past, whatever happened between the two of you, and be the bigger person. We both know Marcus isn't capable of that."

Maggie would have to deal with some backlash later for her comments, but right now, the best way to acquire Eddie's help was appealing to his ego by using his dislike of Marcus to their advantage. She hoped Marcus would see that later, *after* they'd enlisted Eddie's help.

Eddie leaned back and steepled his fingers. "I'm always happy to help officers of the law. When possible."

"We have a mass murderer with a connection to a San Francisco crime boss they call Mr. King."

"I've heard of him. Supposedly very reclusive and ruthless. But I don't know King or anything about his activities."

"That's not what we need from you. We just want to use you as a reference to get close to him. A simple testimonial kind of thing."

"And what are you supposed to have done for me?"

"Contract killing."

Eddie chuckled. "Why on earth would I need a contract killer?"

Taking a deep breath, Maggie said, "Let's not chase our tails here. You run a powerful criminal organization with your hands in everything from drugs to money laundering. Mr. King has similar interests on the opposite coast. We hear he's not a very trusting man, and we don't have the luxury of time. If you were to vouch for our undercover agents, it would help us at least get our feet in the door."

Eddie shook his head. "I have a reputation to uphold. I

don't know your friend, Mr. King, but we could possibly do business with some of the same people. I don't know. Hypothetically, if I was involved in anything like what you mentioned, which I'm not, I couldn't go around helping the feds. It would be bad for business, and from what I've heard about King, he would hold a serious grudge."

"We understand that. The thing is, we're not after King. We're after someone who works for him. We're only trying to get a lead about our killer. King will never know we're not who we say we are or that you vouched for the other side."

"And why would I stick my neck out? Sounds like a lot could go wrong in that scenario. What's in it for me?"

Marcus said, "How about the satisfaction of, for the first time in your life, *not* being a worthless sack of monkey—"

Ignoring him, Maggie interrupted with, "The Shepherd Organization has pull with pretty much every government agency. We would owe you."

"What? I never agreed to—" Marcus started, but again Maggie intercepted his comments.

"Our Director asked me to extend this offer to you. We could be a powerful ally, or we could make sure that you're on the radar of agencies like the FBI and the IRS."

"Is that a threat?"

"No, I'm just trying to explain that it's better to be our friend. Our Director has the Attorney General on speed dial. I think that would be the kind of relationship a man like yourself would find valuable."

She looked over at Marcus. His eyes were on fire, and his jaw was clenched. He had never been happy with the lengths to which the Director would go to stop a killer. Marcus didn't have a problem bending a few rules, but when it came down to it, he had his own code of righteousness that often didn't fit within the SO's shades of gray.

"If I were to provide you with this reference," Eddie said, "that favor would have to be a damn big one."

"I can't offer you a get-out-of-jail-free card, but the Director can move a lot of mountains under the right circumstances."

"Fair enough, but I have another minor stipulation. I'm going to need Marcus to admit that his father, Detective John Williams, was a dirty cop who liked to plant evidence."

Marcus balled his fists. In a whisper, he said, "My father was a man of integrity. Something you'd know nothing about."

Eddie's calm demeanor toppled like a house of cards. He slammed a hand on his desktop and screamed, "I treated you like family, and you betrayed me. You squealed like a good little piggy. Went running right to your daddy. But when he didn't have an actual case, he decided to make one. Except your filthy pig father got caught."

Marcus shot to his feet, knocking over the leather chair, and before Maggie could intervene, he vaulted over the top of Eddie's desk.

Grabbing the crime boss by the lapel of his tuxedo, Marcus lifted Eddie from the chair as if he weighed nothing. Then Marcus drove his former friend back against the large window that occupied the space behind the desk.

Using leverage, Marcus wrenched Eddie's arm up behind his back, soliciting a crack of tendons and a cry of pain.

Marcus whispered, "I know what kind of man you are. The same one you've always been. Weak and afraid. You're all talk and no action. You see that rod iron fence down there. I bet I could throw you through this window hard enough to make you land on that. I want you to imagine being impaled on that fence while I tell you the way things are going to be. Now, you're going to take our deal, and you'll get your all-important favor from on high. I'm going to let you go, and we're going to have a nice ride back to the airport in your limo. But if you call me or my father a pig one more time or even try to act like the tough guy I know you're not, then you're either going to sprout wings or become intimately acquainted with the top of that fence."

41

Junior hadn't been kidding about losing his way in the warren of secret passageways. Marcus had to crawl through some, and sometimes he had to slide down or climb up. He thought he was close behind the other boys, but sound carried strangely in the dark skeleton of the house. Within two minutes, he realized he had taken a wrong turn. But even after trying to correct his error, he quickly lost the sound of Eddie's and Junior's voices completely.

"Great," Marcus said to himself. "I'm going to get trapped in here and have to live on rats and cockroaches. I'll become like the Phantom of the Opera, only inside the walls. The Ghost in the Walls. Sounds like a scary movie."

By the end of his little speech to himself, his voice had begun to tremble with fear.

Darkness terrified him more than anything else. So much so that he carried a flashlight with him everywhere he went. But even under the protection of the miniature Maglite's warm glow, the darkness was always creeping up behind him. The shadows seemed to pulsate with unseen dangers. The darkness seemed to reach for him. Something about the unknown. He couldn't fight what he couldn't see.

He told himself he was being stupid.

Sometimes he would get angry about being scared and

chase the shadows into the basement with his fists in the air, ready for a fight. Of course, he had no idea what really would've happened if he found anything down there in the dark. He suspected it would involve a lot of screaming and a little pee in his pants.

He summoned all his courage to keep moving. He turned around, trying to trace his steps, but that had merely gotten him lost in the other direction.

And then his flashlight flickered and went out.

He slapped the Maglite over and over and was rewarded with a few flickers of illumination. But with every flash, his mind's eye saw something moving toward him through the darkness.

The beam came on just long enough for him to see that there was nothing there. Then the light was gone, and his world became pitch black.

Marcus tried to remain calm as the input from his other senses threatened to overwhelm him. Every small sound seemed amplified. The dark corridors smelled of mold and mouse urine. He could taste the dust in the air. His hands shook. He felt what he hoped were imaginary spiders crawling over his body.

But then he realized that his real fear should have been the rats. The giant subway rats lived just across the water from Jersey. Rats could swim. And New York had some of the biggest damn rats anybody had ever seen.

Spiders couldn't kill and eat him. It wasn't as if there were tarantulas in Jersey.

Stories that other kids had told him popped to the forefront of his mind. Stories of rats eating babies and gnawing off children's legs in the night. He had often *imagined the rats crawling up under his covers and slowly devouring him. He often imagined their whiskers touching his feet. Often so vividly that Marcus would pull back the covers to check.*

Getting to sleep was an incredible chore for him that sometimes took hours.

Then he heard voices ahead and stumbled his way forward. As he grew closer, he realized the sound wasn't voices but whimpering.

Or was it squeaking? His mind projected images of a mountain of rats flowing toward him like a tidal wave.

Forcing himself to move, he crawled forward on his hands and knees, feeling his way through the space between the walls. He stopped every few feet to examine the walls for a way out. Repeating the same procedure for what felt like miles, he worked his way through the house, but the only things he found were peepholes and entrances sealed off well enough to require tools to open them again.

And along the whole journey, tiny pinpricks of sensory input made him feel the spiders crawling over him, the rats gnawing at him.

Marcus yanked his hand back as his fingertips brushed against something sharp and cold covering the floor of the passageway. Something metal. He cautiously probed the surface and discovered the inwardly spiked ribs of a vent. It felt like a giant upside down cheese grater. Testing the metal to make sure it would hold his weight without slicing his hands and knees to shreds, he cautiously inched out over the metal barrier, and then he heard the squeaking sound again.

No, not squeaking.

Now that he was closer to the source, he recognized the sound of a woman sobbing.

42

Baxter Kincaid sat atop his black-and-red 1947 Harley-Davidson Knucklehead parked in front of the almost fluorescent-colored facade of Amoeba Music. He checked the time on his phone. Jenny was either working over or enjoying making him wait. It seemed that, although he was technically her boss at Baxtercorp—the actual name printed on his business cards—she delighted in antagonizing, insulting, and discouraging him. Although, technically, he supposed she wasn't an employee, since he didn't pay her anything.

It was more that they were independent contractors providing a mutual service to one another. Jenny used her accounting degree to keep his books up to date along with a few other office-related tasks that would have never been completed if the job had been left up to him. And, in exchange, he agreed to let her tag along in her down time and learn the art of investigation. Why she wanted to learn had remained a mystery. She never mentioned getting her PI license or showed an interest in working on her own as an investigator. He suspected that boredom played a role, which was likely the same reason Jenny had abandoned a cushy CPA job, dyed her hair black, pierced her body, and tattooed over so much of her flawless skin.

As if summoned by his thoughts, Jenny appeared at the front window, cocked her head to the side, and winked—while flipping him a middle finger that had happy-face tattoos climbing up to a nail adorned with a winking emoji.

In that moment, Baxter could have cared less about the lessons for the night and her reasons for wanting them. All he cared about was the fact that, for the next three to four hours, he had her all to himself. If the rest of the world didn't envy him for that, then they had never met Jennifer Vasillo.

He had little doubt that she understood his attraction to her, but she always seemed to let their relationship teeter on the edge of flirtation and consummation.

A new addition caught his eye as she walked, fresh ink on her wrist surrounded by red tissue. He could only see a small, black shape in that brief glimpse, but he made a mental note to ask her about it later. Her skin was the artificial white of cocaine. Her black hair was short and spiky with pink highlights. Her lips bright as strawberries. She wore jeans and a bright, red-leather jacket, the kind that Michael Jackson wore back in the *Thriller* days, the one with all the zippers. Tattoos climbed her neck, and a round nose ring looped around the bottom of her right nostril.

He wondered, not for the first time, what it would take to love a woman who disguised her true self with so many layers.

He said, "I brought an extra helmet, just in case you decided to live free on the back of the bike."

With a shake of her head and a roll of her eyes, she said, "I prefer to keep my internal organs right where they are, instead of squished up against a guardrail like a bug to a windshield. I'll drive. As usual."

He shrugged. "I'm an infinite optimist."

"You're optimistic that I'll decide it's a good idea to have my insides on the outside?"

"Merely hoping that you'll see the light. That you'll choose to live with the wind in your hair and nothing above you but blue skies."

"The wind wouldn't be in your hair. California has a helmet law."

"I was speaking metaphysically."

"You mean metaphorically."

"Whichever you prefer."

"So what are we investigating tonight?"

Baxter chuckled and shook his head. "I honestly don't recall at this point."

43

Ackerman had wanted to rouse the whole group of task force investigators and hold the briefing that night. He had certainly seen investigators called out of bed when they were tracking him. But Emily Morgan had spouted some nonsense about not being ready and respecting the families of the officers.

Ackerman finally said, "Fine. But you tell that FBI agent's kid—"

Emily snapped, "Agent Fuller doesn't have any children, but you wouldn't know that because you've forgotten who it is we're trying to save."

"Nonsense." The little dog yapped and scratched at his leg. "Don't you start, you grubby little hobo. As I was saying, Dr. Morgan, since we can't bother the task force with this tonight, what avenues of exploration and investigation do you propose for this evening?"

Yawning, she said, "Your brother will be coming back on the first flight. We'll get some sleep and be fresh in the morning."

"But I'm not tired."

"Not everything revolves around you, Frank. You may not require sleep, but I do. You're a big boy, and you can decide on your own when you want to rest. But I'm going to my room to lie down for a few hours."

"This is preposterous. Computer Man? Are you in agreement with this?"

From the screen of Emily's laptop, the tattooed tech genius said, "You don't actually remember my name either, do you, Mr. Ackerman?"

He rolled his eyes. "Of course I remember your name."

"Then what is it?"

"It's ... Stan ... Stan Macallan."

The agoraphobe seemed almost touched that he had remembered. But it was merely out of professional and operational reasons that he knew the man's name. He found it strange how such small gestures of respect could serve to brighten a person's day.

He said, "Stan, you're on my side, right? We must press on. Once more into the breach. And so on and so forth."

"Well, I'm pretty wiped myself ..."

Ackerman focused his laser-beam gaze on the computer screen's camera lens.

Stan said, "But I suppose I could stay up for a few more minutes."

Emily sighed and checked her watch, "We can work on the case here in the conference room for a few more minutes, but I might pass out on you."

Ackerman wondered if this was what it felt like for a normal when his or her parents said they could stay up late. Such sensations were entirely foreign to him. His childhood was less slumber parties and sleeping bags and more acetylene torches and melting flesh.

He said, "Let's discuss Mr. King. He's a total recluse, possibly even agoraphobic. Only a few distant photographs of him on the balcony of his mansion are in existence. How are we going to gain access to him, with Eddie Caruso's help or not?"

"We actually aren't hoping to gain access to the man himself as much as his personal network," Stan said.

"Can't you just hack in from the outside?"

"No, it's very secure. Like NSA level secure. The only way inside is to actually get into the building. If you can get a phone or hidden device within range of a computer with admin access, then I could hijack a Wi-Fi signal and—"

Ackerman said, "I get the idea. But the question remains, how do we arrange a meeting in the office of one of King's high-ranking men?"

Emily stretched her arms and yawned, her movements almost feline. She said, "I think they want Eddie Caruso to help with that, but I'm sure Marcus has alternate plans as well."

"I have some ideas of my own."

Emily rolled her eyes. "There's not enough coffee in the world to keep me awake through one of your ideas right now."

"Sticks and stones, my dear. I was merely going to suggest that we send a *one-way message.*"

Stan said, "That sounds terrifying, especially coming from you, Mr. Ackerman. No offense."

"None taken, obviously, but I'm simply proposing that we find someone who is believed to do a great deal of business with King's organization. Then we make an impression on that individual and use them to send a message to King...a one-way message. King's response would be showing up at a designated place or time or perhaps even as simple as adding us to his schedule at a certain time and we go to him. We show up. Chances are that we don't actually meet with the boss, but if the message is sent correctly, he definitely feels inclined to at least charge a competent lieutenant with handling the matter."

Emily shook her head. "I don't think any of us want you to be the one to craft that message or make an 'impression' on anyone."

"I don't have to physically harm the person. I can establish the proper sense of urgency using only words."

"We can talk about it in the morning when your brother's here."

Ackerman said, "We should deliver the message tonight, while the target is sleeping. I find it best to creep into the bedchambers of a victim. It helps to convey the seriousness of the conversation."

Emily stood up. "Speaking of sleep. Sorry, Dracula, no creeping into any bedchambers tonight."

She headed for the door, and he knew it was futile to argue at this point.

But then he noticed the little dog, curled into a furry ball, sleeping in one of the conference room chairs. He said, "You forgot your foul creature."

Without turning back, she said, "He's not my anything. He's yours." As she pushed into the hallway, letting the door swing shut behind, she added, "He wants to sleep with his new daddy tonight."

He called after her, "I'm no one's daddy. I'm very careful about that for exactly this reason."

The dog had raised its head and rolled its oversized eyeballs toward him with a look that was so "cute" it made Ackerman's teeth hurt. Not because of the figurative sweetness, but due to the literal bad wiring in his brain. Whatever wires were crossed made the sight of adorable things fill him with some strange and undesirable form of pain.

Lips curled back in disgust at both the animal and the woman who had forced it upon him, Ackerman said, "Computer Man, before you go, can you give me the name of a possible target for the plan I had described. Someone who does business with King. Preferably a lot of business. But not someone who would have a great deal of security. I'd like to have the information ready to present to my brother in the morning."

Stan smiled. "I'm way ahead of you." A picture of another man popped up on the screen. "Guy's name is Willoughby."

"Like a small kangaroo?"

"No, that's a wallaby. His name is Willoughby, like 'Willow Bee.' He's been suspected of running guns from King down to the cartels, but the cops have never been able to make anything stick. He runs his own gun shop and firing range. It's about forty minutes to the east of you, between Oakland and the Sibley Volcanic Regional Preserve. He has his business and residence at the same address."

"And what is that address, Computer Man?"

Stan read it off while Ackerman wrote it down on a stray folder and then added, "By the way, you can just call me Stan. Although Computer Man does make me feel a little like a superhero."

Ackerman said, "I haven't been calling you that because I forgot your name. I just don't like it."

"Don't like what?"

"Your name. It doesn't properly roll of the tongue. Stan. May I call you Stanley instead?"

"Well, my name is actually just plain Stan. That's what's on my birth certificate. I've always liked my name. You know, Stan the Man."

Ackerman said, "I still don't like it. So it's settled. I'll just call you Computer Man, which honestly feels much better to me. And you can interpret it as a gesture of respect."

Stan seemed confused. He said, "Uh, okay, I guess. By the way, Mr. Ackerman, your brother wanted me to remind you about the chip in your spine and that your location is constantly being monitored."

"Thank you for relaying the message, Computer Man. Sweet dreams." He closed the laptop without waiting for a response. Staring at the address—which Computer Man had so naively provided—Ackerman committed the street name and digits to memory.

44

Marcus battled against his natural urge to feel exhilarated by having exacted a small measure of revenge against his former friend. In truth, he felt alive and free, but he could never allow himself to feel pleasure at someone else's pain. That was the darkness talking.

Maggie sat across from him in the back of Eddie's limo, throwing daggers with her eyes. For a moment, he thought he could see visible fumes emanating from her body. She hadn't spoken a word since they had left the club.

He said, "I probably could have handled that better."

"Ya think?"

"Take it easy. Everything worked out fine."

"You're telling me to take it easy? That's just beautiful. What the hell was he talking about anyway? Why would he say your dad was a dirty cop?"

"He was just trying to push my buttons."

"Obviously, but that's not the whole story. He mentioned 'Junior's family.' Junior Who?"

Marcus cracked his neck and sighed. He wished the past could just stay in the past, but old skeletons had a way of bobbing to the surface.

He said, "Tommy Juliano, Jr."

Her eyes went wide.

"Yes, that Juliano. I went to a birthday party once with Eddie at Tommy Jewels's house. I got lost and saw something I shouldn't have. Eventually, I broke down and told my dad about it. He told me he'd handle it from there."

"So it's very possible that your dad did plant some evidence."

"Don't you start too."

She said, "I'm not judging. We've all been there. You still talk to your dad's old partner a couple times a month. Give him a call and ask him."

"What the hell is that going to prove?"

"It seems to me like you and Mr. Caruso have some unresolved issues and neither of you knows the full truth. I know you. Those unanswered questions will gnaw at you and interfere with this case. Call your dad's old partner. It's always better to know the truth."

He considered that and was reminded of a Bible verse, John 8:32: "And you will know the truth, and the truth will set you free." But Marcus also knew that the journey to the truth was always a painful one.

45

Baxter admired Jenny's driving skills as she whipped her 1982 "Fox Body" Mustang into a parking spot. The car was too boxy for his tastes and sported a headache-inducing shade of red for a paint job. The interior looked as if Jenny lived in the automobile. Gesturing to the building in front of them, he said, "I give you the location for this evening's riveting investigation."

As they exited the car, Jenny asked, "Does this have to do with that deal for Faraz, the pimp?"

"It does, actually. He wanted to hire me to find the missing sister of one of his ladies. The sister's name is Corin Campbell."

"And Corin lived here?"

"Up until two weeks ago, when she disappeared."

Jenny pursed her lips. "Cool. Missing persons case. Are we thinking the boyfriend?"

"I peg him as clean. Just a gut feeling."

Baxter walked out into the road and looked both directions. It wasn't a heavily trafficked street, but there were still cars traveling by every few seconds. He wasn't concerned about the vehicles. He needed to get a look up and down the road a ways, and the best place to do that was from the center lines.

"What witnesses have you talked to?"

He replied, "Only the boyfriend, Blake, and the sister.

I've been holding off on going any deeper."

"Why?"

"Baxter's Rule #7084: never trust what is squishy and fragile over what you can see with your own eyes."

He could hear the rattling of all her zippers as she hurried along behind him. "I have no idea what that means."

"Never trust someone's memory, or story, over some good camera footage."

She grabbed him by the Hawaiian shirt and manhandled him over to the curb, saying, "Get out of the road, you jackass."

"Your concern is touching."

"I'm not concerned for you. I'm worried about the dent you might make in somebody's hood."

"I believe all cars are equipped with those new-fangled brakes I've been hearing so much about. You may have read about it on the Tweeter."

"Cars have *always* had brakes. And it's Twitter. What were you doing in the middle of the road?"

"Surely the very first car ever built didn't possess brakes. An inventor who built the brakes first probably wouldn't have created such a modern marvel." Baxter pulled a joint from the breast pocket of his white-and-red Hawaiian shirt and added, "And I was deciding which direction someone may have driven off in Corin's car. Earlier I found something that made me wonder if Corin had been taken from here. You actually just parked in her reserved spot. Security footage at the school shows her leaving there. The boyfriend doesn't think she made it home, but I'm not convinced the investigating officers believed him."

"You said he was clean?"

"I said that I believed him. I just think he may be wrong. But that's the difference between me and the cops. They have procedures and due diligence. I just go with my gut. They have to thoroughly check out the boyfriend. But I think he's clean, so I'm moving on."

"Your gut ever wrong?"

"Of course, but sometimes you just need to sit back and let the Universe take the wheel."

"So now your gut has the ability to communicate with 'The Universe?'"

"We all have that kind of connection, Jenny. But most people don't trust that the Universe has their best interests at heart."

She raised her eyebrows. "So you just go with the flow and trust that some higher power has your back, so you'll be good?"

"Well, yeah, in a way. I mean, it's like solar eclipses."

"You lost me."

"The study of our sun is a natural and integral part of learning more about the universe and making new scientific discoveries. In their book 'The Privileged Planet,' astronomer Guillermo Gonzalez and philosopher Jay Richards argue that our place in the cosmos is designed for discovery. Eclipses make it possible to gain knowledge about the sun in ways that aren't normally observable. That's how they validated Einstein's theory of relativity, which predicted that gravity bends light. The same with solar flares and coronal mass ejections. Scientists were only able to observe those phenomena during an eclipse."

"So what? Eclipses are the Super Bowl for scientists. I knew that."

Baxter smiled. "But did you know that, in order for an eclipse to occur, the moon has to be just the right size, orbiting a planet just the right distance from its host star. You see, the sun is four hundred times larger than the moon. In order for the two objects to appear roughly the same size in the sky, the sun has to be four hundred times further away from us. Which, just so happens, to be our approximate distance from the sun. Is that just coincidence or does somebody have our backs? I don't expect that choirs of angels are going to protect me, but I think the concept of goodness is universal. And we should trust that the Universe wants good for us."

"If God does exist, he's indifferent."

"That's a horrible thing to say. Think of it like this. Everyone has some sense of what is fair and good. Every culture in history from remote South American villages to the Romans to modern Americans have a general sense of what is right and wrong. We have a measuring stick by which we judge what is good and what is evil. That inherent facet of humanity has to come from somewhere. I just take what's thrown at me and let the Universe direct my path. Everything's worked out so far."

She shook her head. "What about a tribe of cannibals out in the jungle?"

"What about them?"

"Some of those tribes murder and devour any outsider they come across. They have a pretty radical view of good and evil."

"I know. Whatever happened to their ancestors must have been pretty horrible for them to be so untrusting. But even under those circumstances, they have a measuring stick. It's just one we don't fully understand."

"Fine, Mr. Universe, which direction does your gut signal say we should go?"

"Away from the city. So, toward the closest interstate or major thoroughfare. Cover the greatest ground in the least amount of time. North or south, in regard to their final destination, doesn't really matter. We just need to think about where they would pass by for the first few blocks." Baxter pointed up the street to the north. "My gut says there's better camera potential in that direction."

Jenny said, "Didn't the cops check for that kind of thing?"

"I'm sure they did, but I'm looking for the things they didn't see. For example, they would draw a circle on a map based on time and distance, then try to check everything they could without a court order. We're just trying to walk in her shoes through space and time. If she was here and left, where did she go next? Plus, the cops would have checked during the daytime. We're here at the same time she would have been taken."

"I don't think they have cameras that only come out at night."

"You never know, my dear."

They walked to the end of the block. Jenny was studying the buildings for cameras, but Baxter was only studying her. He said, "Four-way intersection, fair Jennifer. Which way now?"

"Keep going straight."

"Why?"

Jenny said, "Because left and right turn off onto side roads. This one is the fastest way out of here. Putting the most distance between me and the scene of the crime in the fastest time."

"You are strong in the ways of the Force, young Jennifer."

"Shut up. I already knew that. What about that ATM machine?" she asked, pointing out the blue-and-gray box sitting across the street. "Or that gas station on the next block. Or there's also a company called RJ Transportation Services up there that has a little truck depot. Any of those would have good camera angles."

Baxter stopped walking and considered that. Something didn't feel right. He held out his hand and said to Jenny, "Will you pray with me?"

"Excuse me."

"Just take my hand. Humor me."

She made a face but reluctantly placed her hand in his. Baxter said, "Lord, some dangerous cat who has lost his way has done crept in on your child, Corin Campbell. Help us get her back. Like Frampton said, 'Show me the way.' Amen."

Jenny said, "Do you feel better there, Mr. Universe?"

Baxter lit the joint in his mouth, inhaled deeply, and held the smoke. He had never understood Bill Clinton's response about never inhaling. All Clinton was admitting was that he was a poser who wasted his buddy's weed. Sounded like kind of a dick move to Baxter. He held out the joint to Jenny. She took a hit and passed it back.

He said, "They didn't go this way."

"How do you know that?"

"Because the police would have checked those cameras. And since we can assume they didn't see Corin's car on any of that footage, we can also assume she didn't go this way. We need to find the cameras they didn't check."

Turning back toward Corin's condo, Baxter walked to

the first intersection and examined the other two paths. They were both small side streets, barely more than alleyways. Cars and reserved spots lined the western path. The eastern path was bordered by brick walls and held ample parking. The next street in that direction was a one-way road heading south.

He started walking to the east.

Jenny said, "I thought the abductor would want to put as much distance—"

"I'm just following my gut, darling."

They reached the next intersection, and Baxter heard the whoosh of air brakes. A bus stop sat to their left. One of the city's many electric trolleybuses was picking up a line of passengers. Two sets of electrical lines hung suspended above the street. A harness atop the bus connected to the wires and supplied the bus with a steady and environmentally friendly stream of power.

Baxter chuckled and rubbed his hands together like Sylvester the cat staring at Tweety Bird. "I just found the camera the cops didn't check. Also, do you think Tweety Bird has an account on the Tweeter?"

"It's Twitter, you idiot. And try to stay focused. What camera? Do the bus stops have cameras?"

"Yeah, but the police would have checked that one. I'll just have to show you."

"I hate surprises."

"But I feel the need to impress you with my genius."

"I'm not impressed."

"You haven't even experienced the genius part yet."

"I won't be impressed. Just tell me."

"Okay, but you're ruining it … We don't want the camera

at the bus stop. We want the videos from the bus itself."

"I didn't know they had cameras on the buses."

Baxter nodded. "Eight cameras, actually. All wide angle. Two inside the cabin of the bus and six along the exterior sides. The city saved enough in insurance premiums to more than pay for the whole camera system. The digital footage is stored on the actual bus as a failsafe but is also broadcast to a central data repository."

"How is that you say the wrong name for Twitter, but you have the inside scoop on mass transit security?"

Baxter grinned. "Because my neighbor is possibly the next Unabomber."

46

Ackerman could never sleep in a bed. He wasn't sure if it was because of his childhood of nightmares and the subconscious trauma, or if his developing bones had merely become accustomed to a harder sleeping surface. He had also removed all the pictures from the walls of his temporary domicile. Emily and the others had acquiesced to his unusual requests and had allowed him to curl up in the corner of a room with no pictures.

While in Arizona, he had simply curled up somewhere on the floor beside Marcus and Maggie's bed, but that had quickly made him feel like some sort of pet. He had demanded to have his own bed, even if he didn't sleep in it.

His brother would be back in California within a few hours, and they would be heading to meet with the task force handling the abduction and hacking case. But even though this was merely a rest stop, not a full-on surrendering of the day, he couldn't help but feel that man's most precious commodity—time—was slipping away from them.

The squished-faced little vermin lay beside him on the floor. And the dog continued to inch closer as time ticked on. Then it started making high-pitched mewling noises and scratched at his arm.

"Do you not have the proper instincts to realize that I am a danger to you? Danger, you ignorant rat. Danger!"

He tried to just ignore it, but there was something about

that mewling sound that sent chills of anger through his body. He had tried locking the thing in the closet, but then it simply scratched incessantly at the door.

Ackerman finally sat up and said, "You're lucky this hotel room doesn't come with a microwave or refrigerator. What do you want from me?"

The dog's tail wagged and his ears perked at the attention. Ackerman started to get up, and the thing ran toward the exit door. When he sat back down, it simply returned to him, and the whole process started over again.

Ackerman growled in frustration, which only seemed to enliven the canine. "I'm starting to wonder if Emily was sold a defective model. Maybe there's a return policy on you. Come on, do I seriously have to take you out every time you need to evacuate your waste?"

The small dog barked and ran toward the door again.

"Piss in a corner like a good hobo. Live like a rock star. Trash the place. I don't care. But I refuse to pander to your petty demands for attention!"

He stood and took the creature into the bathroom, holding it over the toilet. "Go," he said, but the vermin merely stared at him. After a few seconds, he growled again and deposited the small dog in the bathtub. "There. Easy clean up. Go nuts."

He returned to his spot on the floor, but it only took a moment before he heard a rustling in the bathroom and the sound of paws on fake tile. He didn't open his eyes, but he could feel its presence in front of him, its eyes staring at him expectantly.

Still, he ignored the creature and turned his thoughts to other things.

In his head, he began listing popular methods of torture from the sixteenth century.

Then the vile creature started back in with the whining and scratching. Opening his eyes and releasing a deep breath, he said, "Fine. But if you get carried off by a bald eagle or hit by a car, I'm not helping you. That's where I draw the line. I promised not to kill you, but that doesn't mean I have to save you from all the other things that could kill you."

The dog barked and ran again toward the door. Ackerman didn't bother putting on a jacket or shoes. His jeans and gray long-sleeve T-shirt alone would have to suffice. He wasn't afraid of a little cold, and he welcomed the pain of sharp gravel and broken beer bottles against the soles of his feet. He tried to pretend that was the sole reason for this late-night stroll.

He stood by the door, trying to forget about the dog, but it barked and whined and broke the illusion. He said, "We'll go when I'm damn good and ready." Remaining still, he took a few deep breaths and then said, "Okay, I'm ready now, but by my own will, not yours."

The dog just wagged its tail and panted, bouncing all the while with that happy, expectant energy. The look on its face seemed *smug* to Ackerman, and he contemplated whether such a beast could, in reality, be a skilled manipulator.

47

As he stood in the corner of the Westchester County Airport's private charter terminal, Marcus's world fell apart. His dad's old partner had given it to him straight, and Eddie had been right. His dad had planted the evidence, and he felt as if his father's memory had been forever tainted with that knowledge.

It wasn't that Marcus judged his dad, especially considering that he knew the suspect was guilty of the crime. Still, his father was the one constant beacon of hope and righteousness in his life. Now, that light was gone, and the darkness had crept in.

He dropped into one of the terminal's chairs, hung his head, and began to cry.

The memory of his dad finding him in a similar position—crying alone in his second-story bedroom—was as vivid in his mind as if it had just taken place. He could still feel the breeze from the open window, the wind carrying with it the melody of the city traffic and distant sirens, a sweet chorus of buzzing humanity.

His dad had asked what was wrong, and he had broken down, happy to finally unburden himself of the things he had witnessed. Every time he had closed his eyes, he saw the blood. He tried to fill his nose with Vicks to mask the smells of copper and vacated bowels that had infected the concrete slaughter room he had found down in the dark.

The slightest sensory reminder of his time in the Mad King's castle would send him to the edge of a panic attack or to the verge of losing his lunch.

He had told his dad everything, and John Williams had hugged Marcus close and told him that he was so proud of him. After which, his detective father had his young son look through countless mug shots until he found a picture of the woman he had rescued. His dad had told him that he would handle it from there and that he shouldn't worry about it anymore.

Marcus hadn't heard another word about the case, until one day his dad pulled him aside and informed him that the woman he had saved from the basement had been found dead. Marcus felt responsible. Perhaps he shouldn't have told? Perhaps he should have told sooner? She had been their best chance at finding someone to testify against Tommy Jewels, but then she was gone. His dad had said, "But that doesn't mean I'm giving up. I'm stubborn that way when it comes to justice being done."

Apparently, his father had then decided that seeing justice done was worth breaking the law and falsifying evidence.

"Looks like you received some bad news."

Maggie's voice startled him, and he quickly wiped the tears from his eyes, not wanting her to see him cry. "You were right. Eddie was right. My father planted the evidence, and he almost lost his job over it."

"I'm sorry."

"For what? No such as thing as heroes, right."

She lowered her eyes, unsure how to respond. Finally, she said, "The FBI pilot said he's ready when we are."

"Good. Let's get the hell out of here."

48

As they pulled up to his reserved spot, Baxter realized he hadn't recorded the additional Baxter's Log episode that Kevin had requested. Before Jenny could exit the Mustang, Baxter said, "Hold up, sunshine. I gotta do a thing for the guy."

"Huh?"

Baxter looked deep into Jennifer Vasillo's eyes, cleared his throat, and then pressed the record button on his iPhone.

"Baxter's Log. Stardate … I gotta be honest here, I never could understand the whole stardate thing. Not that I ever really gave it too much thought. Anyway …

Why don't people see that we are, in actuality, an infinitely complex mass of infinitesimally small particles? A scientist would agree with me on that much, I expect. However, I propose that at the most basic level there is a particle that is the originator of all the others. Call it Alpha. Call it Omega. Call it God.

The point is that something beyond our comprehension set this whole train in motion. We have trouble wrapping our small minds around that because our limited thinking is governed by time and space. We simply can't comprehend a being who exists beyond a linear timeline, a being like the one who wrote the laws of physics. What is there beyond time and space? How do we possibly understand the will of a fifth-dimensional entity? These are realities that we may never fully explore before humankind blinks out. But we still owe it to ourselves to search out some of those answers. My assertion is this: If you honestly seek, you will most definitely find. And if you're honest with yourself and follow your heart, the right path will just open up to you, one small step at a time.

I'm Baxter Kincaid, and I approved this message. Baxter out …"

As he ended the recording, he noticed Jenny looking at him as if a tiny Jimi Hendrix had just sprouted from his shoulder and started in on "The Star-Spangled Banner." She said, "You are a total weirdo, you realize that."

Baxter giggled. "You know, we spend about half our lives trying to be just like everybody else. Trying to blend in and survive. But then we realize that all we really want to do is be different. As the late, great Jimi Hendrix said, 'I gotta be stone free to do what I want.'"

"Do you ever go back and listen to those recordings, so that you can actually hear the way you sound?"

Baxter said, "Nah, that's in the past. And you know time is like a river, ever changing as it flows. And we time travelers are like vessels that must follow where it goes."

"Did you just paraphrase a Garth Brooks song?"

With a laugh, he said, "Oh yeah, that is a song. Good thing I didn't say that on the recording."

After ascending the stairs, Baxter knocked on Kevin's door, and they waited as the sound of a platoon of deadbolt locks were undone. With two chain locks still in place, Kevin peeked out at Baxter from beneath his trademark hood. The only difference was that he wasn't wearing his usual sunglasses.

Kevin said, "You scared the crap out of me, man. Do you have a new post for me? They are eating the last one up. I think we should really get another one up quick."

"Yep, I just recorded one for you. Why don't you let me in, and we can transfer it over or whatever you need to do?"

"You can just email it to me or use that file transfer app that I showed you."

"Well, I was wanting you to do another little thing for me. It's related to a case. I know you expressed interest in becoming more involved here at Baxtercorp, and so I thought—"

"Do you have someone with you?" Kevin asked.

"It's just Jenny from Amoeba Music. Remember, I told you that she was kind of job shadowing me. Let us in, Kevster."

"You know how I feel about the uninitiated, Baxter."

"Yeah, I know, brother. But she's straight, man. I'm telling you."

"Are you vouching for her?"

"Yeah, man, that's what I'm saying. I totally vouch for her. If she were a contract, I'd be like signing all over her. Come on, Kevarino. I guarantee she's the hottest chickadee you've ever had in that apartment. And the ones on your computer screen don't count."

"Wait there."

Kevin shut the door, and they stood there for a full minute before Jenny said, "I thought this guy was a friend of yours? And what was that job-shadowing crap?"

"Kevin's a good dude. He's just a little eccentric and a whole lot paranoid."

The door opened, but instead of inviting them in, Kevin

stepped out into the hallway with a scanning wand. It looked like the type used at airports, except that this one appeared to have been modified by Kevin himself. He said, "I'm just going to check you guys for bugs."

"I know she looks a little Seattle grungy, but I don't think that the fair Jenny has any parasites crawling on her."

"I mean like government bugs. Recording devices. Things you may not even know they planted on you." Kevin started scanning them with his homemade wand. After a moment, he said, "Okay, you're clear. But no sudden movements, don't leave my sight, and I'd like both of you to sign nondisclosure agreements."

49

As he watched the vermin pace back and forth, back and forth, Ackerman wondered what instinct told the little dog which spot was best. Was the canine actually choosing a spot or merely working itself up for the deed? He shouted, "You disgust me, creature."

As if in response, the dog stopped and squatted. A woman in high heels and a red jacket passed on the sidewalk beside the motor inn. Ackerman called to her, "You don't know whose dog this is, do you? I think it's in need of a good home."

She merely diverted her gaze and kept walking.

"See that. She didn't like you either."

The dog started prancing around as if it had achieved some great accomplishment in finding the perfect spot to defecate. It barked and pranced in his direction. It looked up at him, tongue hanging and tail wagging.

"I don't have time for this. You know I should be out there securing our meeting with Mr. King, right now, not talking to an inbred mutt who has no idea what I'm saying."

The dog barked.

"Are you trying to say that you do understand? Bark once for 'Yes' and twice if I'm just losing the last of my sanity."

The dog barked twice.

"Are you being facetious?"

The dog barked once. Ackerman merely stared at the creature a moment. Then he said, "The car is just across the street. I could hotwire it, and be on my way. I'm sure with a little finesse I could be back in an hour and a half. Two hours tops."

The dog issued a low growl, whipped its head around, and started barking. The fit lasted about three seconds, until it lost interest and returned to him.

"I know what you're saying. And you're right. They are watching us. Tracking me with some kind of chip embedded in my spine."

The dog whimpered.

"Don't cry for me. I don't mind the chip. It was a necessary evil. The one thing I don't like is that I have yet to figure out a way to beat their system. They say that someone is monitoring my movements. But are they really? Maybe it's time to test the fences. See how far the leash really stretches."

The dog issued some strange and whiny "ro-ro-ro" sound.

"Your concern is touching, but don't worry, my little parasite, your meal ticket isn't going anywhere. They would never actually enforce a kill option. Not unless I had gone completely off the rails. For goodness sakes, these people have studied me for years. They know me. They're going to have to expect a certain level of rebellion and disobedience. Right?"

Ackerman sat on the curb. The dog pranced in front of him and barked twice.

"That's not a very polite thing to say. And totally subjective."

The dog ran and jumped at him, its front paws coming to rest on his chest. Then it licked his face and rubbed against his chest.

Ackerman pushed it away. "No apologies necessary, but I appreciate the gesture of respect. If we're going to be doing this for at least a period of time, then we might as well establish some rules. I'm the alpha. You are not even a beta in this pack. Do you understand? You are an omega. The lowest rung of our pack's social hierarchy. You should fear and respect me. And be happy that I'm allowing your existence."

The creature tried to lick him again. "Okay, wonderful. Thank you."

He stood to escape the dog's reach, and as he did, he spotted their rental car across the road. It was right there for the taking. The address was in his memory. The car was equipped with GPS.

But if they were monitoring him as they claimed, or even if they checked his movements periodically, they would find out that he had been a bad boy. A sudden overwhelming urge to sever their leash seized him. Taking deep breaths, he fought with himself to keep from digging the tracking chip out with his fingers.

He was no one's dog.

In his ear, he heard Father's voice: *You are the night, Francis. Kill them all. Kill them, and the pain will stop.*

The dog looked up at him strangely and voiced a low growl of disapproval.

50

Bang, bang, bang.

Bang, bang, bang, bang.

Faster this time and with more force. Ackerman added an extra bang as a sort of period on the message.

He heard movement inside the hotel room, and the door cracked open. Emily Morgan stood on the other side, holding an arm up to block the light from the motel's sign. She was still in the same clothes, including her shoes, as if she had literally fallen into bed. Her small Glock 19 pistol was in her hand.

The little dog nosed its way inside her room.

She said, "This had better be good, Frank."

"Computer Man gave me the address of someone who would fit into my plan of sending a message to Mr. King. I'm going to pay him a visit. With or without you. I'm no one's pet."

"Trust me. No one thinks of you as our pet."

"I should hope not. Are you going to drive or give me the keys?"

With a sigh, she said, "Let me grab my jacket. What about the dog?"

"It can come with us."

"Sounds like you're warming up to him."

"Not at all. We've merely reached an understanding."

"Glad to hear that, but the dog will be fine alone for a

while. We'll put him in the bathroom."

Ackerman added, "And one more thing. I'm going to need a gun."

"I'm not authorized to give you a gun, Frank. No weapons of any kind. I would give the dog a gun before I gave one to you."

Ackerman looked down at the furry beast and said, "That's ridiculous. It doesn't even have thumbs."

51

The past…

Marcus followed the sound of a woman crying into the depths of the Mad King's castle. The air was growing colder and fresher. He felt the breeze on his cheek. He reached a junction that seemed to descend into the monstrous property's lower levels. He could still hear her crying, but the closer he came the more he realized that it wasn't merely a sad sobbing but a wailing of agony.

In the little over a decade that Marcus had been alive, he had never felt fear like this. He was trapped, unable to find his way back out, and some creature was obviously down here sharpening its claws on a living subject. If he followed the sound, he could be the next victim. The fear made his legs want to run. He stared into the depths of the home. The shaft was perhaps four feet by four feet wide with metal rungs anchored to the wall every couple of feet.

Within the totality of darkness, Marcus couldn't see the bottom of the shaft before him. This could be the entrance to hell.

A memory floated to the surface of his terrified thoughts. Something his father had said. Detective John Williams had leaned over to him at the dinner table, and in relation to a story he had been telling, he said, "Sometimes, you gotta do what's right. Even when it's stupid."

Steeling his heart, he thought about his father's words. Even if this was hell, that was a person in need of help, and he couldn't walk away even if he had the option.

He reached out, grabbed the first rung of the ladder, and descended to the lowest level. Once on the bottom floor, he saw a vague light ahead, and it called to him like a flame to the moth. After a moment of nearly blind stumbling, he found himself inside a concrete panic room. There was a massive steel door that could seal off the entrance to the secret passages. He guessed that this was the real reason for the so-called Mad King deciding to build his home with hidden passages behind the walls: as a secret means of defense and escape.

The room reminded Marcus of a bomb shelter, but bigger. Rows of canned food and provisions lined one wall. The opposite wall was covered with guns, like the back half of a sporting goods store.

Marcus knew about guns. His father had showed him how to use them, and they had always been around the house. But not guns like these. These were weapons of war.

He approached cautiously. He wanted to pick them up, but he didn't. He stood transfixed before them, considering the implications. His father had said that Eddie's dad and the people he worked for were bad men. But how bad did you have to be to need this many guns and a fortress to keep them in?

A massive steel door, like that of a bank vault, stood in front of him. Beyond it, he heard the screaming.

Looking back to the wall of guns, his fear of what monster waited in the darkness convinced him to choose a weapon. He tested a few of the big black guns and finally found one that was small enough for him to handle. He didn't bother to load it. He had no intention of shooting anyone. He didn't even like to kill insects. But he was also relatively certain that he could bluff his way past any man. A crazy child with a machine gun could be pretty frightening, or so he imagined. Still, he wondered: What if the thing beyond the door was no man, but some sort of demon? If that were the case, there would be no reasoning with it, no bluffing his way past. He would be dead.

This time, he heard Eddie's voice saying, Don't be stupid, freak.

With the gun in his right hand, he reached out with his left to spin the door's release. On the other side, he found a series of concrete tunnels. The corridors were lit by bare bulbs hanging from unfinished ceilings. He came first to some storage spaces filled with boxes and old filing cabinets.

But it didn't take him long to find the source of the screaming. He peered around the corner and saw a large man with no neck and gray hair wearing a simple black suit. The big man stood beside another steel door and was mumbling to himself about the B-word driving him crazy.

Marcus listened for a moment and waited. He jumped as the big man slapped the door twice and yelled, "Shut up. Or I'll give you something to cry about!"

There was no doubt in Marcus's young mind that whoever was in pain beyond that metal door would not live to see another day unless he did something about it. It might've been stupid to think that he could take on a behemoth of an adult like the man in the black suit, but he also knew that, even though it was stupid, it was the right thing to do.

52

Francis Ackerman Jr. stepped from the vehicle and sucked in the cool night air. The infamous serial murderer had once doubted he would ever taste free air again, and he had especially never expected to be working for the federal government the next time he did.

The wind picked up dry gravel and swirled it around them. The air carried a strange, sweet scent. To Ackerman, it smelled like a crematorium. He knew the smell well. He had burned many people alive during the dark days of another life.

But now, he had found purpose. A use for his unique talents. Not to mention that he felt propelled by divine purpose to show the demons of society that redemption was within reach. If not in body, certainly in spirit.

Emily Morgan, his counselor and babysitter, said, "Remember, you're not allowed to touch him."

"That doesn't sound like much fun. No touching. It's like an Amish courtship."

"I'm serious. You cross the line, and you'll be back in a cell by the end of the day. Or they may just decide to explode that chip in your neck."

Ackerman rubbed the base of his skull at the thought.

He was relatively certain that he could find a way around the machinations of the Department of Justice and the CIA, who had supplied the technology. There wasn't a security system in the world that couldn't be bypassed by a determined mind. And his mind had always served him well. Still, he was in custody because he chose to be, because this was where he belonged. For now, at least.

"Fine," he said, "I'll play nice. But what if he tries to get frisky? I would be honor bound to protect you."

"I can protect myself. Stick close to me. And since when do you have any honor? What is it you always say? 'Losing is just an excuse for not cheating hard enough?'"

Ackerman laughed. "Yes, but my father also told me to always keep my word. I promised to protect you, no matter what, and I promised my brother not to kill anyone without permission."

"Who made you promise to protect me?"

"No one made me. It was just a promise I required of myself. And I've always felt that promises you make with yourself are the worst kind to break."

Once upon a time, Ackerman had tortured and killed Emily's husband and endangered the lives of herself and her child. Emily even carried a scar across her forehead from the encounter, which she covered with her hair as best she could. That seemed like a lifetime ago now. Another life in another world. At the time, he had been wandering with no purpose through a darkness without borders. But the light had found him, and the journey had changed him.

It had changed Emily as well. She wasn't the same woman he had held captive and forced to play one of his games. Although, he wasn't sure if her changes had been for the better. It seemed that she had grown harder over time. He had once thought her to be fragile, something he would never accuse her of now.

Emily added, "Sometimes I can't decide if you're actually starting to think like a person or if you're only trying to manipulate me. Make no mistake, Frank, I'll kill you before they can ever activate that implant if you step out of line. I don't want to, but if I have to choose between your life and the life of some innocent person, I'm going to save the someone else every time."

"Fair enough. But you should know that if it comes down to my life over yours, I will choose your life, every time."

She was quiet a moment, and he wondered if he had done something wrong. Finally, with tears forming in her eyes, she said, "Well, let's just try to make it so we never have to face either circumstance."

Willoughby's Exotic Gunsmithing and Firing Range sat at the end of a long, dead-end lane with mountains in the background, nothing but dry dirt surrounding it, no wind breaks. The main building was made of corrugated metal, weather beaten and worn. The paint had long since faded and chipped, and the proprietor hadn't bothered with repairs. Ackerman imagined that, like many small businesses these days, the majority of the man's sales were done online, which didn't facilitate the need for a beautiful storefront.

Emily said, "So what's your plan?"

"I was thinking a simple knock and kick."

"What's that?"

"It's where you knock, and when they answer the door, you kick it in on them."

"This guy is the owner of a gun shop and firing range, and you want to just kick his door down?"

"Shortest distance between two points is *always* a straight line."

"Let's at least try the diplomatic approach. And I told you not to touch anyone. Kicking a door into someone's face would classify as physical contact."

"Fine. You can kick the door in."

"That's not what I'm saying. Listen, I'll get us inside and then you do your thing with him to send a message. Just make sure that whatever you do at that point is all bark and no bite."

53

Emily repeatedly rang the bell at the delivery entrance. Hearing movement inside, Ackerman stepped to the side of the door and turned his head away. She gave him a look of confusion, and he said, "I'll bet you a dog that he comes to the door with a shotgun."

"He has a camera. You're probably making him think that we're bandits from the way you're acting."

"*Bandits*? I kind of like the sound of that. I'm Bonnie, and you're Clyde."

"I think you mean that I would be Bonnie and you would be Clyde," Emily said.

"If you prefer. I was just trying to mix things up a bit."

The door flew open, and someone yelled, "Don't move!" A man Ackerman presumed to be the business's proprietor stood a few feet inside the doorway with a sawed-off, double-barrel shotgun in one hand, and a small remote control in the other. He was a short man with stubby arms and a face that reminded Ackerman of a species of small monkey known as the common marmoset. Like the small primate, Willoughby was flat nosed and wide faced, with tufts of unkempt hair sticking out each side of his head.

The man said, "There's a shaped charge of C4 beneath your feet, and this shotgun is loaded with the latest in home security shells. If one doesn't get you, the other will. Now, you better have a damn good reason for waking me up."

Emily looked down at the shotgun and hesitated. "Uh … We're …"

Ackerman said, "We're part of Mr. King's crew. He said you were the man to see about getting some clean and effective long-ranged weaponry."

The marmoset narrowed his eyes and said, "I have no idea what you're talking about. Are you two cops? I've told you guys before—"

"Do I look like a cop?" Ackerman said, giving him a predator's stare. "I assume you're Mr. Willoughby?"

"That's right. You make any sudden movements and your tombstone will read, 'Shot to Death by Mr. Willoughby.'"

Ackerman replied, "We were told that you run guns from King to the cartels. And that you have recently received a shipment of products that would be perfectly suited for a particular task we need to accomplish."

"What shipment are you talking about? What are you looking for?"

"Let's step into your office and discuss the details like gentlemen."

"And you say you heard this from Mr. King?"

"No, I said we work for King. Oban told us about you. Nobody sees Mr. King."

Eyes narrowed, Willoughby said, "Come inside, but keep your hands up and no funny stuff. No sudden movements."

As he stepped inside, Ackerman saw that the owner had left only a token amount of ammo on the shelves. The gun wall behind the register and display case, however, was fully stocked with all manner of rifles and pistols, ranging from the mediocrity of the Glock to the exotic enticement of the 8-mm Nambu.

"So what are you after?" the stubby man said. "You said it's part of a shipment of guns I'm supposedly smuggling from King to the cartels?"

"Can we cut the bravado? Do you sell guns or not?"

"Oh, I sell guns. But I don't sell guns for King."

"Whatever, friend," Emily said, hands raised and voice trembling. "If you're not our guy, we'll head on down the road."

"No, you see, you misunderstand me. I do run a smuggling operation for Mr. King. But just because I run a gun shop doesn't mean that I smuggle guns. I know nobody would have sent you here for a gun. I have a strict policy of keeping my legitimate business, this shop, which my father founded in 1971, separate from my other dealings. That tells me that this doesn't have a squirt of piss to do with Mr. King. So why are you really here?"

"I'm looking for a hunting knife," Ackerman said. Emily shot him a scathing glance, but he ignored her.

Willoughby said, "Get down on your knees."

Ackerman saw a display of cheap pocket knives on a shelf within arm's reach. He said, "I'm getting very tired of people telling me what to do. May I share a secret with you, Mr. Willoughby?"

"Talk."

"I don't wish to purchase your wares. I'm here for two reasons, actually. One, I need information. And two, I need to send a message."

"The only thing you need to do, pal, is shut your hole. I'm calling King's real guys. They'll deal with the two of you."

Ackerman said, "Look into my eyes. Do you honestly think I would allow you to reach a phone?"

"I'm the one with the shotgun."

"I don't see your point. May I show you something. I think you'll find it very interesting. I'm just going to pick up one of these little pocket knives."

"You aren't picking up a damn thing. I told you—"

With a flash of calculated and non-threatening movements, Ackerman snatched up one of the blades, flipped it open, and sliced through his shirt and across his massively scarred forearm. The blood burst forth and trickled down onto the concrete floor.

Willoughby raised the shotgun and said, "What the hell!"

The shop owner was a good ten feet away, but Ackerman had no doubt he could kill the man with the small pocket knife at this distance, shotgun or not.

"Just look into my eyes," Ackerman said as he ran another bloody slice across his forearm. He pulled up his left sleeve to expose the wounds and show the shop owner his scars, his small smile never wavering. In fact, the pain was a welcome distraction. He sliced another gash across his forearm, just for the fun of it.

Willoughby's sunken eyes were wide with shock.

Ackerman slashed another line of blood. "I enjoy pain, Mr. Willoughby. I only feel truly alive when I'm inflicting or experiencing it. But, I have to admit, I prefer the administration of suffering. The fear and agony in the recipient's eyes is indescribably glorious."

"Is that supposed to scare me? You have a little pocket knife, and I have a shotgun."

Ackerman's smile widened, and he gave Willoughby a wink. "Once upon a time—in my opinion, how every good story should begin—I extracted information from this ghastly pedophile by placing him naked atop a wooden structure that came to a sharp point. I then added weights to his feet, and the pressure slowly eviscerated him, starting at the groin."

Willoughby didn't respond. He was statue still. Ackerman hadn't even noticed the man breathe.

He said, "I love that story. But I also feel that if you want the story to be a good one, you need to tell it yourself, in the moment. So, with that in mind, I'd love to try something with you, Wallaby, that I've been dreaming about."

He very slowly ran another slice across his forearm and licked the blood from the knife. Willoughby scowled defiantly, but even the little man's facial movements had become increasingly erratic.

Ackerman continued, "In another life, I think that I was likely a member of a barbarian horde. Perhaps riding alongside Genghis Khan or someone like Cyrus the Great, the first emperor of Persia. You see, it is the Persians who devised the method of torture I would like to inflict upon you this evening, Mr. Marmoset."

Willoughby cocked his head to the side and whispered, "You're batshit crazy, mister. I tell you what … If you leave now, I won't call anyone. I'll forget this ever happened."

Ackerman chuckled as he stuck the knife into his arm again. "Are you familiar with the concept of 'scaphism,' my dear Mr. Marmoset?"

The stubby man said nothing, but took a cautious step backward.

Ackerman said, "The ancient Persians developed a most insidious method of torture, which they deemed 'scaphism.' The way it commonly worked was to have the victim tied down in a small boat and force-fed milk and honey, with a portion of the honey spread across the victim's naked body. The excessive ingestion of milk and honey caused the poor soul to defecate furiously into the boat. All the while, insects of many varieties, drawn by both the sweet and putrid, feasted upon the victim's honey-and-feces-covered flesh. There's a small lake just up the road. I saw some john boats tied up by the water as we drove past."

Fear and sweat covered the stubby man's features like a burial shroud, but he remained defiant. He said, "This is your last chance—"

"It wouldn't take long before you were assaulted by several different species. Arachnids, bees and hornets, carrion beetles, flies of every kind. They would burrow inside you and lay their eggs in your flesh. And every day, I would return to shove more milk and honey down your gullet."

Ackerman could see the doubt slowly creeping over Willoughby's face as the man with the shotgun tried to understand why the man with the pocket knife was unafraid.

"Some historical records indicate that certain individuals of a strong constitution would survive up to three weeks. Although, I wouldn't let that number trouble you. I'm sure the onset of delirium mercifully came within a week. The smell of your own rotting feces and gangrenous limbs would be quite overwhelming. But, to me, smells aren't good or bad, they are just … intriguing. And some of the most fascinating smells overwhelm the senses in a way that I can only describe as pleasure. I would kill a thousand of you just to experience that smell once."

"If you move another muscle, I will—"

"You will what? You honestly haven't figured this out yet, have you?"

"Figured out what?"

"Ask yourself this question … If we were professionals, perhaps sent here by a competitor looking for information on Mr. King, would we knock on your door in the middle of the night?"

Willoughby's grip tightened around the wood of the double-barreled shotgun, but he said nothing.

"Think about it. If we were going to use some kind of ruse, would we come in the middle of the night—putting you on guard and coming to the door with a shotgun—or would we come during business hours, where we could walk right up to the counter and have you at a disadvantage? Obviously, we would come during the day."

"That's enough. I'm going to use the phone. Don't you move."

"Or you'll what, Mr. Marmoset? You're still not getting the picture. When someone comes in the night like this, they don't ring the bell. They slip in like a shadow and attack you while you're most vulnerable."

"But you didn't do that."

"No, we came to your door in the middle of the night, rousing you with your shotgun. But you see, we paid your errand boy, Tyson, to remove the firing pins from the loaded shotgun you keep at your bedside."

Willoughby's eyes went so wide that Ackerman thought they may slip from his skull.

Ackerman had noticed the employee's name beside the door when they came in, on a cheap plaque proclaiming "Employee of the Month." He had known at the time that

Tyson would serve as a perfect distraction. The betrayal and the seemingly inside information would combine to put Willoughby over the top.

"Tyson would never do that."

"You know the two of you look a bit alike. Don't be too hard on the little hobbit. He's not disloyal. He's just gullible and ignorant. Much like his mentor. We came to him with a wonderful story about a television show called *Scaredy Cat* where we scare people and then film it. We told him that we needed his help with safety concerns, like your loaded weapons and security systems. He's probably waiting on his front porch as we speak. I told him we would pick him up and let him join in the fun. Maybe we'll pick him up later. Maybe have some fun with him too."

The shop owner looked to Emily Morgan for rescue, but to her credit, she maintained an unsympathetic and impenetrable mask. Tears formed in the man's eyes. "Please. Leave him out of this. He doesn't know."

"He doesn't know what? That you're a criminal?"

"No, he knows about that, but he doesn't know that I'm his biological father. It was a college thing that started at a party, and I think she put me down on the birth certificate. Not sure, but I know the info is out there somewhere, since Oban threatened me the same way. That's why I gave Tyson this job and …"

Ackerman glanced at Emily, confusion causing him to break character. "And he doesn't know you're his father?"

Willoughby, his grip on the shotgun loosening, said, "Please. I can't tell you anything. Mr. King would kill me and my son. That's the way he works. Vengeance is swift and absolute."

"Look into my eyes. Do you think that whatever they did to you could approach the horrors which my imagination could devise?"

"You're insane."

"Probably. Many have said so. But it's a very vague term based purely on your perspective of what is sane and normal. And where's the fun in being just like everyone else?"

Willoughby licked his lips, his breathing labored and short, his eyes darting back and forth between Ackerman and Emily.

"We're not here to hurt you. Put the gun down, and we'll talk. King doesn't have to know that you spoke a single word about him."

The barrel of the shotgun moved slowly up and away. Willoughby looked down at the gun as if it had chosen to betray him. But then his expression changed, and he said, "Wait. Tyson's been out sick all week."

With a quick flick of his wrist, Ackerman hurled the pocket knife at the shop owner. The blade embedded itself into the center of Willoughby's right hand, traveling through the soft flesh and into the wooden stock of the shotgun.

Emily pulled her Glock 19 pistol but seemed unsure where to aim it.

54

The single bedroom of Kevin's apartment had been converted into what he called his "Command Center." Electronic components, soldering guns, swivel-mounted magnifying glasses, wires, tools, and multiple working computer systems. The rest of the apartment seemed to simultaneously be very normal and yet very wrong. It took Baxter a moment to realize why, but when he made the connection, it made perfect sense. The kitchen and living room contained all the normal items: refrigerator, table, couch, television, coffee table. What the rooms lacked was a single decoration or photograph. The walls were beige and bare. All in all, Kevin's domicile reminded Baxter of a well-kept crackhouse.

Unlike the rest of the apartment, movie posters adorned the walls of Kevin's Command Center. Beneath the posters, a metal cage lined the interior walls of the former bedroom. Kevin explained that it was a Faraday cage and went on to describe the importance of the countermeasure. At which time, Baxter zoned out for a moment.

After completing his spiel, Kevin led them to the living room, pulled the blanket and pillow off his gray suede couch and said, "Please, sit. Would you like a refreshment?" Kevin spoke in a clipped, unnatural tone, like a waiter on his first day, as if he were reading from a script.

Baxter dropped onto the couch and put his feet up on the

coffee table. He said, "I'd love a Fresca or something like that, if you have it."

Kevin was silent a moment, his face hidden behind the shroud of his hood. Finally, he said, "All I have is coffee, Jolt Cola, and bottled water."

"Don't worry about it, little buddy. Have a seat. Let's communicado."

Kevin reluctantly sat on the edge of the coffee table, his hooded face only a couple of feet from the couch. Baxter said, "Are you sure you don't want to just sit between us?"

Kevin seemed to consider this.

Baxter shook his head and continued, "Never mind that. Remember a couple weeks back when you were telling me about how you had hacked into all of the bus cameras, and that you are basically big brother, and how you were sure that the government was using those cameras against us."

"Right. They claim that all the extra cameras are because they're beta testing some type of automation software, but I don't buy that for a second. These asshats basically have mobile surveillance vans traveling all over the city."

"I read in the paper it had something to do with insurance liabilities."

Kevin said, "What's 'The Paper?' I'm not familiar with that group."

"The newspaper."

"I didn't know they still made those."

With a roll of his eyes, Baxter said, "Kids these days. Anyway, doesn't really matter. Important thing is that I want to exploit those mobile surveillance vans for my own gain."

Kevin didn't seem to be following.

"I want you to help me use their system to save a young woman's life. So I just got one question for you, Kevmeister, are you ready to be a hero today?"

Kevin shrugged. "I guess. What do you wanna see?"

Fifteen minutes later, Kevin had accessed the transit authority video systems and recalled the archived footage from the night Corin Campbell went missing. Unfortunately, the video from the bus nearest Corin's house showed nothing of interest.

Staring at one of Kevin's massive flat screen monitors, Baxter said, "Can you pull up a street map with the Muni lines over the top?"

Kevin, sitting in his command chair in front of the four twenty-seven inch screens, said, "No problem." A few seconds later the map appeared on the screen.

Leaning close, Baxter studied the different colored lines. "Can you print this out for me?"

"I don't have a printer. What's the point anymore? If you have a coupon or something, you can just show it to the cashier on your phone."

"Kids. No worries. I'll make do." After a moment of staring at the map, he said, "We know that Corin's car wasn't there. So whoever took her must have also taken the car. If we trace back the cameras, and we map that out, and we kind of think fourth dimensionally, then I ascertain that we could track his path with the car and then maybe find a bus that intersected with them. We could get lucky. But what bus do we need to check next?"

Kevin said, "While you were yammering on, I pulled up the exact hexadecimal color of Corin Campbell's car. Now I'm going to run a search through all the archive footage from that time period searching for that specific color. We'll get a lot of false positives, but if I narrow those results by geographic area, that will give us the best chance of finding her car on the footage."

With a nod, Baxter replied, "I have no idea what you're talking about, but it sounds beautiful."

"The search is running now."

A few moments later, after having sorted through a couple of false positives, Kevin said, "And there is Corin Campbell's car." He pulled the video up on the screens and added, "This is all the footage they caught."

The video played on, showing Corin's car as it passed one of the city's electric trolleybuses. Baxter studied the video, searching for any reflections or views into the car, but unfortunately, all the angles were wrong. They didn't have a clear shot of who was driving.

"Can you replay that again? This time in slow motion."

The video played at a slower speed. Baxter watched again and said, "Stop it there."

Pointing to a spot on the monitor, he said, "Can you zoom in here and enhance?"

Kevin complied, and when he was finished, they had a clear picture of a man's hand reaching across the car to close the glovebox.

But, more importantly, the hand was inked with a very distinctive tattoo.

Baxter, slapping his hands together excitedly, said, "There it is, *dos compadres*. Bingo, bango, bongo. Now, all we have to do is take this down to a Kinkos or Staples or something, get a printout, and head over to see my old partner."

Kevin said, "Absolutely not. No cops. I have a strict no police policy. It was in the waivers that you two signed."

Having mostly just hung back, taking it all in, Jenny asked, "Why do we need the cops anyway?"

Baxter said, "It's time we get the proper authorities involved. We've proven that there's more to this case than just a missing person, and we've given the cops a great lead. I've earned my pay and done my duty. And now it's time for the cops to step in and do their thing. Plus, I need Detective Ferrera to run that crazy tattoo through the database. With a little luck, we may have a suspect in custody this time tomorrow."

"How about I run the image of the tattoo against all social media photos in the San Francisco area?" Kevin asked. "Then we'll have the guy's name and know everything about him."

Jenny said, "You can do that? How? Do you pull all the images and run some kind of pixel recognition for the tattoo?"

"Something like that. Who's asking? Are you affiliated officially or unofficially to any kind of law enforcement agency?"

Jenny raised an eyebrow and looked at Baxter. He said, "Take it easy there, Kevieronymus Bosch. Go ahead and run your search."

"It'll take a few minutes," the young computer expert said, still eyeing Jenny cautiously from beneath his hood.

"We'll wait," Baxter said as he walked over to the one item in Kevin's living room that wasn't a cookie-cutter bare necessity. It was an old record player hooked up to a new sound system. A stack of worn records sat beneath the record player's stand. Baxter mused, "I'm gonna take a minute to explore your record collection, Kevin."

"Those are sorted and alphabetized by genre and band name."

"You just go do your thing. I'll put them back exactly as I found them."

Sorting through the stack of timeworn records, Baxter was careful to keep them in the same order. It wasn't long before he found a nice Hendrix album and placed it on the turntable. Moving the needle into place, he closed his eyes and listened to Jimi sing about castles made of sand.

Jenny came up beside him and said, "Funny that we may catch that woman's killer based on some tattoo."

"We don't know she's dead. There's always hope. But I certainly wouldn't envy the torment she's endured if she's still alive after all this time."

"That's one heck of a creepy tattoo. It was like the bottom half of some mangled skull."

"Yeah, it seems somehow familiar to me, but I can't quite place it. Speaking of tattoos, what's with your new ink?"

"Noticed that, huh?"

"I'm a detective."

She rolled up her sleeve and displayed her wrist. The new tattoo was small, barely larger than a half dollar in size, but intricate. The artist clearly had tremendous talent. The swirls and flourishes of ink, which were now outlined in irritated skin, depicted a Yin Yang symbol. Only the emblem was composed of the images of a white and black dog.

Admiring the artistry, Baxter said, "It's gorgeous. What was the thinking behind it? What's its significance?"

Jenny stared out the window as she bobbed her head along

with Jimi. "My grandmother used to tell me that we all have two dogs inside us. A white dog and a black dog, good and evil, love and fear, that kind of thing. She would say that the one who survives will be the one we choose to feed."

"I like that. Think I'm going to steal it. Next time you hear it, just go along with me and pretend like I made it up."

She punched him in the arm and shook her head. "Do you really like the tattoo?"

"I think it may be my new favorite," he said with a big smile, showing off his dimples.

Kevin stepped back into the room and said, "I know this sounds crazy, but I don't think this guy has a social media account. And he apparently doesn't have any friends who take pictures either."

Baxter shrugged. "Why is that so strange? I don't have a Facebook or Tweeter account."

Jenny curled her lip and looked him up and down. "Yes, you do. You're always posting on there about your blog stuff."

"Damnit, Kevarino, I told you not to do that."

"It's a requirement for the blog. It's not like I'm using it to pick up chicks."

"I don't like having my name and face on stuff that isn't me. I don't even know the username and password for my own accounts."

"I programmed them to all be accessible through your cell phone."

Baxter shook his head. "I barely know how to answer that thing."

"But you texted me directions earlier. How did you do that if you can't work your phone?" Jenny asked.

"I saw your message come in, and I saw that my phone sent you the directions you wanted."

"Your phone doesn't just do that."

Kevin cleared his throat. "I thought you knew all this, Bax. I've been handling that kind of thing for you for a while now. I manage your calendar, help with tech stuff, read your messages. I—"

Holding up a hand to stop his pale young friend, Baxter said, "So you responded to Jenny's message for me, and you've been monitoring all my phone conversations."

"Just doing my part to help out."

"Stop helping me, Kevin. We're going to have a long talk about this later, but for now, it looks like I have no choice but to go see a cop about a tattoo."

55

Marcus considered merely running up and trying to scare the big man with the useless weapon he had taken from the panic room. But his father had also taught him a thing or two about fighting. One of the most important lessons was to use your weaknesses as strengths. If you're small, you have a lower center of gravity, and you needed to use that to your advantage. If you're big, you have a longer reach.

In Marcus's case, he was a scared little kid, and he intended to use that weakness to kick the man in black's ass.

He pinched his arm until he drew blood, and then repeated the procedure until his eyes were full of tears. Then he ran screaming down the concrete corridor, straight toward the big man in the black suit. The guard started to reach into his coat, but Marcus ran right up and buried his tear-soaked face in the big man's stomach. He said, "Please, help me! I'm so scared."

The big man asked, "What the hell, kid? How did you get down here?"

Under his breath, Marcus mumbled, "Have you ever been punched in the nuts?"

"What?"

Then Marcus reached into his New York Yankees jacket, grabbed the handle of the gun, and using it like a club, he *attacked the big man's crotch. The blow connected with a crunch and rattle.*

Marcus stepped back as the behemoth of a man leaned over as if he was going to retch. He looked at Marcus with confusion in his eyes.

Marcus smiled and said, "Hurts, doesn't it?"

And then he hammered the side of the gun into the big man's temple. The guard toppled forward, slamming his head against the concrete wall.

Marcus backed up several steps, keeping the gun trained on his opponent, but the man didn't move. He was out cold.

Wasting no time, Marcus ran to the steel door and pulled it open. There was no handle on the other side. The room beyond was lit with two red bulbs, the kind Marcus had seen on emergency signs, giving everything a hellishly red tint. The space was nothing more than a giant concrete box with a drain in the center. There were two people strapped to gurneys in the middle of the room. The young couple—a man and woman, much older than him but still what his dad would call "kids"—were naked and bleeding, their blood flowing toward the drain like watercolors. The man's head had nearly been cut off.

Marcus was too terrified to be disgusted, too frightened to feel anything else.

The woman was alive, despite wounds that covered her whole body. She still screamed and moaned.

When he spoke, it didn't seem to be his voice, but someone older. "I'm here to help."

The sound must have broken death's hold on the woman because she stopped screaming and bent her head up in his direction. Her face had been severely beaten, causing her words to sound as if she had a mouth full of gum. She said, "Thank God. Dude, you gotta help me."

"No shit," Marcus said.

He ran forward and clawed at her restraints.

The only time he had ever seen a woman without her clothes on was in some of Eddie's *Playboy* magazines. The woman on the gurney was like one of them—young, beautiful. At least, he guessed she would have looked like that if it wasn't for pieces of her flesh being cut away. She had a dark tuft of hair between her legs and large breasts. Or, at least, they seemed large to him.

Her chest had drawn his focus not merely because he was a boy in the presence of a naked woman, but also because he would have to reach over her to unclasp one of the restraints.

Seeming to read his thoughts, she said, "It's okay, kid. Just get me out of here."

"Who are you? Why are they doing this to you?"

As he spoke, he undid the last of her restraints. She didn't answer him. Instead, she dropped her trembling legs to the floor and staggered toward the nearly decapitated man. Giving no thought to the blood, she laid her head on his chest and wept.

He heard her mumbling a name under her breath, but he couldn't quite catch what it was. He repeated his previous questions, and this time she responded, "None of that matters now, kid. We tried to steal from Tommy Jewels, down at one of the casinos in Atlantic City. The less you know, the better. How do I get outta here?"

He said, "How the hell should I know?"

"You had to get in here somehow."

He shook his head. "You don't want to go that way. But if you go out the door and take a right, I thought I heard the sounds of engines coming from that way. Maybe it's a garage or something?"

She stumbled through the steel door and over to the guard. She felt inside his jacket until her hand came out with a long black pistol with a sound suppressor threaded onto the end of the barrel. Marcus recognized it as the kind of gun that James Bond villains used when they wanted to kill someone and not have anyone hear.

She didn't bother to cover her naked body. She said, "Who are you, kid?"

"I'm just a guest here at the party. But my dad's a cop. He can help you."

"Nobody can help me. All I can do is run. Your dad is probably on Tommy Jewels's payroll. And even if he's not, his boss probably is. That's the way this world works, kid. You fight the system, you end up dead. And Tommy Jewels runs the system, or at least his boss does."

She glanced down the hall, checking both ways for more guards, and then she continued, "Here's what we're going to do, kiddo. You're going back to your party, and you're going to forget that you ever saw me."

"No, you need help. I can't just—"

She grabbed his head and twisted his neck toward the hellish room that held the bloodied body of her companion. She said, "I talked him into this. His blood is on my hands. And I'll be damned if I have your blood on my hands to. I'm the adult, and I have a gun now. Just go back to the party and keep your mouth shut. That's the best way you can help me."

Marcus said, "But what about the guard? I knocked him out. I think he's going to remember me when he wakes up."

Without the slightest hesitation, she raised the gun and squeezed the trigger. There was a small flash and a thump and a ping, and then blood splattered out from the man's head onto the concrete floor of the corridor.

She said, "Problem solved." Then she rolled the guard over, removed his jacket, and slipped it over her bare shoulders. He was a big man, and she was a small woman, and so the jacket functioned more like a dress. She ejected the magazine from the gun and checked the number of rounds. She did it in the same way his dad had showed him. Slamming it back in hard, she said, "I'm not a damsel in distress, and no offense, but you aren't a knight in shining armor. Now get your ass back to that party and keep your mouth shut."

"But I could at least call my dad. I could—"

"You listen good, kid. The only way that we survive is that you don't tell a soul that you ever saw me."

56

Ackerman leaped toward the stubby marmoset man, not worrying about breaking the rules to disarm the man with the shotgun. Besides, he had always found that it was better to ask for forgiveness than permission.

Instead of wrenching the weapon from Willoughby's grasp, he grabbed both ends of the shotgun and placed his entire weight into pulling it to down to the floor. To his great satisfaction, the knife remained affixed in both the gun and Willoughby's hand.

Face to face, his prey totally at his mercy, Ackerman whispered, "I will accept nothing less than total surrender. You live and the pain stops if you give me that. But nothing short of it. That means that if I let you up and even think that you are holding anything back, I will feel that you have violated the terms of your capitulation."

He slid the gun across the concrete floor, pulling the blade slowly through the soft tissues of Willoughby's hand. The stubby man yelped and said, "Please."

"Total surrender. Everything you know, I want to know."

"Okay. Okay. Total surrender."

Ackerman smiled. "You know, if we were in ancient Sumeria—"

Emily said, "That's enough, professor. Let him up."

He sighed as he ripped the knife out of Willoughby's flesh and punched him in the chest in one arcing motion.

Willoughby landed on his rear and scuttled back a few steps like a crab. Ackerman held up the bloody knife and said, "Total surrender. Sealed in blood and vowed under threat of death. I consider that to be a warrior's oath. Or a knight's code if that analogy better suits you. In either case, I would feel honor bound—if you were to break such a vow—to cut off your hands and feet, cauterize the wounds, and then have some fun with you. Do you like milk and honey?"

"Whatever you want to know, I'll tell you."

He narrowed his eyes. "First off, I'm going to write down a message for you to deliver. I want to stress to the letter's recipient the kind of people with whom he's dealing. I want you to stress that to him upon delivery."

"A message for who?"

"For your associate, Mr. King."

"I don't have access to him. No one does. He has his top people who deal with him, and then you meet with them."

"Then deliver the message to his intermediary."

"That would be Oban."

"Tell us about him," Emily said.

Willoughby swallowed hard, clutching his bleeding hand and mewling like a wounded animal. "Can I tend to my hand?"

"After we're done," Ackerman said. "Now answer her question. Total surrender."

"I only know what I've heard about his past, but he's Egyptian. Word is that he started out as a boss in Cairo before being recruited by Mr. King to be his right hand."

Ackerman licked the blood from one side of the blade. He did it slowly, allowing the point to rest on his tongue and penetrate his flesh. "Anything else we should know about him?"

"One strange thing. A mutual business partner told me that the name *Oban* means 'King' in Egyptian."

"Are you suggesting that Oban could actually be Mr. King?"

"That's what my friend thought. But I've spoken with King on the phone, and the voice on the other end wasn't Oban."

"Why would a little pauper like you receive an audience with the king?"

"He makes a phone call to every person who starts working for him at a certain level. He pretty much just stressed how seriously he takes revenge."

"I want to know every word."

Willoughby stammered around the subject a bit but finally said something that caught Ackerman's interest: "I don't remember exactly, but there was this big story that involved Attila the Hun or someone like that."

Ackerman searched his own memory banks. He had read much about all the great conquerors and killers throughout history. His memory couldn't compare with his brother's, but he still prided himself on his ability to recall details.

But he couldn't conjure from memory a story about Attila the Hun that focused heavily on revenge.

But Genghis Khan ... He was famous for holding a grudge.

Ackerman said, "Could it have been Genghis Khan that he told you about?"

"Could be. I really can't remember for sure."

"The Mongol emperor, Genghis Khan, once sent a

trade caravan through the Khwarezmid empire that never returned. The traders were killed when their caravan was seized by the governor of one of the cities. To exact revenge, Genghis Khan invaded the empire with two hundred thousand men and killed the governor by pouring molten silver in his eyes and mouth. He even went so far as to divert a river through the Khwarezmid emperor's birthplace, completely erasing it from the map. He redefined the idea of getting on someone's bad side. Could one of those instances be the story he told you?"

Willoughby raised his hands. "Total surrender, but I can't remember."

Ackerman said, "Very well then. Next question. Why haven't you talked to Tyson about you being his biological father?"

"Frank!" Emily snapped.

He growled deep in his throat. "Fine. Since we can't discuss the Tyson situation, I want to know everything you know about Mr. King's organization. But hypothetically, about the whole Tyson deal, you should definitely tell him the truth. Honesty is always the best policy."

57

Willoughby lived up to his end of the bargain. Total surrender. Ackerman listened as Willoughby gave a full account of King's operations, which ranged from running guns from Mexico up to California's inner cities to human trafficking of Eastern European and Asian women by way of the Canadian border. And these were merely the activities of which Willoughby, a lowly corporal in King's empire, was aware. All of it being accomplished through intermediaries while the King remained in his castle.

Ackerman was impressed. The alleged agoraphobe had built quite the criminal empire. He mused that in another life, he could have easily built his own kingdom through similar tactics.

Willoughby droned on about the way King had banded several scattered groups together, typically brokering the deals between the different criminal outfits. The tactics seemed familiar to Ackerman, but he couldn't yet ascertain the historical template that King had used to construct his business model.

Emily asked, "So where do you fit in, Mr. Willoughby?"

Their informant had shied away from that information previously and seemed physically affected by the mere question. Ackerman said, "You had mentioned previously that you wouldn't associate your criminal and legitimate enterprises. So, no guns. Must revolve around human trafficking, correct? Remember, total surrender."

Willoughby licked his lips and said, "Sometimes, but it could be anyone that King needs disposed of. He brings me people that he wants erased."

Ackerman cocked an eyebrow. "Do tell. You incinerate them somehow, don't you?"

Willoughby curled up his front lip. "I have a license to use exotic weapons on the range. So I have a flame thrower. Then I built a hidden pit out on the back of the property. The bottom is filled with my own patented formula for dissolving bone and charred flesh. Atop the solution is a steel cage. We drop people in, burn them down to nothing, and sweep what's left into the *Sludge*."

"Fascinating. I would love to—"

A familiar sound echoed through Willoughby's store and stopped Ackerman mid-sentence. It was the reverberation of metal rolling over a hard surface. He knew the sound of a grenade or gas canister well. But which was it?

He searched the floor, homing in on the sound, and found a gas canister coming to rest only a few feet away. But then he heard several other canisters joining the first and beginning their rotation.

With a roll of his eyes, he said, "Well, excrement."

Then he took a deep breath and scanned the room for the person or persons who had thrown the tactical devices. Part of him hoped it was Tyson—Willoughby's illegitimate son and apprentice—then they could have some in-depth family therapy.

He spotted a massive man standing among the rows of army surplus gear. The attacker wore a hooded sweatshirt and a gas mask. Knowing his only chance at preventing their capture at this point would be to disable their uninvited guest and retrieve his mask, Ackerman rushed forward and engaged the interloper.

He came in hard and wild with a series of jackhammer blows. But the newcomer in the gas mask deflected each blow with an expert's hand. Ackerman switched tactics to Muay Thai and then Indonesian Sulat, but he failed to connect with a single direct blow.

He came in for another attempt, his lungs screaming for air. His third blow of the series had just missed when his opponent engaged in his first offensive maneuver. One that was perfectly planned and timed.

The man in the mask ducked under the blow and lunged forward with a punch aimed at the space just below his ribs. The blow was executed with a perfect upward motion, as if his opponent was attempting to push his stomach up into his chest. But Ackerman instantly saw his mistake and recognized the brilliance of the assault—a blow designed specifically to knock the wind out of him.

He took four steps backward and rode the wave of pain. But, in the end, he had to breathe or pass out. As he finally dropped to the floor, Ackerman wasn't sure if it was the hypoxia or the gas from the canisters that would ultimately lead to his unconsciousness, but he was fairly certain where he would wake up. Which was fine by him. Ackerman had wanted to get a good look at Mr. King's private crematorium anyway.

58

Ackerman awoke in a pit of corroded and charred metal. The only light came from the few over-achieving rays that had snuck in around the hinges and edges of the metal trapdoor which formed the ceiling of the dungeon. The grated metal floor smelled oddly of wintergreen, the aroma of who knew how many people's erased remains simmering in a chemical soup below.

Emily Morgan slumbered beside him on the steel cage. She looked so peaceful when she slept. He had always thought so. Her red-tinted hair swept over her pale Asian cheekbones, which were speckled with freckles that were only visible when her face was ruddy.

He reached out, brushed the hair away from her face, and then flicked her ear with enough force to make an audible *thwap*. She instantly came awake and said, "Ouch, damnit, Jim!"

Ackerman felt a stab of some unidentified emotion at the mention of her dead husband's name—one of his many victims during the dark years.

Emily's eyes slowly revealed recognition of their current predicament. She looked up at him with a frown and asked, "Did we survive?"

"Nope. Welcome to hell."

"Then I know we survived. Hell is one thing I don't fear because I know I'm not bound for that place."

"Not sure I can say the same. But I still don't fear it."

Pushing herself up into a sitting position, she said, "I would suggest that escaping from this pit would be your area of expertise."

"I woke up ten seconds before you did, but give me a minute. Maybe two. You can't rush brilliance."

He stood and felt his way around the walls, examined the hinges to the trapdoor over their heads—which he could barely touch on tiptoe—and then he turned his attention to the floor. It was a solid cage, except for a small trapdoor secured by a small but formidable lock, which required a key. Finding no weaknesses exploitable using their current resources, he turned his attention to the sludge beneath the metal floor. He wasn't sure what he hoped to see, but within thirty seconds, he found what he had been hoping for.

With a smile, he said, "Actually, my dear, our escape is going to depend solely upon you. My arms are too thick to reach through the grate, down into the sludge, and grab that piece of metal, but your slender appendages will slip right through."

"What piece of metal?" She moved closer, and he pointed down through the cage floor. She said, "What is that?"

"My guess is that it's a metal support rod, which had been implanted into the leg or hip of one of Mr. Willoughby's victims. How often do you think they're alive when he burns them? Considering that I find pleasure in pain, perhaps I would be best served by a fiery demise."

"Nobody is meeting their demise tonight. Fiery or otherwise. What do we do with the rod if I'm able to reach it?"

"You'll have to get on my shoulders and pry out one set of hinges. They're only held in with four screws."

"That could take forever."

"I estimate we have less than five minutes."

59

Maggie was growing increasingly worried about Marcus. She had rarely seen him so ... *deflated*. It was as though a fire in him had gone out. He sat across from her on the FBI jet headed to San Francisco, and he had actually fallen asleep. She had rarely seen him sleep, let alone pass out anywhere but in a controlled environment. He simply wasn't the kind of guy who dozed off, and the ease with which he had done so scared Maggie. She had seen Marcus push forward with bullets still embedded in his flesh, broken bones, and everything in between. But to deal with this wound, he had passed out like a machine shutting down for repairs.

Maggie couldn't allow herself to sleep, but not because she wasn't exhausted. She had work to do. After Ackerman had informed her of the hole in the Taker investigation, she had pulled the files and reviewed them again for herself, still unable to trust Ackerman at his word. But he was right. And she had overlooked it for years.

She needed to track down every one of her childhood neighbors and, eventually, her father. Unfortunately, she couldn't involve Stan, and so she would have to do the leg work herself.

With that in mind, Maggie pulled out her laptop, connected to the jet's Wi-Fi, and set out to find someone who may have caught a glimpse of the Taker on the day he stole her brother.

60

The metal ceiling flew open and blinding artificial light filled the pit. The time in near darkness was enough to make Ackerman's vision go white. He closed his eyes against the sudden illumination and tried not to move. He had advised Emily to do the same.

Through squinting eyes, Ackerman saw a reject from a 1950s robot movie. Based on stature, he assumed the mechanized intruder to actually be Willoughby wearing a face-shield and protective acrylic clothing. The flame-thrower in his hands was a long vented tube with a pistol grip and hoses running back to a metal tank on his back. The end of the weapon held a lit flame in front of the barrel.

Willoughby cursed and pulled back his protective mask. He said, "They're gone."

In order to hear the conversation above, Ackerman had turned his head so that one ear poked out of the sludge in the bottom of the pit. Emily had been correct. They hadn't the time to dislodge the hinges from the metal door over their heads. But he did have ample time to pick the lock in the cage floor, allowing them to drop into the sludge pit of chemicals and human remains. They had then pulled themselves back into one corner and waited, their heads just above the surface. The strange-smelling soup was lumpy and blackened, and the cage didn't offer much of a view of the liquid resting three feet below. To all appearances, they had disappeared.

The big man who had bested him earlier while wearing the gas mask stepped forward. Now some type of surgical mask covered his face. Cocking his head, the expert fighter stared into the empty pit and said, "Oh well. Oban said to let them go anyway. You're just lucky I was dropping off a package and was halfway here when you triggered that silent alarm."

"But how in the hell did they ..."

The man in the mask said, "Not our problem. Oh, and one more thing, Mr. King wanted me to give you a message."

He punctuated the sentence with a perfectly placed blow to Willoughby's Adam's apple. The tiny marmoset man was caught completely by surprise. Clawing at the air, Willoughby struggled to breathe as he choked to death on his own dislodged body part.

The big man in the mask calmly but forcefully pulled the flamethrower from Willoughby's grasp, slipped the tank from the choking man's back, and shoved him into his own pit. The marmoset man was still fighting for air when the man in the mask aimed the flamethrower downward.

Ackerman quickly looked at Emily, took a deep breath, and ducked under the surface. He felt her following suit beside him shortly before the flames scorched the air above their heads.

Waiting for the heat to subside, Ackerman wondered how long Emily could hold her breath.

He received his answer when he felt her start to move toward the surface, but the heat was still pushing down on them, and there would be no air to find above. He grabbed hold of Emily and held her underneath the surface until the fire stopped.

Finally, the flames relented, and they both tried to gasp in the hot air without alerting the man standing high above them with the flamethrower. Ackerman had to admit that he somewhat enjoyed the smell of Willoughby's blackened flesh.

The man in the mask said, "I assume you can hear me down there. If so, Mr. Oban has you on his calendar for tomorrow at 1:00 p.m. Enjoy the rest of your night."

The overhead doors closed, and he and Emily waited in the darkness for several minutes. Finally, judging that it was safe to make their escape, Ackerman said, "All in all, I would say we had a productive evening."

61

Sunday

Special Agent Jerrell Fuller couldn't find his way to the sleep his mind so desired. It wasn't that he was tired. He had slept more than enough over the past couple of days, waiting for whatever trials his captor had prepared for him. It was just easier to sleep, easier to dream, than to stare into complete darkness.

For a while, he had searched and plotted escape, but there was nothing to help him. He was basically inside a concrete shower stall with a smooth steel door on one side. One weak point might have been the window in the center of the door, but he was sure that the Gladiator or whatever his tormentor called himself would have paid the extra cash for reinforced glass, which pretty much meant he would break his hand before he could punch through it.

As he lay in the darkness, coveting a dream, Jerrell went over the cell's design again for what might have been the millionth time. There was a speaker in the wall by the door, but it was flat and smooth and dotted with pencil-sized holes. He couldn't get any leverage on it. The only other possible flaw he could find was the drain in the center of the floor. It was smooth, no screws, which meant that it was probably glued down. The holes in the drain were large enough that he could slip his figures inside and pull up on the circular metal grating.

Under normal circumstances, Jerrell conditioned his body as if fitness was a religion. Not because he wanted to impress anyone. He worked his body so hard in his down time because he knew that a few extra muscle fibers could be all the difference when wrestling with a murderer.

But the glue was apparently stronger than his workout regimen. He had twisted and pulled, but there was no give in the drain's housing. After a few seconds, he had given up on the idea.

When he had first awoken in this nightmare, he had suspected the drain was there to rinse away his blood. As time ticked on, he realized it was actually his toilet.

He slapped a fist down on the concrete floor, again for what was probably the millionth time. He stood and paced the cell. Then he did some pushups and sit-ups. Then he lay back down.

As he fought for breath from working his body, he again considered the drain in the floor. If he could pull it free, he could perhaps sharpen it down to a cutting edge. Or, at the very least, it would act as a set of brass knuckles. Perhaps giving him a chance at shattering the glass in the door.

Pulling himself to his feet, he walked around the drain for a moment. He did the same thing while maxing out when lifting weights. He needed to get his adrenaline going a bit, work up some anger at the obstacle.

After a few seconds, Jerrell squatted over the drain and wrapped his fingers through the cover. He intended to use the muscles in his legs and arms in tandem, putting all his strength and conditioning to work.

He counted to three and then pulled up with everything he had. His skull shook as every muscle tensed. After a moment with no give, he relaxed, adjusted his grip, and changed tactics. This time, he pulled up and twisted the cover at the same time, wrenching against the glue from every angle.

And this time, he was rewarded with some movement. He continued pulling and twisting, throwing the last of his energy into removing the possible instrument of his salvation.

Jerrell stumbled backward from his own built-up momentum when the drain cover finally came free.

He leaned his left hand on the concrete wall and smiled to himself, his right fist gripping the sturdy metal grate. He tested the weapon with a few shadow punches and smiled some more. Then he set to work at sharpening the front edge of his new best friend.

62

The little dog jumped as Marcus stormed in and slammed the door. The panels of frosted plastic covering the conference room's fluorescent lighting rattled, and the dog issued a sound between a growl and a whimper.

Ackerman and Emily occupied two of the conference room's faux-leather desk chairs, the little dog in another chair between them. They both still carried a putrefying chemical aroma even after showering. Their complexions were ruddy from irritation caused by the exposure to Willoughby's magic soup.

Marcus could feel his anger level rising, and he urged himself to calm down. Taking a deep breath, he pulled out a chair on the opposite side of the oblong Formica table. Then he sat and leaned back, trying to find the words. His brother wouldn't respond to anger, which was one of the only emotions Marcus seemed able to muster these days. How do you explain the world to a man who is addicted to pain and has no fear?

Finally, Marcus whispered, "Do you have anything you want to say to me?"

Ackerman quickly replied, "I find the situation with this canine vermin to be completely unacceptable. Time is man's most precious commodity. Benjamin Franklin said, 'You may delay, but time will not.'"

With a roll of his eyes, Marcus said, "And Einstein said, 'Time is an illusion.' You can't win the famous quotes game with me. You don't have the memory for it."

"I do feel that my recollection isn't what it once was. I find myself forgetting a great many things."

"Unfortunately, my memory is as clear as ever. Anything else you want to tell me?"

"Why would I tell you something else when we haven't adequately explored the first issue of this dog?"

Marcus closed his eyes and imagined his fist pummeling Eddie's face. He said, "Fine, let's talk about it. What did you name your pet?"

The dog, sitting in its own chair, seemed enthralled by the whole conversation.

"I don't want to name it. I want it to go away."

"He's not going anywhere, which is honestly more than I can say about you. You should pick a name for him."

"How about Dropkick? Please, return this thing to the puppy penitentiary where she found it."

"It's a full-blooded Shih Tzu. It came from a pet store, and Emily paid a lot of money out of her own pocket to get it for you."

She said, "It's really not a big deal. I just looked in his eyes and had a sense that he would be a good companion for you. If the burden is too much, then I'm sure I can still return him."

Ackerman actually seemed to be at a loss for words. "No, it's fine. I think we've reached a level of mutual understanding. Perhaps we could just get some sort of cage for it. And some diapers."

"The way I see things going right now," Marcus said,

"you're going back into a cage before that dog does. Do you understand?"

Ackerman said, "What makes you think I would allow that?"

"Someday—maybe a year from now, maybe tomorrow—your overconfidence will be your downfall."

"I don't start fights I can't win."

"The problem is that you aren't afraid to lose, so you believe you can win any fight. Just because you aren't afraid to die doesn't mean you won't."

Ackerman shrugged. "Of course not. Everything dies. Such is the way of the flesh. The cost of our mortal coils. Most would say that a life well-lived is the goal. To live, not merely to avoid death. But what does it mean to live well? Efficient management of the precious seconds of one's life certainly comes to mind."

Marcus growled and rubbed his temples. "Are you still talking about the damn dog?"

"What else would we be talking about?"

Marcus snatched up a ceramic coffee cup from the table and threw it against the wall. It didn't shatter, since the conference room walls were padded with sound-absorbing material. The dark liquid stained the beige cloth, and the cup fell to the floor with a crunch.

Ackerman said, "That was Emily's mug."

"You almost got Emily and yourself killed last night. You basically forced her to go in the first place."

Emily said, "That's not true, sir. I could have—"

Ackerman interrupted, "What does it matter? I could have gone on my own, but I thought involving her would be the politically correct maneuver."

"You should have sat tight and waited for me. First, you convince her to go to some gym, and you pick a fight there. Then, you endangered both your lives at Willoughby's."

"Some would say I saved her life."

"You should have followed orders. You're not here to get your hands dirty."

"Then why am I here, little brother? Dirty is pretty much all I do well."

"Not anymore. Now, you just consult. You let me do the dangerous stuff."

"I don't need your protection, baby brother. In fact, I feel the opposite to be true. And I don't ever want to see anything happen to you. I won't allow it. You, Dylan, and this team are all I have."

Marcus leaned back in his chair and rubbed his temples. "I know, Frank, and I don't want to lose you either. I don't want you to get killed, and I also don't want you to lose control."

"It seems to me that my grip upon the darkness within exceeds your own, as of late."

With a shake of his head, Marcus replied, "When I lose control, coffee cups are the only ones in any real danger. Nobody gets killed."

"It's been a long time since I've let my own personal demons see the light. And if you want to discuss putting this team in danger, then let's talk about your handling of the Demon situation. I told you that we should have walked away from anything to do with him. We should have handed the case off or let him go or anything other than kick that hornet's nest. But you're too stubborn to see when you've hooked a fish big enough to pull the whole boat under with it."

"Damnit, Frank, you've always said that destiny or fate or God brought us together. What if this is why? What if stopping Demon and burning his sick little empire to the ground is that one thing that you and I were meant to do together? What if this is our destiny?"

The little dog hopped onto Ackerman's lap, and he scowled down at it for a long moment. Marcus hoped Ackerman was pondering the question and not thinking of snapping the dog's neck. Finally, his lip curled in disgust, Ackerman picked up the dog as if it was a piece of roadkill and dropped it back onto the neighboring chair.

To the dog, Ackerman said, "What have we discussed regarding personal space?" Then, looking back to Marcus, he added, "Good talk, brother. Now, can we get on with the day's activities? Destiny doesn't fulfill itself, and we have dragons in need of slaying."

63

Corin Campbell sat with her broken legs criss-crossed atop the silk sheets. She thought of escape and tried to recall every detail of the compound. Sonnequa, whom Corin had mentally started referring to as "The Good Wife," had shown her to a private, four-poster bed of her very own. All of them were oversized, probably two California king beds shoved together under a custom-made canopy. Her entire world had been concrete for the past weeks. Now it was all soft and white, an ocean of silk. The veils even provided a sense of privacy, as if she had her own tent, along with her own set of white silk dresses hanging on a rack beside her new bed.

Still, she had a strange sense that this silk existence would end up being much worse than her previous life of concrete and nakedness.

The Good Wife had told her to rest and be ready for breakfast with the Master in the morning, but Corin couldn't sleep. Her mind kept searching for ways to kill a man during breakfast. At times, she could hear other girls sobbing into their pillows, but she refused to cry, refused to let self-pity overcome her.

Before now, she had also refused to believe her tormentor's proclamation of a pregnancy. That hope had crumbled when she had seen one of the other girls with a swollen stomach. She needed to accept that a child was growing inside her. *His child*.

But that was a decision and a worry for later.

Right now, she had more pressing concerns. Like figuring out how to open a man's jugular with a plastic spoon.

She was surprised when Sonnequa parted the veil. Corin hadn't heard the other women's footsteps. The Good Wife said, "Breakfast is ready. Follow me to the dining hall. And—this is important—no one speaks before the Master does. He likes to eat in silence, and you had better not be the one to break that peace, or he'll break you."

Corin nodded and said, "I understand. I'm ready."

64

Marcus knocked on the hotel room door in a coded sequence, for security purposes. Two knocks followed by three would signal the agent to open the door. Two knocks alone would alert her to danger. And the five other FBI agents on loan from Valdas now patrolled the perimeter and had the entire floor blocked off, so there was no chance of a maid bumbling in and getting shot.

Within a couple of seconds, Agent Lee was at the door, opening it cautiously, her gun at the ready. The beautiful young black woman had short-cropped curly hair and bright-green eyes. She gave Marcus a nod and then let the door swing open. Walking back to a small table where a Subway sandwich sat half eaten, she said, "Let me just grab this, and I'll take it down the hall. Give you guys some alone time."

"You're fine. Don't worry about it. Finish your sandwich," he said.

Dylan didn't even look up as Marcus entered the room. The boy was too engrossed in his own little world. He wore a black ninja costume with Apple earbuds attached to his skull. Dylan sat atop the bed, but all the hotel's comforters and blankets had been stripped away, leaving nothing but the bare sheets. All manner of Lego vehicles, fortresses, and play-sets covered the bed. Heroes and villains of all kinds were represented in Lego form, from Star Wars to Robin Hood.

There was just enough room on the bed behind Dylan for Marcus to slip in and take a seat, looking over his son's shoulder. He pulled out Dylan's earbuds and said, "Do I even get a hello?"

Dylan looked back at him with a smile and said, "*Hola, Padre*. That means: Hello, Father. Agent Lee has been teaching me some Spanish."

"That's awesome, buddy. It's a good skill to have. What are you doing here? You got what looks like SpongeBob on the TV. Then you're listening to your iPhone. And all while you're building this magnificent fortress here."

"I wasn't actually watching SpongeBob. Agent Lee turned that on. She told me I needed to watch some cartoons instead of the History Channel."

With her mouth full of sandwich, Agent Lee said, "A boy your age should only watch so many World War II documentaries in one day."

Marcus ran a hand through the boy's hair. It was the same color as his own. He said, "She's right, buddy. It's great to learn, but sometimes you need to let your brain rest."

"That's what I'm doing," Dylan said, going back to his work on the Lego kingdom.

"What were you listening to?" Marcus asked.

"The *MythBusters* podcast."

Marcus didn't know how to respond to that. It didn't really seem appropriate for a boy who wasn't even double digits yet, but he also didn't know what kids were into these days. Maybe watching World War II documentaries and listening to podcasts was perfectly normal. When he was a kid, he had spent hours memorizing encyclopedias, so he had no room to judge.

"I'm sorry I've been away so much with work."

"That's okay. I don't mind. I like being on the road with you where I don't have to be at school, and I can spend all day working on my Legos. I've been able to try out a lot of new ideas that I've been wanting to do for a long time."

Marcus said, "That's good, buddy. But it's still not okay for me to be gone. I should be making more time for you. It's just that we've had a lot going on lately with this case. A lot of things hitting all at once. To be honest, I don't know if I'm coming or going. But that's no excuse. I guess I'm just trying to say that even though I haven't been hanging out with you as much as I would like, I want you to know that it's not always gonna be like this. And it definitely doesn't mean that you're not important to me. You are the most important thing in my world. I want you to know that. I love you, kid."

Dylan didn't look back at him, didn't pause his building, but the boy said, "I love you too, Daddy."

Closing his eyes and thinking of how much of a failure he was as a father, Marcus said, "How about I help you out. Maybe we could put this piece over here." Then he picked up a large blue Lego and attached it to the flying fortress that Dylan was creating—which reminded Marcus of one of those flying aircraft carriers from the Marvel movies.

As soon as the block was in place, Dylan began shaking. The boy's breathing became rapid and his whole body trembled. Dylan snatched the block from his Lego masterpiece and threw it across the room. Through clenched teeth, Dylan said, "That doesn't go there. I have these things all planned out. What, do you think I'm just sitting here sticking pieces together? No, there's a certain way that all of it needs to fit together."

"Okay, my bad. But it's really not that big of a deal, buddy. It's not permanent. I put it there, and you took it off. You don't need to be so angry about it. That's the cool thing about Legos. There's no set way that you have to do it. You can't make any mistakes when building these things. And if you do, you can just tear it down and build it again. It's not permanent."

"You don't understand. Can I just get back to work? I'm sure you have a lot of things you need to do on your case."

"I don't understand why you're so upset. You're much more important to me than some case, and I—"

"I need to use the bathroom. I'll see you later. Love you," Dylan said, and then he grabbed his iPhone and earbuds and headed for the bathroom.

Marcus just nodded and watched him go. After Dylan slammed the door and turned on the exhaust fan, Marcus said, "What am I doing wrong, Agent Lee?"

The young agent raised an eyebrow and said, "Don't look at me. I don't even have a cat."

"Great, thanks. I'll leave you to it, but if he starts requesting weapons grade uranium to go into some of his Lego creations, be sure to drop me a text and let me now."

"Agent Williams?" she called after him. "Has there been any headway in finding Jerrell? I mean, Agent Fuller?"

He could hear a tremble in her voice. He said, "The two of you were close, I take it. I didn't know."

"They wouldn't let me be an active participant in the investigation to find him, because of our ... relationship. But I volunteered to help with his case in any way I could, so they gave me this job."

After explaining the few twists the investigation had

taken, he said, "I can't promise that we'll find him alive. Not at this point. But I haven't given up hope, and I never will."

Grabbing him with an unexpected and awkward hug, Agent Lee wiped a tear from her eye and said, "Thank you, Agent Williams. Jerrell is one of the best men I've ever known, if anyone could survive something like this, it's him. And don't you worry a bit about your boy. I'll keep him in line, and if anyone wants to get to him, they'll have to go through me."

65

Corin knew that the man who had repeatedly brutalized her could walk. She had watched him stroll naked toward her a few times in the beginning, but she had quickly learned to close her eyes and find distance. Even then, she heard his bare feet padding into her concrete world.

So who was the guy in the wheelchair?

The other girls had already set the table and prepared the meal by the time Sonnequa wheeled Corin into the ornate dining room. A long table covered in a white linen cloth occupied the center of the room. The walls were are a dark, rich wood, and a crystal chandelier hung over the formal place settings.

Sonnequa had wheeled her up to the table, and the other girls took their assigned seats. Once everyone was in place and silent, The Good Wife left the room and returned, this time pushing a man in a wheelchair. Sonnequa walked with an air of superiority, as if she were escorting royalty. The man in the chair took his spot at the head of the table, with Sonnequa filling the seat at his right hand.

He was perhaps the most beautiful man Corin had ever seen. An expertly groomed head of sandy-blond hair sat above bright-blue eyes and a combination of other flawless features that would have been the envy of cinematographers everywhere.

The others seemed to fear and respect this man. They

treated him as though this was the *Master* they had told her about. She had assumed that the Master and the man who had raped her were one and the same, but she also knew that her tormentor could walk.

Was this really the man in the skull mask playing some kind of sadistic game with her? Was he faking an injury? It had to be a trap of some kind. He was testing her—her obedience, her self-control, her patience, her fear.

The young Asian girl named Tia, the one with no tongue, served the food to the Master. Corin could taste his dominance hanging over them like a cloud of noxious fumes. The other girls seemed to be holding their breath as the man in the wheelchair savored his first bite and finally said, "My compliments, ladies. Enjoy."

He continued eating and the rest of the girls started passing around the porcelain serving trays filled with eggs, potatoes, bacon, biscuits and gravy, sausages, and all manner of rolls and croissants.

Corin burned to show at least a small gesture of defiance—perhaps ask a question when she knew not to speak, or refuse to eat—but she fought the urge. She needed to play the role of the mouse: quiet, patient, waiting.

They ate in silence until the man in the wheelchair tossed his napkin atop his plate and said, "As you all know, we have a new addition this morning. Welcome to the table, Corin."

In unison, the other girls said, "Welcome to the table."

She said nothing. She just stared down at her plastic fork. Maybe she could pierce his eye with it, or ram it into his ear? She didn't necessarily have to kill him, just slow him down, incapacitate him.

He said, "You're now part of something very special, Corin."

One of the girls who hadn't been present the day before—a tall, thin woman with red hair and freckles—began weeping at the end of the table.

The man in the wheelchair said, "Let's not be rude, Estelle. This is Corin's moment."

"You killed my baby," the redhead whispered.

"Now, my dear, I did no such thing. I would never harm one of my children. We've been over this. It wasn't your fault or mine."

"You let him die. You're a doctor. You could have saved him."

"Estelle, you know the rules. If the child doesn't have the will to survive, then it's not worthy of life. Your baby was weak. But don't worry. There will be plenty of opportunities in the future to bear children. Let us not forget that we are only a few days away from going to the *Island*."

"Who are you?" Corin said abruptly, unable to hold back her words any longer.

He laughed. "She *can* speak. And this is a time to speak freely, Corin. In answer to your question, I am Dr. Derrick Gladstone. I'm a geneticist and fertility specialist."

"What is this place?"

"The facility is an abandoned luxury resort. There was supposed to be a golf course and spa and the whole nine yards. Unfortunately, black mold spread through its heart like a cancer. Board of health condemned the whole place. But don't worry, the dangerous areas are locked away."

"But what is this? What are you trying to do here? And what the hell is the 'Island'?"

"The answer to that is quite simple and yet infinitely complex. I'm building a better world, one child at a time. I call it the Eden Project."

"You're insane."

Sonnequa snapped, "Show the Master respect!"

"It's okay, my dear. This is a time to speak freely. She merely lacks understanding."

Corin said, "I *understand* that this whole thing is about as sick and perverted as it comes. It doesn't matter what religious message you try to dress it up with."

"Religious message? Hardly. I don't believe in that sort of thing. What I'm doing here is saving the human race."

"See, right there. Listen to that statement. Doesn't that sound a little insane to you."

"If spoken by a lesser man, perhaps. Let me explain. First of all, are you acquainted with the basic concepts of evolution?"

Corin said nothing, but as he spoke, she slipped a plastic fork from the table and concealed it beside her leg.

"Crash course. Evolution 101. The core idea is that all species evolved to what they are today by means of natural selection. Now, natural selection is very observable in nature. I could quote you many clearly defined cases from the classic examples of the peppered moths during the Industrial Revolution to Darwin's finches to Italian wall lizards and the cane toads in Australia. All examples of species adapting to better survive in their environments. You may have heard that 'only the strong survive,' but that's not necessarily the case. Oftentimes, it's genetic mutation or viral outbreak or some other random factor that determines which distinct subset of a population will survive. Unfortunately, our species has created a society where the poor and ignorant are those most likely to reproduce."

"What are you planning to do? Release a virus to kill the world and create your own Noah's Ark?"

"Nothing quite so dramatic. No, I'm not trying to kill the world. I'm merely attempting to right the ship. You see, all living things evolve. The difference between humankind and any other species in history is that we have the knowledge and means to affect our own evolutionary course for the better. How do we do that? It's very simple. We control breeding."

"One guy and a few sex slaves can't influence humankind."

"First of all, you're not slaves. You're the *Chosen*."

"Chosen by who?"

"By your genes, and by your will to survive. Everyone at this table has been tested thoroughly using the most advanced genetic screenings available. We are all free from genetic markers causing disease or defect. As you can see by the diversity, this has nothing to do with the color of one's skin. I could care less if two hundred years from now the Caucasian race is a small minority. All I care about is that the individuals who are in the majority are healthy, well-educated, productive members of society."

"So you're basically trying to rape humankind as a whole ... That's wonderful. I'll kill myself before I let my DNA become part of this insanity."

Derrick wheeled away from the table and pushed himself closer to her. "I don't think you have suicide in you, Corin. You're a fighter. Unlike your mother."

"What the hell do you know about my mother?"

"I know everything about you, Corin. I know who you

really are and all that you've done. Everyone at this table is a survivor. By whatever means necessary. That's the kind of people I need to correct the evolutionary destiny of our species."

She wondered what he really knew. Her mother's suicide was public record. He could have gotten that information from newspaper archives. But there was no way that he could truly know all that she'd done to survive over the years.

Derrick said, "My plans go much farther than merely this compound. But consider this before you decide the issue of my sanity and the validity of my plans. About eight percent of men in Asia can trace their lineage back to the great Genghis Khan, a personal hero of mine. He reportedly fathered hundreds of children, but that doesn't always correlate with a strong genetic legacy. After all, fathering a multitude of sons doesn't always mean that those sons will sire their own multitudes of offspring. Establishment of such successful lineages often relies on social systems that allow powerful men to father heirs with many women. Unfortunately, most societies which present the necessary circumstances are considered barbaric by the modern world. So I decided that the only way to move forward was to form my own society. From the ground up. And through technology and the current crumbling of our culture, I intend to leave an even broader legacy than the great Khan."

"You're disgusting."

"Am I? Why is that?"

"What you're doing is wrong."

"How do you define right and wrong, Corin?"

"It's pretty widely accepted that kidnap and rape are wrong."

"Right and wrong are religious concepts. In order for something to be 'right,' there has to be an inherent measuring stick by which one assesses what is right and what is wrong. For many, that's where God comes in, but the truth is that we are nothing. Mankind is but an enlightened animal with a tendency toward delusions of grandeur. If you want something in this world, you have to take it. You see, 'only the strong survive' actually isn't anything that Darwin ever said or even a core concept of evolution. But on a personal level, on the level of our individual generation, it's still the truth of a finite, mortal existence. The law of the jungle. The strong prey on the weak. And if I'm strong enough to affect the genetic destiny of our entire species for the better, then why is it wrong for me to do so?"

"They're going to catch you. It's not just wrong. It's illegal." Corin turned her wheelchair to face his, her muscles coiled and ready to strike.

Derrick smiled. "The police or feds or whoever are welcome to try and stop me. If I'm not strong enough and smart enough to carry out my plans, then I don't deserve to be the genetic father of millions. You see, I intend to …"

She had heard enough.

While he basked in his own glory, she readied her weapon. Then, picking her moment, Corin lunged forward and grabbed him by his perfect mane of golden hair while thrusting the end of the plastic fork toward his ear.

66

Baxter's memory of Detective Natalie Ferrera was of a woman a bit younger and a few pounds lighter, but his former partner was as still as beautiful as ever. Her skin reminded him of white-sand beaches after the tide came in—pure, moist. Natalie was born in Cuba, but her parents had defected when she was in junior high. He had often thought of her family, washed up on a Florida beach like a message in a bottle.

Natalie wore a red blouse beneath a coal-black pantsuit. As she approached, she caught him admiring her. He could see it in her eyes. The beautiful brown mirrors to her soul filled with a warmth that he remembered fondly. But then her memory must have landed on one of the bad times because her eyes went cold.

Beside him, Jenny said, "That's your old partner? She's gorgeous."

"Yes, she is."

"You ever hit that?"

Baxter had tried to talk Jenny out of coming along to the police station, but it was her day off, and he couldn't find an adequate explanation for wanting to leave her behind. He didn't know why he should feel awkward. Jenny wasn't his girlfriend. She was just his secretary, apprentice, or whatever. And Natalie was no longer his partner. She hadn't been for quite some time.

In response to her blunt question, he smiled over at Jenny and winked. "A gentleman never tells."

Detective Ferrera reached them and immediately said, "I don't need your shit today, Baxter. This had better be good."

"With me, darling, it's always good."

Natalie rolled her eyes. "Except when it's bad. I remember a lot of bad, Bax."

He glanced over at Jenny who was still questioning him with her eyes. "Well, I suppose this is kind of a bad case, but it's a hell of a good lead."

"I'll bite. A lead on what?"

"An abduction. Girl's name is Corin Campbell. It's one of your cases, kiddo."

"Cut to the chase. What do you want for it? You need a favor or something?"

"I want full access to the case."

Jenny said, "*We* want full access."

"My apologies, Jennifer. May I introduce Detective Natalie Ferrera, and Nat, this is Jennifer Vasillo. She's my ... apprentice."

"Partner," Jenny said.

Natalie grunted and looked Jenny up and down. "Good luck with that, little girl."

Jenny attacked Nat with her eyes. Before things got out of hand, Baxter said, "This is the kind of lead that solves a case. I could pursue it on my own, which is what my client is paying me to do. But I figured that we might as well work together and possibly save this poor kid's life."

Nat's gaze finally shifted from Jenny back to him. She said, "Don't try to manipulate me, Bax. If you don't inform us of something that could help save a life, then I would feel obliged to arrest you as an accessory."

Baxter chuckled. "I always love it when you talk all professional like that, but as you said, let's cut to the chase. I'll give you the info. You know I will. Even if you shut me out. You have resources I don't. Ones this case needs. But I have resources you don't. Somebody else is paying my bill. Why not let me help you for free? You need me on this."

Shaking her head and grinding her teeth, which he recognized as her tell for reluctant acceptance, she said, "Fine. I'll let you in. But it's your eyes only. Lose the girl."

He immediately said, "No deal. She's my partner, remember. She goes where I go."

"A good partner would understand."

"It's not up for discussion."

Natalie once again shook her head and ground down on her teeth. "Fine, but she keeps her mouth shut and touches nothing. You got that, little girl?"

Jenny, thankfully, raised her hands in surrender. Nat pursed her lips and, turning away, said, "Follow me."

Jenny winked over at Baxter, a small grin and a blush warming her pale skin. In the process, he had probably further pissed off and alienated his old partner, but Grandpappy Kincaid had always told him that you dance with the one you brought. And Baxter had always found it wise to heed Grandpappy's advice.

67

It wouldn't have been the first time Corin Campbell had committed cold-blooded murder. But in those instances, her victims had been helpless. This time, Dr. Gladstone was far from feeble. He caught her arm and wrenched it up, nearly popping the joint out of the socket.

A strange vision flashed before her eyes as the pain erupted. Her mother hung above her, kicking and clawing at the rope around her neck, hands reaching toward any would-be savior.

Now, fighting the wave of pain as her shoulder slowly dislocated, she was merely mimicking the movements of someone who had died before her eyes. But she needed to learn from her mother's mistakes. Her flailing hand caught the armrest of Gladstone's wheelchair, and she suddenly realized where her mother had gone wrong. She had been reaching out for something to save herself, while all Corin really cared about at this point was hurting Dr. Gladstone.

She wrapped her slender fingers around the armrest and jerked upward with all the force she could muster. At first, the chair didn't move, and she thought she would die helpless just like her mother, despite anything she did. But then she felt the armrest rise, and she pushed harder, tipping the chair over and throwing Gladstone to the floor.

Clutching her dislocated shoulder, Corin wheeled for the closest door. She knew she'd never escape in her condition, not with the hellhounds patrolling the perimeter. But Gladstone must have transportation between the compound and the city, a vehicle of some type. If she could find that, she would have a chance.

A steel exit door with a sign warning "Alarm will sound" was the her closest way out. She pushed through the door. No alarm shrieked, but something did growl.

Corin slowly backed away from the door as the beast followed her through the opening, its hackles raised and its teeth bared.

"Easy, boy," she said to the massive black dog. Still backing away, she bumped against something hard and unmoving. Looking over her shoulder, she saw another snarling face. This one belonging to Gladstone, who towered over her now, apparently only faking the need for a wheelchair.

He grabbed her by the shoulders, his large hands trembling with barely contained rage. He said, "Sonnequa, get a fire going. It's time our new addition gets a lesson in negative reinforcement."

Corin spun on him, punching and clawing at his eyes.

The muscular Dr. Gladstone easily deflected her blows, and then unleashed one of his own. She felt the impact of his fist against the side of her head. Then her world became a kaleidoscope of exploding colors, and she dreamed of falling into a well with no bottom.

68

San Francisco's Richmond Police Station was a Romanesque building of red and white brick. Based on the architecture, Ackerman guessed that the structure had been erected sometime in the early 1900s. It had no doubt undergone major renovations since then, considering that most buildings in San Francisco were now seismically reinforced.

The desk sergeant had led them back to a large briefing room. It was the same kind of space he had seen in countless police stations across the country, and at least one time in Mexico. They all, of course, had their unique flourishes and differences in size and amenities, but they all still served the same basic form and function. The walls here were a pale-yellow plasterboard, and the ceiling was the standard two-by-two speckled tile, which seemed to be a favorite of schools, hospitals, and office buildings alike.

Bulletin boards, calendars, schedules, announcements, photos—they smothered the walls, only allowing small glimpses of the pale yellow to shine through, like clouds blocking a rising sun. Coffee and donuts rested in the corner. A little cliché perhaps, but he supposed it was probably as true for any office setting as it was for those in law enforcement.

They were alone in the large space, and Ackerman had refused to sit until the so-called task force arrived.

He said, "This is ridiculous. How long have we been waiting?"

Maggie, pouring her second cup of coffee, said, "It's only been like twenty minutes. Just relax. Have a donut or something."

"My body is a temple. I'm very selective about what I put into it. I don't eat donuts."

In response, Maggie flipped open the box, plucked one out, and said, "Ooh, Krispy Kreme's. Your loss." She punctuated her statement by taking an indulgent bite of the pastry.

Ackerman turned his attention to his brother, who sat at the conference room table. Marcus had a full cup of coffee in front of him and was again rubbing his temples, likely fighting off another migraine.

He said, "Why are we wasting time with this, brother? Can't Computer Man just break into their files?"

Marcus didn't even pause his rubbing. "I'm not in the mood for a big philosophical discussion here, but let's just say that the intuition and personal knowledge of the local investigators can make all the difference."

"I see. So we plan to use them for our own ends."

"No, I plan to help them do their jobs."

Marcus opened his eyes and lowered his hands from the sides of his head. He looked up at Ackerman and said, "I cannot take you seriously in that shirt."

"I think it's patriotic."

"You look like you're going to a barbecue ... In Texas ... At the house of a guy named Roy. I can't believe Emily let you buy that."

Ackerman replied, "She didn't. I stole it."

"What? First of all, you were there shopping for clothes on the government's dollar. Why in the world would you steal instead of just having Emily pay for it? And second, why in the name of all that is holy would you choose that shirt?"

Looking down at the garment in question, Ackerman couldn't understand what all the fuss was about. It was a long-sleeve button-down dress shirt, covered in red stripes with denim patches and white stars on the shoulders and on each breast pocket.

He would never admit it out loud, but he knew the real reason he had stolen the shirt and chosen something so flamboyant was to get a rise out of the team. He found it difficult not being antagonistic.

With a mouthful of donut, Maggie dropped into a chair across from Marcus and said, "I forgot to mention it earlier, Ackerman, but Kenny Rogers called. He wanted his shirt back."

Marcus chuckled, but Ackerman didn't get it. He said, "I'm not familiar with this Rogers fellow, but you can tell him that if he wants something of mine, then he's welcome to pry it from my icy death-grip."

Marcus said, "Okay, take it easy. Let's not get our panties in a twist."

"I don't wear underwear. I don't like feeling restricted."

"Too much information," Maggie said. "And would you sit down already!"

"As you wish," he said, taking a seat beside his brother. Maggie kept stuffing the donut in her mouth, and Marcus had gone back to rubbing his temples. Ackerman wasn't used to these kinds of situations— working in a team environment, making small talk. He found it all so exhausting. His gaze traveled over the room, searching for some subject of discussion.

Finally, thinking of an amusing anecdote, Ackerman said, "This ceiling reminds me of a particularly interesting encounter I had in Mexico, during which I wore a man's face. I had carefully removed the mangled visage of his corpse and then placed it over my own. Then I crawled up into a suspended ceiling, much like this one. I distributed my weight until the right moment, and then I allowed myself to fall through, appearing to be the dead body of a police officer. Then—"

"I really don't want to hear stories like this, Frank. I'd rather think of you the way you are now."

"All of us, dear brother, are the sum of our parts and pasts. You, like me, have been tempered by the fires of pain. I find that sharing such feelings is a rather cathartic exercise, which—"

"Please stop talking."

"Oh, come on now. It was actually a really good story. It even revolved around my first love."

After a long swig of her coffee, Maggie said, "Okay, now I'm a little bit interested. You are referring to a woman and not, like, death or pain or something like that."

Marcus snapped, "Don't encourage him. Even if he wasn't wearing that ridiculous shirt, I still wouldn't want to hear the story."

"I could take the shirt off, if that's the problem."

"Just shut the mouth. That's the problem."

Ackerman turned to Maggie and said, "He hasn't been sleeping, has he, little sister?"

"I think it's been days since he's slept for more than an hour," she replied.

Marcus cocked his head to the side, loudly cracking his neck, and then he started balling up his fists and popping all his knuckles. Ackerman recognized it as a sign of his brother nearing a meltdown. Marcus said, "I'm going to shoot the next one of you who speaks."

Waiting only a few seconds, Ackerman said, "I believe that type of escalation is what my counselor would classify as an inappropriate overreaction to the situation."

69

Jerrell had thought long and hard about the reinforced glass that separated him from freedom. The floor drain was now filed down to a cutting edge and ready for action, but the more he had considered it, the more he felt that using his new weapon against the barrier was the wrong play.

If he tried to break through the window, the Gladiator would know what he had done. He would be exposing his hand. Jerrell concluded that the better strategy was to keep his ace in the hole. So he had slipped the drain cover back in place, testing to make sure he could easily pull it free.

He didn't have to wait long.

A dim blue light stung his eyes for a second as his vision adjusted. He went to the window and this time, instead of the skull face, he saw the next chamber. The space beyond was perhaps ten by ten, but a similar design to his current prison. The difference was that a chair occupied the center of the room. A life-like straw-and-burlap dummy dressed in Jerrell's clothes had been propped up cross-legged atop the chair. In front of the faux person, sitting at attention inside two circles painted on the floor, were the two biggest Rottweilers he had ever seen.

Bathed in the blue light, the massive dogs were like statues of ice, except for the occasional turning of a head or licking of the lips.

"Do you like dogs, Agent Fuller?" the voice said over the

speaker in the wall. He saw now that his host stood on the opposite side of the chamber, behind another steel door and security window.

"I have an acquaintance who trains this particular breed to be the most loyal killers money can buy. He calls them 'hellhounds.' Would you like to see what they can do?"

His thoughts on the drain in the floor, Jerrell said nothing.

The blue light in the next room turned to red and a high-pitched hum reverberated through the chamber.

The two hellhounds flew into action, working together to tear the dummy apart. The dogs crushed what could have been bone between their massive jaws and whipped their heads from side to side. Instead of focusing on what would've been the soft parts of a human body first, the hellhounds directed their attacks only on the throat, head, arms, and legs. They tore those extremities away from the dummy, but left the torso intact. Jerrell imagined them tearing into his own flesh in the same way, their muscular snouts and razor teeth gnawing pieces off him. He wondered if this explained why the limbs of the former victims had been removed.

The Gladiator said, "My best friend was a man who went by the name of Judas. He helped me design these proving grounds. You passed the first test by pulling the drain cover free and refusing to die. You may retrieve your weapon now and ready yourself for the next test."

On the Gladiator's last words, the door clicked and slowly swung free. Jerrell looked around the edge of the door at the two hellhounds. The dogs had returned to their circles painted on the floor and again stood at attention. The light in the chamber had changed back to blue.

Straw was everywhere, some small pieces still lazily floating to the floor.

Jerrell bent down, retrieved the sharpened metal cover, and tried not to consider that his blood and flesh could soon be spread across the concrete chamber just as easily as that straw.

70

Baxter Kincaid, as if he were in some old Charlie Chaplin movie, nearly stumbled in surprise as he walked into the briefing room. He hadn't expected to find a room full of people. He assumed he'd present the photos to Natalie and her new partner, Detective Olivette—whom Baxter referred to as Detective All-a-that. Instead, he found what he recognized as the best detectives from all ten districts of the San Francisco Police Department.

As she ushered him toward the stage, Baxter leaned over to Natalie and whispered, "You didn't tell me there was a task force. How did you get all these people together so fast?"

She rolled her eyes. "Not everything is about you, Baxter. We've been summoned here by the feds, who supposedly have an interconnecting case. They throw out a little cheese and expect all of us rats to come running."

He said, "I only have one set of photos."

With a shrug, she replied, "We could try to scan them and show them up on the big screen."

"No worries. I'll make it work. I always do. But if I'm going to do this, I need a little herb first."

Natalie jammed her finger in his face and said, "No, no, no." Each time she said the word "No" she bounced the finger, as if she were scolding an insolent puppy. "Baxter, do not embarrass me up there. Do you remember, back when you were on the job, seeing actual professionals? Please just pretend like you're one of them. Act the way they would."

"I find that terribly offensive. In the immortal words of Popeye, 'I ams what I ams.'"

Natalie looked toward the ceiling, let out a long breath, and said, "I've always respected you, Baxter. But if you embarrass me up there, I'm going to punch you in the balls. And I'm not kidding."

Eyes going wide, Baxter said, "Damn, girl. I'll be on my best behavior."

He followed Natalie to the front row of chairs. Her new partner Detective All-a-that had saved her a place, but the rest of the chairs were filled, which forced Baxter and Jenny to sit three rows back. Detective All-a-that seemed a bit overly satisfied at the minor snubbing.

"Which ones are the feds?" Jenny whispered.

"Not sure. I recognize most of the people in here."

"So ... how long were you and Natalie together?"

"Well, we worked together for about—"

"No, Bax, I mean for how long were the two of you fornicating?"

"A gentleman never tells. And, oddly enough, neither do I."

"Don't give me that 'Grandpappy Kincaid says don't kiss and tell' crap. I'm not asking for all the gory details. Just trying to get a lay of the land."

Baxter winked at her. "In that case, the land is a little rocky, some ups and downs, rolling hills, but the soil is dark and rich, and the crops are ready for the harvest."

"What the hell does that mean? That makes no sense."

A door opened beside the stage, and Baxter watched his

old captain escort a group that had to be the federal agents onto the dais. Looking over at Jenny, he placed a finger to his lips. "I would love to explain it to you. But the show is about to start."

Jenny gave him a look that Baxter interpreted as her considering boiling his balls and serving them in a bowl of Brussel sprouts.

He found something about the look on her face incredibly funny, and he almost snorted trying to hold back his laughter. He pointed toward the stage.

Part of him supposed he should have been kissing Jenny's ass. He found her fascinating in every way and hoped their relationship would grow to be something more. But if they were going to form anything meaningful, she would have to accept him for the man he was—one who sometimes enjoyed being a bit obtuse.

Focusing his attention back on the case, Baxter watched the federal agents take the stage. There was a row of chairs behind the podium, where the speakers normally sat. The whole thing made Baxter think of a high school graduation, with the principal and school board sitting in their places behind the valedictorian. In this case, however, the school board was a very dour-looking crew, and the valedictorian, who had just stepped up to the microphone, was Baxter's old commanding officer.

When the little man opened his mouth, his voice was high pitched and nasally. To Baxter's trained eyes, the captain looked more like someone who should be tending bar in Philadelphia than a man in charge of San Francisco's best detectives. But the captain had political connections. Baxter couldn't remember the details—nephew of a senator, son of the mayor's golfing buddy, or some such. Still, it wasn't his place to judge, and in his experience with the captain, the little man had actually been surprisingly adequate.

With a scratch of his unkempt beard, the captain said, "First off, thank you all for coming in on a Sunday. I'll let the lead agent explain to you why such urgency was necessary, but let me just say that I think all of you have done a great job on this case. And I think your hard work is about to pay off. So, let me introduce you to the agents from the Department of Justice, and then I'll turn this briefing over to their team leader, Special Agent Marcus Williams."

71

After instructing Jerrell to sit in the chair, which was bolted to the floor, the Gladiator had demonstrated his control of the situation by switching the lights to red and filling the room with the high-pitched tone. The dogs charged at Jerrell with frightening speed and ferocity, but Jerrell didn't remain in his place. He rushed to a corner of the room. Putting his back to the wall, he hunkered low, arms guarding his throat, his makeshift weapon at the ready.

But, at the last moment, the tone lowered in pitch and the lights flicked back to blue. The massive Rottweilers shook with denied fury as they snarled and growled at him, saliva dripping from the beasts' fangs, but the hellhounds would come no farther. The tone sounded again, and the dogs reluctantly returned to the painted circles.

"Make your choice," the Gladiator said over the intercom. "Brawn and blood, or brains and imagination. You can either fight my pets to the death or you can pass my test."

Not seeing any other options, Jerrell sat back down. The eyes of the hellhounds followed him all the way as he crossed in front of them and sat.

"Good. First question. A murderer is condemned to death. He has to choose between three rooms. The first is full of raging fires, the second is full of men with loaded guns, and the third is full of lions that haven't eaten in three years. Which room should he choose and why?"

Jerrell sat dumbfounded a moment and then said, "Is this a joke? What kind of question is that?"

"This test is designed to establish a number of factors regarding your brain power, including your IQ and cognitive flexibility. Do I need to repeat the question?"

"I'm not playing some stupid game with you!" Jerrell screamed. "Come in here and face me like a man, you little bitch! All big and bad with two bodyguards and a steel door between us. Why don't you come in here and face me yourself?"

"All in due time. Do I need to repeat the question?"

"The answer is: Go screw yourself."

"Once again, your choice is simple. Fight the hellhounds or pass the test. Refusal to participate is a choice that results in failure. If you fail the test, the lights turn red and you face trial by combat instead."

Jerrell gritted his teeth with rage. He squeezed the sharpened drain cover in his right fist. Then he looked at each of the dogs. Their eyes were wide and alert, and they made soft mewling sounds, as if they were watching and waiting as their master dumped kibble into a bowl. Maybe if he struck first and took one of them down he would stand a chance against the sole survivor. Against one of the dogs, he felt he had a chance. But taking on both would be suicide.

He leaned forward in the chair, and the dogs growled. Over the intercom, the Gladiator said, "I wouldn't do that. Unless, of course, you're choosing to fight."

Jerrell leaned back and reconsidered his options. He'd never make it to one of them before they both pounced.

The Gladiator said, "Do you need me to repeat the question?"

"Yes," Jerrell said. "Repeat the damn question."

72

Sitting in the chair closest to the podium, Marcus tapped his leg and tried not to focus in on individuals in the crowd or any of the other sights, smells, and sounds that threatened to overwhelm him. Over the years, he had learned to filter out the distractions and maintain his composure. But the less he slept, the less he could focus.

The captain introduced each member of the team—minus Ackerman, who Marcus wouldn't allow on stage wearing that ridiculous shirt. He wasn't sure why the young captain felt the need to make such a drawn-out introduction, but maybe the little man was just smart enough to make himself look in charge.

Marcus zoned out for a moment. He looked out onto the assembled detectives and noticed a man in a Hawaiian shirt sitting with some goth chick. He wondered if they were undercover agents.

Once the little man was done making himself look important, the captain called for Marcus to take over the briefing. He heard his name, but at first, it didn't register. He was off in his own little world. After an awkward pause, Marcus finally collected himself and stepped up to the microphone.

Clearing his throat, he said, "Let's cut right to the heart of it. We're from a special unit within the Department of Justice, which is focused on serial murderers. We've been tracking down a killer known as 'The Gladiator.' A friend within the FBI knew about our case and informed us of a tape which was recorded three days ago by an undercover agent. The Bureau had inserted this agent into a local criminal organization run by a man known as Mr. King."

As he looked out across the room, he saw that he had everyone's attention. He was certain they had all heard of the infamous and reclusive crime lord.

"The agent who recorded what you are about to hear has gone missing. The FBI believes, and we concur, that this agent is now being held by the Gladiator. We also believe that the Gladiator and your 'Skullface' could be the same killer."

A wave of murmuring swept over the crowd, with a few of the detectives attempting to ask questions, but Marcus silenced them with a raised palm. "Our technical director has control of your computer system, and he's going to play the recording, which is between Oban Nassar—who is King's right-hand man—and an unknown party. I'll go into more detail afterward, and so I'll probably end up answering most of your questions then. Go ahead and play that recording, Stan."

...Hello. Yes, sir ... I understand ... That is very unsettling news ... Decisive action is certainly required, sir. He's already seen too much. He must be dealt with quickly, in order to mitigate the damage ... With all due respect, sir, I don't believe that this is a job that would require the services of the Gladiator ... I wouldn't argue that, sir, but you know how I feel about the prices that the Gladiator and his handler have been charging us for their services ... Do you think it's

*wise to send this man to the Diamond Room? ... Of course,
sir ... I understand. Consider it done ...*

"The man referred to on this recording—The Gladiator—
is a contract killer, but we also believe that he's killed just
as much for his own pleasure as he has for money. And
although he obviously doesn't choose the type of target he
gets *paid* to kill, his personal tastes, we believe, align with
the profile of your missing girls."

73

Corin crawled out of a bad dream about falling and awoke into a full-fledged nightmare. Last she remembered, they were in the ornate dining room. Dr. Gladstone had struck her, and then she must have passed out.

But now where was she? Her vision was blurred. She could only see vague shapes and silhouettes swimming in a pool of light.

Her mind was still falling when Gladstone said, "Corin, my dear, wake up. It's a good morning."

She tried to raise her arms, but they wouldn't move. She tried to move other parts of her body, but below her neck all movement had been restricted to only a few centimeters of leeway.

Blinking herself awake, her breathing became short stabs of air that smelled like blood and fire. In front of her, she saw water. The same small lake that had been beyond the glass of the triangular windows of the ballroom. But now, she could see blue sky and smell the algae and muck growing along the lake's boundaries. She was outside. To her left she saw Gladstone, back in his wheelchair, her fellow captives behind him. The other girls wouldn't make eye contact with her. The looks of fear on their faces made Corin wonder if this was less a punishment and more an execution.

She said, "What's up, Doc?"

Gladstone smiled and shook his head. "You've been a

very bad girl, Corin. You didn't even let me fully explain the situation. As I was attempting to elucidate earlier, my work goes far beyond this compound and a few kidnapped women. I'm confident the work I'm doing here will one day lead to the salvation of humankind."

Her world still spinning, she said, "Do you actually hear the words that are coming out of your mouth? I mean, your cheese has slid way the hell off your cracker, Doc. I kind of wonder if you were just born without the cheese."

"You're not in a position for mocking, my child. Once again, you rush to judgment without hearing all the details."

As Corin's mind began to clear, she studied her restraints for weaknesses. Her skin felt like ice. She was completely naked, mounted to a piece of curved metal. Only her head was free to move.

They were somewhere in Northern California; she was sure that. She recognized the climate and the kinds of trees. In her youth, Corin had spent time in a foster home nestled just outside the Redwood National Park. Her foster parents had been survivalist-types, and she had always been a quick study when it came to surviving.

Gladstone said, "I don't enjoy this sort of thing. I really don't. I'm not a sadist, but there has to be law. In order for our new society to function, you all must accept me as your universal ruler."

She said, "People like you may live on in infamy, but in my opinion, that's even worse than being dead."

He laughed. "You are so naïve, little girl. I mentioned Genghis Khan earlier. In many ways, he's a model for what I'm trying to accomplish. In Mongolia, the great conqueror is seen as a hero and the founding father of their nation."

"I'm going to kill you."

His smile faded. "I'll make you a deal, my pet. If you can tell me the capital of Mongolia—the name of the city—then you're free to go. I'll drive you home myself."

She didn't trust his word for a second, but she still searched her memory for the answer. All those moments she had spent studying, memorizing textbooks and arbitrary facts. But when was the last time she had been exposed to that kind of information? Freshman year of college? Senior year of high school?

"Do you give up?"

"I'm thinking."

The capital of Mongolia?

Was it some derivative of their founding father? But she couldn't recall ever hearing the names Khanopolis or Genghisia.

Finally, she whispered, "I don't know."

"Too bad. Ulan Bator is the capital of Mongolia. But how about I give you a second chance. A slow pitch right down the middle. This one is for your life. What's the name of Mongolia's international airport, university, and vodka?"

"Screw you," she said, her voice trembling, no longer able to hold back her tears.

"Oh, come now, my dear. This is an easy one. No tricks. I'll give you another hint ... His portrait also appears on all Mongolia's currency."

She said, "Genghis Khan."

"That's correct. In Mongolia and most of Asia, Genghis Khan is revered as a hero and known as the great unifier. His legacy is not only found in the DNA that he passed down to a large percentage of the population, but also through the revolutionary ideas he put in motion."

"And he was also known as a ruthless butcher. Everyone lived in fear of the Mongol horde. He slaughtered countless innocent people."

"So what?"

"Listen, Doc, if I have to explain to you why it's not okay to slaughter thousands of innocent people, then I'm not sure where to go with this conversation."

He chuckled. "I'm very much enjoying our little dialogues, Corin. I'm glad I chose not to kill you outright for your defiance."

"I'm glad you didn't kill me too. Then I would have missed the chance to watch you bleed out. And I want nothing more than to look in your eyes as you die in your own shit."

Gladstone gazed down at her like a parent secretly amused at a child's insolence. He said, "Sonnequa, if you would be so kind, please give Ms. Campbell a small taste of the pain to come."

74

As the federal agent's presentation steamrolled forward, Baxter Kincaid leaned back in his seat and looked down at his folder full of grainy photos. Agent Williams was a tough act to follow—guy was all business and knew what he was doing. Baxter decided that he better up his game just a bit. But how to accomplish such a feat?

Some unseen technician had magically taken control of the department's computer systems. The mounted LED display screens overflowed with photos of victims and persons of interest. Special Agent Williams explained the facts and their conclusions in a no-nonsense way. Baxter got the sense that the man was actually telling them everything and doing whatever he could to help in their investigation. Unlike what was often shown on film and television, Baxter had found that, the biggest percentage of the time, law enforcement officers considered themselves to be on the same team, despite jurisdictions and bureaucracy. There were, of course, rivalries, pissing contests, and territorial disputes perpetrated by men with big egos and bigger guns. But, for the most part, he had always found officers of the law to have good hearts and share a genuine desire to stop crime.

As he considered how to up his own game, he absorbed all the information presented. Agent Williams passed the mic off to some of his team members, who discussed other aspects of the profiles. One theory that caught Baxter's ear was that the Gladiator—or Skullface as the San Francisco Police Department had come to call him—may think of the skull mask as his "true" face, and that this could be indicative of a facial deformity, real or perceived.

It was a detailed and astute presentation, complete with all kinds of fancy graphics and photos. The damn thing was a work of art. And now Baxter was going to have to get up there and make all these guys pay attention to a few grainy photos that he believed might lead to the man that they were all yammering about.

Baxter had already made up his mind that his involvement in this case was about to come to an end. It was way out of his league and not his job. But he also wanted to make sure that the people whose job it actually was paid attention to the juiciest leads.

Watching Natalie take the stage, thank the agents for their presentation, and introduce him, he still had no idea how to leave an impression upon the assembled group of men and women.

She called him forward, and Baxter jogged up the two steps to the slightly elevated stage as if he was about ready to receive an MVP trophy. He grabbed the mic and said, "What's up, y'all. Most of you know me, personally or by reputation. And so you should realize that I wouldn't be bringing a lead to this task force if it wasn't straight legit. So …"

Looking down at his folder, Baxter had a thought. The photos showed a time progression, sort of like time-lapse photography. And when he was a kid he always liked to play with time-lapse photography in a cool and special way. He just needed something to bind them together.

Glancing around at the expectant, tired, and just plain grumpy faces of the gathered officers, Baxter's gaze came to rest on Detective All-a-that with his slicked-back black hair, dimpled chin, and golden tan. The dude reminded Baxter of a soap-opera actor, and not the hunky cool type, but the one in the role of the villain. A white, three-ring binder rested atop All-a-that's lap. It was exactly what Baxter had been looking for, perfect for holding his 8 x 10 inch photographs.

Into the mic, he said, "Just one sec, everybody."

Baxter then stepped down from the stage and snatched the binder from Detective Olivette's unsuspecting hands. He turned it upside down, flipped the releases, and dumped the stack of paper onto Olivette's lap. The handsome young detective struggled to catch a few stray sheets and then looked up at Baxter as if he had just replaced the boy's morning cereal with kitty litter.

The thought made Baxter grin from ear to ear.

Retaking the stage, he laid the binder on the podium and forced the printed photos over the rings. Natalie wore an expression that seemed to Baxter to say, "You have embarrassed me, and I am definitely going to punch you in the balls for this."

But Nat had yet to see the finished product.

Pointing to the computer sitting at the podium, Baxter said, "This is one of those MacBooks, right? Can you bring up that Photo Booth program for me, Detective Ferrera?"

She glared at him a few ticks longer—with that strange look of testicular vengeance in her eyes—but then she stepped over to the computer and did as he asked.

Turning the binder over, Baxter placed his homemade flip book in front of the MacBook's webcam and cycled through the photos as if they were a stop action movie. He flipped through a few times at different speeds, letting everyone get a good look at all the pictures.

Then Baxter laid the binder on the podium and said, "What you just saw was a flip book of still photographs which was taken from a video. My technical consultant told me to bring the video in on something called a flash drive. Looking back, that may have been my bad, but we've improvised, adapted, and overcome. So ... the photos show the vehicle of one of your missing girls, Corin Campbell, driving away from her apartment on the evening she went missing. The footage shows a man behind the wheel of Corin's car, a man with a very distinctive tattoo on his right hand. And, icing on the cake, the tattoo looks a bit like the lower jaw of the dude you've been calling Skullface."

Baxter paused to let the info permeate, while resisting the urge to drop the mic.

A few of the crowd members shouted questions, and so Natalie grabbed the microphone and said, "We've already run the tattoo through all of our databases with no luck. Now we need all of you to hit the streets and start asking your informants about a guy with the jaw of a skull on his right hand. This could be it, people. This could be our one shot at this guy."

75

Corin had started to protest when she felt a cold fire ignite on her right calf muscle. Then the cold retreated, leaving only the excruciating pain that seemed to be eating its way through her leg. It felt as though the bit of a drill press was being run all the way through her flesh.

With exhausting effort, she fought the cresting waves of agony. She felt slick with sweat, as if she had just run a marathon. Darkness threatened to overcome her, but she fought the urge to shut down and sleep. It seemed like several moments before she could think over the agony, but pain also had a way of stretching time.

Dr. Gladstone said, "The Mongols were brutal for sure. But think of them in comparison to Rome or Alexander the Great. It is said that Alexander the Great wept when he looked at his domain. *For there were no more worlds to conquer.* That's legend. In terms of actually leaving your mark on our species, let's judge by the extent of the conquered area, the number of years taken to conquer it, the number of years the area was under the rule of the king or his lineage, and his military efficiency and effectiveness. If you consider all those factors, then Genghis Khan is the clear winner. His was the largest land empire in history!"

Still panting, Corin said, "And how many people had to die for him to feel important?"

"I've seen some articles which propose that the great Khan and his horde were responsible for the deaths of as many as forty million people."

"And he's your role model?"

"I don't necessarily wish to cause anyone's death. But I also have no problems killing anyone who gets in my way. Genghis Khan was actually a just and fair ruler who sought to bring the entire world under his umbrella of protection and peace."

"He was a butcher."

With a shrug, Gladstone replied, "It is said that, in a city that was about to be sacked by the Mongol horde, women would walk up to the tallest points on their outer walls and fall to their deaths. They preferred death over the rape and suffering that was in store for them."

A freezing wind blew over the water and attacked her naked body, but Corin didn't mind the cold. It actually numbed a bit of the pain.

She asked, "Why are you telling me all this?"

"Because I want you to understand. I don't want to hurt you, Corin. I want you to be part of something that will never pass away. Something grand and beautiful. A new society."

"And torture is your sales pitch," she replied, still out of breath and feeling increasingly lightheaded.

"Our rules here are strict because we can't allow one scared and naïve child, who doesn't even know what she believes, to jeopardize all we're building. But once we get to the Island, everything will change, and you'll see that this is your opportunity to do something with your life."

Corin started to explain that she planned to survive this, kill him, and write a bestselling book about it. But the hate she was about to spew caught in her throat. A small voice in her head told her that losing a little dignity was a small price to pay for survival, and Corin could sense that further defiance would incite Derrick Gladstone into killing her slowly and painfully while trying to act as though he wasn't enjoying it.

Choosing her words carefully, she replied, "Fine, tell me all the details of this kingdom you're trying to build. Then I can make an educated decision."

"I like that attitude. After your punishment has been administered—and you've had some time to recover—I'd be happy to explain everything. We have no secrets here."

"I thought you just gave me my punishment."

He laughed. "No, my dear, that was merely a small taste. As I was explaining, I have learned much from studying the ways of the great Khan. One very popular method of execution among the Mongols was to pour molten silver into the eyes of the condemned. You've just experienced the pain of a few drops of that same melted metal."

"And I suppose if I decide I don't want to be part of your kingdom, then I get the silver in my eyes."

"It's important that I establish treason as the most deplorable of offenses."

"I didn't ask to be part of this."

"Soldiers are often drafted against their will. In fact, one of Genghis Khan's largest battles was a war with an already conquered province that refused to send him troops for one of his campaigns."

Tears streaming down her face, Corin said, "I don't want to go to war. I'm not a soldier."

"Oh, Corin, this fragile little mouse act of yours doesn't

work on me. And the war I'm referring to isn't one that requires battle. It's more a war of ideas. And ensuring the survival of our species can be a messy process."

"I've learned my lesson. Please, show me mercy. I'm begging you."

Gladstone brushed the hair from her face and wiped away her tears. Then he said, "Rules are rules. There are no exceptions. And believe it or not, seeing this through is going to hurt me worse than it hurts you. I hate to see perfection defiled, but sometimes scars and disabilities serve to make people more interesting. I have a few phone calls to make, and so Sonnequa will be completing your punishment. But don't worry, my dear, you'll survive, and we'll talk again real soon."

76

After the task force of SFPD detectives had asked their questions and dispersed, the rest of the team went to work, speaking with detectives and making connections. Marcus decided to approach the strange man in the Hawaiian shirt and chinos—who was currently having a heated discussion with Detective Ferrera—but Marcus wasn't looking to make friends.

He already disliked Kincaid, after that little presentation. This hippie stoner, dressed like the lost member of the Beach Boys, had stepped onto the stage and openly mocked him with a flipbook. Marcus considered Kincaid's little show to be the briefing room equivalent of thumbing your nose at someone in the schoolyard.

He said, "Detective Ferrera, I haven't had the pleasure of meeting your consultant here."

Trying to smile while still glaring at Kincaid, she said, "Yes, Baxter may act and dress like an idiot, but he actually has a large network of informants and connections. He occasionally helps the department."

Kincaid, who smelled like a Bob Marley concert, stuck out his hand, and Marcus shook it a bit too firmly. The private investigator didn't seem to notice. Instead, he said, "Call me Baxter." Then he pointed over at the goth chick— who was now sprawled out across a few of the padded chairs, swiping at her phone—and added, "That lovely lady is my partner, Ms. Jennifer Vasillo."

Marcus said, "That was a … *unique* presentation, Mr. Kincaid."

"Mr. Kincaid was my *grandpappy*. I'm just the Bax, man. But, thank you, and while we're on the subject, your presentation was damn impressive as well, Agent Williams. It even had little transitions and graphics and such. It was a work of art. Really, man, I dug it."

Unable to decide if Baxter was still making fun of him, Marcus clenched his jaw before he could respond with an insult.

After an awkward pause, Baxter asked, "So is this your first time in our fairest of cities?"

"It is my first time, but I don't know if I consider this a *real* city."

"Excuse me? San Francisco has been one of the world's premier cities since the time of the gold rush in 1849."

"I'm from New York. It was founded in 1624 and *is* the world's premier metropolis. To me, this isn't a city. It's more like a borough."

Baxter chuckled, which only further irritated Marcus. Then the private investigator said, "I hate New York. It's like drowning in concrete and business suits. My city is more for people who enjoy beauty and culture."

"You saying New York is ugly and lacking culture?"

"For me, New York is like being a rat in a maze."

Beside him, Marcus heard Ackerman say, "It feels that way for me as well, only the entire maze is made out of cheese. And I need to chew my way out."

Looking at the newcomer, Baxter said, "I like this guy

already. I adore that shirt, brother." Then, instead of a handshake, Baxter stuck out his fist for Ackerman to bump.

With a small wink at Marcus, Ackerman returned the gesture and bumped fists with the investigator.

With a roll of his eyes, Marcus said, "Baxter Kincaid, this is our special consultant Mr—"

"Francois Dantonio. Pleased to make your acquaintance," Ackerman interrupted.

Marcus resisted the urge to growl. Instead, he changed the subject. "If you have such a large network, Mr. Kincaid, why don't you put them to work finding our suspect?"

From beside Baxter, Detective Ferrera said, "You know what you're going to have to do about this tattoo thing, Bax."

Marcus noted the irritated, yet intimate, way that Natalie Ferrera spoke to Kincaid.

"Don't say it."

"You're going to have to pay a visit to Illustrated Dan. He'll be able to tell us exactly who's hand that is."

"I wouldn't count on that. Even Dan doesn't have complete files. And he's still pissed at me about that poker game we busted up during the Hutchinson case."

Marcus asked, "Who's Illustrated Dan?"

Detective Ferrera said, "He's an old friend of Baxter's, a lowlife biker whose entire body from the neck down is covered with tattoos."

Baxter said, "That's not completely accurate. He's saving a few spots on his thighs for future inspiration." Checking his watch, he added, "Even if we did pay a visit to Dan, it would have to wait until later."

"Why is that?" Marcus asked.

"I'm not sure where to find him right now. We'd probably

spend all morning looking. But I know exactly where he'll be this afternoon."

"Do you have his number?"

"He doesn't believe in cell phones. He has a pager for emergencies, but only his boys in the MC have those digits."

"I didn't know they still made pagers."

Ackerman said, "Actually, they're widely available. I've used them as detonators on several occasions."

Marcus, trying to quickly cover up his brother's odd comment, said, "Okay, we'll go with you this afternoon to meet with him."

"I don't think he'd appreciate me bringing feds around. No offense."

Looking at Ackerman, Marcus said, "Don't worry. We'll dress casual."

"He'll smell you from a mile away."

Detective Ferrera said, "We'll all go together, Baxter. Official business. He'll be down in Tenderloin, right?"

Baxter sighed and said, "Fine, but you're picking me up in your convertible, Nat. And after this, I'm done being an active part of this case. Homicides and kidnappings aren't my bag. The pimp hired me to find Corin and—"

Natalie interrupted, "Wait, what did you say? What pimp? Who's your client?"

"Crap, sorry, that was a slip-up on my part. I'd prefer my client's identity remain confidential on this one."

"Baxter, listen to me. Who is your client? Is it Faraz, that pimp who lives off Haight and Ash?"

Marcus noticed a subtle shift in body language and posture come over Kincaid. A second ago, the man seemed to not have a care in the world. Now, Kincaid appeared to have been struck with conviction and everything about his mannerisms had turned deadly serious.

Baxter asked, "Why are you asking me about Faraz?"

"Because Faraz Tarkani, his guys, and nearly all of his girls were gunned down last night."

77

In preparation for the meeting, Marcus had stressed to all of them that they needed to make inroads with the locals after the briefing. But, when the officers had been dismissed, Maggie only wanted to speak with one person: Baxter Kincaid. Unfortunately, she had been intercepted by a detective named Olivette, who wore way too much cologne, and possibly eyeliner.

When she noticed Baxter and his goth companion rush from the room after conversing with Marcus and Ackerman, she excused herself and hurried to catch up. Not because she cared how Marcus or his big brother had offended Kincaid, but because she was in need of a private investigator.

She finally intercepted the strange pair on the front steps of the old brick building. She shouted, "Mr. Kincaid!"

He turned back, and she saw a fire in his eyes that hadn't been there previously. She quickly said, "I'm sorry for whatever my colleagues may have said to upset you. But—"

"It's nothing like that. I just heard about an emergency that needs my attention. If you'll excuse me."

"Wait," she said. "I want to hire you. I need you to locate someone for me."

A look of confusion fell over his face, but he fished a business card from his pocket and handed it to her. "My cell is on there."

"Hold up. This will only take a second, I promise."

"Why do you need my help anyway? You have more resources than I do."

She quickly said, "I have my reasons, but I'd like to keep this between us. It's a personal matter." She held out a business card of her own. Only this one listed her info on the front, and on the back, she had already written her father's full name, date of birth, and a few last known addresses—having planned to hire Kincaid from the moment he was introduced as a private investigator.

She said, "I need you to find the man whose details are on the back of that card."

"How quickly do you want it done, and how much are you willing to spend?"

"As quickly as possible, and money is not an issue."

Baxter narrowed his eyes. "Who is this guy, and why do you need to find him so badly?"

"Does it matter?"

He shrugged and, after a glance down at the front and back of her business card, said, "Doesn't matter to me. I just ask because it may help me find him. But no worries, I'll flush out your wayward father like an old coon hound."

"How did you know the man I'm looking for is my father?"

Stuffing the card in his pocket, he said, "I'm a detective. That's how I roll. I'll be in touch real soon, Agent Carlisle."

78

The pictures of the two mansions, which the task force had pinned to the walls of the conference room, didn't nearly do the properties justice. Mr. King's estate jutted from the hills overlooking the bay like the nest of a large predatory bird. They had traveled up a private drive to reach a massive black security gate. The walls around the rest of the property were fifteen feet tall and made of concrete, but because of the steep slope of the hills into which the mansions had been built, the two massive white homes were on full display.

The structures reminded Ackerman of a white whale with her baby nestled under her fluke. The mansion closest to the security gate was the baby, and Mr. King's personal residence was the mother resting on the hill's summit. The baby was still a mansion by anyone's standards, but King's home was more than a mansion; it was a palace. The buildings were almost vulgar in their opulence, each adorned by massive white pillars and intricate carvings, with King's residence looking like a bastardized child of the White House and the Roman Coliseum.

Ackerman could sense that his brother was still angry with him over the Willoughby incident. He imagined that he should be concerned or ashamed or something of that nature, but he couldn't bring himself to worry about it. All he could do was follow his personal north star and hope to find his way through the fog of this life. He couldn't go around worrying every moment, afraid that he would offend one of the normals. Not only because he was incapable of such fear, but also because he refused to live according to the flawed standards of a broken world.

He had, however, acquiesced to his brother's request to change into a suit for the meeting with Oban. Ackerman suspected Marcus intended to burn his patriotic shirt of denim. A shame, but it was only a piece of fabric sewn together in a sweatshop somewhere. It was nothing worth fighting over.

Alongside the drive—before they reached the security gate—there were several parking spaces. Marcus pulled into one and said, "Let me do the talking."

Ackerman shrugged his shoulders. "That's fine. I'm more a man of action anyway."

"First, I don't want you to take *any* action. Second, you are definitely a talker."

"If I'm not supposed to do anything, then why am I here?"

"Because that's how the Director wanted it."

"You didn't want me on this case?" Ackerman asked.

"It's not that I didn't want you here. I just … You're kind of like an alcoholic. Or a drug addict. And you wouldn't expect an alcoholic to work at a bar and not give in to that constant temptation. I want to limit your exposure to situations that may tempt your darker nature."

Ackerman heard his father's voice, a memory from one of his childhood lessons. From somewhere over his shoulder, Thomas White's voice said, *You jam your fingers in here and here. That's good. Now rip out his trachea.*

He still kept his nails a little long to make easy work of penetrating flesh and killing with his hands, just as his father had instructed.

Ackerman shook his head. "Would you put Michael Jordan on the bench because he might be tempted to play basketball? I think not."

Marcus's expression traveled from confusion to annoyance.

Deciding to further explain, Ackerman said, "It reminds me of something Theodore Roosevelt once said—"

With a roll of his eyes, Marcus opened his door, stepped from the rented Chevy Impala, and started toward the intercom panel beside the security gate, which looked as though it could withstand the onslaught of a tank.

Thomas White whispered, *Now rip out his trachea.*

Ackerman sat dumbfounded for a moment. Having killed so many people due to slights of much less magnitude, he was discovering that his little brother's desire to "protect" him really meant locking him in a cage of a different kind. But he supposed it didn't truly matter. He would keep doing his thing until someone killed him. And he had always found it better to ask for forgiveness than permission.

To the empty vehicle, he said, "Don't worry, Father. I'm sure there will be some trachea ripping on the agenda soon."

By the time he reached the gate, Marcus had already pressed the button and said, "We have a one o'clock appointment with Oban Nassar."

Ackerman added, "The scheduling was done by a mutual acquaintance of ours named Willoughby."

The guard on the other end of the intercom paused for a moment, likely verifying their appointment and clearance with a superior, and then said, "Mr. Oban will meet you in the lobby. Leave your vehicle where it is and enter through the small door to the right of the main gate."

Ackerman whispered, "They must be worried that someone may drive a bomb into the inner courtyard."

Moving directly to the metal walkthrough door, Marcus said nothing.

The darkness swelling inside him, Ackerman followed his brother but said, "Have you been sleeping well? You're especially pissy today."

"You already disobeyed my orders at the intercom."

"I merely felt that you should stress who had delivered the message."

"No more talking."

"As you wish, baby brother."

With a low growl, a flare of his nostrils, and a crack of his neck, Marcus opened the security door. It led to another checkpoint where two armed men wanded them for metal and performed a set of thorough pat downs. Then they were escorted into the lobby of the smaller mansion. A long staircase flowed like a snake along the three-story room's right side. There were two guards at the top of the staircase and more in the corners of the massive foyer. All were well armed and alert.

The interior of the mansion was just as color starved as its exterior. White marble floors, gold trim and crown molding, crystal chandeliers, and a smell like fresh linen hanging in the air. With two more guards armed with H&K assault rifles at his side, Mr. Oban entered from a twelve-foot-tall archway opposite the sprawling staircase. Oban wore a charcoal suit over a black shirt and purple tie. His skin was the color of amber, and his hair matched the gray and black of his tailored suit.

With the smile of a desert fox, Oban said, "Welcome to King and Associates. Please, let's speak in my office."

He led them up the stairs and past two more guards, who fell in step behind them. Ackerman wondered what would come next. Would Oban feel the need to establish dominance and have them seized and searched? Maybe even killed on the spot, just to be safe?

Normally, Ackerman would strike first, but then Marcus would be upset. So he decided it best to let things play out a bit further.

Without a word, Oban led them down a long hallway and past a series of closed doors with gold plates displaying the occupant's name and position in the company. The last door on the right, toward the back of the mansion, read "Oban Nassar - Chief Operations Officer."

One of Oban's personal guards opened the door, while the others stepped inside. Then the COO gestured for his guests to enter. Once they were all inside the office of white marble and dark wood, Ackerman counted a total of six armed opponents, plus Oban himself, who looked to be in excellent physical condition.

The guards raised their weapons. Closing and locking the door behind them, Oban said, "Please, remove your shirts and get on your knees."

"Screw you," Marcus replied.

"Let me rephrase that. Get on your knees now or my men will shoot you in the legs, and I'll have all the skin removed from the lower halves of your bodies. Then we'll talk again and see if your attitude has been properly adjusted."

Ackerman laughed and said, "That certainly sounds exhilarating. I've skinned victims before, but I've never been flayed myself, at least not to such a degree. I would suggest hanging us upside down when you perform the act. If you plan to start at our feet, that is. Less blood that way. And the other way around, we would be dead before we could have another conversation."

79

Dr. Derrick Gladstone unlocked the steel security door and wheeled into the compound's control room. This was the nerve center of his sanctuary. From here, Derrick could see every inch of his kingdom. And thanks to an old friend—the brilliant killer known as Judas—the compound, especially the Diamond Room, was equipped with the latest and greatest in monitoring technology.

What had once been the resort's executive offices now pulled double duty as the control center and his mother's cell. He had provided the old witch with a comfortable bed in the corner, three square meals, and a wheelchair. What else did she need? Mother had Parkinson's so bad that she had basically lost all control of her own movements anyway. What more would she receive in a nursing home? Perhaps a television, but she had something better: a front row seat to everything happening inside her son's kingdom.

"Hello, Mother," Derrick said. "Are you enjoying the show?"

Her eyes were already filled with tears. The terrible truth of Parkinson's disease was that it attacked the body but left the mind intact.

Derrick followed her shaky gaze and saw Sonnequa on one of the monitors administering Corin's punishment. The sound feed wasn't active for that monitor, but with a turn of a dial on the control board, the sound of Corin's screams filled the room. With a small grin creeping onto his face, he reduced the volume and said, "I'm so happy you're able to bear witness to the culmination of your legacy."

It seemed to him that Mother tried to shake her head *No,* but he found it difficult to know for sure among all her involuntary movements.

"Don't bother thanking me, Mother. What's that you said? Oh, you'd like me to read you a story? Perhaps your favorite?"

She closed her eyes.

Derrick wheeled over and opened a desk drawer, from which he removed an old leather journal. Opening to a marked page, he began to read aloud: "I don't know how I will ever explain to the boys. I know they idolized their father, but they didn't understand him the way I did. He was a terrible man. What I did, I did for my boys as much as for myself. The bastard wanted to trade me in for a younger model and was planning to abandon us. So I shot him in the back of the head."

Tears rolled down Mother's cheeks.

Derrick whispered, "I just love that one, don't you? I'm surprised you didn't read that to us as a bedtime story when we were boys. And in case you're wondering, Mother, I am knowingly torturing you. Yes, I enjoy it. And yes, I think you deserve it."

She opened her eyes and twitched.

"I want you to remember everything, Mother. I want to constantly remind you that you showed me all that is broken with this world. And Father ... he showed me how to make it right. I could perhaps forgive you for the murder of such a great man. I suppose, in some twisted way, I can understand your feelings on the matter. But your hatred could have died with him instead of turning its attention on your sons."

She tried to raise her arm, but all her muscles would do was tremble. Derrick respected the ruthlessness of Mother's affliction.

He said, "I heard from Dennis this morning. Your precious baby is wanting to pay you a visit. At first, I was rather upset about the whole thing, but with our declaration of independence forthcoming, a visit from my worthless brother actually presents an interesting opportunity. Dennis is without a doubt the weakest link in our genetic chain. He exemplifies the weak, ignorant complacency that is eroding our society. I think I'm going to kill Dennis and his family, while you watch. Kill two birds with one stone, so to speak. I'll get to taste your pain as the favorite child dies, and I'll also be ensuring that his inferior genetic makeup isn't allowed to spread."

She shook violently and turned her eyes from him.

"And don't worry, Mother, once we reach the Island, I'll find plenty of other ways of making your life interesting. Perhaps I'll start by slowly removing pieces of you. I could begin with your toes and work my way up. Average life expectancy is now 81.2 years for women in the USA. If you even get close to that, it will mean that we have ample time for me to remind you of past sins."

80

Oban Nassar walked over to his desk—a black-and-gold marble monstrosity that screamed of decadence and power—and picked up a handful of dates. He took a bite of the sweet fruit as he walked around and leaned against the front of his desk. He said, "I'm sure you gentleman can understand our concern for security, considering the audacious and insulting nature of your attack on one of our associates merely to get our attention."

Ackerman could feel the telepathic bullets Marcus was sending his way. Perhaps he had been a bit overzealous, but the message seemed to have been received in the manner he had intended.

He said, "Sometimes a situation calls for a certain level of audacity."

Marcus snapped, "Shut up, Frank. My partner didn't mean to insult you, Mr. Nassar. He can be a bit … abrasive."

Oban raised a date to his mouth and bit down to the pit. "Are you aware of our company's reputation, gentlemen? There are some horrible rumors floating around. Jealous competitors and governmental bureaucracies claim that our methods are extreme, but I feel that we have always displayed a measured response dictated purely by the nature of our business."

Turning away from Oban, Ackerman faced the nearest of the armed guards, who stood beside a row of dark bookshelves. With a smile, he said, "The nature of the business we have come to discuss warranted a proper introduction."

"Attacking one of our associates is how you like to introduce yourselves?"

Ackerman replied, "No, that was merely setting the appointment, and the stage. This is the introduction."

On the last word, he leaped toward the closest bookshelf, pushing off the third level and diving toward the nearest guard. His bicep collided with the gunman's throat. Ackerman squeezed and used the stunned man to change direction again, pulling the guard off balance and coming up directly behind the man. Just as he had mentally choreographed, he then grabbed the man by the gun arm, wrenched up, and tore the shoulder from its socket. In the same motion, he grabbed the H&K rifle by its grip and, holding it like a handgun, pointed it toward Oban.

Ackerman said, "Here's the thing. Well, the first thing. You don't really want to kill us, because you need to know who we actually work for. These men have been ordered to harm us only if absolutely necessary. That creates a hesitation in their actions, which leaves an opening for attack."

Oban took another bite and said, "I'll make a note for future reference."

Ackerman kicked the guard away and made a show of disassembling the assault rifle, piece by piece, dropping each component to the floor. His fingers flew over the weapon with intimate knowledge. While in various institutions and in other down times throughout his life, he had studied all manner of weapons to their exact specifications. In those days, his access to the Internet was extremely limited, but a keen intellect could find ways to learn most anything.

He named off the components as his fingers gripped and pushed against the release mechanisms.

Once the last piece of the weapon had hit the floor, he continued, "Second thing. If the kind of service we have come to offer states that we can reach out and touch anyone, anywhere, anytime … Then how better to prove ourselves than by showing how easily we could kill you. But if we had come to harm you, then we would have done it already. Now, can we dispense with this nonsense and discuss business?"

Oban finished off the last of the dates and, to his men, said, "Stand down." Then he gestured for two chairs to be brought over. "Please. Have a seat. You were right about my desire to know more about who employs the both of you, along with the Asian woman from last night."

Ackerman dropped into one of the chairs. Marcus seemed hesitant, his jaw clenched and his face growing red. But, after a moment, he too sat down in front of Oban Nassar's desk. Ackerman said, "Let's just get the obvious question off the table. Are we cops or law enforcement of any kind? Well, I can assure you that I'm not on the side of any law beyond God and nature."

Oban crossed his arms. "Why would you ever think that our company would want to hire a service that can, as you said, 'reach out and touch someone?' We're an investment and asset-management firm. We have no need of such services."

Marcus said, "We've done work back east for Eddie Caruso. We're branching out, and he told us that you own north Cali. He suggested we reach out to you."

"Yes, your associates mentioned that to Mr. Willoughby. But I also knew because Eddie—or The Great Caruso, as they call him now—contacted me this morning. He let me know to be expecting you."

Ackerman maintained his expression despite the urge to roll his eyes. Marcus didn't seem to be keeping his composure quite as well. His brother's voice was almost a snarl when he replied, "And what did dearest Eddie have to say about us? Nice things, I hope."

Oban smiled. "I assume that you're Marcus. Eddie told me all about you. He said you were a cop."

81

Stefan Granger pulled his second Buick in two days to the curb, having ditched his other car and purchased a replacement after the brothel mission. He considered what weapons he would need for his current undertaking. After some thought, he decided on his bare fists, with the silenced Beretta in his coat as a backup. He wasn't excited about what he was about to do, but it was a necessity. Unser had grown increasingly bolder with his threats, and now the old man had sealed his fate by sending federal agents to the cemetery. Normally, cops at the graveyard weren't a problem for Granger, because they were either dead or grieving. It did bother him, however, to have officers hunting him down and discovering the place where he had spent half his life.

It was a rare stroke of luck that the agents hadn't probed deeper or asked to speak with the caretaker.

Granger had once considered Leland Unser to be a friend, but now his old mentor had betrayed him to his enemies. And Father had always taught him that revenge should be swift and complete.

Stepping from the Buick and locking the old vehicle's door manually with the key, Stefan Granger walked toward the brick-and-glass facade of Unser's Gym. The place had undergone three makeovers since the days when he had started his training. He didn't particularly like the new look. There was something a bit too girly and self-absorbed about it. But Granger also understood that anyone in the service industry had to adapt to the needs of their clientele.

He knew the door would be locked and the gym closed. Unser, a devout Catholic, refused access to his facilities on a Sunday to all but his chosen few.

Through the glass, Granger saw Unser and several of his guys practicing footwork. He removed his silenced Beretta and shot out the glass of the gym's entry door. As he stepped over the broken shards, pistol still in hand, he had everyone's attention. There were five of them, not including the old man. He recognized the group as one of Unser's primary trainers and his four top guys.

Granger smiled as he rolled his shoulders and stretched his muscles. If he was going to murder his mentor, he might as well have some fun while doing it.

Unser stepped forward and yelled, "You crazy son of a bitch! You have some real balls busting in here. But I guess anyone can pretend to be a big man when he's holding a gun."

Still smiling, Granger undid the slide on the Beretta and pulled back the mechanism, essentially rendering the weapon useless until it was reassembled. Then he gently laid the gun atop one of the nearby weight benches.

Granger saw the fear in Leland Unser's eyes. The old man had trained him during his youth and knew what he was capable of. Or, at least, the old man thought he did. In truth, Unser had only seen a fraction of the methods of destruction at Granger's disposal.

He ran his fingers across a straight bar, which rested on the supports above the bench. It was a standard Olympic-sized bar that someone had apparently been using to bench-press.

It was much like the one he had at home, except this one had started to bend slightly from neglect.

He could hear the other men scuttling about and arming themselves, but he ignored them. Unser said, "Why are you here, kid?"

"You know what you did. Don't add insult to injury by playing dumb. Do you remember what you told me when I came to you to be trained? I could never afford your fees, but I begged you to let me work off the debt. Do you remember the warning you gave me?"

Unser looked toward the floor, regret in his eyes. Then he whispered, "I told you the thing about making a deal with the devil is that, one way or another, the devil always collects."

Stefan laughed. "You always did have a way with words, old man."

"And you always had a way with your fists. You're the best fighter I've ever trained, and yet you're my biggest disappointment."

Granger had been prepared to hear something along those lines, but the insult still stung. He had once idolized the barrel-chested old boxer. But he had outgrown fighting for sport, preferring battles with higher stakes. For him, fighting wasn't a game; it was a way of life, an existential philosophy.

Unser asked, "Who told you about the feds?"

He replied, "One of your stable of young studs informed me about the visit and the information you gave them. You really can't trust anyone these days."

To Unser's credit, he didn't try to deny the allegation. He said, "I always suspected that some kind of cop would show up asking questions about you and your Diamond Room. I think I always knew you were a monster. I just thought maybe you could be *my* monster. I thought maybe I could beat that out of you, show you a better way. But I made up my mind a long time ago that if anyone ever came asking about you, then I would send them out to your dad at the cemetery. I figured he would be the only one who really knew what rock you were hiding under and how to find you."

"Why do you take such offense to my choice of profession?"

"'Profession'? You use the skills I taught you to kill people. That practically makes me an accessory."

"You realize the consequences of your actions?" Granger looked up and saw that all of Unser's top guys had armed themselves. One gripped a baseball bat that he must have retrieved from the back office. Another held a switchblade. Another had grabbed two thirty-five pound dumbbells, apparently planning to use them like weighted gloves. Granger recognized the final opponent as Unser's number-one contender prospect. This last man simply cracked his knuckles and stepped forward.

Stefan Granger removed his jacket and rolled up his sleeves. Then he stepped up to the Olympic straight bar and snatched it up one-handed. Then, to test the weight and balance of his new weapon, Granger spun the forty-five pound Olympic bar as if it was a bow staff, twirling it through the air and around his body.

After a few seconds of showing off, Granger looked at his opponents with a lopsided grin and whispered, "Get over here."

The young prospect with the aluminum baseball bat rushed in first, ready to hit a homerun. An aluminum bat wasn't a bad weapon, in the right hands. The thing about a bat or club was that the wielder needed lots of room for the swing, which wasn't a problem in the open gym.

Unfortunately for him, the softball slugger had completely underestimated the speed at which Granger could wield his makeshift bow staff. What his opponents didn't know was that, between sets, Granger would often grab a bar and spin it like a weapon. Not that he had ever intended to use one while in combat, but the heavy training increased the strength of his blows with a lighter staff.

Now, just as he had practiced so many times, he whipped up the end of the Olympic bar and connected it with the onrushing power of the baseball bat. The two metal objects collided with a resounding clang. The young man holding the bat screamed in pain as the intense vibrations traveled up the bat to the muscles in his arms. Obviously, he had forgotten how well aluminum bats transferred force.

The attacker's arms dropped to the ground as they absorbed the vibration. But Granger wasn't done yet. He spun on his heels and twisted the other side of the Olympic bar back to collide with his attacker's skull. Metal connected with bone in a sickening crunch, and Granger drove the blow home, pushing the man all the way to the floor and slamming the bar flat against the concrete, crushing his opponent's skull.

Blood spattered all over Granger's face and torso.

Thinking of his days as the undisputed *Mortal Kombat* champion, he said, "Flawless victory. Who's next?"

82

Marcus could feel the grim reaper close by, hovering in the shadows, watching with hungry eyes. And he couldn't blame this screwup on anyone but himself. Except maybe Eddie. Trying to say something to save their lives, he offered, "I was drummed out of the NYPD a lifetime ago."

Pausing a moment, Marcus analyzed the room and their available options. Ackerman had already made his play with one of the guards, who had rushed from the room seeking help with his dislocated shoulder. The other gunmen would be on edge, and even Marcus's big brother couldn't outsmart a bullet.

Taking his seat behind the black-and-gold desk, Oban Nassar said, "Once a cop, always a cop."

Ackerman said, "Do I look like a cop to you? Don't worry about him. You can deal with me if you don't like my associate's previous profession."

"I don't know anything about either of you."

Marcus asked, "What did Eddie tell you? I'm sure this is just a misunderstanding."

With a nod to some of his men, Oban said, "It doesn't matter what Mr. Caruso had to say. I don't trust anyone. So if you really want to do business with this company and myself, then you'll have to prove yourself with something more than words."

The door to the office opened and two of the armed

guards carried a hooded and bloody man into the room. They laid out a plastic sheet and propped the hooded man up in a wooden folding chair in the center of the plastic. Then they placed a small stand between the desk and the hooded man. An ornate box rested atop the stand. Marcus gauged the dimensions and estimated the box was large enough to hold anything from cigars to a .45-caliber Colt 1911 pistol.

The hooded man smelled like vinegar, and Marcus could hear him softly whimpering beneath his covering.

Marcus asked, "What's in the box?"

Oban replied, "This man has stolen from Mr. King, which means that if you wish to do business with us, then he has also stolen from you. But more than that, he has endangered our operations and leaked information. Consider this your job interview. Pass or fail. Anyone with whom we would want to do business already knows what's in the box and what they need to do with it."

Ackerman said, "Oh, I see. He's wanting a freebie, Marcus. Would you like the honors or shall I? Wait, are we responsible for cleanup as well, because I refuse to cleanup afterward for free. Plus, I would need to grab my overalls from the car—"

Oban said, "We'll discuss those details once the interview is complete."

"That's all well and good, but you see, I'm a professional. I don't go around rubbing DNA evidence with dead men. Please, don't misunderstand me. I'd be all for scooping out this man's intestines and bathing in his blood, but only if I'm assured the proper methods of disposal will be implemented after the fact."

It took Marcus a moment to realize that his brother's rambling was actually orchestrated to buy him time to formulate a plan, and so he decided not to waste the opportunity. He analyzed every aspect of the situation, every variable, every action they could take, every consequence, every outcome, every motivation, every flaw to be exploited.

They couldn't shoot someone just to prove themselves, no matter the circumstances. He could take the gun and use it to shoot his way through the five men armed with assault rifles, but that sounded like a good way for everyone to get very bloody.

He forced himself to look at the scenario from Oban's perspective. What was the underworld COO trying to accomplish? Even by suggesting that they execute this man, Oban was making himself vulnerable for prosecution under the RICO guidelines established by the Racketeer Influenced and Corrupt Organizations Act. As federal agents, they could arrest him on the spot for such an order. And not only Oban, but under RICO statutes, they could also go after everyone affiliated with Oban. A mistake like that could topple Mr. King's whole empire like a house of cards.

Unless that was the whole point...

If they did have some kind of micro transmitter and listening device embedded in their clothing, then a SWAT team would already be storming the building. Or if they left and made a move, they would be revealing themselves as cops.

Marcus's mind flipped through the possibilities at rapid speed, disregarding ideas, searching for a solution.

As he replayed exactly what Oban had said, he realized

that the COO had actually not told them to harm the hooded man at all. He had merely suggested that a friend of their organization would know what to do.

Which also meant that the box couldn't contain a loaded gun. If it did, that could be used as evidence against Oban and re-open the RICO possibilities.

And that clue lead Marcus to further examine the hooded man sitting atop the plastic.

Ackerman was still arguing about some small aspect of the proposed murder. But Marcus, having found his solution, interrupted and said, "How about I tell you how this plays out, Mr. Nassar?"

With steepled fingers, Oban said, "By all means, enlighten us."

"The box contains a gun. Probably one loaded with dummy rounds, otherwise the weight would be off. You're an intelligent man, not the type to make mistakes. A man like you would be intimately familiar with the RICO laws. If you actually thought we were cops, you wouldn't risk prosecution. But you haven't really risked anything, have you?"

Oban said nothing in reply, and his expression gave nothing away.

Marcus continued, "That brings me to our hooded guest. Did you really think I wouldn't notice your hands, body language, and bone structure, Eddie?"

He let the revelation of the hooded man's identity hang in the air a moment. Then the man whose face was hidden beneath the black cloth started laughing. Eddie Caruso reached up and removed the hood from his head. Chuckling and shaking his head, Eddie said, "After how much fun we had last night, Marcus, I simply couldn't resist flying out and surprising you. Plus, it gave me a chance to check on my business interests on the west coast."

83

Maggie Carlisle ran the tub up to the point of overflow, and then she sat with her knees to her chest and sobbed quietly, not wanting the FBI protective detail outside the door to hear her. Early that morning, after the briefing at Richmond Station, she had told Marcus that she wasn't feeling well. She knew he wouldn't object. He didn't need her, and she couldn't bring herself to care what was happening with the Oban Nassar meeting.

As her gaze traveled around the tub, a long-lost part of her brain told her that she was probably sitting in a venerable Pandora's box of microscopic invaders. But she couldn't make herself care about that either.

All she seemed able to care about these days—all that occupied her thoughts—was her brother, the man who took him, and the family that was destroyed.

Stretching a naked arm out of the tub, she rummaged through her bag, searching for her flask of vodka. Instead, her hand came back with her switchblade knife.

Maggie had always heard of women committing suicide in the bathtub. They would slash their wrists, and the warm water would cause the blood to flow more quickly or something like that. She had heard the explanation on one of their cases, but she couldn't recall the details. She suspected that both Marcus and Ackerman could have rattled off the exact reasons. Different parts of her seemed to simultaneously envy, pity, and despise both of them.

Stowing the switchblade, she retrieved her flask and took a long shot of cheap vodka.

She spilled a bit of the liquid into the tub as the sound of a thumping rumble reverberated around the bathroom. Quickly screwing the metal lid in place, she grabbed for her cell phone, which was vibrating against the tile floor of the bathroom.

Maggie didn't recognize the number, which meant it could have been the call she was waiting for. Leaning out of the tub and sticking the phone to her ear, she said, "Hello?"

"Agent Carlisle, this is Baxter. I found your father for you."

She was struck speechless for a moment but was finally able to say, "That was … wow … that was fast. I'm impressed, Mr. Kincaid."

"Mr. Kincaid was my *grandpappy*. Actually, he was *Professor* Kincaid, but that's a long story for another time. You can call me Baxter, cuteness. Or the Bax. Or El Baxterino—if, you know, you're not into the whole brevity thing." This made him chuckle uncontrollably and add, "Classic."

Maggie had no idea what he was talking about at this point. She said, "That's great, Baxter. Can you send me—"

"My associate has already instructed the magical email faeries to deliver all the pertinents directly to your account posthaste."

"I'm sorry. Are you saying you emailed it to me?"

"I'm sure it's already waiting in your inbox."

"Thank you, Mr ... Baxter. I really appreciate your help. Please send me a bill to the same address, and I'll—"

"It's on the house, cuteness. No worries. But you could let me take you to dinner tonight. Your charming company would be more than adequate compensation for a humble servant's time."

Again, the strange private investigator had struck her speechless. Stumbling over her words, she said, "I really appreciate your help and the offer. No offense, but I already have enough ... big personalities in my life."

An infectious laugh started on the opposite end of the line. A smile involuntarily crept across her face. Maggie couldn't help but feel cheered up just by talking with the strange man.

After a moment of chortling, Baxter said, "I can definitely understand that, Agent Carlisle. If you change your mind, you know where to find me. But I warn you, don't you dare go out on the town with me expecting not to fall madly in love. The fact is that once you go Bax, you never go back."

She chuckled. "Is that so? Then why are you single?"

"Because I'm picky about who I take out on the town and *allow* to fall in love with me."

"It looked to me like you had taken at least two of the ladies in that room today 'out on the town.' Whatever that means."

"It's complicated. One was an old flame, and the other was a fire not sure whether it wants to spark. I'm not currently in a relationship with either one."

"Do they know that?"

He laughed. "See, this is why I wanted you to have dinner

with me. You're delightful. What about you and your team leader? What's the status on that fire?"

"Now you're just grasping at straws, there's no way you—"

"The Bax can sense these things. Don't try to deny it."

Maggie was quiet a moment, trying to think back on the briefing for what she had done to give away her and Marcus's relationship. Finally, she said, "That flame is still flickering."

"Well, Agent Carlisle, it's none of my business, but maybe you should do some deep pondering on the fact that you've been flirting with me all this time, and you just now offered that you're in a relationship. If I were you, I'd either fan those flames or let them go out."

84

The Great Caruso smiled and asked, "Are you surprised to see me?"

Marcus replied, "Oh, Eddie … If I woke up tomorrow with my head sewn to the carpet, I wouldn't be more surprised than I am right now."

Ackerman laughed and said, "'Head sewn to the carpet,' that's a good one. The victim would need to be drugged while they slept in order to accomplish something like that without waking them, though. Perhaps one of those curare-related drugs."

"Shut up, Frank. Don't get me wrong, Eddie, it's wonderful to see you again so soon, but to what do we owe the pleasure?"

Eddie stood from the metal chair and said to Oban's guards, "Can one of you please bring me a clean shirt and a more comfortable chair?" The gunman closest to the door nodded and hurried from the room.

Moving to the front of Oban's marble desk, Eddie leaned on the edge of the massive piece of furniture and crossed his arms. "To be honest, I really enjoyed catching up with you. And I really like the business plan you're developing. So I thought: *Hey, I've got a private jet.* Why not fly out and make this a personal introduction? It was Oban's idea to have a little fun with you, but I was happy to play along. And I was right, wasn't I, Mr. Nassar?"

King's righthand man nodded and said, "I was most impressed by both your mental acuity and physical demonstrations. The two of you appear to be quite the team, Agent Williams."

Marcus made his face stone, betraying no emotion. But on the inside, his brain scrambled for a reply. What the hell had Eddie told Oban Nassar? Marcus had always learned that if you weren't sure what to say, then you should keep your mouth shut. And that's what he did. He let the silence hang in the air, hoping that his brother wouldn't break it before one of their adversaries.

After a moment, Eddie chuckled and said, "Don't blow a gasket, *Rainman*. I told you that you should have revealed yourself as feds from the start. That's the biggest reason I flew out. I figured you'd do something stupid like this. But don't worry, I explained everything to my associate."

Marcus said, "We appreciate that. Anything come out of that discussion I should be aware of."

"Well, I told Oban all about your current position within a corrupt federal outfit funded by black budget funds. And how you're leveraging that to eliminate the criminal competition. I told him you're a good man to know and do business with, that you have a lot of connections and power. I even explained how you're a second generation dirty cop. Ain't that right, Marcus?"

He wanted to scream, to ram his fist into Eddie's face over and over again, but he remained stone. "I suppose so. It was kind of you to pave the way for us. Did you tell Mr. Nassar that we're here hunting the Gladiator and have plans to dismantle Demon's whole network?"

"No, I'll let you fill him in on the gory details. But I tell you what, it's a darn good thing I decided to make the trip. Oban was planning to execute you. You see, a few of King's men have been following you since the Willoughby incident and saw your group head over to Richmond Station to meet with the cops. Oban had already dug up what he could find about you and your team and was planning to have all of you put to bed before you even reached this meeting." Eddie shrugged and grinned from ear to ear. "You could say that you owe me your lives."

85

Corin lay atop an ocean of white silk, weeping, and trying to regain some of her lost fortitude. The pain was now only a dull ache. After administering punishment, the Good Wife had dressed her wounds and given her some type of sedative. She couldn't imagine the eventual scars that would come from this incident, both physical and emotional. She wondered if she'd spend the rest of her life in a wheelchair. If so, Dr. Gladstone would probably have her put down like a horse with a broken leg.

Still, through all the pain, the unbreakable girl at the beach house kept her distance from reality and continued making plans.

Gladstone had mentioned that he was headed to his office to make some calls. That made it pretty evident that he had a communications rig of some kind. But then again, as batshit crazy as Dr. Derrick was, it could've meant that he was going to consult with the ghost of Genghis Khan. Perhaps it was best that she just gave up. Perhaps she should just let exhaustion drag her down to sleep and hope to never wake up again …

A voice in Corin's head whispered, *Get up*.

She needed to find Derrick's office. She should explore the halls and take inventory, always searching for everyday items that could be used as weapons.

Again, the voice whispered, *Get up*.

Despite many attempts to make her body respond to the urgency that her mind felt, her muscles refused to move. Perhaps she should just rest her eyes a moment …

She awoke to Gladstone parting her white curtain and saying, "No rest for the wicked, Corin. Let's go for a roll. And I apologize if I made that sound like a request."

Fearing the punishment non-compliance would bring, she struggled her way over to the edge of the bed and lifted herself into her wheelchair. Gladstone occupied his own chair, but his was much more sophisticated than her own. She examined his chair for the first real time, admiring its modern design and utilitarian elegance.

As she fell into her chair, Corin closed her eyes and said a quick prayer to a God whom she didn't really know. *Please give me the strength to kill this man.*

"Roll with me, my dear," the handsome young doctor said as he used his tightly muscled arms to roll away from her silk cell.

She had little choice but to follow, but she struggled to keep pace with Gladstone, who seemed to consider wheelchair ballet an Olympic event. She wondered why he was keeping up the ruse. He obviously didn't require the chair, unless he had some condition where he couldn't stand for long periods of time. But that didn't seem to make sense. She wasn't sure what to think. She wasn't sure what was real anymore. From time to time, the fact that she was in hell still crept into her mind.

Gladstone was halfway across the ballroom before he realized that she had fallen behind. Spinning around on a dime, he smiled and said, "What's wrong, Corin? Do you not have the strength to keep up? If so, I would like to remind you that only the strong survive."

Unable to hold her hate inside, she snapped back, "Is that the way it's going to be in your new society? The strong preying on the weak, pushing them down to raise themselves up. Sounds like the same old world to me, just a different tyrant."

As he waited for her to catch up, he said, "I think if you look at all of these so-called tyrants throughout the ages, you'll find healthy doses of insecurity, mania, religiosity, and, most of all, selfish motivations."

"And your motives aren't selfish?"

"The only way for a human life to have meaning is to have a positive influence upon your society and your species as a whole. My own plans and selfish motives are always secondary to my primary goal."

"I still don't see how one group of kidnapped women forced to carry your children has a positive influence on either our species or our culture."

"As I said previously, Miss Campbell, this compound and your sisters are merely the tip of my iceberg."

Gladstone led her through the condemned resort to an elevator she had spotted earlier. The thought had crossed her mind to slip inside and see if any of the buttons were labeled "Parking Garage." They took the elevator to the top floor. Gladstone said, "This used to be the resort's presidential suite, but I found it lacking. So I had it retrofitted to serve as a true *presidential* suite."

"Is that what you're going to call yourself? President Gladstone? Or maybe President Doctor Derrick?"

"I've actually given that quite a bit of thought, and I haven't decided yet. King Gladstone, perhaps. Maybe

Emperor Gladstone. Once we get to the island, I suppose we could take a vote."

"'Emperor' doesn't really imply democracy."

"I sometimes like to re-use antiquated terminology, in order to help us remember the past. Those who forget the past are doomed to repeat it. And human history is certainly full of mistakes to learn from. But words like *Emperor* and *Democracy* will take on a new meaning. I suppose the most accurate term would be *Progenitor*."

As the elevator doors parted to reveal the presidential suite, Corin stared at the room beyond and said, "Is this your room or a seafood restaurant?"

Derrick laughed. "I find the underwater motif to be quite soothing."

The presidential suite looked as if it had been designed by Captain Nemo. It was all shades of blue and flowing lines. The ceiling was recessed and shimmering lights shined across it, creating the impression that it was made of water. A massive fish tank rested in the center of the room and bustled with all manner of tropical fish. The massive space contained two sitting areas and was configured as a kitchen and dining room, complete with an ornate crystal chandelier. It even smelled like an ocean breeze within Derrick's personal domain.

"I've always loved the ocean," he said. "I used to be quite the surfer, before my accident. This is, of course, a central gathering area. My bedroom is to the left, and Sonnequa's room is on the right. I consider that the First Lady's suite. But that is an appointed position that is always in flux, Corin. I could easily see you as my first lady instead of Sonnequa. But one step at a time. Before we get into that, I'd like to show you something very important in my bedroom."

86

Marcus felt dead tired, exhausted enough that a few moments rest was a real possibility. He had a little over an hour before they were to be picked up by Detective Ferrera, and he planned to squeeze out every second of sleep he could. As he stumbled into the hotel room—which he shared with Maggie—and pulled off the suit that had been strangling him all morning, he didn't even bother to flip on the lights.

The meeting with Oban certainly hadn't gone as expected, but the result was more or less what Marcus had hoped. Eddie had been his usual blustering self, but Marcus had to admit that his old friend had probably saved their lives and unlocked a door that they could have never opened on their own. In fact, Oban Nassar had graciously invited them to a private viewing of the Diamond Room, a break which could make all the difference between finding the missing women and Agent Fuller dead or alive.

It wasn't until he reached the bed that he noticed something about the space was off.

The bed had been made hotel-room style—two standard pillows and sheets beneath a floral bedspread. The problem was that Maggie never allowed the room to be attended by the maids or for the beds to be made. The first thing she had done upon their arrival, as was the case in every hotel room they stayed in, was to strip the sheets and bedspread and disinfect the room with a special concoction of her own that was supposed to kill 99.9% of bacteria as well as the infamous bed bugs that were making a comeback in the US in recent years. Maggie had been growing increasingly concerned about the tiny invaders and was constantly sending him articles on the subject.

After disinfection, Maggie would cover the bed with a set of sheets and blankets that had been sterilized and coated with anti-bedbug juices at home.

But now, the hotel sheets and bedspread had been draped over the mattress. As he stared at the outline of the floral shapes in the nearly dark room, he thought of the woodgrain of his aunt's coffin on the day he had placed her body to rest.

He flipped on the lights and also found Maggie's suitcase missing. His heart seemed to stop beating at the strange finality of the moment. He remembered the same heartbreak upon losing his aunt, the woman who had raised him and loved him like her own.

Scolding himself for such thoughts, he rationalized that there must be a reasonable explanation. He asked himself why his thoughts first turned to Maggie leaving him. Was it guilt? A sense that her leaving would be what he deserved?

Checking his sidearm—as he almost compulsively did at the smallest sign of danger—Marcus moved to the hallway and then over to Dylan's room. He gave the proper knock code, and a few seconds later, Agent Lee—the beautiful young black woman with the short-cropped curly hair—opened the door. She must have seen something strange in his eyes because she immediately said, "What's wrong?"

"Have you seen Agent Carlisle today?"

"Yeah, she spent some time with Dylan and then left. She told me to let you know that she emailed and explained why she had to rush off."

He asked, "Why wouldn't she have just texted me?"

Agent Lee looked almost as tired as he felt. She said, "You ask me a lot of questions that I couldn't possibly answer."

"Sorry, I'm talking to myself here. Don't worry about it. I'll check my email. Is Dylan doing okay?"

"Last I saw, a Lego pirate ship was battling a Lego Star Destroyer."

With a weak smile, he said, "Thanks. I really appreciate your help."

"Show me your appreciation by bringing Jerrell home. Find him, Agent Williams. Please."

Marcus had contemplated conversations like this for hours upon hours. As a homicide detective and then a federal agent, he had made a lot of promises he couldn't keep while staring into the eyes of a victim's family. After all that analysis, he had yet to find a suitable response that was able to comfort the bereaved and yet properly convey the realities of the situation.

He said, "We're closing in."

87

From: maggie.carlisle490@justice.gov
To: "Marcus" <marcus.williams22@justice.gov>
X-Mailer: WolfMail 7.8.0.1
Subject: READ ME ...

Marcus,

I know you'll blame yourself for this, but it's not your fault. Your tendencies to push people away haven't helped, but at the core, this is about my brother. I don't feel that I've done enough to find him, to learn the truth. I once believed that joining the SO would help me find the man who took him, but in reality, being part of this team has only drawn me farther from where I need to be. I have to catch the person or persons who did this, no matter what it takes, no matter how long it takes. So you can consider this my resignation. In regard to me and you, I love you, and I always will. But I don't expect you to wait for me.

PS - Tell Ackerman that I hope he endures an extremely painful death in the very near future ;-)

Yours Always,
Maggie

88

Ackerman had been immediately impressed by the roominess of the hotel's closets. Most establishments didn't provide the space necessary for proper sleep, and so he would curl up in a corner or beside one of the beds. But whenever reasonable, he preferred to slumber in the confines of a nice closet. The benefits included a greater sense of comfort and rest accompanied by various tactical advantages. Most interlopers looked to the beds and bathrooms. The closet was a secondary concern during a surprise attack, which gave him ample opportunity to plan his counteroffensive.

Now, however, he was not alone in the closet and was consequently unable to properly enjoy the spaciousness. The vermin had insisted on joining him inside his small sanctuary, and the dog now lay curled against his midsection.

Ackerman wanted to roll over, but he didn't move for fear of waking the furry beast, which could result in more licking and tail wagging. He hated to admit that his tolerance of the thing was growing. He still considered the canine to be a tumor, but at least a benign one—a remora to his great white shark.

The little dog popped to attention a full second before Ackerman heard the sound of breaking glass.

Sliding open the closet door, he crawled across the beige carpet and listened. Then, still staying low and out of the line of fire, he rolled toward the source of the crash: his brother's room.

He and Marcus shared an adjoining door, but it was currently locked. Ackerman was considering whether he should kick it in or merely knock when Emily burst into his room with her weapon drawn and ready. She scanned the whole room before making eye contact with Ackerman. He pointed toward the room allocated to Marcus and Maggie.

Emily stomped forward and propelled the door inward with an impressive spin-kick.

Following her inside, Ackerman saw Marcus in the bathroom, sitting atop the toilet with blood gushing down his face and dripping from his right fist. Resisting the urge to check the closet first—there were not many with thought patterns similar to his own—he accompanied Emily as she rushed to his brother's side.

Marcus said, "I'm fine. It's just a little cut. Looks worse than it is."

"What happened?" Emily asked.

The bathroom mirror had been shattered and bloody pieces filled the sink. By the patterns of the breakage to the glass, Ackerman could see that at least one of the impacts had been caused by Marcus's forehead. He said, "Brother, we need to know whether or not you've been attacked."

"I tripped. Just let me wash off the blood and—"

"Quiet," Emily snapped. Then, as she tended to Marcus's wounds despite his objections, she said, "What really happened?"

His brother's gaze was locked on the brown tile floor.

Ackerman noticed the slight odor of disinfectant and insect repellant which he had come to warmly associate with his little sister. He asked, "Where's Maggie?"

After a moment, Marcus reluctantly offered, "She's gone. The email is still up on my computer screen. You might as well all see it."

Returning to the bedroom, Ackerman located the MacBook and read Maggie's message. Most of what she said he had seen coming for some time now. But he hadn't expected the kind sentiment of the postscript.

… PS - Tell Ackerman that I hope he endures an extremely painful death in the very near future ;-) …

A moment later, Emily joined him and read the message. Ackerman said, "Wasn't that sweet at the end. I must really be making an impact on her."

"It doesn't sound very sweet. She hopes you die painfully."

"Exactly. Death would be a grand adventure. To live is Christ and to die is gain, as written by … I can't recall if it was John or Paul … No matter … As you've said, pain is my drug of choice. Therefore, a painful death would be a most satisfying beginning to my afterlife."

Emily narrowed her gaze but said, "It's sad that the first part of that note you comment on is about yourself. Maggie could be in serious danger. Not to mention that she's suffering enough emotionally to abandon us during an active investigation."

"That's the thing about warriors and hunters, my dear. When aren't we warring and hunting in one way or another? It's hard to focus on anything else when you're constantly faced with situations of life and death. Maggie merely needs to do some soul searching. It's really no surprise. I saw this coming all the way back in Chicago, and I assumed you had as well."

Marcus—a towel wrapped around his head like a red-and-white turban—joined them at the hotel room's desk and slammed the lid of his laptop. "Everybody out. I need to lie down before we meet with Detective Ferrera and their source."

"You're not lying down after suffering a head trauma," Emily said. "You need a hospital."

"For what?"

"You need stitches."

"I'm fine."

Ackerman said, "I can stitch him up. I've performed the procedure many times. On both the living and the deceased."

Marcus nodded. "Well. There you go. No hospital."

Emily's ability to endure never ceased to amaze Ackerman. She said, "Fine. Enjoy that Frankenstein scar. But while he's sewing you up, I need to know what really happened in there? When it comes to the team's mental and physical safety, I'm the boss, remember?"

Ackerman interjected, "Marcus said that he's fine. Besides, you know why he did it. It was just yesterday morning I was informing you of the article I read on the relationship between head-banging and a sense of relief for those with my brother's particular neurodiversity."

"That's enough, Frank."

"No, it's not. I've held my tongue on this subject long enough. Head-banging is a survival strategy used to deal with the devastating amount of sensory and emotional input attacking my brother on a daily basis. Head-banging is a pain that he can control. The brain of an individual with ASD shows higher brain activity, even while at rest. It's no wonder Marcus can't sleep. And the more emotional stress and sensory overloads he suffers, the more he can't sleep. With lack of rest comes the breakdown of his filtering and coping mechanisms. It's a vicious cycle. You want to discuss the mental and physical safety of this team. I believe that keeping the truth from my brother is endangering every one of us on both counts."

Emily wouldn't meet his gaze, but Marcus said, "What the hell is he talking about? I'm really not in the mood for this, and I tuned about three quarters of that nonsense out, but from what I did hear, you're both keeping something from me. From now on, we all need to be more open with each other. If I had been more open with Maggie, well … One of you is going to tell me what's going on."

Sensing that this was Emily's moment of truth, Ackerman held his tongue. After a deep breath and a long silence, she said, "Marcus, I wanted to wait to share this with you until a more opportune and private moment, but I've diagnosed Dylan with Autism Spectrum Disorder. And although this is far from confirmed, there is a genetic component to ASD. You certainly display some of the outward signs, but it's impossible for me to give a diagnosis with any certainty without—"

Marcus interrupted, "I've heard enough. There's not a damn thing wrong with me or my son. Everyone out. Now."

"But your stitches?"

"I'll do it my damn self! I've survived this long without anyone's help. I think I can make a go of it a bit longer. I'll see you both in the lobby in one hour. Now, get out."

89

Corin now suspected that she had been given more than just a mild sedative. The world had been spinning from the moment she rolled off the elevator. Or perhaps the underwater motif had simply hypnotized her into a state of utter disorientation. Either way, she felt at first as if she was aboard a submarine, and then as if the room was full of water and she was floating out of her chair.

The good news was that she could no longer feel her ruined legs.

Derrick, his voice taking on a dream-like reverberation, said, "It's this way. Don't doddle. What are you waiting for?"

She tried to answer, but her mouth seemed unable to form the proper shapes.

Apparently seeing the signs of her intoxication, Gladstone finally said, "Oh, dear. It seems that Sonnequa may have given you an excessive dose."

His hands wrapped around her head and held open her eyelids. He said, "Pupils are dilated to the max. Sonnequa was likely trying to kill. She's become the protective matron of our little wolf pack."

Corin blinked herself back to semi-consciousness. She felt as if she was drowning. When she opened her mouth, it sounded as though someone else was speaking in slow motion. "Why would she want to kill me?"

"Obviously, she sees you as a threat for my attentions, and I can understand why she would be jealous. Plus, to let you in on a little secret, she should be worried. You're tough, resourceful, willful, beautiful. You're exactly the kind of woman I envision helping me build my brave new world."

Her inhibition and fear waned as the drug took hold. Without any forethought, she said, "I'm not a professional, but I've taken several psychology classes, and I can't determine whether you're a narcissist or a psychopath."

He slapped her hard across her left cheek. She felt the impact like a meteor striking a planet's surface. Her wheelchair rocked to the side and nearly toppled over, but Derrick grabbed her hand to keep her from tipping.

"Remember your place, Corin. You need to learn that I am the supreme ruler here. You will show me respect at all times."

With a little chuckle, she said, "That's exactly what a narcissist or psychopath would say."

He slapped her again, harder this time, but the pain was starting to grow oddly enjoyable. It was helping to wake her up from the drug-induced stupor.

She said, "I am *so* going to kill you."

This time, he struck her with a closed fist.

Gladstone was well built, and he threw every ounce of his muscle into the punch. Corin thought at one moment, when she saw the blow coming toward her, that he was literally going to knock her head off. When his fist connected, she felt herself levitating across the room as the chair tipped over and her body took flight.

She landed on the floor beside one of the suite's sitting

areas. The impact with the tile floor reminded her that pain and pleasure were seldom good bedfellows. It was as if all the pain of the past weeks came rushing back at once. She ground her teeth and fought to keep from passing out.

Dr. Derrick wheeled over to her and said, "Stop your crying. This isn't pain. You don't know what pain is."

At first, Corin didn't know what the man in the wheelchair was talking about. *Crying?* Had she been crying? As the haze cleared from her brain, Corin realized she had apparently curled herself up into a ball and begun sobbing uncontrollably.

Still, she couldn't find words.

King Derrick said, "I chose you for a number of reasons, Ms. Campbell. First of all, you had donated blood to a local charity, which I oversee. I've studied your DNA at length, and I found that you have the purest genetic material of any of the ladies here. Purest of any woman I've tested. That's why I've been taking it easy on you, trying to cut you some slack. But through my research, I've also discovered that humans possess an attribute that science cannot adequately measure at this time. I call it the *Will to Live.* I've seen a lot of things during my tenure as a doctor. I've seen patients who had no business living make a full recovery, and I've seen people go in for a simple procedure and fail to wake up. Sometimes, there is just no explanation for it. I've noticed this in several other ways as well. You see it in an opponent's eyes during a sporting event. It's a determined fire. A will to win, to survive at all costs. You're a survivor, Corin."

She tried to move but suspected she had sustained broken ribs in the fall. She hurt all over. Her legs were a ruined mess, she couldn't breathe, and the drugs couldn't hold back the pain any longer. Corin threw up all over Derrick's tile floor.

He scowled down at her, shaking his head in disgust. Then he removed a small black pistol from the right side of his jacket. Bending over in his chair, he pressed the barrel to the back of her head and said, "I don't feel like you're listening to me."

In a choked whisper, she managed to say, "I'm ... all ... ears."

He smiled. "And that brings me to the main reason I think you're special. When I saw the results of your genetic tests, I decided to learn every detail of your life. I probably know more about you than you know about yourself. I learned all about the sins of your past."

She said, "Please, help me. I think I'm dying."

"Let's start with your sister's boyfriend. The one who introduced her to the spiraling hell that is her life. You murdered him in cold blood. He had been shooting up for years. I've heard you need to do something for ten thousand hours to be considered an expert. Sammy's deceased boyfriend was definitely an expert in pumping poison into his veins. He would never have given himself such a large dose, and he had no suicidal indicators. Your protective instincts have always been as strong as your desire to survive. You would do anything to keep your sister safe, including taking the life of her junkie boyfriend. Did you protect sweet Sammy from your own mother as well, Corin?"

Still gasping for air, she said, "You don't know anything. You don't know me at all."

"It would be a real shame if that were true. Because then

I would have to move on to *Plan B*. Your sister, Sammy, doesn't possess that same desire to thrive as you, but I'd be willing to bet her genetic material is worth harvesting. No guarantees, but considering that you have such clean DNA—a code that lacks all the genetic markers for handicaps and other medical conditions—chances are that sweet Sammy would have a similarly flawless double helix."

"Stay the hell away from my sister."

"There go those overactive protective instincts again. I'll make you a deal. You be a good girl, and I'll forget all about sweet little Sammy."

"Fine, whatever you want. Just … please … help me." She held out her arm, but he slapped it away.

Derrick aimed the gun down at her and said, "If you truly want to live, then demonstrate your desire. If you have the fire in you, then crawl your way back over to that chair and pull yourself up. And if you can't do it, if you aren't strong enough, then I'll put a bullet in your brain and feed you to my dogs."

90

Ackerman had never truly owned much of anything, let alone an automobile. He had forcefully commandeered several of them over the years. Still, stealing a car was a totally different feeling from purchasing one. At least, he supposed it would be. To actually earn the money to purchase a vehicle sounded oddly appealing. He would have to ask Marcus later what they planned to give him for a salary. Because, if he was going to save up for a car, he would want a classic piece of machinery like the one owned by Detective Natalie Ferrera.

Leaning forward from the back of the convertible and speaking over the wind, Ackerman asked, "I respect your choice in automobile, Detective Ferrera. What is the make, model, and year of your vehicle?"

The beautiful Hispanic detective replied, "Thanks, and it's a 1964 Ford Falcon Futura."

From the passenger seat, Marcus added, "This is the same car used in the 1987 movie *Summer School* starring Mark Harmon."

Natalie Ferrera said, "Wow. I didn't know that."

"Really? I assumed that was why you had bought it."

As she wheeled the fifty-three year old automobile onto Haight and Ashbury, Natalie replied, "No, it was my dad's car. We restored it together."

Ackerman resisted the urge to point out that his brother's

obsession with particular subjects was a common ASD indicator, much like Dylan's obsession with Lego. Marcus hadn't said much since hearing the diagnosis bombshell, and so Ackerman decided to let him process the info a bit more before calling out observations of symptoms.

As they rolled down the street, the skunk-like smell of marijuana was prominent in the air. The sidewalks bustled with conspicuous tourists and obvious locals alike. Natalie slowed to a crawl beside one storefront and yelled, "Baxter Kincaid!"

Most of the sidewalk's occupants glared over at the convertible as if they were escaped mental patients—which Ackerman supposed was accurate in his case. But what he found especially interesting was the three people who pointed up the street, directing Natalie towards Kincaid.

Marcus said, "Popular guy."

Driving slowly and scanning for Baxter, she said, "I suppose, depending on your perspective."

Spotting the private investigator hurrying up the street beside a Ben and Jerry's Ice Cream parlor, Ackerman said, "He's right there. Didn't we have an appointment with Mr. Kincaid? Why is he running from us?"

Focused in on Baxter and increasing speed, Natalie replied, "We're not chasing him, and he's not running from us. Sometimes he loses track of time, and he hasn't been answering his cell. I think he's upset about the shooting in his neighborhood. He gets this way sometimes."

Natalie closed the distance and brought the Falcon to a screeching halt beside the curb. The sudden noise drew Baxter's attention, and that of everyone else on the street. Ackerman noticed a tall black man about thirty feet ahead of Baxter turn around, notice the car and Kincaid, and take off sprinting in the opposite direction.

Shaking his head, Baxter approached the convertible and said, "You just scared off someone with whom I needed to have a serious discussion."

"Then why aren't you chasing him?" Ackerman asked.

Baxter laughed and shrugged. "That dude is a member of the gang that controls the machine-pistol trade in the city. It's a Kenyan gang. As in, that dude is straight up from Kenya. His spirit animal is the *gazelle*. Sometimes, you got to know when to fold 'em. Plus, if I'm supposed to catch up to him, the Universe will give me another shot."

Natalie said, "You were supposed to meet me at the station. We're going to see Illustrated Dan, remember?"

"Sorry, Nat, I've been a might distracted with this shooting business."

"I know. But let's get going. The feds here have an appointment for a special viewing of their Diamond Room."

Baxter hopped over the trunk and landed in the back seat beside Ackerman. "Then let's go talk to Dan the Man."

91

Corin Campbell didn't want to die. Neither did she desire to live like this. But there was always hope. She just needed do what she always did, take one step and then another, roll with the punches until circumstances changed.

The pain had become so intense, the external casing of her soul so devastated, that she could almost feel her brain shutting down certain parts of her body. Just like a submarine captain sealing hatches to save the rest of the vessel.

Gladstone said, "What shall I do with you, Ms. Campbell? Would you prefer to be put out of your misery? I always have *Plan B*. With you gone, there won't even be anyone left alive to miss sweet Sammy."

Calling on the last bit of strength held by the unbreakable girl in the beach house, the girl who still refused to die, Corin put one hand in front of another, digging her nails into the rug, crawling for her life and the life of her little sister.

When she reached the wheelchair, Corin had no idea how to pull herself up. Her legs were useless. Any movement in them caused more pain than it was worth. She was a weakling by most standards, and she was also five foot four and a girl. Upper body strength had never been a priority.

Derrick had at least righted the wheelchair for her.

She tried to climb into it, but each time it started to roll away. Searching the wheel, she activated the brake by pulling back a black lever. After which, she was able to get to her knees, turn to her side, and pull herself up by gripping the armrest.

Corin felt as if she had run a marathon. She struggled to right herself and place her feet on the wheelchair's rests. When she was young, she had battled asthma, but just as the doctors had said, she had eventually outgrown the affliction. Despite so many years without an attack, she now felt one coming on.

She didn't hear Derrick's slow clapping until she was able to get her breathing under control. He beamed with pride as he said, "That's exactly what I'm talking about. Just from looking at you, your petite frame, and then accounting for your injuries … Well, let's just say that no doctor would bet on your true strength and ability. But they would all be wrong. I may be the only person in your life who has ever truly believed in you, Corin. The *real* you. I want you to see what I see. I want to help you realize your true potential."

Between ragged gasps, Corin asked, "What do you see?"

He smiled, a hint of madness shining through. "I see a potential Eve to my Adam."

The wave of nausea that struck Corin at the thought was almost worse than the pain. But this time, she held her tongue, and her bile.

Then Dr. Derrick wheeled himself toward the master bedroom, saying over his shoulder, "That's enough rest. Onward and upward."

She had little choice but to follow and play along with whatever lunacy he had in store for her. The same disorientating sea motif carried through into Derrick's master suite. Same tray ceiling with lighting and shadows that made it seem as if one were underwater. A California king bed rested along the back wall, and beside it was a sitting area. The bedspread and furniture were sea-foam green and salmon red. She swore she tasted salt in the air.

Gladstone wheeled into the center of the room and turned to face the wall opposite the bed. As Corin moved closer, she saw that the entire wall was lined with hundreds of photos.

Each photo was marked with a name, a date, and a birth weight. The ceilings in the presidential suite were at least ten feet tall, and the bedroom was at least thirty feet wide. Children's photos—boys and girls, all varying skin tones and hair colors—stretched from floor to ceiling, wall to wall.

Trying to fight off a wave of despair even more powerful than the wave of pain, Corin said, "What am I looking at?"

"These," Derrick said, "are all my children."

92

The true story of how San Francisco's Tenderloin district received its name was a matter of contention. Some tour guides spun the yarn that officers who worked in the Tenderloin received "hazard pay" for working in such a violent area, which allowed them to purchase the better cuts of meat. Marcus knew that it actually got its name from an older New York neighborhood, but the apocryphal reasons for the name remained. He had heard every explanation from bribery benefits to the "tender" loins of the district's prostitutes and strippers.

Marcus supposed the history of the district's name didn't hold any real significance to the case, but he still felt compelled to analyze and ponder it. For a moment, he wondered if that desire to understand how things worked was a characteristic of the diagnosis Ackerman had revealed—a diagnosis which Marcus didn't believe to be accurate. There was nothing wrong with him, or his son. At least not with internal wiring. Externally, a lot was wrong. His girlfriend had just left him, his brother and biological father were both serial murderers, and his team was at odds with a whole network of the world's worst killers.

All of those problems had been exacerbated further by the private detective sitting behind him in Ferrera's convertible, who kept sparking up pinch hitters full of marijuana.

As Detective Ferrera pulled the Ford Falcon to the curb

beside a line of homeless men and women waiting in front of a soup kitchen, Marcus asked, "Is your informant a vagrant?"

Baxter laughed. "No, he volunteers down here a couple times a week. His shift will be starting soon. While we're waiting, do y'all mind if I record an entry for my blog?"

Marcus said, "Only if you stop blazing it up back there. You're giving me a headache."

Putting away his paraphernalia and starting up a recording app on his phone, Baxter said, "I think that big gash on your forehead may be a more likely culprit, but I can dig it …"

Baxter's Log. Stardate 7016.niner.alpha.12 Anno Domini.

(Chuckling)

I heard a lost soul talking on that Your Tube thing the other day and giving all his thoughts on God, as the song says. This dude claims that: if there was a God and he had a chance to stroll up to the pearly gates, well, old boy says that he would tell the almighty, "How dare you!" Then he goes on to blame all human suffering on the Creator, as if we have no responsibility in the matter.

But I say, think about it like this, man. If you had a kid, you have to tell the kid what's right and wrong and then let them do their thing. They're going to go their own way no matter what you do.

This guy blames things like insects that attack

humans and bone cancer in children on God. He called the Universe evil, and the Creator an utter maniac for building a world which contains so much suffering that isn't our fault.

Unlike that gentleman, when I look around, I see the immense beauty of God's creation. I see order and design. I see scientific truths and processes—the basic laws of physics and mathematics—established by some kind of Force beyond our current comprehension. And I see a world which mankind has corrupted. Why did those insects evolve to attack humans? Why are there parasites in this world which drill holes in children's eyeballs? Was there a "man" factor involved there? Pollution, deforestation? Did a previous link in the chain have to evolve into that menacing creature because we took away its ancestor's food supply?

I don't know, but I think of it like this ...

I'm small. Even in terms of my city, the incomparable San Francisco, I'm not going to be remembered. Not a hundred, a thousand, or, possibly, not even one single year after I'm gone. I will pass away after having lived a life that was mostly spent chasing the wind.

To think that my mortal existence and comfort has more significance than the laws of nature and the Creator's design—in this unimaginably vast universe, which is likely only one universe in a limitless multiverse—well, that seems pretty damn arrogant to me.

But here's the thing. Just like a parent loves his child, that Creator loves each and every one of us. Because he's part of us, and we're part of him. So how do we live on and make a difference?

I say that we make our story become part of the story that the Universe is telling, man.

Maybe rather than sitting on our butts bitching about the suffering of this world, maybe we should start doing something about it. You have a passion for fighting childhood cancer, then maybe you should set out to cure it. Or at least give a lot of money to that cause.

But here's the thing ... The very nature of life is struggle. If you believe the story of Adam and Eve, with either an allegorical or literal interpretation, then our own arrogance—thinking we were smarter than our Pop—is what caused suffering to come into our world.

But let's not even get into that.

If you believe in any kind of afterlife and eternity, then this world is just the first step in a long journey. Who can say what wonders are yet to come for us. I know I want to find out. If this existence is only the baby steps, the job interview, or training wheels period, if you will, then maybe we should stop and ask ourselves what our Pop is trying to teach us.

Because if there is an uncreated being who built all of this—or at least a being whose existence is beyond our limited understanding—then that Creator would live beyond space and time. Beyond our universe, beyond our multiverse. I don't know about y'all, but I imagine such a Big Dude like that would be pretty smart. I think that a being like that would have a lot to teach me, if I only chose to listen.

Read the book of Ecclesiastes with an open mind and heart, and you'll see what I'm talking about.

Or don't. That's your bag, man.

I guess I'm just saying that before we go questioning the thoughts of the man upstairs or dismissing the idea of a benevolent Creator, we owe it to ourselves to explore the real truths that Papa Bear is trying to show us.

So keep it real out there, baby girls and boys. Let your freak flags fly, but make sure your flag is displaying a banner you truly believe in. As for me, I'm going to use my story, passions, and abilities to become part of the kickass rhythms the Creator is laying down.

Baxter ... out.

When Kincaid was finished with his rambling, Marcus said, with a grunt of disgust, "*The Pothead Prophet.* Do people actually listen to your bullshit?"

Baxter shrugged. "They read it, I think. It's a blog or something. I don't know though. Maybe they listen to it as well? I just give my thoughts at the moment and cash the checks."

"You get paid for doing a blog? How does that work?"

"My technological wizard sells advertising space on the website or something like that."

Ackerman asked, "How much money do you make from this weblog?"

"Frank!" Marcus snapped. "Even I know not to ask questions like that. How about we all just sit quietly?"

Baxter waved his hand in dismissal. "No worries. My cut last year was a little over two hundred thousand."

The car went completely silent.

Baxter added, "Before taxes."

Ackerman broke another long silence by asking, "Would

you put me in touch with your wizard? I would also like to start a weblog."

"That's not happening," Marcus said.

"You're not the boss of me."

Marcus glared at his brother and glanced toward the car's other occupants. "Actually, Mister …" He searched for the exotic name Ackerman had given at Richmond Station. He finally said, "Mr. Tonydanzio, I am literally your superior in the chain of command."

"Dantonio."

"I know that, jackass. Just be quiet, please, before my head explodes."

Baxter said, "You have trouble sleeping, don't you, Agent Williams? A little herb would likely alleviate your affliction."

"I don't do drugs. The nuns taught me that your body is a temple, and drugs desecrate that. They alter your perception and sever any connection you could possibly have with God. Drugs are just crutches for the weak of mind and spirit."

"There's a difference between drugs and medicine. And God gave us all the medicine we need directly from the earth. Genesis 1:29: 'And God said, Behold, I have given you every herb bearing seed, which is upon the face of all the earth, and every tree, in the which is the fruit of a tree yielding seed; to you it shall be for meat.' I believe in organic medicine. In my mind, a little natural remedy is far better than the man-made prescription drugs that doctors are pumping into every soccer mom in the suburbs. Still, you're correct that even medicine can alter one's perceptions. Although, I would argue that there are many whose perceptions need a little altering. But to each his own, Agent Williams. To each his own."

Spotting a man dressed in a biker's vest and jeans and covered in tattoos—and hoping for a change of subject—Marcus said, "Is that our guy?"

"That would be the illustrious Illustrated Dan," Baxter said. "Now, when we approach him, he's going to punch me in the face. Nobody make a move. Just pretend you're watching a National Geographic special on silverback gorillas."

Not waiting for a response, Baxter vaulted from the convertible's backseat before Marcus could open the passenger door. Ackerman followed suit on the other side.

Marcus rolled his eyes as he calmly opened his door and he and Det. Ferrera took up stride behind the strange private blowhard and Ackerman.

He could see the fascination growing in his brother's eyes the more they were in the presence of Mr. Kincaid. And he didn't feel that a stoner in love with the sound of his own voice would be the best influence on a man with enough addictions and afflictions of his own.

The man they called Illustrated Dan saw Baxter from about fifteen feet away. The biker's lip curled, and his eyes narrowed. Dan was an older man with a white beard and shoulder-length white hair pulled back into a samurai-style bun. The tattoos started at his neck and covered every exposed inch of the man's body. His skin was an eclectic representation of pop-culture icons and symbology, including movies, music, motorcycles, Biblical references, skulls, dragons, and everything in between. All the work had been done by true artists with an incredible level of detail.

Just as the stoner prophet had predicted, Dan closed the

gap between them in two strides and struck Baxter with a powerful right hook. Kincaid spit blood onto the sidewalk and said, "Is it out of your system now, or would you like another free shot?"

Through clenched teeth, Dan said, "You have a lot of nerve showing your face around me, Bax."

"I won the damn thing fair and square. Don't gamble with what you're not prepared to lose. You know that."

"You cheated me."

"I never cheat. You know that too."

"I was drunk! You took advantage of the situation and stole Doc's bike from me. Knowing full well what that old Panhead means to me!"

Baxter shrugged. "Once again, I don't see how your choices having consequences is my fault. You *chose* to drink too much and play poker with a superior player. Then you *chose* to gamble away your prized possession. I tried to talk you out of it."

Dan punched Baxter again and started to push past them to the door of the shelter. Detective Ferrera stopped him with her ID held out like a talisman. She said, "We're here on official business."

"I don't associate with cops. You wanna talk, call my lawyer. I pay him a lot of money for all that. Now get out of my way."

Detective Ferrera stepped aside but glanced at Baxter with a look that seemed to scream, "*Do something!*"

With a sigh, Baxter said, "If you help us on this, I'll give you the bike back."

Stopping dead in his tracks, Dan turned around and asked, "What do you want?"

After handing him an enhanced photo of the tattoo from the bus footage, Baxter said, "We need you to check your whole network and put a name to that tattoo."

"Nothing I find would be admissible as evidence."

"We just need a name or list of names, depending on how many men you can dig up with that tattoo on their hand."

"And if I give you this information, then I get Doc's bike back?"

After a moment's hesitation, Baxter said, "That's right. Lives are on the line, Danny. If you lead us to our guy, then it's a small price to pay."

Dan looked down at the photo and said, "I'll put the word out. Wait for me at your place, and have my bike ready to go. You'll get your name."

As Illustrated Dan walked away, Detective Ferrera said, "We owe you big on this one, Bax."

"I didn't do it for the department, and it's just a possession that I've had the privilege of enjoying for a period of time. Plus, now I don't have to take a punch every time I see Dan. But since the bike is my main mode of transportation, you do owe me a new motorcycle. I trust there's something down at the impound that will suffice."

93

Corin bent over and threw up. Not because of the effects the drugs had on her system or the pain of her ravaged body, but at the thought of so many children born of rape.

Sitting back in the wheelchair and wiping the bile from her lips, Corin said, "You've kidnapped and impregnated this many women? Where are all the babies?"

Derrick laughed. "Heavens no. There are photos on this wall showing the offspring of your sister wives, but the vast majority of these are simply women who have been implanted with Gladstone brand semen."

"Implanted?"

"Yes, did I fail to mention that I am one of California's premier fertility specialists. I own twelve clinics across five states. My real claim to fame within that field of expertise came from a test that I developed for spotting certain genetic disorders."

"You're saying that a couple will come to see you or one of your employees at this clinic, but instead of fertilizing the egg with the husband's sperm, you replace it with your own?"

"In most cases, we function much like any other clinic. Although when we discover a red flag in the genetic makeup or the personal history of the prospective father, I simply intervene with genetically superior material. And it's not always my semen. I've also found a few other worthy individuals whose DNA has been disseminated among the population through insemination. It's really a service I'm doing for these people. Especially the women. They found a genetically inferior mate. And instead of having to reproduce and create genetically inferior children, they get to elevate themselves with a child of superior stock. I can't wait to see the wonderful things the boys and girls on this wall will do for humanity."

"You really believe the sewage that spews out of your mouth, don't you? You've convinced yourself that playing God and screwing with people's lives without them knowing is in their best interest. You're sick."

"That would depend pretty heavily on your definition of what is healthy. I look around and see a world that is dying, and I want to do something about it. I, as a scientist, have an obligation to our species to attempt the circumvention of an evolutionary disaster. Look at the world today. People of lower class, lower intelligence, and who are of no benefit to society, are reproducing at alarming rates. But intelligent, educated, and worthy individuals are choosing career paths over children, or, choosing to be socially conscious, are only having a single child. It may take a couple of centuries, but eventually, evolution will always favor those who are able to reproduce in greater number. That is the essence of natural selection. We've deluded ourselves with these concepts of love and monogamy. But, in reality, males are built to sire many children while females are built to only reproduce a set number of times."

"I'm going to kill you. I really mean it."

Rolling his eyes, Derrick said, "If you see a flaw in my logic, please let me know."

"You can't just go around choosing who is worthy. You don't have the right. And who's to say that the genetic abnormality that you want to filter out isn't the mutation that will ultimately lead to the survival of humankind?"

"I'm not choosing who is worthy. Nature is doing that for me. You act as if I'm meddling with natural selection, but what I'm actually doing is abiding by those laws. The strongest and most intelligent of the species have an obligation to ensure that the faction in which they were born wins the evolutionary race. It's all of you who have deluded yourselves with fairy tales about angels and demons and bought into the lie that human beings are anything more than highly intelligent animals. Simply because we stand at the top rung of the ladder doesn't mean we're not still driven by the same instincts and bound by the same scientific truths."

"You remind me of this other guy you may have heard of, Adolf Hitler. He also thought that the world needed cleansing and that only certain people deserved to live."

"Yes, and he forced those beliefs on others and murdered millions. I'm not trying to hinder or harm anyone. I'm simply trying to give my genetic line a leg up over the competition. It's perfectly natural. Think about natural selection and the types of people we would view as enlightened, intelligent, and productive members of society. Are they having children? Or are the dregs of society the ones who are flourishing and spreading like wildfire. Every generation, we are going to get dumber and dumber because of natural selection. Every generation, there will be fewer educated people and more illiterates. Unless we take back natural selection."

"You're a pig. A Neanderthal. You think you can just hit

women over the head and drag them back here to be your wives?"

Derrick looked up at the wall of baby pictures one last time and then said, "Obviously, I can. No one has stepped up and stopped me yet."

"Your precious Darwin would be ashamed of the way you've corrupted his ideas."

With a shake of his head, Derrick said, "You're only succeeding in putting your ignorance on full display. I'm taking the natural next step of his work. Let me recall a few of Charles Darwin's own words …"

Closing his eyes, Dr. Gladstone recited from memory, "We civilized men … do our utmost to check the process of elimination; we build asylums for the imbecile, the maimed, and the sick … Thus the weak members of civilized societies propagate their kind. No one who has attended to the breeding of domestic animals will doubt that this must be highly injurious to the race of man."

He paused, taking a deep, reverent breath. Corin noticed that Derrick seemed to recite the words of Darwin with the same fervor that a gospel preacher may quote the Bible.

After a moment, he added, "According to Soloway in *Demography and Degeneration*, Alfred Russel Wallace reported that: 'Darwin was gloomy about the prospect of a future in which natural selection had no play and the fittest did not survive. He talked about "the scum" from whom "the stream of life" is largely renewed, and of the grave danger it entailed in a democratic civilization.'"

"What about compassion?" she asked. "That's one of humanity's finest qualities. It's one of the many things that separates us from mere animals."

"Darwin believed the same thing. He never called for the eradication of any subset of the species. At the same time, he hoped that the weaker and inferior members of society might refrain from reproducing. He often cited Francis Galton's *Hereditary Genius*, which introduced the concept of eugenics. Darwin warned that if we don't 'prevent the reckless, the vicious, and otherwise inferior members of society from increasing at a quicker rate than the better class of men, the nation will retrograde, as has too often occurred in the history of the world.'"

Corin wasn't sure what else to say. She had tried numerous times to appeal to Gladstone's conscience and humanity, but it seemed that part of him had never existed.

Checking his watch, he said, "I'll direct you to some further reading materials, but we have all the time in the world to debate the subject. We have the rest of our lives together."

94

Marcus and Ackerman waited at the southwestern corner of Washington Square Park, two unmoving rocks in a flowing river of tourists and shoppers flocking into the niche stores and cart vendors that lined both sides of the street. The air smelled faintly of funnel cakes, which masked the scent of the ocean and fish market that was only a few blocks away. Following Oban's instructions to the letter, they were both dressed in tuxedos. Oban had suggested a neutral location and said he would send a limo for them at 6:30 sharp.

Checking his Apple watch, Marcus said, "Two minutes to game time. By the way, don't damage that tux. It's a rental. And the Director has become very budget conscious lately."

"You can't be serious."

"I'm hoping we can handle this without getting any bullet holes in our clothes."

Admiring his reflection in a passing city bus, Ackerman said, "We do look rather dapper."

Rolling his eyes, Marcus replied, "Oh yeah, you're ready for the cover of GPQ...Gentlemen Psychopath's Quarterly."

"I'm not a psychopath. You know how I feel about the misrepresentation of that term. I'd wager there are more CEOs of Fortune 500 companies who are suffering from psychopathy than those who are serial murderers."

"Okay, okay. I should've just kept my mouth shut."

"Not to mention," Ackerman continued, "that true psychopaths are born that way, whereas I was forcefully designed and sculpted into my current glory."

"I know, I think. I'm just being my normal grumpy self."

"We are what we are, brother. Whether we like it or not. Do you blame me for what I am?"

"I really don't know what the hell that means."

"Let me rephrase." Ackerman hesitated, apparently considering his words very carefully. "Do you believe that I had any choice in the things I've done?"

Marcus took a deep breath and said a quick prayer while rubbing the cross tattoo on his chest. "That's a deep question. Honestly, I don't know, Frank. I don't blame you for anything that happened while you were under Father's thumb. But after you got away from him, that's when *you* really got started. You could've gone to the authorities. You could've explained things to people. Hell, you might've even been seen as a hero."

"In other words, I could have played the role of the victim."

"I'm just saying that you had a choice."

"I've thought long and hard about that, brother, and I honestly don't know if I did. When you've been taught to do one thing your entire life, and you're dropped alone as a teenage boy into the world … Can that boy be expected not to do the one thing he's been trained to do?"

Marcus said, "I don't know that it really matters. It happened. It's over. All we have is right here and right now. The past is gone, and tomorrow may never come. What you do in this moment and every moment after is all that matters, and I do believe that you genuinely want to do good. That's all that counts right now."

"That means a lot to me, little brother. If I were a person who was ever so inclined as to lovingly embrace someone, I suppose this would be such a moment."

Marcus said, "Please don't hug me."

"I didn't intend to actually embrace you. I was merely observing that I feel a vomit-inducing sensation that I can't quite define and require your assistance in identifying it."

"I don't know, Frank. Could be happiness. Or pride. Or love. All I know is that if you try to hug me, I will take you down."

As a long black limo pulled to the curb in front of them, Ackerman said, "That's so cute. He thinks he could take me down. Adorable. It's like when dogs wear people clothes."

Under his breath, Marcus said, "That's enough, jackass. Remember, be on your best behavior."

A well-groomed young man, dressed in a classic chauffeur's uniform, got out from behind the wheel and walked around the car. He didn't say a word. He merely nodded and opened the door for them.

Ackerman bowed his head in thanks and then dropped into the back of the limousine. Marcus, however, took off his jacket and looked into the vehicle's interior. It was all dark leather and smelled of hard liquor and ArmorAll. He also noticed a rubber floor mat just inside the door. He had been hoping to find one, which meant he wouldn't need to use his tuxedo jacket. It really was a rental, and Andrew had been up his ass lately about accurate reporting and overspending.

Looking up at the chauffeur, Marcus put on his best tough-guy face and said, "I don't turn my back on anybody, kid. You go get back behind the wheel, and I'll be inside by the time you get there."

The young man's expression remained neutral. He simply bowed and walked back to the driver's door.

Tossing his coat at Ackerman, Marcus bent down to step inside the vehicle. As he did so, he snatched up the floor mat, rolled it up twice, and stuffed it between the door and the latching mechanisms. Then, with his right hand, he gripped the door to make sure it was pulled tightly enough to keep an alert from sounding to the driver. But, if all went as planned, the rubber mat would also keep the locking apparatus from fully engaging.

Ackerman said, "It would appear, dear brother, that you are expecting a trap."

"I'm always expecting a trap. And, according to my research, seventy-five percent of the time there is a trap."

"Is that an actual statistic?"

"Be useful or be quiet."

Ackerman said, "Very well. All the glass in here is bulletproof and impact resistant, so I hope your little trick works. Otherwise, we will be at their mercy."

"What are you thinking they'll use? Some kind of knockout gas pumped through the vents?"

"That would be the safest and most effective method. Lock us back here and pump in the gas. We're restricted from shooting our way out. And we can only hold our breath for so long. Not very sporting, but effective."

"Okay, if they try gas, we'll take turns breathing at the crack in this door."

Ackerman leaned forward and grabbed one of the crystal carafes, which contained a light-brown liquid. He popped the top and sniffed. "Smells like twenty-five-year-old Scotch."

"Don't drink that."

With a little shrug, Ackerman sat the bottle down and started fiddling with the controls for the entertainment system.

Marcus asked, "Are you taking this seriously?"

Grabbing a handful of mixed nuts from a tray beside the liquor, Ackerman leaned back and said, "I'm taking it very seriously. If you are holding the door open so we can breathe, couldn't they just stop the car, roll down the little divider window, and shoot us?"

Marcus considered that for a moment, and then he said, "Here's what we'll do. If they start pumping gas, and it's safe, we'll jump for it. Then we'll have the advantage. We'll have time to get set up before they can come back at us."

"What if the gas is odorless, and they've already activated it?"

"You're getting on my nerves more than usual today. I just want you to know that."

"It's likely a side effect of your self-inflicted head trauma.

"Never mind that. I always keep an extra burner phone on me. We'll stash it back here, just in case."

Marcus fished into his jacket to grab the burner phone, but then the limo pulled over to the side of the road, and he heard the front passenger door open and close. They had just picked up another passenger.

The protective glass began to roll down, and Marcus, releasing the door, snatched a hidden pistol from his sleeve and aimed it at the glass. On the other side of the glass waited a muscular man holding a Beretta equipped with a long sound suppressor. The driver stared straight ahead, as if none of this was happening.

Marcus suspected this was the same man Ackerman and Emily had encountered at Willoughby's. The newcomer's face was round with a large, overly pronounced chin. His countenance was oddly childlike and menacing at the same time. His nose had clearly been broken on multiple occasions. Scars etched his skin. Some small, perhaps from fighting. Others—surrounding the lower jaw—appeared to be surgical. During his analysis, Marcus also noted the presence of cauliflower ear, a condition often suffered by wrestlers and MMA fighters.

The new passenger said, "So you're aware, every surface in the rear of the limo is actually coated with a mild neurotoxin. It won't kill you, but it will render you unconscious and give you a hell of a headache. You both should be asleep within the next thirty seconds, give or take. You wanted to see the Diamond Room. This is how that happens."

The man with the facial scars and the gun started to roll the window back up, but then he stopped and added, "And, before you pass out, please pull the mat out of the door. It makes this awful buzzing sound up here. Appreciate it, gentlemen."

Marcus gritted his teeth so hard that he thought he was going to snap them to pieces. They had been thoroughly and completely outplayed. Again.

He said to Ackerman, "Do we stay or do we go?"

"Our new friend wasn't bluffing. We won't get far,"

Ackerman said. Then, throwing another handful of nuts into his mouth, he added, "I say we sit back and enjoy the ride. Hopefully, this neurotoxin has some psychotropic effects."

95

Her world had become blurry, the lines between nightmare and reality slipping out of focus. She didn't know where she found the strength to push the wheelchair forward and keep up with Dr. Derrick, but she could hardly feel a thing now anyway. The hall seemed to travel on forever, the world shrinking and contracting all around her.

But even in a reduced state, Corin never lost sight of the goal. She analyzed everything along the way. Every door, every room, searching for anything that could be used as a weapon or become the instrument of her salvation.

The wheels of her chair whirred and squeaked down the forever corridor. It had once been beautiful but had fallen into ruin, a creeping black rot staining everything. Dr. D wheeled on in front of her as if he didn't have a care, or fear, in the world. She wanted to shove that overconfidence down his throat, but she also knew that he wasn't the only demon prowling these halls.

They took an elevator to the sub-basement—a place of concrete, pipes, conduits, and the odor of wet soil. She was afraid to ask any questions, not trusting what she might say. But eventually, after Derrick had led her into another elevator and down another decaying hallway, she said, "Where are you taking me?"

"I just wanted to introduce you to another of our guests, before he has to depart. I think it would do you some good to see firsthand what happens around here when someone wears out their welcome."

"You really don't have to prove anything to me. I've gotten the point about defying you."

"I'm not sure you have. You still think that you're going to kill me. You don't seem to understand the futility of such an act. There is no escape from this place or from me. But words are cheap, and seeing is believing. We're here."

The doors to the next room were encased in a massive stone archway, the words VIP lounge etched into the rock. The Good Wife stood beside the door like a subservient subject, wearing her white dress and her comfortable shoes. With a nod, Sonnequa said, "Your brother has been waiting for you, sir."

"Thank you, my dear one."

The French doors to the VIP lounge were inset several feet, and video screens covered the walls of the alcove. The LED displays were dark, but Corin wondered about their purpose. When The Good Wife parted the French doors, the screens came to life. The effect was dizzying, as if a bevy of new dimensions just opened up beside her. What had once been the entrance to the VIP lounge was now a giant viewing window. The screens, she now realized, showed every angle of the room beyond the window. The massive lounge had two occupants: a metal chair bolted to the floor and a shirtless black man, his face covered by a hood.

Dr. Derrick said, "Welcome to the Diamond Room. Of all my business endeavors, this room perhaps hasn't made me the most money, but it's damn close, and it's certainly the most fun. It's amazing what the rich and sadistic will pay to watch someone die." He gestured toward the video displays and added, "Notice the shape in the center."

Corin, still trying to determine if this was a dream or reality, studied the room on the video monitors. The center of the large space was sunken and shaped like a diamond. The rest of the floor was built in three stair-stepping levels, which she guessed had once held tables for dining and viewing the entertainment in the center pit. She could easily picture the place as a swank club for the resort's elite.

Derrick said, "My boyhood home possessed some unique architecture. In the very center of the house, there was a sunken sitting area in the shape of a diamond. It was the hub of the place, a central gathering point. But our mother turned it into our own personal battle arena. She called it the Diamond Room. When I saw this place, I immediately knew what I wanted to use it for. The symmetry was just too much to ignore."

"I don't understand. What am I looking at?"

"This is my own personal ThunderDome. And I figured, why not charge admission? So I put one of my team on it, and they set up this wonderful portal on the Dark Web, which is basically the Internet for criminals. People can log in for a price and witness a live feed of two men fighting to the death. It's like pay-per-view murder and mayhem."

Corin watched as a door on the other side of the Diamond Room opened and a massive man entered. He wore a twisted skull mask, the same one she had seen in the background of her photos, the one that had haunted her nightmares. The same one he had worn as he raped her. His body was all muscle. Not huge like that of a bodybuilder, but lean and lithe like a fighter. He wore only a pair of spandex shorts.

The man in the skull mask descended to the center of the room. Then, after pulling off the black man's hood, he snapped his fingers. Instantly, like a team of obedient shadows, the hellhounds poured through the open door and took up positions along the raised levels like an expectant audience.

Beside Corin, Derrick whispered, "I love those dogs. A business partner, who actually helped me get all my endeavors off the ground, trains them and gave them the 'hellhound' name. I suppose the nomenclature shouldn't be surprising, considering that my associate's name is Demon. I'm not sure if he trains them personally or if he just designed the regimen, but they are truly amazing creatures. Although, the real killing machine in that room is my baby brother. Simon 'The Gladiator' Gladstone."

"Why did you have your brother rape me, instead of doing it yourself? Is it because of your disability? Are you not able to function below the belt, Dr. Gladstone?"

"I'll forgive your insolence because I know you're impaired at the moment, but no, I *function* just fine. My spinal cord injury occurred during a college football game as a result of damage to my T7 vertebrae. I have no feeling below my waist, but I'm still able to move my legs and *function,* as you so eloquently phrased it. However, walking is difficult and disorienting for me because of the lack of feeling, that's why I require this chair."

"Do you really not see how sick and depraved all of this is?"

"Like I've told you previously, in order to make such

judgments you have to have some kind of measuring stick. Many use moral codes and religious beliefs as that measuring stick. That all hinges on there being some kind of purpose or higher power. When you realize the truth of our existence, you also realize there are no ends that don't justify the means. I'm not a sadist personally. I don't enjoy watching people suffer. But I won't refuse millions of dollars in profits for providing the service of suffering to those who are into that sort of thing."

Corin considered throwing up again, this time forcing herself to do it all over Derrick. Instead, she asked, "And who's tonight's victim?"

"He's an FBI agent who crossed me. As you can see, despite his training, he was unable to escape this place." Derrick looked at Sonnequa and asked, "How much time?"

She replied, "The feed goes live in sixty-three seconds."

"Excellent. I think you could be in for a real treat here, Corin. I do hope you get to see the hellhounds in action. They are truly remarkable. Mr. Demon takes them through very rigorous training, but the real trick he employs is so deviously simple. He establishes the dogs as loving and loyal protectors over the client. My brother and I were the first people that each of these dogs saw after they were born. Then, as the dogs received their training under what I'm certain were most brutal circumstances, Simon and I would visit them and essentially bring them all kinds of treats and shower love on them. The effect was that the dogs associated us with love and safety. They would die for us. We are the bright center of their universes. It kind of works in the opposite way that advertising sponsorship does. A company may choose a celebrity to be a spokesperson for their product. What they're doing is taking a known figure associated with positive feelings and getting people to view their product in the same light. This, of course, is a logical fallacy, but an effective advertising method. It's the same with the dogs. They associate us with happiness and full stomachs. And that, to a dog, is an almost unbreakable bond."

"It's really not much of a fight if your brother needs attack dogs backing him up."

"Oh no, you misunderstand. The dogs won't participate in the fight. But after my brother is done with Agent Fuller, they'll get to clean up the mess. So, sit back and enjoy the show."

96

FBI Special Agent Jerrell Fuller was tired of waiting around to be killed. First, he had been confined in darkness and a concrete cell. That cell had opened into another in which a long and very strange test had taken place. It consisted of several questions which seemed like something you would find on an IQ test or maybe something designed to gauge cognitive development. Jerrell couldn't see the point to any of it. Unless the point was to piss him off. Then he had been escorted at gunpoint to this room where he had sat ever since. It was almost a relief when he heard his tormentor enter, the little black death machines right on his heels.

The light blinded Jerrell's eyes as the hood was pulled off. The man in the skull mask didn't say a word at first, but Jerrell heard him moving about. As his eyes adjusted, he saw that the Gladiator carried a small wooden table atop which sat food, water, washcloths, and a wash basin. The Gladiator then removed his restraints, and if his legs hadn't been asleep, Jerrell might've made a move right then and there, but it was pointless in his current state.

The man in the skull mask unrolled a yoga mat in front of Jerrell and crouched down into the lotus position. The deep voice behind the mask said, "Prepare yourself for combat, Agent Fuller. Get cleaned up. Take as long as you wish, but I wouldn't get too close to my pets. They'll tear you to shreds if you try to leave this room. I always feel it appropriate to give my opponent the opening move, and so I will be here meditating. When you're ready, make your move."

"And what happens if I don't? What happens if I just sit down and don't do a damn thing?"

"Then we'll sit here until our four-legged friends decide that their hunger is more important than their training. At which time, they will eat you."

Jerrell said, "At least I'd be taking you out with me."

"I'm afraid not. It's not that I feel that the hellhounds and I have some kind of unbreakable bond. But the animals have been conditioned to the point that they would never harm me until other food sources had been exhausted."

"And what happens when I make my move?"

"We fight until one of us emerges victorious."

"Right, but I'm not allowed to leave, so even if I win, daddy's little monsters will still eat me."

"Actually they've been trained quite well on *how* to kill and *who* to kill. In this instance, they know that once the fight starts, there is one winner and one loser. The winner is allowed to leave, and the loser is lunch."

Jerrell started by waking his legs. He walked over to the small table, ate some of the food, had a drink. Then he did some stretching and limbering up. He paced the floors around the sunken, diamond-shaped portion of the room.

The hellhounds lay across the stair-stepped levels of the room, looking down reverently, like spectators at the coliseum as Caesar spoke. The beasts' eyes were alert, watching everything. When he strayed too close to the edges of the sunken platform, the dogs would growl and bare their teeth, their breath stinking like a slaughterhouse.

Other than that, they merely waited patiently for their next meal to be tenderized.

Through all of Jerrell's pacing and preparing, the man in the skull mask didn't move, didn't even flinch. He sat there, meditating, and waiting for his opponent to make his opening move.

Jerrell new that this first move could theoretically be the last. All it would take was one perfect blow to the right spot. He still had the grate cover that he had sharpened to a knife's edge against the concrete floor. It wasn't nearly as sharp as a real blade, but he was still confident that his improvised weapon would penetrate flesh. Then there was the metal washbasin and the small wooden table. They could also be used as weapons.

Or he could just do it the old-fashioned way. A sucker punch or a kick to the scrotum.

Jerrell paced and thought, paced and thought, and the more he walked, the less sure of himself he became. The confidence of his opponent had unnerved him. He felt like the only person who didn't understand the joke. As if everyone but him was seeing the world in a totally different light ... and laughing at him.

Finally, Jerrell settled on a plan of attack, slipped his hand down the back of his pants, and retrieved the sharpened grate covering. Then he took up a position behind his opponent and made his move.

97

Marcus woke up feeling as if his head had been used as Metallica's bass drum. He lay atop one of two mattresses inside a dimly lit concrete cell. Ackerman occupied the other. His older brother sat on the concrete with his legs crossed and his arms in some kind of strange yoga pose.

Marcus asked, "What the hell are you doing?"

"I'm meditating upon the present circumstance."

"Wonderful. Any revelations?" His voice was harsh, and his throat felt like sandpaper.

"I suspect I already know the answer, but the device you implanted into my spine … It doesn't actually track all my movements, does it?"

Rubbing his eyes against his palms, Marcus replied, "If you're asking whether or not anyone knows our current position, the answer is probably not."

"I feel something there, a foreign object. I'm going to be rather annoyed if your Director friend risked paralyzing me in order to insert a placebo."

"It's a real device. We're actually still trying to get the funding for the more sophisticated chip and monitoring capabilities from the NSA, but after Foxbury, the powers that be wanted you in the field asap. So they put in last year's model, in a manner of speaking. The implant can still track you and kill you, but it only sends and receives small bursts of data whenever you're in range of a Wi-Fi network or cellular hot spot. Basically, the device hijacks an Internet connection and transmits your GPS coordinates. It then receives back a code of whether to detonate or not. As long as it doesn't receive the kill code, you're fine. But if you screw up, that chip would eventually end you. You wouldn't be able to hide from it forever."

"But I could kill all of you and strategically make my way to Washington in order to deactivate such a termination order. Hypothetically."

"You're not traveling across the country without hitting some kind of wireless network. Not in this day and age."

"Where there's a will, there's a way."

Trying to steer the conversation back onto the right track, Marcus said, "The good news is that we just need to get you within range of a network. That security camera probably runs off Wi-Fi. Maybe a team is already on their way."

"Doubtful. An internal network in a private compound would have restricted access to the Internet. Our captor may even employ signal jammers. Such devices are easy to come by and inexpensive to build."

"We'll figure something out. We always do."

Ackerman said, "In light of this new information, my opinion is thus: we should now behave in the same manner that a scuba diver would when coming face to face with the massive jaws of a great white shark. Or, if you prefer, the hiker coming nose to nose with a grizzly bear and her cubs."

Marcus had no idea what his brother was talking about, which was a common occurrence, even when he wasn't groggy from being drugged. He said, "Are you waiting for me to answer? I don't know. You poke it in the eye?"

"No," Ackerman said. "Try again."

Marcus snapped back, "You pull out a knife and jam your arm into the shark and/or bear's mouth with the blade pointing vertically. So when it bites down, the knife is stabbed into its brain."

Ackerman chuckled. "I like your line of thinking, if you and I were actually encountering one of those situations. However, I was speaking more metaphorically. Sort of like that old joke about what to do when you're on a plane going down … you put your head between your legs and kiss your ass goodbye. We have now come to such a moment."

"Bullshit. I've never seen you give up before."

"I've never met anyone who could beat me before."

"I beat you."

Ackerman chuckled again. "You really believe that, don't you?"

Marcus growled and cracked his neck. "We really don't have time for that discussion right now. What makes you think we can't outsmart or outfight this guy?"

"Past experience is usually the best indicator, and our new friend has consistently beaten me."

"Don't you mean: beaten *us*?"

Ackerman said, "If you prefer. The point is that I have evaluated all the variables, and based upon everything I've observed from this opponent and given our limited resources, I see no way that we can possibly defeat him and survive this encounter. Well, perhaps a ten percent chance."

"We've been in worse situations than this, and we've always come out on top. I will never stop fighting, until they cut out my heart and drop my cold ass in the ground."

"You misunderstand, dear brother. I'm not giving up. I'm merely preparing myself for the possibility of defeat. There's a significant difference."

With a shake of his head, Marcus paused to consider his brother's words. He never treated the moments he had with people as if they could be his last. And maybe he should start. He said, "I want to tell you something, just in case."

"I know."

"You know?"

"It's a *Star Wars* reference. You were going to say, 'I love you.' And I replied, 'I know.' I've heard you and Maggie do it before."

Marcus rolled his eyes. "I do love you, in some weird way, but that's not what I was going to say. I want to tell you that I think you were right all along. I should have listened to you."

Ackerman cocked an eyebrow. "You're going to have to be much more specific."

Marcus continued, "We should have turned the Demon case over to another agency. Maybe we still can. I'm sure Valdas could get some team at the FBI on it. You were right. There is no case that's worth sacrificing any of the people I love. Maggie is off chasing phantoms. We're in this situation. And I can't shake the feeling that Dylan is in real danger. If we make it out of here, I think we should walk away from this case. I say we let this dragon sleep."

With a shake of his head, Ackerman closed his eyes and said, "It's much too late for that."

"What do you mean 'too late'?"

"That ship, as they say, has sailed. Demon allowing us to walk away was a one-time offer. He's going to destroy all of us and everyone and everything we love, merely on principle."

Marcus rubbed the cross tattoo on his chest. "Then what do we do?"

"Now, the only way out is through. We're going to have to kill them all, little brother, before they do the same to us."

98

Jerrell Fuller had shown an aptitude for martial arts at an early age, and by the time he was in attendance at the FBI Academy, competing for Quantico's unofficial hand-to-hand combat championship, he was a black belt in Muay Thai and trained in Brazilian Jujitsu. He had faced opponents who were among the best in the world, but he had never seen anyone move like the man in the skull mask.

Jerrell had thought long and hard about how the fight would go down. He had decided that he would attack with the sharpened grate cover, but not straight on or directly from behind his opponent. Instead, he would start behind and run diagonally toward the hellhounds, then he would jump into the air, kick off the next level, and come down on the Gladiator from above with the full weight of his body. The bastard would never see that coming, and even if he did, he wouldn't have time to react.

Jerrell's first move worked out exactly as he had planned, with the exception of the blow never connecting. He had been flying through the air, coming down right on top of his adversary, and then the man in the skull mask had simply disappeared.

Before Jerrell could process what he had actually witnessed, the Gladiator had hold of him, using his own momentum to slam him to the polished hardwood floor.

Pain shot through his whole body, and the air abandoned his lungs as he belly flopped off the ground. The Gladiator was right on top of him, riding him down, and striking him repeatedly in the back of his head.

Then the weight was gone from his back, and Jerrell rolled to his feet.

The Gladiator, or Skullface, or whatever the hell he called himself, stood there with a smug little grin on his face. Or at least, Jerrell imagined there to have been some kind of cocky look of self-assurance beneath that mask.

Deciding that it was about damn time he saw his tormentor's real face, Jerrell took off in a dead sprint, as if he were going to tackle the larger man. Instead, he came up short, faked a head-butt, and landed a few quick jabs to the abdomen.

The man in the skull mask barely flinched at the blows.

Using every trick he knew, Jerrell responded with a long series of punches, kicks, and feints. The Gladiator simply fended off each attack without making any purely offensive moves.

After a full three minutes of watching his expertly planned and perfectly executed blows be slapped away or absorbed, Jerrell finally realized that the Gladiator was merely playing with him. The thought drove him to hit harder and faster. He used his wrestling skills, trying to grapple, trying to take the fight to the ground. But his opponent was always one step ahead of him, never taking advantage, but always making sure that the attack fell short. Without landing any significant blow, Jerrell managed to expend a tremendous amount of energy, completely exhausting himself—while his adversary was barely even winded.

Changing tactics and buying time to recuperate, Jerrell grabbed the items from the small table and threw them at the Gladiator. Then he scooped up the wooden table itself with his left hand and swung it like a club as he slashed with the grate cover.

The Gladiator disarmed him easily, grabbing him by the wrists and wrenching his arms in the wrong direction until he could no longer grip either item. Then, in his first offensive move, the Gladiator struck Jerrell with an open palm to the throat.

Not even breathing hard, the big man in the metal mask waited for his opponent's next move. Jerrell had never wanted to kill someone so badly in his life. He had never felt rage like this.

He stepped forward, and with renewed vigor, he unleashed an onslaught of quick combinations, all leading up to a major knockout blow.

But it appeared that the Gladiator had let the show go on long enough, because this time when Jerrell went in for an uppercut after two feigned rabbit punches, the man in the skull mask caught his arm, twisting it up into position. Then Jerrell watched helplessly as, with incredible strength and speed, his enemy used his forearm as leverage to snap Jerrell's arm in half.

As an FBI Special Agent, Jerrell Fuller had been trained to deal with pain. He'd been trained to overcome it, to push through it. But he had also seldom experienced such an all-encompassing pain as this.

Perhaps for truly the first time since his ordeal began, Jerrell now knew, beyond any hope, that he was going to die.

Still, he couldn't give up. He wasn't built that way. He pushed past the sharp stabs in his left arm and swung the right with all his might. The Gladiator merely slapped the blow away and brought the outside of his foot down onto Jerrell's knee, snapping it just like his arm.

The world became pain, and then he was falling, collapsing back against the hardwood floor of the Diamond Room. The woodgrain was stained with blood. His blood. The blood of others. Old blood and new. He couldn't breathe. He didn't know what was happening. He had to get up; he had to keep fighting. He scanned the ground for the grate cover, found it, and dragged his broken body toward the weapon. As he had just reached his destination and slipped his fingers through the metal of the grate, a shadow fell upon him.

It was the Gladiator—dropping from above and driving his knee down on to Jerrell's right hand, the one holding the sharpened metal drain cover.

Jerrell could do little but watch as his hand was mangled, crushed, and broken.

The pain was secondary now. He still felt it, but only in a distant, detached sort of way. Jerrell wasn't sure if his fingers were gone completely or still hanging on by the skin, he just knew that he could no longer feel them in any way to indicate that they remained attached.

Despite all his injuries, he refused to lie down and die. He clutched his mangled hand to his chest and used his unbroken leg to push himself away from his opponent. His back found the wall separating him from the upper platform.

Hearing a growing snarl, Jerrell jerked his head away as a

Rottweiler's jaws closed on the empty air where his face had just been. He scuttled from the edge of the sunken platform like a crab, fleeing this new threat with all his remaining strength. Luckily, the animal must've simply been warning him to get back from the edge because the beast didn't follow him into the pit.

His limbs had grown cold. He was no doctor, but that didn't seem like a good sign.

Still, if he could just hang on a little longer …

But he wasn't sure there was any point in continuing to fight. No one was going to suddenly burst in and save him, just in the nick of time. But he refused to give up hope; Jerrell Fuller just wasn't built that way.

99

Emily Morgan laid her cell phone atop the conference room table and resisted the urge to cry. The person on the other end of the call had been the Director, and he had instructed her to "use local resources" to locate and assist the brothers, adding that she was a field agent now and needed to be able to "stand on her own." He had screamed most of the instructions. Then he had hung up.

Perhaps she was being overly cautious and worrisome? Marcus and Ackerman had only been out of contact for a matter of hours, and they were certainly capable of taking care of themselves. Still, she was the rookie agent and had been left alone trying to hold together all the threads of a complex investigation. She could call in additional support from the FBI, but that felt like giving up. If Maggie hadn't abandoned them, she wouldn't have had to face the case alone.

She stared at the phone, hoping for an update of any kind from Marcus, a message she feared would never come. The screen lit up with a San Francisco number she didn't recognize. Emily snatched up the device and said, "Hello?"

"Agent Morgan, this is Baxter. I've been trying to reach your colleagues to no avail. Was beginning to think I had made a bad impression."

"I'm sorry, Mr. Kincaid. The other members of my team are out of contact right now, working on the case."

"Right, they had that rendezvous with Oban Nassar. Have you heard any word from them? They had any luck?"

"No, I haven't heard anything."

"Did they go in without backup? That seems a might reckless."

"What can I help you with?"

"Well, I wanted to let your boss know that I have a name connected to the hand and tattoo on the video. Stefan Granger. Unfortunately, the guy is a ghost. Appears to be a fake identity, and we have no known address on him. But at least now we have a name and a face, and we're beating the bushes. According to Illustrated Dan, Granger was an undefeated contender in the MMA world, and so he definitely fits the mold for our Gladiator."

Emily considered what the Director had told her about utilizing local resources, and then she thought of the display of Baxter Kincaid's eccentric skills she had witnessed earlier. She said, "Mr. Kincaid—"

"Call me Baxter or Bax, my dear. Every time someone calls me Mr. Kincaid, I sprout a gray hair and lose a pound of muscle."

"Okay … Baxter … I need your help."

100

Corin Campbell couldn't decide if her adrenaline levels, increased heart rate, and rapid breathing were lessening or multiplying the effects of the drug. All she knew was that her world had become like a stone skipping over water, ever closer to going under.

She was a protector; that was the way she was built. She needed to do something. A man was about to lose his life. But her body wouldn't cooperate.

Her gaze traveled from screen to screen and then over to Dr. Derrick, who sat in front of the looking glass, a sadistic little smile across his face.

She had to do something. She forced her arms to move, to grab the rails and propel the wheelchair toward Derrick. Forcing herself forward a few feet felt like climbing Mount Everest. Finally, she bumped into the back of Derrick's chair, but he merely turned back and winked.

"This is the best part," he said.

"Please," she whimpered. "Spare this man. You have the power to show him mercy. You're our universal ruler. Do it for me. I can make it worth your while."

"And how would you do that? What could you give me that I don't already possess?"

"I could start being a good wife to you."

Corin glanced over her shoulder at Sonnequa, whose face was curled up in a hateful snarl, and then her gaze returned to Derrick. She said, "I could be your number one wife. Your First Lady. Your Empress."

"I'm fully aware of your potential, my dear, but I still don't see how letting this man live helps you realize that destiny."

"Consider it a wedding gift to me."

With a wistful and almost compassionate expression, Derrick paused and seemed to consider her offer. Then, turning to his brother beyond the viewing glass, Dr. Derrick Gladstone, like a tyrant of old, held out his arm with the thumb pointing down.

The giant in the mask nodded and walked past the salivating but patient canines.

Corin said, "Please, Derrick. Please, you can save that man."

"Yes, I could, darling. But this is business. Our clients have paid a lot of money to see a show. I can't simply pull the plug. Especially not when the Diamond Room's big finale is coming up tomorrow night." Rotating his chair toward Sonnequa, Derrick said, "Turn on the red lights, and ring the dinner bell. The boys have earned their supper."

"No!"

Ignoring her, Derrick turned back to the glass, waiting for the show.

With a reverent nod, Sonnequa touched the surface of her iPad. A distinct buzzer sounded, and all the lights in the Diamond Room changed to a nightmarish shade of red. The hellhounds came alive, flowing toward the center of the room like a tidal wave of sinew and teeth.

Corin closed her eyes against the tears. She didn't want to see what was about to happen. Unfortunately, covering her ears wasn't enough to block out the snarling and the screams of torment.

Over her own sobbing, she heard Derrick say, with a gleeful edge to his voice, "Dogs are actually red-green colorblind, so the hellhounds can't perceive the change in the color of the lights. But I think it adds something, and the viewers love it."

101

Marcus, as always, had started systematically by searching the room for any structural flaws, anything that could be used as a weapon, and any abnormalities. He came up empty on all accounts. Then he dropped to his mattress and listened, scanning for any clue to their surroundings, any information that could give them the upper hand.

A part of him was just glad that they didn't have electric shock collars around their necks.

The only items in the room that he considered using were a flat-screen television mounted to one wall and a small security camera screwed to another. But the destruction of either item would draw a lot of attention from their captors, and a homemade shiv made of broken electronic parts was of little help against a man with a gun.

The flat-screen television abruptly came to life, and Marcus shot to his feet, ready for an attack. Ackerman didn't even budge from his yoga pose. A man in a grotesque skull mask filled the large LED display.

The Gladiator, in an undistorted baritone, said, "Welcome, Agent Williams and Mr. Ackerman."

Marcus glanced over at his brother, but he hadn't even opened his eyes yet. There was no way their captors could have known Frank's true identity. To ensure that, Ackerman had undergone extensive facial reconstruction surgery, and the SO had faked his demise. Unless Frank had told them himself …

The Gladiator continued, "That's right, gentlemen. We know who you are, and why you're really here. We of the *Legion* go deeper than you can possibly imagine. And just so we're clear, Mr. Demon set you up from the very beginning. He learned of the FBI informant and used the mole to send a message to you. To draw you here. So that my brother and I could kill you."

Not even sure that the killer could hear him, Marcus said, "You know where to find us, pretty boy."

The Gladiator continued, "Here's a small preview of what's in store for you tomorrow night. You should be honored. You will be featured as the main event in the series finale of the Diamond Room."

The image on the video monitor changed from the horrifying mask to a grid of video feeds. Marcus stepped closer to get a better look, and Ackerman was right beside him before he even realized his brother had stood. They both watched as Jerrell Fuller was easily bested by the Gladiator and then devoured by the pack of dogs.

After it was over and the screen had faded to black, Ackerman said, "My previous estimates of a ten percent survival rating may have been a bit high."

102

Corin Campbell wept for the man who had just been torn apart. His screams had died away, but she could still hear the gnawing, the snarls, and the sound of teeth against bone. Part of her was relieved that she hadn't been the one on the other side of the glass, but then she felt guilty for that temporary reprieve. She certainly didn't deserve to live over that FBI agent. Derrick was right about one thing. At her core, she was a murderer.

She didn't open her eyes, but she heard Derrick say, "They are such magnificent creatures. Did you know ... Well, of course, you don't, but the Rottweiler can, thanks to their large head, exert more biting power than German shepherds and pit bulls with a force of 328 pounds—that's about half of a shark's, but still pretty damn impressive."

She said nothing.

"Evolution nearly claimed the Rottweiler at one time in history. The breed had been used mainly as herding dogs, but when the railroad invaded the land, the Rotties were out of a job. They're normally gentle giants, but they are also very malleable animals. I find it fitting that a species that fought its way back from the brink of extinction will aid me in doing the same for humankind."

She finally opened her eyes and saw Dr. Derrick's flawlessly handsome face and million-dollar smile. He said, "What do you say we switch gears? I think we've had enough of the Discovery Channel. Let's flip the station to one of those cheesy talk shows with a long-lost reunion episode. Watch the monitors carefully, Corin."

"I don't want to see it. Whatever it is. I don't want to see."

"Trust me. You'll want to see this."

"Just kill me. But please, make it quick. Don't feed me to the dogs."

He said, "I wouldn't feed you to the hellhounds, my dear. You've earned the right to at least become a lady of the lake. But it would be a shame to leave poor helpless Sammy here all alone."

The video monitors changed all at once to the grainy image of a cell much like the one she had occupied for the past two weeks. Sammy sat in the corner, rocking back and forth, knees to chest. Her younger sibling looked pale and thin.

He continued, "I was so very enthusiastic when I discovered your genetic code. In your case, a trait coupled with the desire to survive, an ability to adapt and overcome most any circumstance. Sammy, I don't believe, has your drive to live, but I'm willing to bet her genes are actually in pretty good shape. I think I may collect a sample and run some tests."

Her voice was low and trembled with fear and rage as she asked, "Please tell me that she hasn't been …"

"What? Raped? Is that even possible with a prostitute? I mean, in reality, isn't that merely an equivalent crime to running out of the restaurant without paying your bill."

"If you or your little brother have so much as—"

"Don't worry. Sweet Sammy has been well taken care of.

She is unharmed and unmolested. And she will remain that way. In fact, in a couple of days, she can go free."

"What happens in a couple of days?"

"We'll be free. Present circumstances have moved up my timeline a bit, but—with profits from the Diamond Room at an all-time high and my other businesses flourishing—it hasn't been a problem in the least. I've already secured the purchase of my own private island, which is part of the beautiful Marshall Islands chain. The Marshalls are also a non-extradition territory. Two days from now, we'll all be sitting on the beach of our new nation. One big happy family. And once we're safe on the island, then things will loosen up. You might even start to enjoy it."

She was about to say something she shouldn't have when *he* turned the corner and was coming toward her. It was the man who had haunted her nightmares and repeatedly violated her in every way—mind, body, and soul.

The father of her unborn bastard child.

A wave of protective instinct washed over her, and she hoped that the overdose of sedatives Sonnequa had given her wouldn't affect the baby.

At first, the thickly muscled man merely stood there, breathing hard, the thick cords of his body pulsing, his whole nearly naked form speckled with blood. Unlike his opponent, the man in the skull mask seemed to have come from the fight with nothing that a shower couldn't cure.

Her mind raced for a way to end him right there, but she quickly dismissed the thought. She had seen the way he had effortlessly dispatched the FBI agent, and that man had been trained to fight. What could she do against such a behemoth of a man, especially in her half-coherent state?

Then he pulled back the metal mask to reveal his true face.

She gasped and clamped a hand over her mouth. Part of her had expected there to be nothing beneath the mask, and she definitely didn't expect him to seem so … ordinary. He didn't necessarily have an innocent face, and yet it was somehow childlike, due to a round jaw that gave him the look of the Cupid off a Valentine's Day card. She also noticed cauliflower ears and a nose that had been broken more than once. Beneath his jaw were signs of surgical scars where doctors had apparently operated on his lower mandible.

He glanced down at her once but seemed hesitant to make eye contact. Derrick wheeled over and said, "I know the two of you have bumped into one another on multiple occasions, but I don't believe you've been formally introduced. Go on, say hello, little brother."

"Hello, Corin, I'm Stefan Granger."

Derrick snapped, "Your name is *Simon Gladstone*! That was the name you were born with. That was the name that our father gave to you. While I understand why you had to forsake that name in the past, it doesn't have to be that way anymore. You can reclaim your true name."

"I've been Stefan Granger for decades now. I've been Stefan Granger for a lot longer than I was Simon Gladstone."

"Now's not the time to discuss this, dear brother. Right now, I have business to attend to. Can you please be a sweetheart and see Corin back to the common room." Then, in his nonchalant manner, the whack-job doctor and the Good Wife headed down the hall, conversing in hushed tones.

The massive, blood-covered man looked at her but then quickly diverted his gaze. He ran a hand through his short hair, appearing nervous, like a kid about to ask a girl to the prom. He said, "So ... did you enjoy the fight?"

"I've seen some horrible things in my life, but that was hands down the worst."

He seemed genuinely hurt by her statements. "Well, I guess you better be getting back. But I did have something I wanted to tell you. It's something I tell all the women who've been chosen to carry my seed. I just want to say that I'm truly sorry for having to do that to you. Derrick insists on the insemination being natural. I always try to be as quick as possible, if it makes a difference. But either way, I'm sorry to put you through all that."

Corin wanted to laugh in his face. And she didn't think that desire stemmed solely from the presence of the psychotropic drugs pumping through her bloodstream. The whole situation seemed so absurd. A man like this, acting shy and offering an apology.

Instead of laughing, Corin heard herself say, "My face is going to be the last one you see before you die. The anticipation of that moment is all that's keeping me alive. Your apology is *not* accepted, and in fact, you can consider this to be a formal declaration that I intend to cut your heart out and feed it to your little monsters."

He leaned down into her face, cocked his head to the side, and slapped her so hard that she nearly toppled over. In a whisper, he said, "I better get you back now. But once all this is over, and we get to the island, I intend for you and I to be spending a lot more time together."

103

Monday

Baxter Kincaid pulled his newly acquired Harley Davidson CVO Street Glide to the curb and killed the powerful High Output Twin Cam 103 engine. The afternoon sun warmly caressed the glass-and-brick facade of Unser's Gym. The beautiful Agent Morgan hopped off the back and headed directly toward the newly renovated building. Detective Ferrara stopped her halfway and said, "You don't want to go in there. It's like nothing I've ever seen before. It's a bloodbath, a massacre."

Baxter hopped off the bike and hurried to catch up. He heard Emily say, "Have you identified the bodies? Who's in there? Is it …"

Baxter explained, "Special Agent Williams and Mr. Dantonio went missing last night. Agent Morgan and I paid a visit to Mr. Oban this morning, but he claims they never showed up."

Natalie said, "Why haven't you told me this before now?"

Through gritted teeth, Emily said, "Who's in there? Is it them or not?"

Natalie shook her head. "No, just Mr. Unser and several of his fighters."

Emily shoved Nat aside, saying, "I need to see."

Baxter followed closely behind. If Natalie told him not

to go in there, he would normally take her word for it. He had never been great with all the blood and guts, a younger Baxter having done more than his fair share of yakking into the bushes. But the gentleman in him wouldn't allow Emily to face this alone.

Once he saw the horrors within, part of him wished he had heeded Nat's warnings. Unser's Gym would likely haunt him for years to come. The victims hadn't simply been killed; they had been slaughtered. They had been laid to waste, Old Testament style. Many of their skulls had been caved in. Bones were torn from their sockets and snapped like twigs. Blood was everywhere.

Emily held her composure for a moment before she started crying and ran outside. Baxter followed close on her heels. He did so for two reasons. One: he wanted to console her, that being the way he was built. And two: he was definitely going to throw up.

He followed her up the block a ways until she dropped onto a bench in front of a BUILT Custom Burgers restaurant.

Giving her a moment to calm down, Baxter took the opportunity to puke off the curb. Then he popped five Tic Tacs, chewed them up, and slid onto the bench beside his new friend.

Pulling out a joint, he said, "You know your partners are much tougher than that pack of street fighters."

Wiping away the tears, she said, "The man who did that, who broke those men like they were nothing—that same man is now doing Lord knows what to the most important men in my life."

He rubbed her shoulder with his left hand, while sticking

the joint in his mouth with the right and flicking his Zippo to spark the fire.

He had taken a couple of puffs when Emily looked over at him, cocked her head to the side, and then snatched the joint from his mouth. He thought at first she was going to stomp it out, but instead, she placed it between her lips and inhaled deeply.

Blowing out the smoke and passing the joint back to him without a cough, Emily said, "I'm not a detective. I'm a counselor. A psychologist. I'm not cut out for this."

"Detective work is a lot about trying to get inside people's heads and figure out what they're thinking. Sounds like you're perfectly suited for the job."

She asked, "Are my friends already dead?"

"This *Gladiator* ... seems to me that he never makes it quick for his victims."

"Is that supposed to make mqe feel better?"

Baxter thought about that a moment before he responded. "No, it's not supposed to make you feel better. There's nothing that will do that right now. You're in the valley. But your best path out is to have a clear picture of the world and the challenges we face. I have faith that if we play our parts well, then things will turn out for the good."

She said, "Faith is a funny thing."

Baxter passed her back the joint, and she took another puff, just a small one this time. He replied, "I once heard a preacher tell a story about a class he had in seminary. The professor in charge of the class took all the students down to a pond in the middle of the campus. Then he challenged them to have the faith to walk out onto the water. None of this taking your shoes off or nothing. Just run, and God will handle the rest."

"Referencing the story of Peter stepping out of the boat to go to Jesus."

"Exactly, so the professor tells the students that, if they really had faith, then they should be able to stroll across the water just like Peter did."

With a small smile, Emily said, "I'm betting this professor's office had a clear view of the pond."

He chuckled and continued, "Don't get ahead of me. But, yes, his office window overlooked the pond. The preacher telling the story went on to say that he had personally considered taking a run at it, but he had ultimately decided that his faith couldn't compare to that of Peter. The old professor had also told the students that if they did succeed in this task, then they shouldn't make a big deal out of it or even feel the need to share their success with their peers. He said, 'What happens here is between you and God. Just run, and let Him handle the rest.'"

Emily asked, "So the guy telling the story never even tried it?"

With a wink, he continued, "Then years later, this preacher tells about how he had become successful and saw this old professor at a conference. Preacher walked right up to him and asked how many students the old man had witnessed run out into the water with all their clothes on."

"Hundreds, I'm sure, depending on how long he taught that class."

"Well, the professor didn't answer. He just smiled. Now, that unnerved the preacher a bit because he had been pondering this subject for some time, so he asked the question that had really been on his mind."

Emily completed the thought: "He asked how many students the professor saw actually walk on the water."

"Right, but the professor just laughed and told the preacher that no student of his had ever succeeded, at least not to his knowledge."

Emily asked, "Is this supposed to be making me feel better?"

"Just stay with me, darling. The professor explained that anyone who actually had the faith that it took to walk on water would never feel the need to prove it, especially not to themselves. It's a bit of a paradoxical exercise. After all, the whole point of faith is believing *without* seeing. The professor told the preacher that people who truly have faith ... they just run and let the Universe handle the rest. And those individuals know that if the world drops out from beneath them, they'll always find themselves on solid ground."

After a long moment, Emily said, "How do we find my friends? I'm drowning here, Baxter."

He took a deep inhalation of his organically grown herbs and then said, "You told me that you'd already met Unser, and he basically advised you to drop dead. But then he up and beats you to it. Makes me question what *precisely* he did tell you. I'm just thinking that he obviously knew something if our friend the Gladiator thought it was worth killing him over."

Emily seemed to consider this but then shook her head. "He just wrote an address down and told us our answers were there. When we went to the location he gave us, we found out it was a cemetery. He sent us on a wild-goose chase."

Baxter smiled. "No, I'm not convinced he did. Here's where local knowledge comes into play. Let's say you and I go take a walk among the tombstones."

104

Sonnequa graciously held the door for Derrick, a Walther PPK pistol in her right hand. He wheeled inside the concrete cage with a nod of thanks to his current First Lady. His brother was close on his heels, as always. As Oban had instructed, both Agent Williams and Mr. Ackerman wore tuxedos. He couldn't help but smile at the pair sitting atop the mattresses cross-legged, like two Buddhist monks on their way to the Oscars. He said, "You two look adorable."

Agent Williams held up a hand to block the brighter light from the corridor and asked, "Who the hell are you?"

"Let me put it like this: if you were to follow the yellow-brick road, I would be the man behind the curtain."

Agent Williams scratched his head and replied, "The Wizard of Oz. Is that who you think you are? I remember that guy as really not so much of a wizard. He was a total fraud, to be honest. Is that what you're saying? Was that like a subconscious cry for help?"

"I'm saying, Agent Smart Ass, that I am the one pulling all the strings. You know me as *Mr. King*."

"But," Ackerman interjected, "we've seen surveillance photos of Mr. King at his mansion."

"Yes, the whole thing with the mansion and the agoraphobia rumors and all of that nonsense is a smokescreen. It's my protection plan. You see, I started out as a quite successful businessman. A doctor actually. Oh yes, how rude of me. My true name is Dr. Derrick Gladstone. It's a pleasure to meet the both of you."

"And what are you a doctor of?" Marcus asked.

"I'm a fertility specialist. More specifically, I have my own chain of fertility clinics, which provide a nice insulator for my other business endeavors. And the darker side of my kingdom is where I make the real money."

Agent Williams started to stand but Sonnequa gestured him back down with the barrel of her gun. The DOJ agent said, "If you're supposed to be the King, then what does that make your boss, Mr. Demon? Is he like the Emperor?"

Derrick checked his watch. "I'm so going to enjoy watching the two of you die later. In regard to Mr. Demon, I owe him everything. He found me and my brother and helped us to realize our true potential. But he's not exactly my superior, either. You might think of him more as a major shareholder in my business empire. And as my younger brother informed you, Mr. Demon set all of this in motion. The message intercepted by the FBI's undercover agent was specifically crafted to make you boys think that *Mr. King*, the *Gladiator*, and the *Demon Welkar* were separate entities, and that Mr. King's organization was not happy with the Gladiator's service. When, in reality, we are all part of the same *Legion*. We are all brothers."

Ackerman said, "I'm not sure how I feel about the reckless dilution of the term 'brother' in such a context. But to be clear, the Gladiator, your masked friend here, is your younger biological sibling?"

Showing his perfect white teeth, Derrick replied, "I do so admire your work, Mr. Ackerman. I had so hoped we would get a chance to chat, and I wanted to tell you this very story. Especially considering how you are also working with a brother."

Both sets of brothers remained silent a moment, and Derrick knew he had just scored a point for his team. It was all psychological, but he wanted them to feel how powerful he and all the Legion truly were.

He continued, "This isn't something I talk about often, but you may have noticed that I'm in a wheelchair. It was during my senior year of college football when the spinal cord injury occurred. I was the star quarterback, and I would've probably been scooped up by the NFL, if it hadn't been for a linebacker trying to prove a point. It was a late hit, completely inappropriate, and the refs called him for it instantly. But the damage was already done. My spinal cord was forever broken."

Ackerman said, "It sounds like a godsend to me. If you had been contracted by the NFL, you probably would have suffered from CTE. There's still a possibility if your college years were as you describe. But, well, I'm sure I don't have to explain those studies to a medical doctor."

Derrick wheeled forward and leaned out over his knees as he continued the story. Sonnequa tightened her grip on the pistol, adjusting to ensure a clear line of fire. He said, "While I was lying in a hospital bed, my little brother went out, captured the man who did this to me, and beat him to death with his bare hands. Now that, Mr. Ackerman, is loyalty. That is brotherhood. But even if we weren't blood relatives, the same kind of brotherhood is still found within the Legion. Mr. Demon wanted me to extend to you one last invitation to join us. He can help you to achieve your true potential, just as he has helped my brother and I, and countless others."

Ackerman glanced over at Agent Williams and paused for a long moment, as if he were considering the offer. Then the infamous serial killer said, "I already have all the brothers I can handle. I have a real family. And I've warned Demon what would happen if he ever tried to take what's mine."

With a small nod of acceptance, Derrick said, "Excellent. Now that we have the introductions out of the way, I'd love for you gentlemen to join me for dinner."

105

It was a beautiful day, one her mother would have referred to as jacket weather. The sun had brightened a gray sky, but as they walked among the tombstones, Emily Morgan felt the sorrow of each death as they passed by. She didn't yet know if Marcus and Ackerman were dead, but she had already begun to cycle the stages of grief. But she had to focus. At the moment, her thoughts should remain on the man responsible for the slaughter she had just witnessed.

Emily considered herself a patient woman. After all, it was her job to listen, to genuinely care, and offer whatever counseling service the client required, whether that be a shoulder to cry on or just a sounding board for his or her problems. The nature of her job demanded a humble and understanding spirit.

But even she was ready to strangle Baxter Kincaid.

"Okay," she said, "we're here. Now, tell me what it is that you're thinking. Is the name on one of these tombstones supposed to mean something to me?"

Baxter said, "Well, these were all once people. Every one of them a son, a daughter, a friend. They each had a life, and now they have departed this mortal coil. Onward and upward. You and I will both share their fate one day. So yes, I would expect these names to *mean* something to you. But that's not why we're here."

With a roll of her eyes, Emily said, "You remind me of someone else I know when you act this way."

"I'm sure you're referring to some kind of brilliant detective mentor?"

"Actually, he's more of a mental patient. But he has this way of being horrible and yet likable at the same time."

A sadness filled Baxter's eyes. He said, "It wouldn't be the first time I was called a mental patient."

"I'm sorry. I didn't mean to insult you. I'm just a little distracted."

"No worries, darling. I want to catch this bastard just as much as you."

"I thought you wanted off the case, that your job was over?

"I said that before he went and shot up a brothel in my neighborhood. This might be a bit childish, but I think of myself as sort of the local protector of my neighborhood, kind of like Batman watching over Gotham City. Only without all the gadgets and Kung Fu and what not."

"How is this trip to the cemetery supposed to help us find the Gladiator?"

As they reached the back edge of the property, Baxter opened a wrought iron gate. Then, pointing at a small yet well-maintained home adjacent to the cemetery, Baxter said, "We're here to talk to the caretaker, who lives on the grounds. I've met him a time or two, and I remembered that his name is Granger."

106

Corin completed her chores and acted the part of the good wife, but she was always watching and waiting. Part of her wanted to shut down and give up, to play the role she had been assigned in Derrick's egomaniacal kingdom and simply go along to get along. But, in the end, she had too much conviction to acquiesce to the will of a madman. The very thing that King Derrick seemed to admire about her most was the aspect of her personality which would never allow her to be part of his harem.

Along with the other women, she helped with the preparation of dinner. It was an all-hands-on-deck kind of moment. Derrick was calling it their *Last Supper*. The final meal that they would share together before entering the promised land. She thought it strange that Derrick, a devout atheist, would latch onto such religious language, but perhaps he was doing that on purpose to set himself up as a sort of living god.

The meal preparations went slowly, since they were only allowed to use one knife. And that knife never left the Good Wife's sight. Early on, Sonnequa had caught Corin staring at the potential weapon while one of the other girls had used it to peel potatoes.

The Good Wife had snatched up the knife, held it up to Corin's throat, and said, "Don't you dare get any ideas, little girl. I know you think you're tough, but you should know that Fallujah ain't got shit on where I grew up. Don't believe for one second that I won't kill you."

Corin didn't flinch as the knife brushed against her throat. She didn't even blink. She stared directly into Sonnequa's eyes and said, "We should be allies, not enemies. If we work together—"

The Good Wife applied pressure to the blade until a small trickle of blood ran down Corin's neck. Sonnequa said, "Before I came here I was addicted to heroin. But that wasn't even enough. I had to have that heroin cut with fentanyl. Derrick saved my life and gave me a purpose. We are going to do great things together, and I won't let you stand in the way of that. I won't let you get the rest of us killed."

Corin backed down, but she kept one eye on the knife to see where the Good Wife stored it when they were done.

She set the table with two extra places, having been told they had special guests. Then she had taken an assigned seat along with the others and waited quietly for Derrick and their guests to arrive. The man in the skull mask was the first to enter, only he wasn't wearing his mask. Instead, he wore a black suit with a white shirt and tie. His hair was coiffed and his face freshly shaven.

It was a bit surreal to see the murderer who had repeatedly raped her taking his place at one end of the table as if he was the VP of some Fortune 500 company.

She noticed him stealing glances at her, but she did her best to ignore his eyes upon her flesh.

Derrick entered the dining room next, followed by two men whose hands were secured behind their backs. Sonnequa brought up the rear a few cautious steps behind them, armed with a black pistol.

The newcomers were dressed in tuxedos, as was Derrick. The Good Wife even wore a special dress and silver jewelry for the occasion.

Everyone took their seats at the long table, Derrick at the head, opposite the Gladiator. Corin had noticed that King Derrick used his younger brother like a hammer, little more than a tool for his own perverse ends, which made her wonder if Derrick could throw away his brother—and all of them—just as easily as a used Kleenex.

As he took his place in front of the assembled smorgasbord, Derrick said, "A few introductions are in order. Ladies, these two men are representatives from a federal agency called the Shepherd Organization. As part of this evening's festivities, you will have the privilege of watching these men die."

The two agents stared defiantly at Derrick. Even beneath the tuxedos, Corin could see that they were both heavily muscled and powerful men. Both were handsome, in their own ways. The one sitting closest to Derrick, whom he introduced as Special Agent Marcus Williams, possessed rugged good looks and brooding eyes. The other man, whom Derrick referred to as Mr. Ackerman, was movie star handsome and had an odd, gleeful gleam in his eyes, as if he was actually enjoying the proceedings.

After Derrick introduced him, Ackerman snickered and said, "How is it that your benefactor figured out my true identity?"

Derrick rolled his eyes. "They may have changed your face. But when Mr. Demon saw your scars, he knew exactly who you were. He's a bit of a student of scars, and he has a great deal of respect for your work, as do all of the Legion."

"Thank you. I try."

"I have to say that my brother, whom you know as the Gladiator, is itching to get into the ring with you. Destroying you and your partner will be his crowning achievement."

The big man at the end of the table remained silent, but his gaze was locked on the two newcomers. He looked as though he was ready to spring forward and attack at any moment.

Ackerman said, "That's sweet. Albeit a little sad, considering that after I kill you and your brother you'll be just another name I forget later."

Derrick laughed. "The betting is at an all-time high for this episode of the Diamond Room. And, personally, I can't wait to see how it all turns out."

Then, with a snap of his fingers, five muscular black-and-brown hellhounds burst into the room, taking up positions around the table. With a small smile, Derrick said, "Don't worry, gentlemen, the boys won't beg for scraps from your meal. They know that their supper will come later this evening."

Corin shuddered at the memory of the Rottweilers in action, the sounds of their growls and the tearing of flesh.

Ackerman looked down at the dogs with admiration and warmth, as if he would have nuzzled the hellhounds if he had not been restrained. He said, "They are amazing creatures. Did you train them yourself? I've always found working with animals to be rather unpredictable. A killing machine that loves you based on the contents of its stomach can never be fully trusted."

"Actually, our mutual Scottish friend supplied me with my praetorian guard. I can only imagine what he uses them for, but I find them much more dependable than any human. You've seen what they can do. If I wished it, I could order them to kill all of you. In less than a minute, all of your jugular veins would be torn out and you would be bleeding to death on my floor as the hellhounds slowly devoured you. I've often seen them bury their snouts into the intestines of a meal while it's still kicking."

The agent with the brooding eyes—whom Derrick had called Marcus—asked, "Can we pet them?"

This drew a chuckle from the one called Ackerman and a scowl from Mad King Derrick.

Corin wasn't sure what she thought of their behavior. The two men both seemed fearless, in their own ways. She wondered if they were really so inept as not to see the danger they faced, or were they playing some kind of psychological warfare?

Derrick simply smiled and asked the Good Wife to pass the potatoes.

Marcus asked, "Are you going to undo our hands? I think it's customary for the condemned to be allowed to eat their own last meal."

"I'll have one of the ladies feed you once they're finished," Derrick replied. "Besides, I want to hear how an infamous serial murderer came to work for the government."

"I filled out an application online, but enough about me," Ackerman said. "Have you ever heard the story of the Persian general who trained wolves to fight as part of a northern campaign?"

"I don't believe I have," Derrick said, stuffing a piece of steak into his mouth.

"The wolves were powerful and magnificent beasts,

similar to your hellhounds. The general trained them well and thought them loyal. So, when he knew that they would have to cross over a dangerous mountain pass—and it was impossible to move the full force of his army—he used the trained dogs and his best soldiers to mount a forward assault. The problem came when they were snowed in up on the mountain. The general's second-in-command, who was in charge of the rest of the forces, found them two weeks later. They were nothing but bone. The wolves, however, were fat and happy."

"My animals are well trained and well fed. We won't have a similar problem here."

Ackerman smiled, and Corin caught sight of a terrible shifting darkness in his gray eyes. He said, "But, you see, that's my point. The Persian general thought that he could control his beasts as well. In the end, he was correct in his assumption that the animals could be trained and domesticated. Where the general went astray—a lesson that perhaps you should learn from—was that he failed to see that powerful uncontrollable forces were moving against him, forces which change the rules of every game."

"And let me guess, Mr. Ackerman. *You* are that powerful force?"

Ackerman grinned. "The general in the story under-estimated the power of the cold, of winter, and of hunger. I was once a force of nature just like those. There was a time when I was the embodiment of darkness, living solely by the philosophy of the tooth and claw. And I have to say that the old me would love to drink your blood and eat your heart, but that's not my point. I was merely suggesting that one of your dogs is going to turn on you, and I'm not speaking solely of the canine variety. As they say, live by the claw, die by the claw."

None of the women had touched their food, except for the Good Wife. Sonnequa still held the pistol in her left hand, as she scooped her meal with her right.

The room was silent as Dr. Derrick and Mr. Ackerman stared each other down. All eyes were on them.

Which made Corin realize that *now* was the time for her to act.

The Good Wife had a death grip on her weapon, and the knife they'd used to prepare the food was locked away in the kitchen. All the steaks and other food had been precut into bite-size chunks.

But there was one other weapon within reach.

Earlier, when he had knocked her out of her chair, Derrick had retrieved a small pistol from a shoulder holster beneath his jacket. She had no way of telling for certain it was still there, but there was a better than average chance that the sidearm was still in place, considering tonight's special guests.

The only problem was that her legs were broken, scarred, and basically useless.

The Good Wife sat between her and Derrick, and there was no way she could approach him without drawing everyone's attention.

A strange memory from her childhood struck her mind like a lightning bolt. One of their many foster homes had a small pond in its backyard. Corin and Sammy had affixed a two-by-four to the end of the dock, to create a makeshift diving board. Her younger sister had been too scared to jump, and Corin had told her, "Sometimes, you just have to make up your mind to jump, and let God handle the rest."

With those words in her mind, Corin Campbell built up all her nerve. She summoned strength from the girl who refused to die, the one living in a beach bungalow inside her mind, and then she sprang into action.

107

Russell Granger was a heavyset man with a kind and jolly manner. Baxter had seen Russ around a few times while volunteering at the soup kitchen down in Tenderloin. Dropping onto the caretaker's couch, Baxter said, "You have a really nice place here, Rusty. I can see you've done a lot of work to it."

Pulling over a computer chair, which rested in front of a desk crammed into the living room, Russell said, "Thanks, I've done all the work myself. Well, with my son's help."

"I didn't even know you had a son."

"He's adopted. What's this about, Mr. Kincaid?"

"Is your boy's name Stefan Granger? And does he have a tattoo on his hand like this." Baxter showed him the still photograph from the bus footage.

"Yes, he does, but I'm sure he's not the only guy around with a tattoo like that. And he used to do this thing with his hand, when he wrestled, where he would wrap his hand over the bottom half of his face. Making it look like he had a skull face. It was a psych-out thing. Someone could have easily seen that, thought it was cool, and decided to copy it."

Baxter cocked an eyebrow. "It seems like you're assuming your son is in some kind of trouble. You went pretty quick to the defensive there, Rusty."

"No, I'm just saying if you think he's done something, anybody could have a tattoo like that."

"You'd be surprised. But, first off, would you like to hear why we've come knocking on your door?"

"If it's something to do with my son, I'll give you his address. He's a grown man. I'm not responsible for anything he's done."

"You said your boy used to wrestle. Did he train at Unser's?"

Russell Granger seemed to visibly shrink. He leaned back in his chair and went white. "I saw on Facebook that there were multiple murders at that gym last night. Is that why you're here? You think Stefan had something to do with that?"

"Well, let me ask you this … When you saw that article on the Book of Faces, was your first thought that your son had probably killed those people?"

Shooting to his feet, Russell said, "Okay, I think it's time I give you the name of our lawyer."

"Oh come on now, this is supposed to be the part where you break down and tell us that you always suspected this day would come and you spill your guts. Besides, why would you need a lawyer? Honestly, as the caretaker of a cemetery would you need legal—"

Beside him on the couch, Baxter felt Emily Morgan shift. Then she coughed to draw his gaze and shot him a scathing glance. He ignored her and said, "I want you to understand something, Rusty. I think your boy is responsible for the deaths at Unser's Gym. I think he also shot up a house of ill repute down in my neighborhood. I'm going to find your son and ask him some questions about it. But, as you may remember, I'm not a cop. When the cops come knocking, you are going to have to answer their questions, lawyer, or not."

"I'd like you to leave now."

"Don't be rude, Rusty. How about we talk about something else? What agency did you go through to adopt your son?"

"That's none of your damn business."

"I've heard, from several sources," Baxter said, "that your son—Stefan Granger—has a rare genetic disease called Cherubism, which has affected his lower jaw for most of his life. So I did a little research on the disorder, and found that it's extremely rare. I'm sure we could backtrack our way to some records and see how many kids were treated for Cherubism in the San Francisco area. My guess, man, if we went to all that trouble we'd end up finding out that no Stefan Granger was ever treated for Cherubism. How old was your boy when you adopted him?"

"I could call the police."

Agent Morgan flipped out her credentials and said, "He's not a cop, but I'm a federal agent here on business that is both official and urgent. Who is *your son* really? I have the authority to open all your adoption and medical records."

Baxter could see the old train of thought clattering through Russell Granger's mind. He knew there was no way out now. The truth would be revealed sooner or later, and maybe it would be better for everyone if it were sooner.

Deciding to add just a tiny bit of icing to the cake, Baxter added, "We don't care about past sins, brother. We just want to make sure that no one else gets hurt. And if your boy is hurting people and causing more bodies in graves, more widows and children crying, then I know you're the kind of man who would want to help."

After a long pause, Russell sat back down and said, "He's

not a bad kid. I know that's what every parent says, but he's really not. He has a good heart. It's just the way he was raised and his family. Not my family, but his *real* family."

Russell Granger started at the beginning and explained how he came to know three young boys through a local youth organization. Their father had abandoned them, and their mother had a lot of problems. The rumor was that she was an alcoholic and sadistically cruel. But she was always hardest on the youngest boy, whom she apparently blamed for their father leaving.

One summer day, the eldest brother, Derrick Gladstone, approached him and told a story that broke Russell Granger's heart. Their mother had made them fight like caged dogs for her own amusement. They feared she wouldn't stop until the youngest brother, Simon, was dead, since she'd apparently rolled up all of her hatred toward their father into him.

And the three boys had come up with a plan …

Russell said, "The oldest one, Derrick, he was always a crafty one, always making big plans. But he was also a star athlete and a straight-A student. Derrick and his fraternal twin brother, Dennis, were getting ready to enter high school. They explained to me that they didn't want to go into the system at their age and assured me they could handle their mother. Maybe even help her. The problem was that they feared for Simon."

"So what was their plan?"

"It was supposed to be temporary. They knew Simon and I always had a connection. He had never really known their father. I think the guy left when Stefan was in kindergarten, and he doesn't like to talk about it. The older boy even offered to pay for his brother's room and board while he stayed here."

Emily asked, "What do you mean while he stayed here? Wouldn't their mother notice his absence? What about school?"

"Derrick was a smart kid. He had it all worked out. Their mother would often take them into this special room in the middle of their house and force them to beat each other bloody. Real sick stuff. Their plan was to act like Simon hit his head and died, or something to that effect. They would do it on a day when their mother was particularly inebriated, so she wouldn't ask too many questions. The boys would then pretend to take care of everything for her and dispose of the body. Which, of course, wasn't really a *body* at all, since it was all just for show. They would have their mother tell the school that Simon had gone to live with his father and wouldn't be coming back. After the grief of what she had done set in, their mother was supposed to learn from the error of her ways, see the light, and they could bring Simon home. He was only supposed to be with me for a short time."

Baxter said, "But that's obviously not the way things worked out."

"No, their mother only got worse, and in time, I came to think of Simon as my own son. We enrolled him in a different school across town under the name Stefan Granger—which was his choice, nothing I forced on him—and it became official. He was *my* son."

Russell Granger began to sob softly, almost politely, trying to cover his tears with a smile.

Baxter could imagine this man—who had a kind and

generous heart but no children or spouse—feeling a great deal of pride surrounding the day that *Simon Gladstone* became *Stefan Granger*, the boy choosing to take on his new father's name. The feeling was probably akin to the emotion a mother felt on the day of her child's birth.

The emotion of the moment sweeping him away, Baxter embraced the big caretaker in a bearhug that turned into Russell crying on his shoulder.

After a moment of patting and consoling, Baxter glanced over to Agent Morgan and said, "We might be a few minutes here, but why don't you get on the horn and call out the hounds on a Derrick and Dennis Gladstone. I think they may be some cats with whom we would like to thoroughly converse."

108

Since it was a special occasion, the girls had been instructed to set the table with the fine china. Betting on sturdy craftsmanship, Corin snatched up the porcelain plate from in front of the Good Wife and swung the edge of the plate into Sonnequa's throat. Then she smashed it across the Good Wife's face, keeping hold of one broken shard.

Her adrenaline had been pumping nonstop for days now, all of it building up to this moment. One surge of strength and action, one last chance at survival. Propelling herself off her ruined legs, she leaped forward, out of her wheelchair and toward Derrick.

It had all happened so fast that he hadn't even turned toward the disturbance before she fell on top of him. She jammed the broken plate shard against his throat with her left hand and searched his coat with her right, hoping to find some sort of shoulder holster.

Pressing in the shard, she groped for the gun, but it wasn't there.

All her hope at success had depended on finding the gun in his coat. She wasn't even sure if the plate shard had enough durability to cut his skin or if it would simply break apart in her hands.

Even if it was a suitable knife, Derrick's brother or Sonnequa would shoot her down before she could do any real harm to King Derrick.

The two federal agents would be of no help with their hands restrained, and the other girls would rather go along to get along and survive.

Refusing to give up hope, she ran her hand down Derrick's side and found the gun in a waist holster.

The pain in her legs caught up to her in one enormous, overwhelming pressure that nearly caused her to black out, but she managed to get her fingers around the gun and pull it free.

Then she pushed herself off Derrick and used the grips of his wheelchair to whirl around on the real threat ... the man who had brutalized her, raped her, stolen a piece of her soul, and impregnated her with a piece of his own.

The big man had pulled his gun, but he seemed hesitant to shoot with King Derrick in the line of fire.

Unlike her tormentor, Corin didn't hesitate. She took aim and squeezed the trigger.

Her first two shots sailed wide. But the next three struck the Gladiator squarely in the chest, sending him toppling back and over his chair.

She then jammed the still smoking barrel of the gun against Derrick's right temple and said, "Say hi to Genghis Khan for me."

109

Ackerman had been genuinely surprised to see one of Gladstone's girls spring into action, and he was impressed by the young lady's animal ferocity. He was also amazed that the actual animals in the room had not leaped to Gladstone's defense. He studied the eyes of the hellhounds as the attack took place and made note of the nature of the dog's training. Two of the Rottweilers flanked Derrick while the others stood behind the other three sides of the table. Other than a few whines and growls, the dogs didn't budge from their designated spots. This told Ackerman that the dogs were trained to only attack when given a certain command. Upon further consideration, he decided that made sense considering that the animals often watched people strike their masters in the Diamond Room.

When Corin Campbell—whom he recognized from Baxter Kincaid's presentation—opened fire into the Gladiator's chest, Ackerman was again astonished that Corin's little coup had an actual shot at success.

Turning to his brother, he saw in Marcus's eyes that they had come to the same conclusion at the same moment. Working in unison, they placed their feet against the table and shoved it over on top of the girls on the other side, including the dark-skinned beauty who had just been attacked and was raising her gun.

The table knocked the armed woman back just in time for her shots aimed at Corin to be deflected into the ceiling.

Ackerman tried to use leverage to snap his plastic restraints. Unfortunately, Derrick had spent the extra money on professional-grade flex cuffs, which couldn't be defeated as easily as common zip ties.

Hands still restrained, Marcus surged forward and kicked the gun away from the complicit captive. Ackerman briefly wondered if the young black woman suffered from some form of Stockholm syndrome. She certainly seemed totally loyal to good King Gladstone. He made a note to self that Derrick's methods may be worthy of more detailed study.

Corin now had the barrel of her weapon pressed against Derrick's temple, and Ackerman knew the look in her eyes very well.

Then, before he even realized he was speaking, Ackerman said, "Ms. Campbell, don't pull that trigger. I know you want to. I know it would be the easy thing to do. But killing changes everything. It will divide your life into two sections, the before and the after. And the faces of the dead forever haunt you."

Tears rolled down Corin's cheeks as she said, "He deserves it. And this isn't my first rodeo."

"Don't do it, Ms. Campbell. Keep the gun on him and help us get free of these restraints. Then we can—"

Ackerman heard two small thumps, and Corin Campbell jerked back from Dr. Gladstone, falling to the floor with a scream and a spray of blood.

Directing his gaze at the source of the suppressed shots, he saw that the Gladiator had wisely chosen to wear body armor beneath his black suit. Ackerman seldom bothered with bulletproof clothing himself. Such concerns were for mere mortals.

110

Marcus's face bounced off the floor as the Gladiator picked him up like a rag doll and slammed him to the hardwood of the dining room. A second later, his brother's face slammed down beside his own. Ackerman didn't even put up a fight.

"You could've just let her kill him," Marcus said.

"I thought we were anti-murder now. I can't keep up with your ever-shifting views of right and wrong. Besides, what do you think the hellhounds would be trained to do if both Gladstone brothers were to expire?"

The sound of two more *thump pings* echoed through the dining hall. The two bullets embedded themselves into the floor between Marcus and Ackerman's heads, sending an eruption of splinters into the air.

The Gladiator stood over them and said, "No more talking. Or my next shots are in your skulls."

Ackerman snorted. "Please. What's going to happen to your crowning achievement if you kill us now? Executing defenseless opponents doesn't seem to be your style."

The Gladiator drove the butt of his pistol down hard into the small of Ackerman's back. His brother merely grinned and blew the big man a kiss.

Marcus asked, "Can you see the girl?"

"Yes, she took a round in the shoulder. She's alive for now. I think she passed out from the shock."

"You really think that if she had shot Gladstone, then the dogs would have gone wild?"

"That's what I would have trained them to do."

"But you've got that weird animal magnetism. Couldn't you have put the whammy on them? Like the Crocodile Dundee, hypnotizing thing?"

Ackerman said, "I'm not familiar with the reference, but I understand your meaning. Against one, of course. Against two, probably. But against a whole pack, not likely."

Two more bullets erupted into the floor, and the Gladiator screamed down into their faces, "I may not want to kill the two of you right at this very moment, but don't worry, it's coming. And if you don't shut up, I'll kill one of the girls. Are we clear?"

111

Corin woke from a dream about Sammy protecting a wounded sea turtle that had washed up onto the beach. The memory was a good one, a moment of innocence and love that seemed so alien to her now. The voice summoning her from her slumber was also one that she remembered well, but not one that she recalled fondly. It was Derrick Gladstone saying her name. She tried to hold on to a more pleasant reality, but a spray of water into her face brought the fantasy crashing down.

She opened her eyes to a sky of reds and purples and heard Derrick say, "I'm very disappointed with you, Corin."

She tried to sit up, but a terrible pain in her right shoulder brought her back down to the smooth concrete. Then she remembered the gunshot wound inflicted by the Gladiator. But that had been inside. Where was she now? She was obviously no longer indoors, and she lay upon a sloping surface of stamped brown concrete.

In response to Derrick's message of disapproval, Corin groggily whispered, "I'm not too happy with you either, Doc."

"I'm sorry to say that your little coup attempt was less than successful."

She pushed herself up onto her left elbow and looked into the face of her tormentor. Derrick sat in his wheelchair several feet above her on a railed platform. Beside her, on the concrete which seemed to slope off into oblivion, was Tia, the young woman with no tongue. Sonnequa stood atop a similar platform on the opposite side of the open space, in front of some type of small control panel.

Fearing that Derrick had already taken her to his private island, Corin asked, "Where are we?"

"My apologies," Derrick said, "I'd forgotten that you've only been with us a short time. It truly feels like we've known each other for much longer. Your sisters and I dined here last week, but that was while you were still undergoing insemination."

Corin had discovered that the closer she came to death, the more the filter between her thoughts and her words had broken down. But now was not the time for rash action. She halted the urge to hurl obscenities and stopped herself from once again telling Derrick how she was going to end him. Instead, she gritted her teeth and, sensing what was coming next, latched on tightly to a piece of nearby metal— some sort of sprinkler or fountain system embedded into the concrete.

Derrick said, "If you had enjoyed the privilege of dining with us last week, you could have experienced this magnificent view under better circumstances. We're about five stories up in a restaurant that was once called *Ristorante La Cascata*, which is Italian. It means simply 'Waterfall Restaurant.' I'll give you one guess in which part you're currently resting."

Glancing over her shoulder at Tia, Corin said, "Grab that metal nozzle and hold on for your life."

Derrick laughed. "Clever girl. Sonnequa, if you would be so kind …"

Knowing what was to come, Corin didn't look to the Good Wife for a plea of mercy. She merely closed her eyes and squeezed the small fountain mechanism with all the strength she had left, which wasn't much. Her right hand had grown numb and weak from the wound in her shoulder, and her left arm felt like a limp noodle.

A second later, she heard the rushing of water. A second after that, she felt a gentle stream cascading over her. The cold water actually soothed her ruined extremities, but even the slow trickle was enough to begin pulling her down the slope toward oblivion.

She didn't open her eyes until the flow abated, and Derrick said, "You may have noticed the chain around your ankle."

In truth, she hadn't realized that her right foot was ensnared by a thick metal chain. She had little feeling in her feet now. As she looked down the slippery slope of the man-made waterfall, she realized that the chain had been wrapped through a pair of cinderblocks, which rested precariously on the edge of the five-story drop off.

"The chain is connected to enough weight to easily pull you over the edge of that precipice and into the darkness beyond. You've actually seen what lies at the end of your fall … the lake beyond the glass adjacent to your living quarters. What you may not realize, however, is that this lake is not natural. It was actually an old quarry and is several hundred feet deep. Imagine what it would be like for those cinderblocks to be swept over the edge, pulling you with them. The five story fall wouldn't be the death of you. No, you would ride that train all the way to the inky depths of the pit. There you would drown and die and ultimately be consumed by the creatures of the dark. And, as I've told you, our actions have consequences beyond ourselves, and so poor Tia has been chosen to share that fate with you. I don't enjoy this sort of thing, Corin, but you've given me no choice. Believe it or not, darling, this is truly going to hurt me more than it hurts you."

112

Stefan Granger—as he preferred to be called; his true name, just as the skull mask was his true face—should have been preparing for the fight of his career. Instead, he had been summoned by his egomaniacal brother and told to bring two "things" to the roof. The first was the saw they used to cleanly sever the limbs of the bodies Derrick used for marketing purposes—a 20v cordless circular saw equipped with a diamond blade and no safety guard—and the second of Derrick's "things" was their Parkinsons-afflicted mother.

He took the elevator up to *Ristorante La Cascata* and arrived in time to hear Dr. Death loudly proclaiming, "I read somewhere that it only takes six inches of water on the road to cause total loss of control of your vehicle. I would think far less would be able to sweep those blocks over the edge."

As he grew closer, Granger saw that Derrick had dropped Corin and Tia into the restaurant's fake waterfall fountain and was threatening to send them over the edge.

Hearing them approach over his shoulder, the mad king wheeled around and said, "Just in time, baby brother."

Scowling, Granger replied, "What is this, Derrick?"

In a booming voice, his brother called out, "Sonnequa, keep the ladies moist for me please."

Granger's anger rose as he watched the water cascade down the slope toward Corin and Tia. He felt no moral obligation to protect them; morality was an illusion forced upon the weak minded. Or so his biological father, the professor, had always told him. But both of the women Derrick was playing with had earned their survival through blood and pain. And through that crucible, they had also earned Granger's respect, something his brother had lost long ago.

"Why are you doing this now? We should both be preparing for the broadcast."

"You have to *make* time for the important things in life."

"Mother could have watched your sick little game on the video feed. Why in the hell did I have to bring her up here now? This is my night, not yours. When we get to the Island, you can play genetic messiah all you want. But tonight, I'm going to prove that I'm the best of the best."

"I don't like your tone. You *will* remember your place, baby brother. You may have taken up the *Gladiator* title, but you will never take up the name of the *King*. Now ... I think the time has come for us to re-unite Mother and Father."

"What are you talking about?"

Looking at their mother with a devilish glee in his eyes, Derrick replied, "I say we cut her into little pieces with the bone saw, starting at her feet, going up appendage by appendage. Then we toss the pieces of her over the waterfall like chum. Call it a grand memorial ceremony for Father, a great thinker and a credit to our kind, who was stolen from us long before his time."

"That's not how I remember him."

"You were too young to remember anything."

"I remember everything."

Granger, in fact, recalled this old swimming hole long before an entrepreneur lost his nest egg on the now defunct resort. He had heard the older kids, his brother's friends, talking about skinny-dipping up at a place they called Undertow Lake. The teenagers would dare each other to dive down until they felt the pull of the current against them. It was apparently a harrowing experience, but he'd never heard any stories of swimmers dying beyond the urban legends of what happened to someone's cousin twenty years ago.

How many bodies were at the bottom of the lake? He couldn't say for sure, but he knew there was at least one.

He had ridden in the front seat beside Mother as they had taken a short drive up the mountain and disposed of Father's remains one rainy September evening. The place had smelled like moss and rot even then. They had tied cinder blocks around Father's body, just like the ones now chained around Corin's and Tia's ankles.

Having learned later that merely weighing down a body usually wasn't enough to keep the remains from bloating and decaying their way to the surface, he had lived in fear of that crime being discovered for much of his young life.

Granger said, "If you're going to sentence Mother to the pit, you'll have to do the same with me."

"Speak plainly. What are you mumbling about?"

"I killed our father, Derrick. Is that clear enough for you? The night he left, I overheard everything. He was abandoning us all to have a love affair with another man. I got a knife from the kitchen, and as he was packing the car, I stabbed him in the throat."

Derrick was silent a moment, an expression of confusion and disbelief on his face. Finally, in a feral snarl, he said, "You're lying. You were only five years old. You couldn't have ..."

"Why do you think Mother hated me so much? Why did she want me dead?"

"Because your abnormality is what chased Father away."

Granger laughed, but inside he wanted to snap his brother's neck. "Is that what you think?"

"I'm not suggesting I feel the same way, but, yes, he—"

"She hated me because I know where all the skeletons are buried. Plus, I think she was afraid of me."

"But … why? Why would you have attacked our father?"

"I heard everything that night. He hated us all, Derrick. He never wanted children. He wanted his work and his sexual freedom. He thought of us as a burden to be discarded, a skin to be shed. I don't remember all the words, but I vividly recall the emotions. He wasn't the man you thought he was. Ask Mother."

Turning to the old woman in the wheelchair, Derrick said, "Blink three times if he's telling the truth."

Mother's eyes were cold and defiant as she responded in the positive with the only muscles over which she could still maintain control.

Derrick's facial features quivered with rage, and his eyes showed that he was about to come unhinged. But Granger waited and watched as his brother, the cold and calculating narcissist, worked things out in his mind and then said, "It doesn't matter now. Doesn't change anything. But the old witch can't live to see the Island. We've played with her enough."

We certainly have, Granger thought. It had been Derrick who had first come up with the idea of "haunting" their mother after his supposed death. Derrick would set her up to see her murdered son in the schoolyard as she drove past. He would sneak Granger into the house and hide him under his bed, so that the younger boy could walk past their mother's door like a wandering spirit. It had been Derrick, with his reluctant help, who had truly driven their mother to madness and a crippling abuse of alcohol and prescription medications.

Granger said, "She's paid for her crimes."

"She will never have suffered enough for the way she treated us. It's truly amazing that I was able to pull myself up from the gutter to the pinnacle of our species, but I've had to work ten times harder because my mother, who was an educated woman, should have known better than to spend her meager teaching salary on cigarettes and Everclear over food for her three children! Don't you remember the days of taking whore's baths in gas-station restrooms because she had neglected to pay the water bill? She disappeared for a third of our summer vacation one year, and we found her in—"

Through clinched teeth, Granger said, "None of that matters right now. In a few minutes, I have the fight of my life."

"It matters now more than ever, baby brother. She's not going to the Island. She doesn't deserve to reap the rewards of a harvest she tried her best to spoil."

Every muscle shaking now, Granger whispered, "You love the sound of your own voice, don't you? Just a narcissistic fool who uses a lot of words but says nothing. A man who cares about nothing and no one but himself. Everything you have done your entire life, even when it appeared altruistic on the surface, has always, at its core, been about *you*. Making *you* the center of attention. Putting *you* up on a pedestal. You think everyone else in the world is sick and needs you to cure them. But what you can't see is that people like you are the disease. A head crammed with knowledge, but so little understanding. You genuinely believe that everyone loves you, when, in reality, we barely tolerate you."

Primarily using his arms, Derrick launched himself from the wheelchair onto his unsteady legs. When standing, Derrick was actually a couple of inches taller than Granger and used that advantage now to stand over his younger brother.

But Granger didn't back down at all. He wasn't afraid of his brother. He feared no man.

Derrick ripped the bone saw from Granger's hand and activated it in front of his younger brother's face. Then he said, "You sniveling freak! How dare someone like *you* question *me*. I should have ended you the moment we found out you were defective. I should have put a pillow over your malformed face along with your clearly malformed brain and—"

Even during his hand-to-hand fights, Granger always carried a set of small push daggers concealed in a custom-made quickdraw holster on the back of his fighting shorts, just in case. Rage overtook him now, and without a further thought, Granger pulled one of the daggers with his right hand and punched it in and out of Derrick's chest with a blow intended to puncture a lung.

The surprise and fear that came over his brother's face was one of the most amusing sights Stefan Granger had ever seen.

Derrick stumbled backward, tipping over his wheelchair. And then, with the improvised bone saw still held in a clenched fist, Dr. Derrick Gladstone flipped over the railing and down the concrete waterfall.

113

The frigid waters had stung her skin like a swarm of bees at first, but after the initial attack, the cold helped to dull her other pains. Corin had positioned her abdomen atop her one lifeline—one of two small fountain nozzles in the center of the sloping waterfall. She had instructed Tia to do the same, but she knew that, if those blocks went over the edge, the force would be enough to pull them both from their tenuous perches.

The Good Wife had been uncharacteristically merciful by only turning the water flow up to a steady trickle when she could have easily washed her sworn enemy over the edge. But Corin supposed that Sonnequa's concern was for Tia and not her.

When she heard the two brothers shouting, she dared not look up for fear of losing her unsteady balance.

But then she heard a scream, and her gaze reflexively shot up in time to see Derrick's body falling on top of her.

She braced for the impact. It was only a glancing blow, but his weight still crushed her against the concrete and expelled all the air from her lungs.

As he rolled over her, the madman's left hand clawed her flesh and locked around her bicep, causing the metal fountain nozzle to dig into her hip while simultaneously halting his tumble.

Wheezing for air, his white dress shirt covered in crimson,

Derrick still found the strength to pull himself to his feet, nearly wrenching Corin's arm from its socket in the process. She would have wailed in agony, if she had any breath by which to do so.

King Derrick's eyes were wide and wild. He tried to climb over her toward the opposite railing, where Sonnequa stood. But Corin kicked at his knees with her untethered leg, causing him to fall back atop her in a heap.

The wild-eyed doctor grabbed her by the throat with his left hand and raised a cordless circular saw he held in his right. Time seemed to slow for Corin, and she feared that her brain was being deprived of oxygen to the point she would black out.

She noticed the dried brown blood and gore splattered over the yellow surface of the saw and knew what Derrick was about to do.

He pulled the saw's trigger and thrust it toward her.

Corin dodged the blow, the saw striking the concrete with a high-pitched scraping.

Derrick reaffirmed his grip around her throat and readied the saw for another strike. She wouldn't be able to keep the blade from chewing her flesh for long, and so Corin let her entire weight press into her hip and reached up toward Derrick's chest. Her fingers scrambled over his shirt, searching for the source of the blood.

When she found the wound, she jammed her thumb inside, grasped his flesh, and wrenched against it.

Unable to breathe or scream, Derrick merely wheezed out his anguish.

He released his grip on her neck and dropped the circular saw. The still-spinning blade came crashing down at her, and Corin was just able to arch her midsection in time. The saw spun to a halt and came to rest against the small of her back.

Derrick wasn't so lucky. He tumbled backward, arms flailing. Corin didn't release her hold on his wound until his weight tore the flesh from her grasp.

Sonnequa had turned off the flow of water, but the surface was still steeply angled and slippery as ice. Dr. Derrick lost his footing and fell to his back, sliding toward the edge.

Searching for a handhold, he grabbed onto the only option left to him: the chains connecting Corin and Tia to the cinder blocks. Corin braced herself against the nozzle as she felt his weight yanking her toward oblivion.

But the chains were slippery as well, and Derrick couldn't get hold of them in time to keep himself from rolling into the quartet of concrete blocks and knocking them over the edge of the man-made waterfall.

114

Corin Campbell had endured a lot of pain. She had been kidnapped, raped, beaten, shot, broken, and punished with molten silver. Pain had become an intimate bedfellow. As the weight of the cinder blocks combined with Derrick's weight tore her flesh against the fountain nozzle, she barely recognized the sensation. It felt more like the shock of a cold shower than the ripping of skin and muscle.

But she knew her body wouldn't be able to withstand the pressure for long.

Her only saving grace was that Derrick's weight was distributed between herself and Tia, the tongue-less girl. That changed when Tia slid from her perch. The other girl wailed and clawed the concrete as the cinder blocks towed her across the slippery surface like a child on a Slip 'N Slide.

Corin heard Tia's screams a moment after she disappeared from sight. Then a splash. And then nothing but Derrick's wheezing as he tried to pull himself up her chain.

At that moment, she realized that all she needed to do in order to assassinate Derrick the Tyrant was to let go. She could push herself off the nozzle that was chewing through her midsection and slip into oblivion, just like Tia. Perhaps it was worth her life to put an end to Derrick's madness.

Then she felt the weight of the circular saw against her back and became aware of another option.

Corin twisted her arm around and grabbed the circular saw's grip. Then she pressed the trigger to activate the blade and swung it toward the chain connecting her to the blocks.

The blade's edge sparked against her thick iron restraints, but it only took a second for her to realize that the attempt was futile. She would never be able to cut through the metal in time. And what was the point anyway? Derrick would be dead, but his brother was still alive. There was no escape for her. Perhaps it was best to just let go. Surrender. Give up.

But, from the back of her mind, she heard a small child's voice whisper: *The saw will cut through bone.*

Knowing what needed to be done and not hesitating to act, she met Derrick's gaze and said, "Believe it or not, darling, this is going to hurt me more than it hurts you." Then Corin brought the spinning blade down onto her own ankle.

115

Stefan Granger rushed to the edge of the railing as his brother fell and then watched as Derrick and Corin struggled. He pulled his pistol and took aim at his brother, but he stopped himself from squeezing the trigger. First, because he hadn't really intended to kill his brother, although he supposed that ship had already sailed. Second, he stayed his hand because they were outside and the sound of a gunshot coming from a condemned property could draw a lot of unwanted attention. He cursed himself for removing the suppressor for cleaning.

In the end, he decided that saving Corin and Tia wasn't worth taking the risk. Derrick was dying, drowning in his own blood. If his brother took one or both of the ladies with him, then so be it.

But Granger watched with fascination as Corin—the girl who refused to die—staved off all of his brother's attacks and returned them with a feral ferocity. She was a virile and tenacious specimen. He hoped to get to know her better on a personal level once they reached the Island, if she survived this encounter.

Those hopes were dashed when the cinder blocks went over the edge. And then again when Tia soon followed.

His brother's pointless struggling for life didn't surprise him. The older Gladstone had always displayed a stubbornness of thought and action.

But Corin's desire to survive was nothing short of awe inspiring. Even in the face of what was certainly overwhelming pain, she tried to cut through her chains. And then, upon failing, she spat words of contempt and chopped off her own appendage, dropping the spinning blade down with force and allowing gravity to do the rest.

Derrick Gladstone's life ended with a wheezing gurgle and a splash. Granger felt it a fitting end for his piece-of-shit brother. He imagined Derrick being dragged to the depths, just like his father before him.

And then he turned his attention to Corin, who had passed out and was sliding toward the edge of the waterfall.

Without another thought, Granger leaped over the railing and clamped one hand onto a nozzle and the other onto Corin. He heaved the small woman up and over the railing, dropping her beside Sonnequa.

Then he climbed out of the waterfall and examined the bloody stump where Corin's foot had once been. He wrapped a tourniquet around her shin using his left-push dagger and a piece of her dress. Then, turning to Sonnequa, he said, "Go down where I keep the tools and bring back a hand torch. We need to cauterize her wound to keep her from bleeding out."

116

Francis Ackerman Jr. had been mentally preparing for this moment since he had watched the video of Agent Fuller being beaten and devoured. Fuller had played his cards well. He had tried to calculate the perfect opening move. He had taken his time and thought things through and had tried to get one step ahead of his opponent.

The Gladiator had made a mistake by giving Ackerman the extra time to plan *his* perfect move. It was an error born of vanity, and such arrogance warranted a slight uptick in the chances of their survival to twenty percent.

Ackerman and his brother had been secured to chairs identical to those used with Agent Fuller. And, just as before, the door opened, and the hellhounds entered like a processional of proud warriors. The Gladiator followed close behind. He now wore his typical skull mask, and Ackerman much preferred him with it on. He was shirtless and splattered with blood.

Marcus said, "Where did all the blood come from? You said if we were quiet and cooperative, then you wouldn't hurt any of the girls."

"The ladies are fine. I would worry about yourself right now."

The Gladiator ran through the usual rules of his game, while Ackerman waited, chomping at the bit, yearning to be let off the chain.

"Prepare yourselves for combat, gentlemen. Get cleaned up. Take as long as you wish, but I wouldn't get too close to my pets. They'll tear you to shreds if you try to leave this room. I always feel it appropriate to give my opponent the opening move, and so I will be here meditating. When you're ready, make your move."

Noting that his opponent had used the exact same speech he had used with Fuller, as if it were a planned monologue, Ackerman increased their survival percentage to twenty-two percent.

After undoing their restraints, Granger struck a lotus pose, and they were given their moment to prepare before the match.

But Ackerman didn't need a moment. His plan was already cemented in his mind.

As soon as Granger was in position, Ackerman took off in a sprint and rolled onto the floor, heading straight for his opponent. The Gladiator didn't even have time to close his eyes and enter a state of meditation before Ackerman leaped into action.

He saw a flash of fear in the other man's eyes, and it tasted like blood in the water to a shark.

It seemed like a very long time since Ackerman had witnessed such a look in the eyes of a victim. It gave him strength. It was a small reminder of a fact he had only recently come to realize: his lack of fear always gave him the advantage in a fight.

He adjusted the odds in his head to twenty-five percent.

Ackerman rolled twice before coming to a stop three feet in front of the Gladiator. Then he mimicked Granger's yoga pose and said, "So ... are there a lot of people watching?"

Because of the mask, Granger's voice sounded muffled and metallic as he replied, "You should be honored. It's a record-breaking night. Nearly doubling our next best ratings, which was the death of the FBI agent that you witnessed. It's truly amazing how many people will pay such large sums of money to watch me kill you."

Ackerman chuckled and said, "I'm afraid there are going to be a lot of sick and twisted folks who will be very pissed off when they don't get to see what they want tonight."

"I am undefeated, Mr. Ackerman. But even if you did best me, they would then get to see me die. Which would definitely be a twist ending."

"You misunderstand me. I'm saying that they are not going to see what they want because we are not going to attack you. I'm going to sit here until *you* make the first move. Because you see, I think you've forgotten how to really fight, and so I'm turning your own challenge around on you. I'm going to sit here until you open the fight yourself."

The Gladiator's muscles tensed as if he was ready to spring into action now, but he hesitated. He said, "The rules of the match have been set. Choosing not to attack is a choice in itself, and if you don't choose, then we will turn on the red light, and the Hellhounds will devour both of you."

Ackerman closed his eyes, leaving himself completely vulnerable. Granger would see it as a great sign of disrespect, and even that small action would sow the seeds of doubt in the Gladiator's head. After a few breaths, Ackerman opened his eyes and said, "That wouldn't be much of a crowning achievement for you. Let's be honest, you'd merely be showing everyone what a weak little freak you are. A confused child with both Daddy *and* Mommy issues."

Granger balled his fists and then used a deep breathing technique to calm himself. "Fine, Mr. Ackerman. Let's play a game of *Who's the More Patient Killer*. But I warn you … stalling for time, thinking that one of your friends will rescue you, is pointless. No one's coming to save you."

"I'm merely demonstrating what a weak little freak you are. What is it that you hope to gain out of all this? Do you truly believe that if you prove yourself to be the strongest and toughest, then maybe Mommy and Daddy will actually love you?"

"I won't fall for your bait. In reality, that's a pretty poor attempt to manipulate me. But the longer you draw this out, the more our viewers will love it. So go ahead."

"We'll see. But if you're too afraid to open the fight, then I suppose we'll just sit and chat while we wait for the dogs to get hungry enough to eat us."

"You can talk all you want. But I'm done answering. I'm going to close my eyes and go into a state of meditation, and as I said, you can begin when you and your partner are ready."

"My dear boy, do you have any idea who I am? I was raised in a nice penthouse apartment atop the seventh layer of hell. I spent most of my life in isolation, staring off into oblivion. I could sit here and entertain myself for days on end."

The Gladiator didn't respond.

With a small smile, Ackerman winked at his brother and said, "This is going to be fun. What should we talk about? Or rather, what subject would you like me to explain to you, Mr. Gladiator?"

117

After lecturing on the battle of Appomattox, quantum physics, string theory, and a torture device called the brazen bull, Ackerman decided it was time to start pushing his opponent's buttons again. He was aware of the level of rage the Gladiator held inside. He had seen it in his handiwork. He had witnessed it in his cold and calculated actions that night at Willoughby's, and he had observed it in the man's eyes during dinner. A rage like that could make one sloppy.

Adjusting their odds of survival to thirty-five percent, Ackerman said, "Well, enough about me, let's talk about you. After all, this is not our first date. It's time we get to know one another better. Let's see, considering your brother's personality and the way he dominates you, I'm betting you didn't have a proper father figure during your youth. Did dearest Dad pass away, or did he merely abandon you?"

He studied the Gladiator's minute physical reactions, and as he mentioned the man's father, he made note of a brief tensing of the shoulders. Obviously, a raw nerve.

"I'm betting he left you. Have you ever considered that your deformity may have had something to do with that decision? I'm sure it played a role. Many weak-minded individuals simply can't deal with having a freak for a child."

The Gladiator's muscles screwed down even tighter.

"And what about your mother? Both you and your brother have consistently demonstrated a blatant disregard for the fairer sex. This also gives credence to my absentee father theory. I get the sense that your mother was present, but you would have been better off if she had not been, correct?"

His opponent looked like a volcano ready to blow, the thickly muscled man's skin growing noticeably redder by the second.

"So how did your mother abuse you? Was it physical, psychological, or sexual in nature?"

The Gladiator began deep-breathing exercises. Ackerman saw that as a sign that the mountain was nearing eruption. Keeping a close watch on the telltale markers that his opponent was about to strike, Ackerman readied himself for his pre-planned defense.

He said, "Did they realize you were a mangled monster from birth or did your deformity present itself later? I'm sure it made it even more difficult, considering how your brother is such a pompous—"

The Gladiator sprang from his seated position like a silverback gorilla. He rolled forward, using his left arm like a vaulting pole to propel himself toward Ackerman. It was a straightforward and brutal attack, all the man's weight shoved forward into one locomotive punch.

But Ackerman saw it coming a few milliseconds before it happened.

Rolling away from the attack, he reached back and jammed his fingers beneath the Gladiator's skull mask. Dropping all his weight down, he used the mask as leverage to drive his adversary's head to the hardwood floor. Then

Ackerman started pummeling the back of his opponent's head.

After landing a few brutal blows, he ripped off the mask, and sticking his fingers through the eye holes, he brandished it as a weapon. He drove the metal mask down at the back of the Gladiator's neck, going for the death strike.

But he struck nothing but floor. The Gladiator had rolled away at the last second and was now on his feet, coming at Ackerman for retaliation.

In his peripheral vision, he saw Marcus joining the fray. His brother ran at the Gladiator from behind, wielding the small table as a club.

The Gladiator seemed to be attacking with reckless abandon, but looks were often deceiving. As Marcus swung his makeshift club at the man's back, the Gladiator dropped to the ground in a sweep kick that pulled Marcus's feet out from beneath him.

Ackerman closed the gap and unleashed a flurry of powerful blows, utilizing some of his favorite Indonesian Silat techniques. He had studied many forms of martial arts, but Silat was a personal favorite since it was designed to completely annihilate an opponent. It was an elegant and brutal art for use against someone who desired to take your life.

Unfortunately, the Gladiator easily countered every attack with the perfect counter move. The man's skill and accuracy were astounding, like nothing Ackerman had ever seen before. It was as if the Gladiator was a fighting supercomputer reacting with flawless precision. He felt as if he had picked a fist fight with Deep Blue.

Going on the offensive, the Gladiator deflected one of

Ackerman's strikes and responded with three powerful punches of his own. Then the big man grabbed Ackerman's throat with one hand and his crotch with the other. Picking him up over his head, the Gladiator tossed him across the ring like a rag doll.

Midair, Ackerman readjusted their chances of survival back down to twenty-five percent.

118

Ackerman had now adjusted their chances of survival to eleven percent, following a series of attacks from both he and his brother—working in unison and separately—that had resulted in unequivocal defeat. He felt as if they were fighting a cyborg from the future rather than a man of blood and bone. The Gladiator was without doubt the most skilled hand-to-hand combatant he had ever faced.

Realizing they couldn't best their enemy in a fair fight, he searched for a way to cheat.

He found none.

His instincts told him to discover and exploit a weakness.

He found none.

From over his shoulder, his father—the serial murderer known as Thomas White—whispered, *Then make a weakness, boy.*

Ackerman ignored the voice. It certainly wasn't the first time his father had vividly spoken to him. At times, he could almost feel and smell the old man's cigar-stained breath on the back of his neck. But, in all other instances, his own internal projection of his progenitor merely quoted scenes from his memory, and he couldn't recall his father ever speaking those exact words to him.

Chalking it up to a deteriorating memory—while ignoring the darker possibilities—he rushed in, slid to the ground, wrapped his legs up with his adversary's and twisted the Gladiator to the ground.

Unfortunately, Ackerman soon learned that was a big mistake.

The Gladiator's ground and pound was even better than his standing game.

Barely rolling away before the enraged pit fighter could pummel him like a gorilla, Ackerman shot to his feet, instantly on guard. But his mind seemed foggy, his razor's edge not as sharp.

His father whispered, *That's not at all what I meant.*

Another line from a memory that he couldn't quite recall …

Ackerman said aloud, "The first rule about having delusions is that you don't talk about, or to, the delusions."

He realized a millisecond too late that he was speaking to no one. Luckily, Marcus was too preoccupied getting his ass handed to him by the Gladiator to note him slipping.

The killer formerly known as Francis Ackerman Sr. said, *I meant you should use your brother against him.*

"I'm not listening to you."

You really don't have a choice in the matter. What are you going to do, plug your ears? I'm in your head, child. Let's be realistic here.

Ackerman watched the Gladiator flip Marcus over, nearly snapping his brother's arm.

He said, "I'm open for suggestions."

Use your brother.

"More specific instructions, please."

You need to create a weakness.

"Not a very helpful hallucination, are you? He has no weaknesses. I'm actually quite honored to be killed by an instrument of such pure perfection."

Now, you're getting the idea.

Ackerman felt a strange, piercing pain in his skull, and he stumbled forward, dropping to his knees.

He said, "If you're going to keep doing all this talking but saying nothing, then I welcome my imminent demise."

Just because he has no weaknesses, doesn't mean he doesn't make mistakes. He's just better than you at hand-to-hand combat. Get over it. I know you've been moping about since he beat you at Willoughby's.

"He didn't beat me. I saved Emily and—"

Once again, news flash, I'm in your head. You can't lie to me. Now, if you can't create a weakness, then create an opportunity for one.

"I hope this isn't how I sound when I intentionally annoy people."

Use your available resources, boy. The Gladiator is the best, and he knows it.

The fog starting to clear, Ackerman realized what his delusion-born dad had been trying to tell him. *Vanity. Pride.* Those were the Gladiator's sins. His opponent had complete confidence that he was the best. But he had also never seen Marcus really angry …

His brother, after being swatted across the hardwood pit like a tennis ball, grabbed Ackerman by the shoulder and said, "Are you okay?"

Ackerman looked up into his brother's face, which was bruised and bloody, and then over at the Gladiator who stood at the opposite side of the ring, hands at his side, waiting for them to come to him. Another sign of his opponent's overconfidence.

Knowing what needed to be done, Ackerman began tearing at his throat and waited for the fear to hit his brother's eyes. Then, still pretending to be choking, he faked a blackout.

"Frank! Frank!"

Holding his breath and lowering his heart rate, Ackerman made himself appear dead to cursory examination. He was going for the idea that the Gladiator had damaged his larynx to the point of him choking to death. He had first learned how to lower his vitals in order to appear dead when he was a boy. It was a skill that had served him well in the past, one forcefully learned under the tutelage of his father. The elder Ackerman had hooked electrodes and sensors to his body and then made an electric shock directly correspond to the rate at which his son's heart beat. This essentially meant that Ackerman had to learn how to die in order to live.

"Frank!" Marcus screamed.

Then Ackerman heard the Gladiator whisper, "Flawless Victory."

He fought back the urge to chuckle, but the Gladiator's words stirred an altogether different emotion in his brother.

Marcus let out a battle cry and rushed at the Gladiator with reckless abandon. Hearing the scream and the footfalls, Ackerman opened his eyes and watched as his brother attacked with a feral intensity that could seldom be witnessed this side of hell. It was an attack of pure rage, no technique or planning or out-thinking an opponent. Marcus punched and kicked and fought the Gladiator with pure animal brutality, no consideration for his own life or for the damage he was sustaining. Marcus used his body like a bullet that he intended to drive into the heart of their enemy, no matter the cost.

Still, the Gladiator was an opponent like no other. He couldn't be bested in a fair fight, by Ackerman or his younger brother. The big man absorbed a lot of blows from Marcus, but he was skilled enough to keep them from striking in full force on any vital areas.

Ultimately, the only way to stop his brother's wild attack was for the Gladiator to wrap him up, the massive arms encircling Marcus like a pair of boa constrictors. But that was a big mistake. It presented an opportunity for his brother to create a weakness.

And Marcus seized the moment, using his teeth. Ackerman watched with pride as his brother bit into the Gladiator's neck. Much as one of the hellhounds watching hungrily from the higher levels would have done, Marcus was going for the throat.

The Gladiator screamed and punched, but he couldn't free himself. Marcus followed by kneeing the larger man repeatedly in the groin until their adversary dropped to his knees.

Following him down, Marcus continued his frenzied assault.

It seemed to be over. The big man appeared to be bleeding out on the floor, and Marcus looked to be intent on the job being properly finished.

But Ackerman knew that any predator grew increasingly more dangerous the closer it came to death.

His choking charade successfully complete, he sprang to

his feet and rushed to assist his brother.

Before he could reach them, Ackerman watched helplessly as the Gladiator produced a small push dagger from a hidden sheath and plunged it into Marcus's side.

Marcus didn't even pause his assault at the blow. He kept working his fists like pistons, and then he pulled the small dagger free from his flesh and thrust the man's own weapon into the side of the Gladiator's neck.

As Ackerman pulled his brother off the dying man, Marcus seemed surprised to see him and wrapped him up in a huge bear hug. It took Ackerman a moment to realize that his brother had actually considered him deceased only seconds ago.

Patting Marcus on the back, he said, "I experienced a momentary loss of consciousness. I see that you faired well on your own."

Pressing his left hand over the knife wound in his side, Marcus said, "You weren't breathing."

"Strange. I suppose I experienced a momentary loss of life. How's your wound?"

"I'm fine."

Ackerman doubted that. Blood was pushing past Marcus's fingers, and his brother's skin grew paler by the second. Marcus needed a battlefield dressing and a trip to the hospital. But he had faired far better than the Gladiator, whose remains would be lucky to see a morgue.

The Gladiator had his hand clenched over the weeping wound in his neck. His eyes were wild with terror, but his mind still clung to life.

Kneeling beside him, Ackerman stroked his adversary's hair and said, "I noticed that during your life you've suffered from a bit of an identity crisis. You hate the face you were given, and so you cover it as often as possible. You hate the name you were given and the people who share it, but what you've failed to realize is that neither the moniker you were given nor the one you conjured for yourself is your *true name*."

The Gladiator reached up to Ackerman and, in a choking gurgle, he rasped, "Kill me. Please."

"Shhhh, don't speak. I'll merely ignore you anyway. You're about to die, my friend, with or without my assistance. The important thing is that you listen to me now. When your life functions cease and you're all alone in the darkness, I think you'll hear a voice calling your true name. Not one given to us by parents or the stage or society, but a name you were given by the One Uncreated Being. I know you don't believe in that sort of thing, but perhaps now is a moment for re-evaluation of one's views on the afterlife? Perhaps you should consider answering that voice calling your true name. Or not. Your call."

Then Ackerman kissed the Gladiator on the forehead and whispered, "Enjoy being eaten alive. You know what they say, live by the tooth, die by the tooth."

From behind him, Marcus said, "Come on, Frank, we need …"

Ackerman turned back as his brother's voice trailed away in time to see Marcus faint. He rushed to his brother's side and caught him under the arms. Then he scooped Marcus up and carried him to the next level of the tiered VIP lounge, striding among the hellhounds.

The dogs growled and woke Marcus. Ackerman said, "Don't make eye contact. At this point, we have to trust their training."

A few of the Rottweilers whined and spun in circles, but they would always look back to the bleeding form in the center of the pit. Once through the door at the top-most tier, he sat Marcus down on the filthy Berber carpet and locked the door behind them. As he did so, he caught a glimpse of the predatory black shapes of the hellhounds descending upon their dinner. Regrettably, he couldn't stay for the show.

When Ackerman returned, Marcus had passed from consciousness once again. Slapping his brother awake, he said, "Now is not the time for a nap."

Marcus mumbled something incoherent, and Ackerman responded by asking, "Why are you always biting people? You have no idea where they've been. Not to mention the microbes that could be swirling in their veins. At least tell me you spit the blood out afterward."

"I think I'm dying."

"Nonsense." Then he tore off a piece of his shirt, stuffed some of the fabric into the wound, and wrapped the rest around Marcus's waist as a field dressing.

"We're trapped," Marcus said. "I'll never get to the hospital in time. There are more of those dogs patrolling outside. We can't even walk out."

Ackerman replied, "You don't need a hospital. We just need some gunpowder and a match to burn those veins and capillaries shut."

His voice a ragged whisper, Marcus said, "Where are we going to get those things? Shut up. Just promise me you'll find Dylan a good home. Somewhere he can be normal. I don't want him to be anything like us. He deserves better."

"I'll raise him myself, instructing and teaching him in the ways of both the flesh and the spirit."

"Absolutely not. He needs—"

"You have no say in the matter. You'll be dead."

"Damnit, Frank, can't you just—"

"If you want to make sure Dylan grows up right, then you're going to have to fight for him. I'm not going to let you off easy, little brother."

"Listen to me, please, I'm not ... Do you hear that? Is that the wind?"

Ackerman said, "If it's flights of angels swinging low to carry you home, they'll have to get through me first."

"I'm serious."

"So am I."

"Just listen ..."

Still concerned that his brother may be hallucinating, Ackerman nonetheless strained to identify any abnormal auditory vibrations. And there was something; a distinct thumping sound.

With a smile, Ackerman said, "That's a helicopter, and it's hovering over the roof."

119

The sound of John Fogerty asking if anyone had ever seen the rain pumped out of Baxter's headphones. He hummed along, nodding his head to the beat of the music, and remembered the next song on his record at home as "Born on the Bayou." Unfortunately, his record player wouldn't have fit on the SFPD's Bell 429 helicopter. He supposed that the reduced size of his music library was one win for technology, but vinyl still sounded better.

From the copilot's seat, Det. Natalie Ferrera said, "There's nowhere to put it down on the roof."

Still nodding along to CCR, Baxter said, "You know how I like to make an entrance."

The roof of the defunct resort property was covered with dilapidated tables and equipment. It looked as though someone had cleared a lot of junk out from the building's interior and stacked it on the roof. But Baxter knew a couple of tricks to clear a path. Directing the chopper's rotor wash at the obstacles, he expertly guided the helicopter lower until the force of the blades pushed away the debris like a giant leaf blower. He repeated the procedure and then set the Bell 429 down in the middle of the *Ristorante La Cascata*.

Nat shot him a dirty look and, referring to the helicopter's given name, said, "Air Support will skin you if you damage *Matilda*."

"Would that be before or after you punch me in the balls?"

Dropping her headset, Nat opened her door and yelled, "Thanks for reminding me. I'll be collecting on that debt when you least expect it."

Agent Morgan slid open the door to the rear cabin, and the two women pulled their weapons and headed for the covered portion of the restaurant, which also held the stairway access.

Baxter stayed with the chopper. He was merely the getaway driver. No need for him to stick his neck out. Nat and Emily didn't make it inside, however, as they were met by a pair of women, one clearly unconscious and wheelchair bound and one a gorgeous black women in a white silk house dress and slippers. The woman in the wheelchair wore a similar outfit but hers was stained red and black. He recognized her as Corin Campbell, the person he had been hired to find. He also remembered seeing a photo of the lady in the white dress in Nat's files: Sonnequa Washington. She had been one of the earliest hacking victims and the first to disappear, which made him wonder how many of the other missing girls were also still alive.

Baxter dropped from the chopper and rushed to help. He scooped Corin's unconscious and bloody body into his arms and laid her down gently in the large helicopter's rear cabin.

Corin's eyes fluttered open, and looking up at Baxter, she rasped, "Am I dead?"

With a wink and a smile, he said, "No, darling, you've got a spectacular life left to live."

"Who the hell are you?"

"Just think of me as your guardian angel. Now, lie back, relax, and let old Baxter take care of the rest. You're safe now."

At his back, he heard Sonnequa yelling, "Get this thing out of here. She needs a hospital."

Emily calmed the nearly hysterical woman with a confident look and a hand on her shoulder. Then she held up her phone and showed Sonnequa a photo of the missing members of her team. She said, "Have you seen these men?"

Sonnequa didn't look long at the photo before saying, "They're already dead. We need to leave now. Before he gets here. He had to have heard you landing."

Baxter noticed Emily's features tense and her porcelain cheeks flush at the thought of her friends being dead. Tears filled her eyes. She opened her mouth, but nothing came out.

Nat asked, "Before who gets back? The man in the skull mask? The Gladiator?"

"Yes. I'm sorry, but he's already killed your friends by now."

Emily grabbed the dark-skinned beauty by the shoulders and said, "What do you mean, 'by now?' You didn't see them die?"

"You can trust me on this, little girl. He's like a spider. No one gets out once they're caught in his web. I've never seen anyone else but him walk out of the Diamond Room. He's invincible."

Releasing Sonnequa, Emily said, "You just don't know my friends. Detective Ferrera, we need to hurry."

Sonnequa held up Corin's leg to show the scorched flesh and missing foot, and Corin cried out in pain. "My friend needs a hospital, please!"

Ignoring her, Emily and Nat headed for the stairs, Sonnequa still yelling after them. Then she turned to Baxter and said, "We can't wait. I'm begging you." Her eyes were bloodshot and wild with fear.

He said, "I assume I'm the only one here who can fly this thing. And I'm much more afraid of those two ladies than your pal, the Gladiator."

Tears streaming down her cheeks, she said, "You're a fool. We're all going to die, if you don't get us out of here. Please."

"Listen, there are a whole slew of other cops on their way."

"How did you even find us? I've been here for … I don't even know how long."

"It's over now. You're safe."

"As long as he's alive, we'll never be safe."

"Granger or Gladstone or the Gladiator or whatever he wants to call himself is just a man of flesh and blood. We tracked down the one normal Gladstone brother and triangulated the last times the burner cells used by his siblings were activated. Then I hijacked a helicopter to get us here as fast as possible, but the local cops should only be a few moments behind us. You're safe now. Your fight's over. You won. Both of you. You survived."

Sonnequa closed her eyes to hold back the tears and shook her head. To Baxter's surprise, Corin reached out and took Sonnequa's hand. A long look, pregnant with emotion, passed between the two women. Then Sonnequa nodded slowly, and wrapping her arms around Corin, both women began to weep.

He said, "You're going home, ladies. You beat them. They'll never hurt you again."

Hearing Emily's voice from behind him, he wheeled around to see Mr. Dantonio carrying Agent Williams, who looked deathly pale. Emily yelled, "Baxter, get us to the closest hospital."

With a smile, he said, "It would be my pleasure."

Climbing into the cockpit, he began his pre-flight checks as the others piled in. Slipping on a headset, Emily said, "He's bleeding out, Baxter. We have to hurry."

Pulling back on the stick and lifting off from the resort's roof, Baxter said, "No worries. You know, you never even questioned how I knew how to fly a helicopter. It's not like I learned this shit from reading a book."

Over the intercom, the man who had introduced himself as Francois Dantonio, said, "Actually, Mr. Kincaid, I did learn how to operate a helicopter, and several other pieces of equipment, by reading a book. It's basically just the concepts of lift, drag, and thrust."

Frowning, Baxter said, "No offense, but I don't want to work with y'all no more. You steal my thunder."

120

Corin stared at the hospital room ceiling and wondered if life was worth living, if the benefits of existence outweighed the costs. She didn't question merely the purpose of her life, but that of all life in general. All the pain. All the suffering. Was there a point to any of it?

She had survived, true. She had refused to die and had won the day. The police had rescued Sammy and the rest of Derrick's harem from the compound, after Mr. Dantonio had contacted animal control agents about humanely tranquilizing the compound's four-legged praetorian guard. Her little sister now occupied the hospital room's other bed, having suffered no physical harm but enough psychological damage that it took her three days to speak. Sometimes, Sammy still seemed to be walking in a sort of sick fugue state, but Corin refused to let herself succumb to a similar melancholia.

She had nearly lost the baby during her own struggle for survival, but through some twisted miracle, the Gladiator's seed still clung to life. It was young enough that abortion was on the table, and she couldn't see herself raising a child conceived in such a dark place. But terminating the pregnancy and choosing whether or not a baby deserved to exist seemed too close to something Dr. Derrick would have done. Adoption perhaps. Childbirth couldn't be any worse than what she'd already been through.

And she hated to admit it, but she was starting to enjoy a little pain.

A voice like honey said, "I hear you're getting a new foot, kiddo."

With a small smile, she pressed the button to raise her bed. Baxter Kincaid stood in the entrance to her hospital room, another arrangement of flowers in his arms. He wore a Pink Floyd T-shirt and camouflage shorts, topped off with his trilby hat and mane of curly golden hair. One of the many bright spots of the past two weeks had been the frequent visits from various members of the team who helped locate the Gladstone compound, especially Detective Ferrera and Baxter.

"You didn't have to bring me more flowers, Mr. Kincaid."

"I'm sorry, young lady, but due to some copyright exclusions they have legally removed the mister from out in front of my name. I'm just the Bax, man. Plus, I feel like I should come bearing gifts more often, not just for you but for everyone in general. Which brings me back to my question. Are you receiving a special gift soon?"

Thinking of the prosthetic, Corin looked down at her blankets and the fall of the fabric where her foot should have been. It was strange; she could still feel it. There were moments when she was able to forget.

She said, "You heard right. The Director of the Shepherd Organization stopped by yesterday and said that he had a connection at DARPA who had secured a cutting edge prosthetic for me."

"It's good to have friends in high places. You're going to be back on your feet in no time."

Corin felt the teardrops growing heavy behind her lids. "I don't know that I'll ever find the strength to stand again."

As he placed the flowers on a side table beside an array of other gift-shop purchases, Baxter said, "I don't buy that for a second. Kid as tough as you will be doing triathlons a year from now."

Changing the subject before her thoughts could venture into dangerous territory, she said, "Detective Ferrera was here earlier. She told me that you used to be her partner in the homicide division. I asked why you quit to become a PI, but she didn't have an answer."

"Was there a question for me in there somewhere?"

"I'm asking. Why?"

Baxter cocked an eyebrow and said, "I heard you broke off your engagement. Same question to you."

"The girl Blake wanted to marry died out there in the woods. And the girl who came back in her place doesn't want to marry someone like Blake. Your turn."

Pulling over a chair, Baxter said, "I left the SFPD because I was racking up too many debts I could never pay back."

"Like gambling debts?"

"No, more like debts of honor. Too many victims whose killers didn't meet justice. Too many families who didn't find closure. The brass were happy with passing a fifty percent clearance rate. Some cases we couldn't solve. Some we solved but didn't have the evidence to prosecute, which is basically the same as not knowing who did it at all. I saw a better alternative and struck out on my own."

"Did you ever kill anyone on the job, Mr. Kincaid?"

"That's a rather bold question."

"I've learned that life's too short not to be who you really are and not say what's really on your mind. I've kept my mouth shut long enough."

"Just curious, but why do you want to know?"

"Is there any kind of client confidentiality with private investigators?"

"Well, you're not actually my client. And no, I'm licensed with the state of California and governed by the Private Investigators Act, which means I'm duty bound to report any criminal activity past or present to the proper authorities."

"So if I told you about something I had done in the past that was illegal, you'd have to tell the cops?"

"That's right. But if you told me about some hypothetical situation, just a mental exercise, then I'd simply assume you were seeking wisdom from an elder."

"Okay, I think." She paused and considered how to phrase her question. "Hypothetically speaking, if an older sibling had taken lives in the past in order to protect her sister, would she be any better than Derrick and his demented brother? I mean, how do you put a value on life? How do you justify killing, no matter the circumstance? Is that older sister any better than the Gladstone brothers?"

Baxter's expression grew serious. "Define better. It's not about who we are or what we've done, but rather who we choose to be. Transcending our own sinful natures is a road we can't walk alone."

"I don't have the energy for a God talk right now, Mr. Kincaid. So just let me guess, your particular religion or church is the right one with all the answers?"

"I don't believe in religions. I believe in relationships. And I personally feel that I've learned how to form a relationship with the Source of everything—to commune with the one uncreated being who resides beyond space and time."

"I don't know if I believe in all that."

"Neil deGrasse Tyson—you believe in him, right?— once said, 'The atoms of our bodies are traceable to stars that manufactured them in their cores and exploded these enriched ingredients across our galaxy, billions of years ago. We are atomically connected to all atoms in the universe. We are not figuratively, but literally, stardust.'"

"What does that have to do with God?"

"We all have stardust in us. The light of the Universe. Tyson is an agnostic, and so that may not be the same kind of cool to him as it is to me. But the more I learn about science, the more I'm secured in my faith. I hear him saying that we are in the universe, but the Universe is also in us. We all hold the light of the source of creation. That's a scientific fact. We just need to open ourselves up to it. Surrender to it. Let your let shine, baby girl. You just have to lower your defenses and pick up what the Universe is laying down."

"What about tsunamis, earthquakes, disease? How can a loving 'Universe' allow all that to happen?"

"Let me answer that quandary with another. Where does your hope come from, Corin?"

"I don't understand the question."

"Would you like to?"

She shook her head in confusion. "Like to what?"

"Understand the question."

"I guess so."

"How much time do you have?"

Corin slowly glanced around the room for effect, sat up in her bed, and replied, "I'm not going anywhere for a long time."

With a grin, Baxter pulled out his cell phone, activated a recording app, and placed the device between them. She arched her brows, and he said, "Do you mind if I record this conversation? You know, for posterity purposes. I have a feeling I may say some pretty cool shiznit."

121

The dilapidated resort's presidential suite smelled like a mixture of a pine forest and an ocean breeze. The first was a result of the biohazard cleaning crew that had disinfected the scene after the CSI work had been completed, and the second odor emanated from Derrick's massive saltwater aquarium, which teemed with all manner of exotic fish. The faux nature smells made Marcus feel nauseous. The SFPD crime scene technicians had come and gone while he was in the hospital recovering. They had sprayed luminol-based chemicals and dusted for prints, searching for blood and other trace evidence. Then the cleaning crews had descended with their Tyvek suits and disinfectants.

And now, Marcus could barely concentrate over the scent of cleaning fluid and saltwater piercing one of his senses while the bubbling and humming of the aquarium's lights and pumps attacked another.

Closing the door to Derrick's master suite, Marcus Williams stared up at the wall filled with baby photos. He ached for those families whose dream of parenthood had been corrupted by the egomania of a madman. So far, none of the parents had been notified, pending the results of the investigation. Marcus wasn't convinced that any of them should ever know the truth. It made him feel old and tired to think that only a few years ago he would have insisted that the truth see the light of day, no matter the costs. He had yet to decide if it was better that his views weren't as rigid as they once were, or if it was worse.

The SFPD had been instructed to stay clear of Derrick's personal computer system and to leave that portion of the analysis to the Shepherd team. The Director had insisted out of fear that some of the Judas Killer's files on the SO might have found their way into Gladstone's possession. With Ackerman's help, Stan had been connected to the device using a wireless hotspot and was currently searching for any evidence that could put them on the trail of Demon's other acolytes.

The locals had an entirely different agenda. The SFPD had hoped to find a connection to Oban Nassar or any of Mr. King's other lieutenants. That would have given them probable cause for a warrant to search the mansions and King's business holdings. Unfortunately, so far, all their efforts had turned up nothing. No official ties could be made between Derrick Gladstone and Mr. King's illicit empire.

Ackerman was now helping Stan by inserting a series of USB flash drives that had been located in Gladstone's safe. They had already been at the job for a few hours, but as yet, Stan's computer forensics had turned up nothing more than a collection of video footage and personal documents. It would have been good evidence for a trial—which was a bit unnecessary for dead men—but nothing that could aid them in dismantling Demon and his Legion.

At his back, Ackerman said, "I believe Computer Man has discovered something pertinent."

Turning around too quickly, Marcus felt the stitches in his side tug against his flesh to the point of breaking.

Ignoring the pain, he joined his brother behind Gladstone's mahogany desk and leaned down to the laptop's webcam. He would have sat down atop a folding chair that rested beside his brother, but that chair was already occupied by Ackerman's new best friend, his Shih Tzu puppy, which Emily had insisted he bring with him whenever possible.

Ackerman said, "I'd be happy to remove the vermin for you. Down, Theodore!"

The little dog looked up from his dreaming and wagged his tail. Marcus smiled. "You gave him a name?"

"Yes, I labeled him after two of my favorite historical figures. Ted Bundy and Theodore Roosevelt. One was a United States president, who had actually tasted battle, and the other a cunning serial murderer. I can't remember which is which for some reason. No matter. The dog has a name, and Agent Morgan can now direct her attentions toward more fruitful pursuits."

Theodore had grown bored and gone back to sleep. Marcus didn't want to wake him. He also didn't want to face the fact that his brother was noticeably slipping in very subtle ways. Instead, he leaned into the laptop's view and said, "It's a good name. What do you have for me, Stan?"

"I've found a hidden partition on some of these drives. The data from any one of them is garbage, but when I combined them together and used a deep analysis algorithm, I discovered a coded series of text documents."

"English, please?"

"I think we may have found some additional Judas diary entries. He must have entrusted them with Gladstone for safe keeping."

Ackerman said, "Or Judas is stringing us along with a

trail of breadcrumbs that leads to Demon's doorstep, still working against his old mentor from the grave. For all we know, Dr. Gladstone may have been unaware of the existence of the files."

"Anything concrete in the entries?" Marcus asked.

"You guys will have to read them to determine that, but I did various keyword searches and came up with one match to the word 'Demon' that you may find interesting. There's an entry here referring to Demon and Judas visiting a potential new member of the Legion. But the strange thing is that Judas refers to Demon as *the Demon Welkar*, like it's his last name or something."

Ackerman offered, "Or our scarred-faced friend is actually possessed by a supernatural entity named *Welkar*."

Marcus said, "We have enough devils to fight. Let's leave the supernatural stuff to priests and angels."

"Spiritual warfare should be a primary concern of us all. We are but mere…"

Feeling one of his brother's ramblings coming on, Marcus tuned out Ackerman, and instead, he closed his eyes and dissected the phrase *'Demon Welkar.'* Was it an anagram? A code of some kind?

"… And then the young lady snapped the chains with her bare hands."

"That's great, Frank. But when you were inside Foxbury Prison, Demon gave you a business card. Remind me again what it said."

"One side held a miniature version of a Henry Fusilli painting. The other contained a simple message …" Ackerman's voice trailed off as he caught the connection.

Marcus said, "It said 'A2E,' correct? If we take that name

and switch every letter E for an A and vice versa. It gives us the name Damon Walker."

Ackerman nodded. "But if that is Demon's given name, it's a clue that either Judas or Demon could have planted for us to find. Two killers. One taunting us from the grave, and the other laughing in our faces at every turn."

"Who knows what madness they have in store for us next."

With a grin, Ackerman added, "I know I'm excited."

"Oh yeah, great fun, if we survive."

"I would be of greater assistance in such a fight if you were to give me a gun."

With a roll of his eyes, Marcus said, "Sorry, the Director still says no guns. But I did convince him to allow you to have your bone-handled Bowie knife back. And these." Fishing into a pocket, Marcus held out the small concealed sheath and push daggers that the Gladiator had used. "I figured these would be right up your alley. And … it's your birthday next week, so consider this an early present."

"I've never received a birthday gift before. Thank you, brother." Then Ackerman examined the small blades and grasped the push daggers so that the cutting edges protruded out between his middle and ring fingers. Testing the weight with an elaborate shadowboxing display, Ackerman said, "These are better than a gun anyway, in the right hands."

"Glad you like them. You've earned it. I'm proud of you, Frank. I mean that."

"And I of you, little brother."

From the laptop, Stan said, "We've turned up one more piece of information you may find interesting, boss. Not all of those pictures on the wall belong to Gladstone's biological children. The biggest part of them are babies born as part of a clinical trial."

"A clinical trial for what?"

"A new fertility drug that was apparently designed by Derrick Gladstone himself. It's currently undergoing the FDA's approval process."

Ackerman asked, "What does the drug do?"

"From what I gather, it coats a man's sperm in some kind of protein that makes them have to swim harder or something like that."

"I'm no expert, but that doesn't sound like it would aid in fertilization."

"It's not designed for men with problems. It's supposed to be for a normal couple having a baby. The theory is that a lot of genetic abnormalities can be bypassed by essentially killing off the weaker sperm. It's also designed to support insemination for the healthier and stronger swimmers. At least that's what I gather from their website."

Marcus's lip curled up in disgust. "A drug that ensures that only the strong survive. Even in death, Gladstone is corrupting the world with his views about who deserves to live."

Marcus supposed that neither he nor his son would have a place in Dr. Gladstone's brave new world. Their unique neuropathology would likely have been one of many deemed unworthy of life.

Ackerman shrugged. "Gladstone was merely adhering to the Darwinian concepts revered by the scientific community. Perhaps taking them to extremes, but Darwin himself believed that inferior individuals should refrain from reproducing. I believe one such quote from Darwin, who is an irrefutable pillar of the scientific religion of today, states that hardly any farmer is so ignorant as to allow his worst animals to breed."

With a shake of his head, Marcus replied, "And who determines who deserves to live? Who among us has that right? It makes me sick. Francis Galton's concept of eugenics was built upon the scientific doctrine set forth by his cousin, Charles Darwin. And Hitler's 'superior race' belief was based on the ideas of group inequality that are key to Darwin's 'survival of the fittest' theory. Rudolf Hess, a Nazi party leader, said that 'National Socialism is nothing but applied biology.'"

Ackerman leaned back in Derrick's leather chair and placed his feet up on the desk. Then he said, "Perhaps, but we can't blame old Charles writing about his observations on the Galapagos as having direct causality to atrocities like the Holocaust. After all, Hitler perverted religious ideology as much as he did scientific theory. Darwin didn't directly advocate concepts like eugenics or the Nazi's final solution, but the idea that we are no more than animals of flesh and blood certainly gives rise to the thought that we should control human breeding in the same manner we would any other livestock. Science is a wonderful thing. Such pursuits save lives and make the world a better place. It's the study of God's creation and our universe, and it's beautiful. But science is not a satisfactory standard for quantifying the human condition. We are so much more than these mortal coils. We are beings of light and emotion. If you rob humanity of that ideal, classifying people as nothing more than a subset of intelligent animals with delusions of grandeur. If our lives have little meaning beyond what we can contribute to the herd, then it becomes easy for us to put a value on one life over another."

"And now Derrick Gladstone is going to enact a holocaust of his own. But rather than killing those he deems inferior, he wants to make sure they're never even born."

"Perhaps your Director has an associate at the Food and Drug Administration who can put a halt to Gladstone's brainchild?"

"Hopefully, but I'm not holding my breath. Damnit, Frank, even in death, that bastard is still hurting people. The more I learn about them, the more I think the Gladstone brothers are the most evil men we've ever hunted. It's one thing to take life, but this is … a whole other level of depravity."

"They were certainly a pair of lost souls, but I get the sense that we've yet to see the meaning of the word 'depravity.' Just imagine the perversions a mind like Demon's could dream up."

Marcus said, "Or someone like our father. But even he only brought two broken children into the world."

"That we know of."

"Don't say that. Two of us is more than enough." Marcus sighed and leaned his fists against the mahogany desktop. "I don't know what to do anymore, Frank. Derrick Gladstone used his brother like a hammer to nail down his enemies. I don't want to push you like that. I don't know that this life is the best thing for you."

"Our lives and the direction our paths take is something we can neither control nor hide from. You told me the past didn't matter. All that's important is what we do now. We are soldiers, Marcus, in a war that we can't even see from our limited perspectives. We are those who stand against the darkness by bringing others to the light. It's our job to save men like these from themselves and prevent them from bringing others down into the depths along with them."

"Some people are beyond saving."

"I'm sure everyone said the same about me. Ephesians 6:12: 'For we do not wrestle against flesh and blood, but against the rulers, against the authorities, against the cosmic powers over this present darkness, against the spiritual forces of evil in the heavenly places.'"

"You and I aren't exactly champions of virtue and light."

"I don't believe we were chosen for who we are, but, rather, who we could be. You and I have been called to rage against the dying of the light inside the souls of men."

"It seems more like we're called to be punching bags."

"There's some truth to that. But I think we're more like those inflatable clowns that children pummel. We always seem to pop back up."

"Until the day comes when we don't."

"And what a grand adventure that will be."

"Where do we go from here? Do we head back to ADX Florence and pay Demon a visit, or do we go after Maggie?"

"You're the boss, brother. But if I may be so bold as to offer a suggestion."

"As if you have a problem being bold."

Ignoring him, Ackerman continued, "I'm afraid that little sister may have bitten off more than she can chew by pursuing the Taker on her own. I say we leave Demon on ice and focus on our wayward team member. Because it's my professional opinion that if we don't find her before she finds the Taker … Well, then she'll be the next one who's *taken*."

Tears brimmed in Marcus's eyes. "It's my fault that she left. I should have been there for her. I didn't know how much she was hurting. If anything happens to her, that'll be my fault too. So how do we find the Taker? It's a twenty-year-old cold case that has been poured over by the best minds law enforcement has to offer."

Ackerman smiled. "But sometimes, dear brother, catching the worst of the worst is a job for the best of the bad."

122

Oban Nassar had first cut his teeth as a *baltagiya* working for the Egyptian government and police. The term translated as "hatchet men," who were basically thugs often hired to attack regime targets and stir civil unrest. The baltagiya had even been trained by the police to implement many forms of sexual brutality against protesters and detainees.

With a head for business, Oban had quickly risen above such menial chores, but even after all these years, Mr. Demon still referred to him as the *Hatchet Man*.

As he pushed the wheelchair down the boardwalk leading to the beach, Oban strained to understand people's fascination with saltwater and sand. Growing up in the desert, he had seen enough sand to last a thousand lifetimes. Sometimes, lying in bed, he felt as though the sand had been permanently embedded beneath his skin.

The Marshall Islands also didn't seem like the kind of place to which the Demon would wish to retire. But it was not his place to ask personal questions of his employer. Oban had the paperwork prepared and ready prior to the deaths of Derrick and Simon Gladstone, and so the entire process had taken only a couple of days to complete. When all was said and done, the holdings of each man— which included the private island on which Derrick had planned to build his new society—were legally transferred to their mother. Then the Gladstone matriarch had gladly transferred control over to the Legion and Mr. Demon in exchange for the best treatment and care on the island for the remainder of her life.

An attendant in a white suit met Oban at the end of the boardwalk, ready with Mrs. Gladstone's beach lounger and martini.

Oban was glad he wouldn't actually have to take the old woman all the way onto the beach and risk getting sand in his shoes. For his retirement, he dreamed of the Swiss Alps, but to each their own.

Leaning down to the old woman's ear, he said, "The staff will handle your care from this point on, Mrs. Gladstone. I hope you enjoy the scenery. It's certainly a step up from the dark room in which your sons had confined you. Mr. Demon wanted to pass on his thanks for your assistance. This island and the financial holdings of your sons will certainly aid a great deal in his plans going forward."

As he headed up the path toward his awaiting AugustaWestland AW109 Grand Versace helicopter—which came equipped with every amenity and a 6.3 million dollar price tag—Oban Nassar thought of the old woman barely able to speak or move and willing to sell out her own children in exchange for a place in the sun. As he climbed inside the cabin of the luxury helicopter, he was reminded of a quote from Helen Keller: "Walking with a friend in the dark is better than walking alone in the light."

ACKNOWLEDGMENTS

First of all, I want to thank my beautiful wife—Gina—and my children—James, Madison, and Calissa—for their love and support (especially Gina who has to endure a lot craziness in the name of research and put up with me in general).

Next, I wish to thank my parents, Leroy and Emily, for taking me to countless movies as a child and instilling in me a deep love of stories. Also, thank you to my mother, Emily, for always being my first beta reader and my mother-in-law, Karen, for being my best saleswoman.

As always, none of this would be possible without the help of my wonderful agents, Danny Baror and Heather Baror-Shapiro, my mentor and friend, Lou Aronica, my amazing assistant, Allison Maretti, and my social media guru, Colby Applegate. In addition, I wouldn't be here without the guidance and friendship of all my fellow authors at the International Thriller Writers organization.

To all those who have helped me along the way and to my extraordinary readers, thank you so much. I couldn't be living my dream without your support.

ABOUT THE AUTHOR

ETHAN CROSS's Ackerman thrillers are international bestsellers. Before becoming a full time writer, he was a computer programmer, a Chief Technology Officer and a Marketing Director for a New York publisher. He lives in Illinois with his wife, three kids, and two Shih Tzus.

@EthanCrossBooks www.ethancross.com

VENGEANCE IS IN MY HEART.
MURDER IN MY MIND.

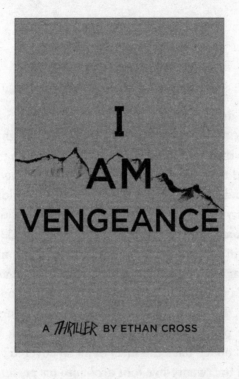

Read the next Ackerman thriller from
Ethan Cross, conjuring one of the most
compelling cop versus killer confrontations
in the pages of crime and thriller fiction.

1

Two days ago…

Maggie Carlisle awoke atop a sea of bones. Some were brittle as kindling and crunched beneath her weight, sending clouds of dust and spores into her face. Rolling over, she discovered that when her captor had dropped her into this pit, she had landed atop a set of remains no older than a couple of years. She dry-heaved from the rancid smell of the pit, which caused starbursts of pain to explode out from a wound in her side. Pulling up her shirt, she found that a shard from a rib bone had punctured her abdomen. As she debated on whether it would be best to pull the bone or leave it in place, the realization struck that she could currently see inside the pit, although it had been pitch black when the Taker had pulled back the sheet of metal covered with sand, which hid the twenty-five foot drop into his personal den of horror, and threw her into the darkness below.

Searching for the source of the illumination and crawling toward the faint glow, she discovered a flashlight with a crank mounted to its side. It was the kind that didn't require external batteries and was instead powered by the wielder manually charging the device by spinning the crank. The flashlight's beam was already growing dim. Without the light, she knew that darkness inside the burial pit would be absolute, but she wondered if that would be for the best. Although, she supposed she still wouldn't be able to escape the smells of the fresher victims.

The entire floor of the teardrop-shaped pit was covered with bones. Some old and white and free of flesh. Others appeared almost ancient, like something from a museum exhibit. But many of the remains were still bloody and stinking of decay. She noticed some kind of black bugs swarming the fresher corpses, slowly devouring the dead flesh. Perhaps, it would be a small blessing to allow the darkness to take her and escape watching the feast for long. Although, she would still see the gore in her mind's eye, and imagining those same black bugs burrowing under her skin for their next meal was not a comforting thought. In fact, the idea caused tears to flow down her cheeks and every muscle in her body to tremble, which caused her even greater pain.

Having decided to leave the bone in place—fearing blood loss and dehydration more than infection—she allowed the light to go out for a moment while she tried to bring her body under control and regain some of her strength. Pushing aside thoughts of her impending death, she instead concentrated on happier times and tried to ignore all the pain and death surrounding her at the moment.

In the darkness, her mind focused in on her baby brother, Tommy. She had always loved playing hide and seek. She and her brother would spend hours playing the game. Each aspiring to be the one to stay hidden the longest. She remembered climbing up into the rafters of the barn at her grandparents' farm, and her brother finally giving up and enduring the shameful process of announcing his defeat and conceding to her superior skills.

But then her brother was taken, and she learned that her hiding and seeking abilities were not nearly as astute as she believed.

After twenty years of banging her head against the wall with little to no progress in the case, help had come from two of the most unlikely of sources: Francis Ackerman Jr.— an infamous serial killer turned government consultant— and a random photograph her mother had received in the mail.

Ackerman had glanced over the same papers that she had spent years of her life studying and had pulled out several new threads for the investigation. During his time as a consultant for the Shepherd Organization, she had witnessed Ackerman save literally hundreds of lives, including her own. Despite all that, and the fact that she had accepted his help as a necessary evil, she couldn't allow herself to forgive the killer for his crimes, which included the murder of one of her closest friends.

She didn't deny that he was a different man than he was during what he referred to as "The Dark Years," and she supposed that a more enlightened person would be able to move forward and start anew. But that was something that she couldn't do. Maggie was amazed by a women like Emily Morgan, who had gone from one of Ackerman's victims to his counselor and friend.

Despite any good he'd done or atonement he'd achieved, she hated him. A part of her felt guilty that she couldn't release those negative emotions. Ackerman had proven himself time and time again. He had been the one who opened the door and sent her on this journey, one she hoped would finally complete the game of hide and seek that she and her brother had been playing for the past twenty years.

Regardless of her feelings, as Special Agent Maggie Carlisle sat in the dark, atop a sea of bones, her only comfort was that she knew Ackerman would find her and kill the man who had stolen her brother—an unsub whom law enforcement had dubbed the Taker.

She knew Ackerman would kill the Taker because that was what he did. He was a hunter, a predator. She simply needed to give him a target and motivation, and her becoming the Taker's next victim would provide both. Her bones were about to join the mass grave of countless others, and when Ackerman found her body, she knew that he would make the Taker pay dearly for his crimes.

And even if Ackerman didn't, she knew that the man she loved would finish the job.

Special Agent Marcus Williams was Ackerman's brother and a hard and dangerous man in his own right, but she had known him in ways that she suspected no one else ever had, even the mother of his son. Marcus was gruff, stubborn, and never passed up the opportunity to make a smartass comment, and yet, he was also kind, funny, and loyal to the point that she had no doubt he would die for her without even the slightest hesitation. The pain of her guilt nearly overshadowed the pain from her wounds, but this had been the only path she could imagine to flush out the man who had taken her brother.

Certain that Marcus and Ackerman would be coming for the Taker hard and fast, she realized that the game was already won, the case all but closed. Like a sacrificial pawn, her demise would pave the way for justice to finally be done. Thinking of all the bones that now surrounded her, all the lives this man had stolen, she supposed that her own life was a small price to pay to ensure that no other families, no other sisters, would be torn apart by the perversions of the Taker's twisted mind and blackened heart.